PENGUIN BOOKS

MAIGRET'S RIVAL

Georges Simenon was born at Liège in Belgium in 1903. At sixteen he began work as a journalist on the *Gazette de Liège*. He has published over 212 novels in his own name, many of which belong to the Inspector Maigret series, and his work has been published in thirty-two countries. He has had a great influence upon French cinema, and more than forty of his novels have been filmed.

Simenon's novels are largely psychological. He describes hidden fears, tensions and alliances beneath the surface of life's ordinary routine which suddenly explode into violence and crime. André Gide wrote to him: 'You are living on a false reputation – just like Baudelaire or Chopin. But nothing is more difficult than making the public go back on a too hasty first impression. You are still the slave of your first successes and the reader's idleness would like to put a stop to your triumphs there ... You are much more important than is commonly supposed'; and François Mauriac wrote, 'I am afraid I may not have the courage to descend right to the depths of this nightmare which Simenon describes with such unendurable art.'

Simenon has travelled a great deal and once lived on a cutter, making long journeys of exploration round the coasts of northern Europe. A book of reminiscences, *Letter to My Mother*, was published in England in 1976. He is married and lives near Lausanne in Switzerland.

GEORGES SIMENON

MAIGRET'S RIVAL

*

PENGUIN BOOKS

Penguin Books Ltd, Harmondsworth, Middlesex, England
Viking Penguin Inc., 40 West 23rd Street, New York, New York 10010, U.S.A.
Penguin Books Australia Ltd, Ringwood, Victoria, Australia
Penguin Books Canada Ltd, 2801 John Street, Markham, Ontario, Canada L 3 R 1 B 4
Penguin Books (N.Z.) Ltd, 182–190 Wairau Road, Auckland 10, New Zealand

Made and printed in Great Britain by
Cox & Wyman Ltd, Reading
Filmset in 10/12 pt Monophoto Sabon by
Northumberland Press Ltd, Gateshead,
Tyne and Wear

CONTENTS

MAIGRET'S RIVAL

Translated by
Helen Thomson

1

The Little Evening Train

Maigret surveyed his fellow passengers with large, sullen eyes and, without meaning to, assumed that stuck-up, self-important look people put on when they have spent mindless hours in the compartment of a train. Then, well before the train began to slow down as it approached a station, men in large, billowing overcoats started to emerge from their various cells each clutching a leather briefcase or a suitcase, in order to take up their positions in the corridor. There they stood, one hand casually gripping the brass rod across the window, without apparently paying the slightest attention to their travelling companions.

Huge raindrops were making horizontal streaks across this particular train window. Through the transparent, watery glass the Superintendent saw the light from a signal-box shatter into a thousand pointed beams, for it was now dark. Lower down, he glimpsed streets laid out in straight lines, glistening like canals, rows of houses which all looked exactly the same, windows, doorsteps, pavements and, in the midst of this universe, a solitary human figure, a man in a hooded cloak hurrying somewhere or other.

Slowly and carefully, Maigret filled his pipe. In order to light it, he turned towards the procession of people in the corridor. Four or five passengers who, like himself, were waiting for the train to stop so that they could slip away into the deserted streets or quickly make their way to the station buffet, were standing between him and the end of the corridor. Among them, he recognized a pale face which immediately turned the other way.

It was none other than old Cadaver!

First of all, the Superintendent groaned:

'He's pretended not to see me, the idiot.'

9

Then he frowned. Why on earth would Inspector Cavre be going to Saint-Aubin-les-Marais?

The train slowed down and pulled into Niort station. Maigret stepped onto the cold and wet platform and called a porter:

'Can you tell me how to get to Saint-Aubin, please?'

'Take the 20.17 train on platform 3 ...'

He had half an hour to wait. After a brief visit to the gentlemen's lavatory, which was right at the end of the platform, he pushed open the door of the station buffet and walked over to one of the many unoccupied tables. He then sat wearily on a chair and settled down to wait in the dusty light.

Old Cadaver was there, at the other end of the room, sitting as Maigret was, at a table with no cloth on it, and once again he pretended he had not seen the Superintendent.

Cavre was his real name, Justin Cavre, but he had been known as old Cadaver for twenty years and everyone at the Police Judiciaire used this nickname when referring to him.

He looked ridiculous sitting stiffly in his corner and shifting from one uncomfortable position to another in order not to catch Maigret's eye. He knew the Superintendent had seen him, that was for sure. Skinny, sallow-skinned, his eyelids red, he made one think of those schoolboys who skulk peevishly at the edge of the play-ground and pretend they do not want to play with the rest of the class, although in reality they long to join in the fun.

Cavre was just that sort of person. He was intelligent. He was probably the most intelligent man Maigret had come across in the police force. They were both about the same age. If the truth were known, Cavre was a little more experienced and, had he persevered, he could well have become a Superintendent before Maigret.

Why was it that even as a young man he already seemed to carry the burden of some kind of curse on his narrow shoulders? Why did he give them all black looks, as if he thought each and every one of them was going to do him down?

'Old Cadaver has just begun his Novena ...'

It was an expression one often used to hear at the Quai des Orfèvres years ago. At the slightest provocation, or sometimes for no reason at all, Inspector Cavre would suddenly begin a course of silence and mistrust, a restorative of hatred, one might say. For a week at a time he would not say a word to anyone. Sometimes, his colleagues would catch sight of him chuckling to himself as though he had seen through their supposedly evil schemes.

Very few people knew why he had suddenly left the police force. Maigret himself did not learn the facts until some time afterwards and had felt very sorry for him.

Cavre loved his wife with the jealous, consuming passion of a lover rather than in a husbandly way. What exactly he found so beguiling about that vulgar woman who had all the aggressive characteristics of a *demi-mondaine* or a bogus film star, one could only surmise. Nevertheless, the fact remained that it was because of her that he had committed serious offences in the course of his career in the force. Ugly discoveries concerning payments of money had sealed his fate. One evening, Cavre had emerged from the Chief of Police's office with his head down and his shoulders hunched. A few months later, he was known to have set up a private detective agency above a stamp shop in the Rue Drouot.

People were having dinner, each customer wrapped in his own aura of boredom and silence. Maigret finished his half-pint of beer, wiped his mouth, picked up his suitcase and walked past his former colleague. He had been less than two yards away from his table, but Cavre had continued to stare down at a patch of spit on the floor.

The little train, looking black and wet, was already at platform 3. Maigret climbed into a cold, damp compartment of the old-fashioned type and tried in vain to shut the window properly.

People were walking to and fro on the platform outside and the Superintendent heard other familiar sounds. The carriage-door opened two or three times and a head looked in. Each passenger was trying desperately to find an empty compartment. Whenever one of them caught sight of Maigret, the door shut again.

Once the train had started to move, the Superintendent went out into the corridor to close a window which was causing a draught. As he did so, he saw, in the compartment next to his, Inspector Cavre who this time was pretending to be asleep.

There was nothing to be alarmed about. It was idiotic to keep brooding on this strange coincidence. Besides, the whole affair was a nonsense and Maigret wished he could extricate himself from his promise with a mere shrug of the shoulders.

What difference did it make to him if Cavre was also going to Saint-Aubin?

In the darkness outside the carriage windows, through which the dot of a light on the side of the road could occasionally be seen, the headlights of a passing car would flash by or, looking even more mysterious and inviting, the yellowish rectangle of a window.

The examining magistrate Bréjon, a charming, good-natured, rather shy man full of old-world courtesy, had repeatedly said to him:

'My brother-in-law Naud will meet you at the station. I've told him you're coming.'

And Maigret could not help thinking as he drew on his pipe: 'But what on earth can old Cadaver be up to?'

The Superintendent was not even on an official case. Bréjon, with whom he had worked so often, had sent him a short note asking him if he would be good enough to pop into his office for a few moments.

It was the month of January. It was raining in Paris as it was in Niort. It had been raining for more than a week and the sun had not once come out. The lamp on the desk in the examining magistrate's office had a green shade. While Monsieur Bréjon was talking and constantly cleaning the lenses of his spectacles as he did so, Maigret reflected that he, too, had a green lampshade in his office, but that the one he was looking at now was ribbed like a melon.

'... am so sorry to bother you ... especially as it's not a professional matter ... Do sit down ... But of course ... A cigar? ... You may perhaps know that my wife's maiden name is Lecat ... It doesn't matter ... That's not what I want to discuss ... My sister, Louise Bréjon, became Madame Naud when she married ...'

It was late. People in the street outside, on looking up at the gloomy façade of the forbidding Palais de Justice and seeing the light on in the examining magistrate's office, would no doubt think that serious issues were being debated up there.

And one had such a strong impression of authority when one saw Maigret's bulky figure and thoughtful countenance that no one could possibly have guessed what he was thinking about.

In actual fact, as he listened with half an ear to what the examining magistrate with the goatee beard was telling him, he was thinking about the green lampshade in front of him, about the one in his own office, how attractive the ribbed shade was, and how he would get one like it for himself.

'You can understand the situation ... A small, a tiny village ... You will see for yourself ... It's miles from anywhere ... The jealousy, the envy, the unwarranted malice ... My brother-in-law is a charming person, and sincere too ... As for my niece, she's just a child ... If you agree, I'll arrange for you to have a week's leave of absence. My entire family will be indebted to you, and ... and ...'

That was how he had become involved in a stupid venture. What exactly *had* the little examining magistrate told him? He was still provincial in his outlook and like all provincials he let himself be carried away by local gossip about families whose names he pronounced as if they were of historical importance.

His sister, Louise Bréjon, had married Etienne Naud. The examining magistrate had added, as if the whole world had heard of him:

'The son of Sébastien Naud, you understand?'

Now, Sébastien Naud was quite simply a stout cattle dealer from the village of Saint-Aubin which was tucked away in the heart of the Vendée fenland.

'Etienne Naud is related, on his mother's side, to the best families in the district.'

That was all very well. But what of it?

'They live about a mile outside the village and their house almost touches the railway-line ... the one that runs between Niort and Fontenay-le-Comte ... About three weeks ago, a local boy – from quite a good family, too, at any rate on his mother's side as she's a Pelcau – was found dead on the tracks ... At first, everybody thought it was an accident, and I still think it was ... But since then, rumour has it ... Anonymous letters have been sent round ... In a nutshell, my brother-in-law is now in a terrible state as people are accusing him almost openly of having killed the boy ... He wrote me a somewhat garbled letter about it ... I then wrote to the Director of Public Prosecutions in Fontenay-le-Comte for more detailed information, as Saint-Aubin comes under the jurisdiction of Fontenay. Contrary to what I expected, I discovered that the accusations were rather serious and that it will be difficult to avoid an official inquiry ... That is why, my dear Superintendent,

I have taken it upon myself to contact you, purely as a friend ...'

The train stopped. Maigret wiped the condensation from the window and saw a tiny station with just one light, one platform and one solitary railwayman who was running along the side of the train and already blowing his whistle. A carriage-door slammed shut and the train set off again. But it was not the door of the next door compartment which Maigret had heard closing. Inspector Cavre was still there.

Now and then, Maigret would glimpse a farm, nearby or in the distance, but always beneath him as he peered through the window, and whenever he saw a light it would invariably be reflected in a pool of water, as if the train were skirting the edge of a lake.

'Saint-Aubin!'

He got out. Three people in all got off the train: a very old lady with a cumbersome, black wicker basket, Cavre and Maigret. In the middle of the platform stood a very tall, very large man, wearing leather gaiters and a leather jacket. It was obviously Naud, for he was looking hesitantly about him. His brother-in-law the examining magistrate had told him Maigret would be arriving that night. But which of the two men who had got out of the train was Maigret?

First of all, he walked towards the thinner of the two men. His hand was already moving upwards to touch his hat; his mouth was slightly open, ready to ask the stranger's name in a faltering voice. But Cavre walked straight past, haughtily, as if to say with a knowing look:

'It's not me. It's the other chap.'

The examining magistrate's brother-in-law abruptly changed direction.

'Superintendent Maigret, I believe? I'm sorry I did not recognize you straightaway. Your photograph is so often in the papers. But in this little backwater, you know ...'

He had taken it upon himself to carry Maigret's suitcase and as the Superintendent was hunting in his pocket for his ticket, he said as he steered him, not towards the station exit but towards the level-crossing:

'Don't worry about that ...'

And turning to the station-master, he cried:

'Good evening, Pierre ...'

It was still raining. A horse harnessed to a pony-trap was tied to a ring.

'Please climb up ... The road is virtually impassable for cars in this weather.'

Where was Cavre? Maigret had seen him disappear into the darkness. He had a strong desire to follow him, but it was too late. Moreover, would it not have looked extremely odd, so soon upon his arrival, to leave his host in the lurch and go off in hot pursuit of another passenger?

There was no sign of an actual village. Just a single lamp-post about a hundred yards from the station, standing by some tall trees. At this point, a road seemed to open out.

'Put the coat over your legs. Yes, you must. Even with the coat your knees will get wet, for we're going against the wind ... My brother-in-law wrote me a long letter all about you ... I feel embarrassed that he has involved someone like you in such an unimportant matter ... You have no idea what country folk are like ...'

He let the end of his whip dangle over the horse's rump. The wheels of the pony-trap sank deep into the black mud as they drove along the road which ran parallel to the railway-line. On the other side, lanterns threw a hazy light over a kind of canal.

A human figure suddenly appeared on the road as if from no-where. A man holding his jacket over his head moved out of the way as the pony-trap came nearer.

'Good evening, Fabien!' cried out Etienne Naud in the same way as he had hailed the station-master, like a country squire who calls everyone by his Christian name, a man who knows everyone in the neighbourhood.

But where the devil could Cavre be? Try as he might to put the matter out of his mind, Maigret could think of nothing else.

'Is there a hotel in Saint-Aubin?' he asked.

His companion roared with laughter.

'There's no question of your staying in a hotel! We have plenty of room at home. Your room is ready. We've arranged to have dinner an hour later than usual as I thought you wouldn't have had anything to eat on your journey. I hope you were wise enough not to have dinner at the station buffet in Niort? We live very simply, however ...'

Maigret could not have cared less how they lived or what sort of welcome he received. He had Cavre on the brain.

'I'd like to know if the man who got out of the train with me ...'

'I don't know who he was,' Etienne Naud hurriedly declared.

Why did he reply in such a fashion? It was not the answer to Maigret's question.

'I'd like to know if he'll have managed to find somewhere to stay ...'

'Indeed! I don't know what my brother-in-law has been telling you about this part of the world. Now that he's living in Paris he probably looks upon Saint-Aubin as an insignificant little hamlet. But, my dear chap, it is almost a small town. You haven't seen any of it yet because the station is a little way from the centre. There are two excellent inns, the Lion d'Or, run by Monsieur Taponnier, old François as everyone calls him, and just opposite there's the Hôtel des Trois Mules ... Well! We're nearly home ... That light you can see ... Yes ... That's our humble dwelling ...'

Needless to say, the tone of voice in which he spoke made it abundantly clear that it was a large house and, sure enough, it was a large, low, solid-looking building with the lights on in four windows on the ground floor. Outside, in the middle of the façade, an electric lamp shone like a star and gave light to any visitor.

Behind the house, there was presumably a large courtyard with stables round the edge so that one would occasionally catch the warm, sweet smell of the horses within. A farm hand rushed up immediately to lead in the horse and trap, the door of the house opened and a maid came forward to take the traveller's luggage.

'Here we are, then! It's not very far, you see ... At the time the house was built, no one foresaw unfortunately that the railway-line would one day pass virtually beneath our windows. You get used to it, admittedly, and in fact there are very few trains, but ... Do come in ... Give me your coat ...'

At that precise moment, Maigret was thinking:

'He has talked non-stop.'

And then he could not think at all for a moment because too many thoughts were assailing him and a totally new atmosphere was closing in on him in an ever tighter net.

The passage-way was wide and paved with grey tiles, its walls panelled in dark wood up to a height of about six feet. The electric light was enclosed in a lantern of coloured glass. A large oak staircase with a red stair-carpet and heavy, well-polished banisters led up to the first floor. A pleasing aroma of wax polish, of casseroles simmering in the kitchen pervaded the whole house and Maigret caught a whiff of something else too, that bitter-sweet smell which for him was the very essence of the country.

But the most remarkable feature of the house was its stillness, a stillness which seemed to be eternal. It was as if the furniture and every object in this house had remained in the same place for generations, as if the occupants themselves, as they went in and out of the rooms, were observing special rites which hurled defiance at anything unforeseen.

'Would you like to go up to your room for a moment before we eat? It's a family occasion, you understand. We shan't stand on ceremony . . .'

The master of the house pushed open a door and two people rose to their feet simultaneously. Maigret was ushered into a warm, homely drawing-room.

'This is Superintendent Maigret . . . My wife . . .'

She had the same deferential air about her as her brother Bréjon, the examining magistrate, the same courteousness so characteristic of a sound bourgeois upbringing, but for a second Maigret thought he detected something harder, sharper in her countenance.

'I am appalled my brother has asked you to come all this way in weather like this . . .'

As if the rain made any difference to the journey or was of any importance in the circumstances!

'May I introduce you to a friend of ours, Superintendent: Alban Groult-Cotelle. I expect my brother-in-law mentioned his name to you . . .'

Had the examining magistrate mentioned him? Perhaps he had. Maigret had been so preoccupied thinking about the green ribbed lampshade!

'How do you do, Superintendent. I'm a great admirer of yours . . .'

Maigret was tempted to reply:

'Well, I'm not of yours.'

For he could not abide people like Groult-Cotelle.

'Would you like to serve the *porto*, Louise?'

The glasses were on a table in the drawing-room which was softly lit with few, if any, sharp lines. The chairs were old, most of them upholstered; the rugs were all in neutral or faded colours. A cat lay stretched out on the hearth in front of the log fire.

'Do sit down ... Our neighbour Groult-Cotelle is having dinner with us ...'

Whenever his name was mentioned, Groult-Cotelle would bow pretentiously, like a nobleman among commoners who takes it upon himself to behave as if he were in a salon.

'They insist on laying a place at their table for an old recluse like me ...'

A recluse, yes, and probably a bachelor too. One could not say why one sensed this, but one sensed it all the same. He was stuck-up, a good-for-nothing who was well satisfied with his peculiar notions and eccentric behaviour.

The fact that he was not a count or a marquis, that he did not even have a 'de' in front of his name, must have been a considerable source of annoyance. All the same, he did have an affected Christian name, Alban, which he so liked to hear, and an equally pretentious double-barrelled surname to go with it.

He was a tall, lean man of about forty and he obviously thought this leanness gave him an aristocratic bearing. The dusty look he had about him, in spite of the care with which he dressed, his dull face and bald forehead gave Maigret the impression he did not have a wife. His clothes were elegant, subtle and unusual in colour; seeming never to have been new, they did not look as if they would ever become old or threadbare either. The garments he wore were part of his character and never changed. Whenever Maigret met him subsequently, he would always be wearing the same greenish coloured jacket, very much in the style of the country gentleman, and the same horseshoe tiepin on a white ribbed cotton tie.

'I hope the journey wasn't too tiring, Superintendent?' inquired Louise Bréjon, as she handed him a glass of *porto*.

And Maigret, firmly seated in an armchair that sagged beneath his weight, much to the distress of the mistress of the house, was prey to so many different emotions that his mind became rather blunted and for part of the evening his hosts must have thought him somewhat slow-witted.

First of all, there was the house, which was the very prototype of the house he had dreamed of so often, with its comforting walls round which hung air as thick as solid matter. The framed portraits reminded him of the examining magistrate's lengthy discourse about the Nauds, the Bréjons, the La Noues, for the Bréjons were connected with the La Noues through their mother. One would have liked to imagine that all these serious-looking and rather stiff faces were one's own ancestors.

Judging from the smells coming from the kitchen, an elaborate meal was about to be served. Someone was carefully laying the table in the dining-room next door, for the clinking of china and cut-glass could be heard. In the stable, the farm-hand was rubbing down the mare and two long rows of reddish-brown cows were chewing the cud in their stalls.

The house embodied the peace of God, order and virtue, and at the same time was the very expression of the petty habits and faults of simple families living encompassed lives.

Etienne Naud, tall and broad-shouldered, with a ruddy complexion and goggle eyes, looked cordially round him as if to say:

'Look at me! . . . Sincere . . . kind . . .'

The good-natured giant. The perfect master of the house. The perfect father. The man who cried out from his pony-trap:

'Good evening, Pierre . . . Good evening, Fabien . . .'

His wife smiled shyly in the shadow of the huge fellow, as if to apologize for his taking up so much space.

'Will you forgive me for a moment, Superintendent . . .'

Of course. He had been expecting it. The charming mistress of the house always goes into the kitchen to have a last look at the preparations for dinner.

Even Alban Groult-Cotelle was predictable. Looking as if he had just stepped out of an engraving, he was the very picture of the more refined, the better bred, the more intelligent friend, indeed the epitome of the old family friend with his faintly condescending airs.

'You see . . .' was written all over his face. 'They're decent people, perfect neighbours ... You can't talk philosophy with them, but apart from that, they make you feel very much at home and you'll see their burgundy is genuine enough and their brandy worth praising ...'

'Dinner is served, Madame ...'

'Would you like to sit on my right, Superintendent? ...'

But where was the note of anxiety in all this? For the examining magistrate had certainly been very concerned when he sent for Maigret.

'You see,' he insisted, 'I know my brother-in-law, just as I know my sister and niece. Anyway, you'll see them for yourself ... But all this doesn't alter the fact that this odious accusation is increasing in substance day by day, to the point of forcing the Department of the Public Prosecutor to investigate the matter. My father was the notary in Saint-Aubin for forty years, having taken over the practice from *his* father ... They'll show you our family house in the middle of the town ... I have got to the stage where I ask myself how such a blind hatred could have arisen in so short a time. It is steadily gaining ground and is threatening to wreck the lives of innocent people ... My sister has never been very robust ... She's highly-strung and suffers from insomnia. The slightest problem upsets her.'

But one would never have guessed that the people present were involved in such a drama. Everything led one to believe that Maigret had merely been asked to a good dinner and a game of bridge. While the skylarks were being served, the Superintendent's hosts explained at great length how the peasants from the fens caught them at night by dragging nets over the meadows.

But why was their daughter not there?

'My niece, Geneviève,' the examining magistrate had said, 'is a perfect young lady, the like of which you only read about in novels now ...'

This was not, however, what the person or persons writing the anonymous letters thought, nor for that matter what most of the locals thought, for it was Geneviève they were accusing, after all.

Maigret was still puzzled by the story he had heard from Bréjon, for it was so out of keeping with the scene before him! Rumour had it that Albert Retailleau, the young man found dead on the railway-line, was Geneviève's lover. It was even said that he came to her house two or three times a week and spent the night in her room.

Albert had no money. He was barely twenty years old. His father had worked in the Saint-Aubin dairy and had died as a result of a boiler exploding. His mother lived on a pension which the dairy had been obliged to give her in recompense.

'Albert Retailleau did not commit suicide,' declared his friends. 'He enjoyed the pleasures of life too much. And even if he had been drunk, as is claimed to be the case, he would not have been so stupid as to cross the railway-line when a train was coming.'

The body had been found more than five hundred yards away from the Nauds' house, about half way between it and the station.

There was nothing wrong in that, but it was now rumoured that the boy's cap had been found in the reeds along the edge of the canal, much nearer the Nauds' house.

There was yet another, even more doubtful story in circulation. It seemed that someone had visited Madame Retailleau, the mother of the boy, a week after her son's death, and had apparently seen her hurriedly hide a wad of thousand-franc notes. She had never been known to have such a large sum of money before.

'It is a pity, Superintendent, that you have made your first visit to our part of the world in winter-time . . . It is so pretty round here in the summer that the district is known as "Green Venice" . . . You'll have some more of the pullet, won't you?'

And Cavre? What was Inspector Cavre up to in Saint-Aubin?

Everyone ate and drank too much. It was too hot in the dining-room. Sluggishly, they all returned to the drawing-room and sat around the crackling log fire.

'I insist . . . I know you're particularly fond of your pipe, but you must have a cigar . . .'

Were they trying to lull him to sleep? But that was a ridiculous thought. They were decent sorts. That was all there was to it. The examining magistrate in Paris must have exaggerated the situation. And Alban Groult-Cotelle was nothing but a stuck-up fool, one of those dandyish good-for-nothings to be found in any country district.

'You must be tired after your journey . . . Just say when you want to go to bed . . .'

That meant that nothing was going to be said that night. Perhaps because Groult-Cotelle was there? Or because Naud preferred not to say anything in front of his wife?

'Do you take coffee at night? ... No? ... No tisane either? ... Please forgive me if I go up now, but our daughter hasn't been very well for the past two or three days and I must go and see if she needs anything ... Young girls are always rather delicate, aren't they, especially in a climate like ours ...'

The three men sat around the fire smoking and talking of this and that. They even began discussing local politics, for apparently there was a new mayor who was acting counter to the wishes of all respectable members of the community and who ...

'Well gentlemen,' grunted Maigret finally, half pleasantly, half crossly, 'if you will excuse me, I think I'll go up to bed now ...'

'You must sleep the night here, too, Alban ... I'm not going to let you go home in this terrible weather ...'

They went upstairs. Maigret's room was at the end of the passage-way. Its walls were covered in yellow cloth and brought back many childhood memories.

'Have you everything you need? ... I forgot ... Let me show you the bathroom.'

Maigret shook hands with the two men, then undressed and got into bed. As he lay there half-asleep, he thought he heard noises, the distant murmur of voices somewhere in the house, but soon, when all the lights were out, these sounds died away.

He fell asleep. Or he thought he did. The sinister face of Cavre, that most unhappy of men, kept creeping into his unconscious, and then he dreamt that the rosy-cheeked maid who served the dinner was bringing him his breakfast.

The door half-opened. He was sure he heard the door open gently. He sat up in bed and groped for the switch to the light-bulb in the tulip-shaped opal glass-covering attached to the wall above the bed-head. The light went on and Maigret saw standing in front of him a young girl with a brown wool coat over her nightdress.

'Ssh ...' she whispered. 'I just had to speak to you. Don't make a noise ...'

And, like a sleep-walker, she sat down on a chair and stared into space.

2

The Girl in the Nightdress

It was a weary night for Maigret, and yet not without its enjoyment. He slept without sleeping. He dreamed without dreaming, or in other words he was well aware he was dreaming and deliberately prolonged his dreams, being conscious all the time of noises from the real world.

For example, the sound of the mare kicking her hooves against the stable-wall was real enough, but the other images that flitted through Maigret's mind, as he lay in bed perspiring heavily, were tricks of the imagination. He conjured up a picture of the dim light in a stable, the horse's rump, the rack half full of hay; he imagined the rain still falling in the courtyard with figures splashing their way through black puddles of water and lastly he saw, from the outside, the house in which he was staying.

It was a kind of double vision. He was in his bed. He was keenly savouring its warmth and the delicious country smell of the mattress which became even more pungent as it grew moist with Maigret's sweat. But at the same time he was in the whole house. Who knows if, at one moment in his dream, he did not even become the house itself?

Throughout the night, he was conscious of the cows moving about in their stalls, and from four in the morning onwards he heard the footsteps of a farm-hand crossing the courtyard and the sound of the latch being lifted: what prevented him from actually seeing the man, by the light of a hurricane lamp, as he sat on a three-legged stool drawing milk into white metal buckets?

He must have fallen into a deep sleep again, for he woke up with a start at the sound of the lavatory flushing. It was such a sudden, violent noise that it gave him rather a fright. But immediately afterwards he was back to his old tricks and imagined the master of the house coming out of the bathroom with his braces round his thighs and going silently back to his room. Madame Naud was asleep, or pretending to be, with her face to the wall. Etienne Naud had left the room in darkness except for the small wall-light above the dressing-table. He started to shave, his fingers numbed by the icy water. His skin was pink, taut and glossy.

Then he sat down in an armchair to pull on his boots. Just as he was leaving the room, a sound came from beneath the blankets. What was his wife saying to him? He bent over her and murmured something in a low voice. He closed the door noiselessly behind him and tip-toed down the stairs. At this point, Maigret jumped out of bed and switched on the light, for he had had enough of these spellbinding nocturnal activities.

He looked at his watch which he had left on the bedside table. It was half past five. He listened carefully and decided that it had either stopped raining or that the rain had turned into a fine, silent drizzle.

Admittedly, he had eaten and drunk well the previous evening, but he had not drunk too much. And yet this morning he felt as if he had drunk a great deal. As he took various things out of his dressing-case, he looked with heavy, swollen eyes at his unmade bed and in particular at that chair beside it.

He was convinced it had not been a dream: Geneviève Naud had come into his room. She had come in without knocking. She had positioned herself on that chair, sitting bolt upright without touching the back of it. At first, as he stared at her in sheer amazement, he had thought she was deranged. In reality, however, Maigret was infinitely more disturbed than she was. For he had never been in such a delicate situation. Never before had a young girl who was ready to pour out her heart stationed herself at his bedside, with him in bed in his nightshirt, his hair ruffled by the pillow and his lips moist with spittle.

He had muttered something like:

'If you'll turn the other way for a moment, I'll get up and put some clothes on . . .'

'It doesn't matter . . . I have only a few words to say to you . . . I am pregnant by Albert Retailleau . . . If my father finds out I'll kill myself and no one will stop me . . .'

He could not bring himself to look at her while he was lying in bed. She paused for a moment, as if expecting Maigret to react to her pronouncement, then rose to her feet, listened at the door and said as she left the room:

'Do as you wish. I am in your hands.'

Even now, he could scarcely believe all this had happened and the thought that he had lain prostrate like a dummy throughout the proceedings humiliated him. He was not vain in the way men can be, and yet he was ashamed that a young girl had caught him in bed with his face still bloated by sleep. And the girl's attitude to it all was even more annoying, for she had hardly glanced at him. She had not pleaded with him, as he might have expected, she had not thrown herself at his feet, she had not wept.

He recalled her face, its regular features making her look a little like her father. He could not have said if she was beautiful but she had left him with an impression of completeness and poise which even her insane overture had not dispelled.

'I am pregnant by Albert Retailleau ... If my father finds out I'll kill myself and no one will stop me ...'

Maigret finished dressing and mechanically lit his first pipe of the day. He then opened the door and, failing to find the light-switch, groped his way down the corridor. He went down the stairs but could not see a light on anywhere, even though he could hear someone stoking the stove. He made his way to where the noise was coming from and saw a shaft of yellow light beneath a door in the dining-room. He tapped gently on the door, opened it and found himself in the kitchen.

Etienne Naud was sitting at one end of the table, his elbows resting on the light wood, and tucking into a bowl of soup. An elderly cook in a blue apron was sending showers of white-hot cinders into the ash bucket as she raked the stove.

Maigret saw the startled look on Naud's face as he came in and realized he was annoyed at having been caught unawares in the kitchen having his breakfast like a farm-worker.

'Up already, Superintendent? I keep to the old country habits, you know. No matter what time I go to bed, I'm always up at five in the morning. I hope I didn't wake you?'

What was the point of telling him that it had been the sound of the lavatory flushing that had woken him up?

'I won't offer you a bowl of soup, for I presume you ...'

'But I'd love some ...'

'Léontine ...'

'Yes, Monsieur, I heard ... I'll have it ready in a moment ...'

'Did you sleep well?'

'Quite well. But at one point I thought I heard footsteps in the passage-way ...'

Maigret brought this up in order to find out whether Naud had pounced on his daughter after she had left his room, but the look of astonishment on his face seemed genuine enough.

'When? ... During the evening? ... I didn't hear anything. Admittedly, it takes a lot to rouse me from my sleep early on in the night. It was probably our friend Alban getting up to go to the bathroom. What do you think of him, incidentally? A likeable fellow, isn't he? Far more cultured than he actually appears to be ... He's read countless books, you know ... He knows the lot, and that's all about it. Pity he didn't have better luck with his wife ...'

'He was married, then?'

Having thought Groult-Cotelle to be the archetypal bachelor living in the provinces, Maigret viewed this snippet of information somewhat suspiciously. He felt as if they had hidden something from him, as if they had deliberately tried to mislead him.

'Indeed he was, and he still is, what's more. He has two children, a girl and a boy. The elder of the two must be twelve or thirteen now ...'

'Does his wife live with him?'

'No. She lives on the Côte d'Azur. It's rather a sad story and no one ever talks about it round here. She came from a very good family, though ... She was a Deharme ... Yes, like the general ... She's his niece. A rather eccentric woman who could never grasp the fact that she was living in Saint-Aubin and not in Paris. She scandalized the neighbourhood on several occasions and then, one winter, moved to Nice, ostensibly to escape the bitter cold here, but of course she never came back. She lives there with her children ... And she's not living alone, needless to say ...'

'Did her husband not ask for a divorce?'

'That's not done in these parts.'

'Which of them has the money?'

Etienne Naud looked at him disapprovingly, for it was obvious he did not want to go into any details.

'She is undoubtedly a very rich woman ...'

The cook had sat down at the table to grind the coffee in an old-fashioned coffee-mill with a large copper top.

'You are lucky. It has stopped raining. But my brother-in-law really ought to have told you to bring some boots. After all, he comes from this part of the world and knows it well. We are right in the middle of the fenland and even have to use a boat in summer as well as winter to reach some of my farms. They're known as *cabanes* here, by the way ... But talking of my brother-in-law, I feel rather embarrassed he had the nerve to ask a man of your standing to ...'

The question Maigret kept asking himself, the question that had been constantly on his mind ever since his arrival the previous evening was: were the Nauds decent people who had nothing to hide and who were doing their utmost to make their guest from Paris feel at home, or was he in fact an unwelcome intruder whom Bréjon had deposited in their midst in a most inconsiderate fashion and whose presence this disconcerted couple could well have done without?

He decided to try an experiment.

'Not many people get off the train at Saint-Aubin,' he commented as he ate his soup. 'I think only two of us did yesterday, apart from the old peasant woman wearing a bonnet.'

'Yes, you're right.'

'Does the man who got off the train with me live round here?'

Etienne Naud hesitated before replying. Why? Maigret was looking at him so intently that he was covered in confusion.

'I'd never seen him before,' he answered hurriedly. 'You must have seen me dithering as to which one of you to approach ...'

Maigret tried another tactic:

'I wonder what he has come here for, or rather who asked him to come.'

'Do you know him?'

'He's a private detective. I'll have to find out where he is and what he is up to this morning. He presumably checked in at one or other of the inns you mentioned yesterday ...'

'I'll take you into town shortly in the pony-trap.'

'Thanks, but I'd rather walk if you don't mind, and then I'll be free to come and go as I like . . .'

Something had just occurred to him. Supposing Naud had been counting on him to sleep soundly so that he could leave early for the village and meet Inspector Cavre?

Anything was possible here, and the Superintendent even began to wonder if the young girl's appearance in his room had not been part of a plot which the whole family had planned.

A moment later, he dismissed such thoughts as foolish.

'I hope your daughter isn't seriously ill?'

'No . . . Well, if you really want the truth, I don't think she is any more ill than I am. In spite of all we've done, she has got wind of what is being said in the neighbourhood. She's a proud young woman. All young women are. I'm sure that's the reason she has insisted on staying in her room for the past three days. And maybe your arrival has made her feel rather ashamed . . .'

'Ashamed, is she!' thought Maigret, as he recalled her brief appearance in his room the night before.

'We can talk in front of Léontine,' Naud went on. 'She's known me from childhood. She's been with the family for . . . for how many years, Léontine?'

'Ever since I took my first communion, Monsieur . . .'

'A little more soup? No? . . . To continue, I'm in a most awkward position and I sometimes think my brother-in-law tackled the case in the wrong way. I know you'll say he knows far more about such matters than I do, that's his job . . . but maybe he has forgotten what it's like in our part of the world now that he lives in Paris . . .'

It was hard to believe he was not speaking sincerely, for he seemed to want to talk over what was on his mind. He sat there with his legs stretched out, filling his pipe, while Maigret finished his breakfast. The kitchen smelt of the freshly made coffee and the two men enjoyed the warm atmosphere of the room. Outside, in the darkness of the courtyard, the stable-hand was whistling softly as he groomed one of the horses.

'I'll tell you straight . . . From time to time, rumours about someone or other are spread round the town . . . this time, it's a serious matter, I know. But I still wonder whether it would not be wiser to

28

disregard the accusation ... You agreed to do what my brother-in-law asked ... You have done us the honour of coming ... Everyone knows you are here by now, that's for sure. Tongues are already wagging. No doubt you intend to question some people and that is bound to stir their imaginations even more ... So that's why I really do wonder, quite sincerely, whether we are going about this whole business in the right way ... Are you sure you have had enough to eat? ... If you don't mind the cold, I'll be glad to show you round. I go on a tour of inspection every morning.'

Maigret was putting on his overcoat as the maid came downstairs, for she got up an hour later than the old cook. The two men went into the cold, damp courtyard and spent an hour going from one stable to another. Meanwhile, churns of milk were being loaded onto a small lorry.

Some cows were going off to market in a nearby town that very day and cattle-drovers in dark overalls were rounding them up. At the end of the yard was a small office with a little round stove, a table, account-books and various pigeon-holes inside. Sitting at the table was a farm-hand wearing the same sort of boots as his boss.

'Will you excuse me a moment?'

Madame Naud was getting up now, for there was a light on in her room on the first floor. The other rooms remained in darkness which meant that Groult-Cotelle and the young girl were still fast asleep. The maid was cleaning the dining-room.

Men and animals could be seen moving about in the dim light of the courtyard and outhouses, and Maigret could hear the engine of the milk lorry running in the background.

'That's done ... I was just leaving a few instructions ... I'll be leaving by car for the market shortly as I've to meet some other farmers ... If I had time and thought you would be interested, I would tell you how the estate is run. I have ordinary dairy cattle on my other farms, as we supply the local dairy with milk, but here we rear the finest thoroughbreds, most of which we sell abroad ... I even send some to South America ... But for the moment, I am entirely at your service ... It will be daylight in an hour. If you need the car ... or if you have any questions you would like to ask me ... I want you to feel at ease ... You must treat this as your home ...'

His face bore a cheerful expression as he spoke, but his smile faded when Maigret merely answered:

'Well, if you don't mind, I'll be on my way ...'

The road surface was spongy, as if water from the canal on the left had soaked the ground beneath. The railway embankment ran along the right-hand side of the road. About a kilometre further on, a glaring light could be seen which was obviously the one in the station, for there were green and red signals nearby.

Maigret looked back towards the house and saw that there were lights on in two other windows on the first floor. This brought Alban Groult-Cotelle into his mind and he began to wonder why he had been so put out to discover he was married.

The sky was brightening. One of the first houses Maigret caught sight of as he turned to the left by the station and approached the village bore the sign of the Lion d'Or. The lights were on on the ground floor and he went inside. He found himself in a long, low room where everything was brown – the walls, the beams on the ceiling, the long polished tables and the benches with no backs. At the very end of the room was a kitchen range which was not yet alight. A woman of indeterminate age was crouched over a log burning slowly in the hearth and waiting for the coffee to heat. She turned round for a moment to look at the stranger, but said nothing. Maigret sat down in the dim light of a very dusty lamp.

'I'd like to sample the local brandy!' he said, shaking his overcoat which the damp dawn had showered with greyish beads of moisture.

The woman did not reply and he thought she had not heard. She went on stirring the saucepan of rather uninviting coffee with her spoon and when it was to her liking she poured some into a cup, put it on a tray and walked towards the staircase.

'I'll be down in a minute,' she said.

Maigret suspected that the coffee was for Cadaver, and was proved right when a few seconds later, he noticed the detective's coat hanging on the coat-rack.

Footsteps sounded above Maigret's head. He could hear voices but could not make out what was being said. Five minutes went by. Then five more minutes. Every now and then Maigret rapped a coin on the wooden table, but nothing happened.

30

At last, a quarter of an hour later, the woman came downstairs again and spoke even less amicably than before.

'What did you say you wanted?'

'A glass of the local brandy.'

'I haven't any.'

'You've no brandy?'

'I've cognac, but no local brandy.'

'Then give me a cognac.'

She gave him a glass that had such a thick bottom that there was hardly any room for the drink.

'Tell me, Madame, I believe a friend of mine arrived here last night?'

'How am I to know if he's your friend.'

'Has he just got up?'

'I have one visitor and I have just given him his coffee.'

'If he's the man I know, I bet he asked you lots of questions, didn't he?'

The glasses left by the previous evening's customers had made round, wet marks on many of the tables and the woman began to wipe them with a duster.

'Albert Retailleau spent the evening here the day before he died, didn't he?'

'What's that got to do with you?'

'He was a good lad, I believe. Someone told me he played cards that evening. Is *belote* the favourite game in this part of the world?'

'No, we play *coinchée*.'

'So he played *coinchée* with his friends. He lived with his mother, didn't he? A good woman, unless I'm mistaken.'

'Hmm!'

'What did you say?'

'Nothing. You're the one who's doing all the talking and I don't know what you're getting at.'

Upstairs, Inspector Cavre was getting dressed.

'Does she live far from here?'

'At the end of the street, in a small yard. It's the house with three stone steps.'

'Do you happen to know if my friend Cavre – the man who's lodging here with you – has been to see her yet?'

'And how do you think he could have been to see her when he's only just getting up?'

'Is he staying here long?'

'I haven't asked him.'

She opened the windows and pushed back the shutters. A milky-white light filtered into the room, for day had already broken.

'Do *you* think Retailleau was drunk that night?'

The woman suddenly became aggressive and snapped back:

'No more drunk than you are, drinking cognac at eight in the morning!'

'How much do I owe you?'

'Two francs.'

The Trois Mules, a rather more modern-looking inn, was right opposite, but the Superintendent did not think he would gain anything by going inside. A blacksmith was lighting the fire in his forge. A woman standing on her doorstep was throwing a bucket of dirty water into the street. A bell, the sound of which reminded Maigret of his childhood, tinkled lightly and a boy wearing clogs came out of the baker's with a loaf of bread under his arm.

Curtains parted as he made his way down the street. A hand wiped the condensation from a window and a wrinkled old face with eyes that were ringed with red like Inspector Cavre's peered through the windowpane. On the right stood the church. It was built of grey stone and covered with slates that looked black and shiny after the heavy rain. A very thin woman of about fifty, in deep mourning and holding herself very erect, came out of the church with a prayerbook covered in black cloth in her hand.

Maigret stood idly for a moment in a corner of the little square by a board marked 'School' which had doubtless been put up to caution motorists. He followed the woman with his eyes. The moment he saw her disappear into a kind of blind alley at the end of the street, he guessed at once that it was Madame Retailleau. Since Cavre had not yet visited her, he quickened his step.

He had guessed right, for when he got to the corner of the alley, he saw the woman go up three steps to the door of a small house and take a key out of her bag. A few minutes later, he knocked at the glass door behind which hung a lace curtain.

'Come in.'

She had just had time to take off her coat and her black crepe veil. The prayerbook was still on the oil-cloth which covered the table. The white enamel kitchen stove was already lit. The top was so clean that it must have been painstakingly rubbed with sandpaper.

'Please forgive me for disturbing you, Madame. It is Madame Retailleau, isn't it?'

He did not assert himself very forcefully, for neither her voice nor her movements gave him much encouragement. She stood quite still with her hands over her stomach, her face almost the colour of wax, and waited for Maigret to speak.

'I have been asked to investigate the rumours that are circulating with regard to the death of your son . . .'

'Who are you?'

'Superintendent Maigret of the Police Judiciaire. Let me hasten to add that these enquiries are for the moment unofficial.'

'What does that mean?'

'That the case has not yet been laid before the court.'

'What case?'

'I am sorry to have to talk about such unpleasant matters, Madame, but you are no doubt aware of the various rumours connected with your son's death . . .'

'You cannot stop people from talking . . .'

In order to gain time, Maigret had turned towards a photograph in an oval giltwood frame which was hanging on the wall to the left of the walnut kitchen dresser. It was an enlarged photograph of a man of about thirty with a crew cut and a large moustache drooping over his lips.

'Is that your husband?'

'Yes.'

'Unless I'm mistaken, you had the misfortune to lose him un-expectedly when your son was still a small boy. From what I have been told, you were forced to bring an action against the dairy that employed him in order to receive a pension.'

'You have not been told the truth. There was never any court case. Monsieur Oscar Drouhet, the manager of the dairy, did what was necessary.'

'And later, when your son was old enough to work, he took him into the business. Your son was his book-keeper, I believe.'

'He did the work of the assistant-manager. He would have been made assistant-manager if he hadn't been so young.'

'You haven't got a photograph of him, have you?'

Maigret could have kicked himself, for as he spoke he saw a tiny photograph on a small round table covered with red plush. He picked it up quickly in case Madame Retailleau objected.

'How old was Albert when this photograph was taken?'

'Nineteen. It was taken last year.'

He was a handsome boy with rather a wide face, greedy lips and merry, sparkling eyes. He looked healthy and strong.

Madame Retailleau stood waiting, as before, and let out an occasional sigh.

'He wasn't engaged?'

'No.'

'As far as you know, he had no relationships with women?'

'My son was too young to be chasing women. He was a serious boy and only thought about his career.'

This was not the impression the photograph gave. Young Albert Retailleau had the impassioned look of youth, thick glossy hair and a well-developed physique.

'What was your reaction when ... I do apologize ... You must see what I am getting at ... Do you believe it was an accident?'

'One has to believe it was ...'

'You had no suspicions whatsoever, then?'

'What sort of suspicions?'

'He never mentioned Mademoiselle Naud? ... He never used to come home late at night?'

'No.'

'And Monsieur Naud hasn't been to see you since your son died?'

'We have nothing to say to each other.'

'I see ... But he could have ... Monsieur Groult-Cotelle hasn't called on you either, I take it?'

Was it Maigret's imagination, or had her eyes hardened momentarily? Maigret was sure they had.

'No,' she murmured.

'So that you consider the rumours concerning the circumstances of your son's death to be quite untrue ...'

'Yes, I do. I pay no attention to them. I don't want to know what

34

people are saying. And if it's Monsieur Naud who sent you, you can go back and tell him what I've said.'

For a few seconds, Maigret stood perfectly still, with his eyes half-shut and repeated to himself what she had said, as if to lodge it in his mind:

And if it's Monsieur Naud who sent you, you can go back and tell him what I've said.

Did she know that it was Etienne Naud who had greeted Maigret at the station the day before? Did she know that it was he, indirectly, who had caused him to make the journey from Paris? Or did she merely suspect this to be the case?

'Forgive me for having taken the liberty of calling on you, Madame, especially at such an early hour.'

'Time is of no importance to me.'

'Good-bye, Madame ...'

She remained where she was and said not a word as Maigret walked towards the door and closed it behind him. The Superintendent had not gone ten paces when he saw Inspector Cavre standing on the pavement as if he were on sentry-duty.

Was Cavre waiting for Maigret to leave so that he, in turn, could talk to Albert's mother? Maigret wanted to find out once and for all. The conversation he had just had with Madame Retailleau had put him in a bad temper and he was in the mood to play a trick on his former colleague.

He relit his pipe which he had put out with his thumb before entering Madame Retailleau's house, crossed the street and took up his position on the other side of the road, immediately opposite Cavre, standing resolutely on the pavement as if he meant to stay.

The town was awakening. Children were walking up to the school gate on one side of the little square in front of the church. Most of them had come from far afield and were muffled up in scarves and thick blue or red woollen socks. Many were wearing clogs.

'Well, old chap, it's your turn now! Off you go!' Maigret seemed to be saying, with a mischievous glint in his eyes.

Cavre did not move, but looked haughtily in the other direction as if he were above any such frivolities.

Had Madame Retailleau summoned him to Saint-Aubin? It was

quite possible. She was a strange woman and it was very difficult to size her up. She had the characteristic, almost inborn mistrust of the peasant, whilst a certain disdain made her more like a well-to-do lady from the provinces. Beneath the cold exterior, one sensed an arrogance which nothing could undermine. The way she had stood motionless in front of Maigret was impressive in itself. She had not moved a step or made any kind of gesture while he had been in her house, but had stiffened as some animals are supposed to do when, confronted with danger, they feign death. She had only said a few words and her lips barely moved as she spoke.

'Well, Cavre, you old misery! Make up your mind ... Do something ...'

Old Cadaver was stamping his feet to keep warm but seemed in no hurry to make any sort of move as long as Maigret was watching him.

It was a ridiculous situation. It was childish stubbornly to remain where he was, but Maigret did just that. Unfortunately, however, this tactic turned out to be a waste of time. At half past eight, a small, red-faced man came out of his house and made his way to the *mairie*. He opened the door with a key and a moment afterwards Cavre followed him inside.

This was the very move that Maigret had intended to make himself that morning, for he had determined to find out what the local authorities had to say. His former colleague had beaten him to it and there was nothing for it but to wait his turn.

3

An Undesirable Person

Henceforth, Maigret refused to discuss this undignified episode. He never spoke of what happened that day, and particularly that morning, and no doubt he would have preferred to forget the occasion.

The most disconcerting thing of all was losing the feeling that he *was* Maigret. For what, in fact, did he represent in Saint-Aubin? The short answer was nothing. Justin Cavre had gone into the *mairie* to talk to the local authorities while he, Maigret, had stood awkwardly outside in the street. The row of houses looked like a line of large, poisonous mushrooms clustered as they were beneath a sky that reminded one of a blister ready to burst. Maigret knew he was being watched for faces were peering at him from behind every curtain.

Admittedly, he did not really mind what a few old ladies or the butcher's wife thought. People could take him for what they liked and laugh at him as he went by, as some children had done as they went through the school gate, for all he cared.

It was just that he felt he was not the Maigret he was accustomed to be. Although perhaps it was an exaggeration to say he was thoroughly out of sorts, the simple fact of the matter was that he just did not feel himself.

What would happen, for example, if he were to go into the white-washed *mairie* and knock at the grey door on which 'Secretary's Office' was written in black letters? He would be asked to wait his turn, just as if he had come in to see about a birth certificate or a claim of some sort. And meanwhile, old Cadaver would continue questioning the secretary in his tiny over-heated office for as long as he liked.

Maigret was not here in an official capacity. He could not say he was acting on behalf of the Police Judiciaire, and in any case, who was to know whether anyone in this village surrounded by slimy marshland and stagnant water had even heard the name Maigret?

He was to find out soon enough. As he was waiting impatiently for Cavre to come out, he had one of the most extraordinary ideas in his entire career. He was all set to pursue relentlessly his former colleague, nay, to follow him step by step and say point-blank:

'Look here, Cavre, there's no point in trying to outwit each other. It is quite obvious you're not here for the fun of it. Someone asked you to come. Just tell me who it is and what you've been asked to do . . .'

How comparatively simple a proper, official investigation seemed at this moment! If he had been on a case somewhere within his own jurisdiction he would only have had to go into the local post-office and say:

'Superintendent Maigret. Get me the Police Judiciaire as quickly as you can . . . Hello! Is that you, Janvier? . . . Jump in your car and come down here . . . When you see old Cadaver come out . . . Yes, Justin Cavre . . . Right . . . Follow him and don't let him out of your sight . . .'

Who knows? Maybe he would have had Etienne Naud tailed too, for he had just seen him drive past on the road to Fontenay.

Playing the role of Maigret was easy! An organization which ran like clockwork was at his disposal, besides which, he had only to say his name and people were so bowled over with admiration that they would do anything to please him.

But here, he was so little known that despite numerous articles and photographs which were always appearing in the newspapers, someone like Etienne Naud had walked straight up to Justin Cavre at the station.

Naud had looked after him well because his brother-in-law, the examining magistrate, had sent him all the way from Paris, but on the other hand, had they not all looked as if they were wondering what in fact he had come for? The gist of what their welcome meant was this:

'My brother-in-law Bréjon is a charming fellow who wants to help, but he has been away from Saint-Aubin far too long and has got quite the wrong idea of the situation. It was kind of him to have thought of sending you here. It is kind of you to have come. We will

38

look after you as best we can. Eat and drink your fill. Let me show you round the estate. Don't, on any account, feel you have to stay in this damp, unattractive part of the world. And don't feel you have to look into this trivial matter which concerns no one but ourselves.'

On whose behalf was he working, in fact? For Etienne Naud. But it was palpably obvious that Etienne Naud did not want him to carry out a proper investigation.

And to cap it all, Geneviève had come into his room in the middle of the night and had admitted:

'I was Albert Retailleau's mistress and I am pregnant by him. But I'll kill myself if you breathe a word to my parents.'

Now, if she really was Albert's mistress, the accusations against Naud suddenly took on a terrible meaning. Had she thought of that? Had she consciously charged her father with murder?

And even the victim's mother, who had said nothing, admitted nothing, denied nothing, had made it perfectly clear by her attitude that she did not want Maigret interfering. It was none of his business was what she inferred.

Everyone, even the old ladies lying in wait behind their fluttering curtains, even the school-children who had turned round to stare as they went by, considered him an intruder, an undesirable person. Worse still, no one knew where this steady plodder had come from or why he was in this village.

And so, in a setting which was exactly right for the part, with hands sunk into the pockets of his heavy overcoat, Maigret looked just like one of those nasty characters tormented by some secret vice who prowl round the Porte Saint-Martin or somewhere similar with hunched shoulders and sidelong glances and cautiously edge their way past the houses well out of sight of the police.

Was he turning into another Cavre? He felt like sending someone to Naud's house to fetch his suitcase and taking the first train back to Paris. He would tell Bréjon:

'They won't have anything to do with me ... Leave your brother-in-law to his own devices ...'

All the same, he had gone into the *mairie* as soon as the ex-inspector emerged with a leather briefcase tucked under his arm. No doubt this would increase his standing in the village, for now he would pass for a lawyer.

The secretary was a little man who smelt rather unpleasant. He did not get up as Maigret entered his office.

'Can I help you?'

'Superintendent Maigret of the Police Judiciaire. I am in Saint-Aubin on unofficial business and I would like to ask you one or two questions.'

The little man hesitated and looked annoyed, but none the less bade Maigret sit down on a wicker-seated chair.

'Did the private detective who has just left your office tell you whom he was working for?'

The secretary either did not understand or pretended he did not understand the question. And he reacted in similar fashion to all the other questions the Superintendent put to him.

'You knew Albert Retailleau. Tell me what you thought of him.'

'He was a good sort ... Yes, that's how I'd describe him, a good sort ... You couldn't fault him ...'

'Did he like to chase women?'

'He was only a lad, you know, and we don't always know what the young are up to, these days, but you couldn't say he ran after women ...'

'Was he Mademoiselle Naud's lover?'

'People said he was ... Rumours were going round ... But it's all pure hearsay ...'

'Who discovered the body?'

'Ferchaud, the station-master. He telephoned the *mairie* and the deputy-mayor immediately contacted the Benet *gendarmerie* as there isn't a constabulary in Saint-Aubin.'

'What did the doctor who examined the body say?'

'What did he say? Just that he was dead ... There wasn't much of him left ... The train went right over him ...'

'But he was identified as Albert Retailleau?'

'What? ... Of course ... It was Retailleau all right, there was no doubt about that ...'

'When did the last train pass through?'

'At 5.7 in the morning.'

'Didn't people think it odd that Retailleau should have been on the railway-line at five in the morning in the middle of winter?'

The secretary's reply was quite something:

'It was dry at the time. There was hoar-frost on the ground.'

'But people talked all the same ...'

'Rumours circulated, yes ... But you can never stop people from talking ...'

'Your opinion then, is that Retailleau died a natural death?'

'It is very hard to say what happened.'

And did Maigret bring up the subject of Madame Retailleau? He did, and the reply was as follows:

'She's a truly good woman. I can't say more.'

And Naud, too, was described in similar terms:

'Such a likeable fellow. His father was a splendid person as well, a county councillor ...'

And lastly, what did the secretary have to say about Geneviève?'

'An attractive girl ...'

'Well-behaved?'

'Of course she is well-behaved ... And her mother is one of the most respected members of the community ...'

The little man spoke politely enough, but his replies simply did not sound convincing. To make matters worse, he kept poking his finger up his nose as he spoke and would then carefully examine what he had picked out.

'And what is your opinion of Monsieur Groult-Cotelle?'

'He's a decent sort, too. A modest man ...'

'Is he a close friend of the Nauds?'

'They see a good deal of one another, certainly. But that's only natural since they move in the same circles.'

'When exactly was Retailleau's cap discovered not far from the Nauds' house?'

'When? ... Well ... But was it just the cap that was found?'

'I was told that someone called Désiré who collects the milk for the dairy found the cap in the reeds along the bank of the canal.'

'So people said ...'

'It's not true, then?'

'It's difficult to say. Désiré is drunk half the time.'

'And when he is drunk ...'

'Sometimes he tells the truth and sometimes he doesn't ...'

'But a cap is something you can see and touch! Some people have seen it ...'

'Ah!'

'It must have been put into safe-keeping by now ...'

'Maybe ... I don't know ... May I remind you that this office is not a police-station and we believe in minding our own business ...'

This unpleasant-smelling, silly individual could not have spoken more plainly and was obviously delighted he had given a Parisian such short shrift.

A few moments later, Maigret was back in the street, no further on with his investigation than he had been before, but by now convinced that no one was going to help him find out the truth.

And since no one wanted to know the truth, what was the point of his being here? Would it not be more sensible to go back to Paris and say to Bréjon:

'Look ... Your brother-in-law doesn't want there to be a proper investigation into all this ... No one down there likes the idea ... I have come back ... They gave a wonderful dinner for me ...'

Maigret passed a large house built of grey stone and saw from the bright yellow plaque on the wall that it belonged to the notary. This, then, was the house that Bréjon's father and sister had once occupied and in the grey, watery light it had the same air of timelessness and inscrutability as the rest of the town.

He walked a little further on until he came to the Lion d'Or. Inside, he could see someone talking to the woman who ran the inn and he had the distinct impression that they were talking about him and standing by the window in order to get a better view.

A man on a bicycle came into sight. Maigret recognized the rider as he approached but did not have time to turn away. Alban Groult-Cotelle was on his way home from the Nauds' and he jumped off his bicycle as soon as he saw Maigret.

'It's good to see you again ... We're only a stone's throw away from my house ... Will you do me the honour of coming in for a drink? ... I insist! ... My house is very modest but I've a few bottles of vintage port ...'

Maigret followed him. He did not expect much to come of the visit but the prospect was infinitely preferable to wandering alone through the hostile town.

It was a huge, solid house which looked very appealing from a

42

distance. Its squat shape, black railings and high slate roof gave it the air of a bourgeois fortress.

Inside, everything looked shabby and neglected. The surly-faced maid looked a real slut and yet it was obvious to Maigret from certain looks they gave each other that Groult-Cotelle was sleeping with her.

'I am sorry everything is so untidy . . . I'm a bachelor and live alone . . . I'm only interested in books, so . . .'

So . . . the wallpaper was peeling off the walls which were covered in damp patches, the curtains were grey with dust, and one had to try three or four chairs before finding one that did not wobble. Only one room on the ground floor was heated, no doubt to save wood, and this served as a sitting-room, dining-room and library. There was even a divan in one corner which Maigret suspected his host slept on most of the time.

'Do sit down . . . It really is a pity you didn't come in the summer as it is rather more attractive round here then . . . How do you like my friends the Nauds? . . . What a nice family they are! I know them well . . . You would not find a better man than Naud anywhere . . . He may not be a very deep thinker, he may be a tiny bit arrogant, but he is so unaffected and sincere . . . He is very rich, you know.'

'And Geneviève Naud?'

'A charming girl . . . Without any . . . Yes, charming is how I'd describe her . . .'

'I presume I'll have the opportunity to meet her . . . She'll soon be better, I hope?'

'Of course she will . . . of course . . . She's just like any other young girl of her age . . . Cheers . . .'

'Did you know Retailleau?'

'By sight . . . His mother seems to be well thought of . . . I would show you round if you were here for longer as there are some interesting people scattered here and there in the villages roundabout . . . My uncle, the general, frequently used to say that it is in country districts and especially here in La Vendée that . . .'

Pure waffle! If Maigret gave Groult-Cotelle the chance he would start telling him the history of every family in the neighbourhood all over again.

'I am afraid I must go now . . .'

'Oh yes! Your investigations! . . . How are you getting on? Are you optimistic? . . . If you want my opinion, the answer is to get hold of whoever is responsible for all these false rumours . . .'

'Have you any idea who it might be?'

'Me? Of course not. Don't start thinking I have any bright ideas on the subject, please . . . I'll probably see you this evening, as Etienne has asked me to dinner and unless I'm too busy . . .'

Busy doing what, pray? Anyone would think that words in this particular neighbourhood took on a completely different meaning.

'Have you heard the rumour about the cap?'

'What cap? Oh, yes . . . I was lost for a moment . . . I did hear some vague story . . . But is it true? Has it really been found? That's the key to it all, isn't it?'

No, that was not the key to it all. The young girl's confession, for example, was just as important as the discovery of the cap. But would Maigret be able to keep to himself what he knew much longer?

Five minutes later, Maigret rang the doctor's bell. A little maid answered the door and started to explain that the surgery was closed until one o'clock. He must have persisted for he was shown into the garage where a tall, strapping fellow with a cheerful face was repairing a motor-bike.

It was the same old story:

'Superintendent Maigret of the Police Judiciaire . . . I'm here in an unofficial capacity . . .'

'I'll show you into my office, if I may, and then when I've washed my hands . . .'

Maigret waited near the folding table which was used to examine the patients. It was covered with an oil-cloth.

'So you're the famous Superintendent Maigret? I've heard quite a lot about you . . . I've a friend who pores over the miscellaneous news items in the papers . . . He lives thirty-five kilometres away, but if he knew you were in Saint-Aubin he'd be over here like a shot . . . You solved the Landru case, didn't you?'

He had hit on one of the very few cases Maigret had had nothing to do with.

'And to what do we owe the honour of your presence in Saint-Aubin? For it is, indeed, an honour . . . I am sure you would like something to drink ... I'm looking after a sick child at the moment and I've left him in the sitting-room as it's warmer there, so I have had to bring you in here ... Will you have a brandy?'

And that was all. Maigret just drank his brandy.

'Retailleau? A charming boy ... I believe he was a good son to his mother ... She never complained about him, at any rate ... She's one of my patients ... a strange woman whom life ought to have treated better. She came from a good family, too. Everyone was amazed when she married Joseph Retailleau, a commoner who worked in the dairy.

'Etienne Naud? He's a real character ... We go shooting together ... He's a crack shot ... Groult-Cotelle? No, you could hardly call him a good shot, but that's because he is very short-sighted ...

'So, you have met everyone already ... Have you seen Tine, too? ... You haven't seen Tine yet? ... Note that I mention her name with great respect, like everyone else in Saint-Aubin ... Tine is Madame Naud's mother ... Madame Bréjon, if you prefer ... Her son is an examining magistrate in Paris ... Yes, that's right ... he's the one you must know ... His mother was a La Noue, one of the great families in La Vendée ... She does not want to be a bother to her daughter and son-in-law and she lives alone, near the church ... at the age of eighty-two, she's still sound of wind and limb and she's one of my worst patients ...

'You're staying in Saint-Aubin for a few days, are you?

'What? The cap? Oh, yes ... No, I haven't heard anything about that myself ... Well, I did hear one or two rumours ...

'All this was discovered rather late in the day, you see ... If I had known at the time, I would have carried out an autopsy ... But put yourself in my position ... I was told the poor boy had been run over by a train ... It was patently obvious to me he *had* been run over by a train and naturally, I wrote my report along those lines ...'

Maigret scowled, for he could have sworn that they were all in league with one another, that whether peevish or merry like the doctor, they had passed round the story as they might pass round a ball, giving each other knowing looks as they did so.

The sky was almost bright, now. Reflections shone in all the puddles and patches of mud glistened in places.

The Superintendent walked up the main street once more. He had not looked to see what it was called but it was most probably the Rue de la République. He decided to go into the Trois Mules, opposite the Lion d'Or, where he had received such a cold welcome that morning.

The bar was brighter than that of the Lion d'Or, with framed prints and a photograph of a President who had held office some thirty or forty years earlier hanging on the whitewashed walls. Behind the bar was another room, deserted and gloomy-looking; this was evidently where the locals came to dance on Sundays, for there was a platform at one end and the room was festooned with paper chains.

Four men were seated at a table, enjoying a bottle of full-bodied wine. One of them coughed affectedly when the Superintendent came in, as if to say to the others:

'There he is . . .'

Maigret sat down on one of the benches at the other end of the table. This time, he felt the atmosphere was different, for the men had stopped talking and he knew full well that before he came in, they would certainly not have been drinking and looking at each other in silence as they sat at the table.

They looked just like characters in a dumb show as they sat together in a huddle, their elbows and shoulders touching. Eventually, the oldest of the four men, a ploughman by the look of the whip beside him, spat on the floor, whereupon the others burst out laughing.

Was that long stream of spittle meant for Maigret?

'What can I get you?' inquired a young woman, tilting her hips in order to hold her grubby-looking baby.

'I'd like some of your *vin rosé*.'

'A jug?'

'All right . . .'

Maigret puffed furiously at his pipe. Up until now the townsfolk had concealed or at any rate disguised their hostility towards him, but now they were sneering at him, indeed, deliberately provoking him.

'Even the dirtiest jobs have got to be done, if you ask me, sonny boy,' said the ploughman after a long silence, no one having asked him for his opinion in the first place.

46

His cronies roared with laughter at this, as if that simple pronouncement had some extraordinary significance for them. One man, however, did not laugh, a young lad of eighteen or nineteen with pale grey eyes and a pock-marked face. Leaning on one elbow, he looked Maigret straight in the eye, as if he wanted him to feel the full force of his hatred or contempt.

'Some people have no pride!' growled another man.

'If you've got the cash, pride doesn't often come into it . . .'

Perhaps their remarks did not amount to anything very much, but Maigret got the message, none the less. He had finally clashed with the opposition party, to describe the situation in political terms.

Who could know for sure? Undoubtedly, all the rumours flying about had originated in the Trois Mules. And if the townspeople laid the blame at Maigret's door, they obviously thought Etienne Naud was paying him to hush up the truth.

'Tell me, gentlemen . . .'

Maigret rose to his feet and walked towards them. Although not timid by nature, he felt the blood rushing to his ears.

He was greeted in total silence. Only the young boy went on glowering at the Superintendent, while the others, looking rather awkward, turned their heads away.

'Those of you who live round here may be able to help me in the course of justice.'

They were suspicious, the rascals. Maigret's words had certainly stirred them up, but they still would not give in. The old man muttered crossly, looking at his spittle on the floor:

'Justice for who? For Naud?'

The Superintendent ignored the remark and went on talking. Meanwhile, the *patronne* hovered in the kitchen doorway, standing there with the child in her arms.

'In order for justice to be carried out, I need to discover two things in particular. Firstly, I need to find one of Retailleau's friends, a real friend and if possible someone who was with him on that last evening . . .'

Maigret realized that the person in question was the youngest of the four men, for the other three glanced in his direction.

'Secondly, I need to find the cap. You know what I'm talking about.'

'Go on, Louis!' growled the ploughman, as he rolled a cigarette.
But the young man was still not convinced.

'Who's sent you?'

It was certainly the first time Maigret's authority had been questioned by a young country lad. And yet it was essential that he explained himself, for he was determined to gain the lad's confidence.

'Superintendent Maigret, Police Judiciaire . . .'

Who knows? Perhaps luck would have it that the boy had heard of him. But alas, this was not the case.

'Why are you staying with the Nauds?'

'Because he was told I was coming and was at the station to meet me. And as I didn't know the neighbourhood . . .'

'There are inns . . .'

'I didn't know that when I arrived . . .'

'Who's the man in the inn across the road?'

It was Maigret who was being interrogated!

'A private detective . . .'

'Who's he working for?'

'I don't know.'

'Why is there still no proper inquiry into the affair? Albert died three weeks ago . . .'

'That's the stuff, my boy! Go on!' the three men seemed to be saying to the youngster who stood rigidly in front of them with a grim look on his face in an effort to combat his shyness.

'No one lodged a complaint.'

'So you can kill anyone, and so long as no one lodges a complaint . . .'

'The doctor concluded it was an accident.'

'Was he there when it happened?'

'As soon as I have enough evidence, the inquiry will be made official . . .'

'What do you mean by evidence?'

'Well, if we could prove that the cap was discovered between Naud's house and the place where the body was found, for example . . .'

'We'll have to take him to Désiré,' said the stoutest of the men who was wearing a carpenter's overall. 'Give us another one, Mélie . . . Bring us another glass . . .'

Even now, it was a victory for Maigret.

'What time did Retailleau leave the café that night?'

'Roundabout half past eleven ...'

'Were there many people in the café?'

'Four ... We played *coinchée* ...'

'Did you all leave together?'

'The two other men took the road to the left ... I went part of the way with Albert.'

'In which direction?'

'Towards Naud's house.'

'Did Albert confide in you?'

'No.'

The young lad's face darkened. He said no reluctantly, for he obviously wanted to be scrupulously honest.

'He didn't say why he was going to the Nauds'?'

'No. He was very angry.'

'Who with?'

'With her.'

'You mean Mademoiselle Naud? Had he told you about her before?'

'Yes ...'

'What did he tell you?'

'Everything and nothing ... Not in words ... He used to go there nearly every night ...'

'Did he brag about it?'

'No.' He gave Maigret a look of reproach. 'He was in love and everyone could see he was. He couldn't hide it.'

'And he was angry with her on that last day?'

'Yes. Something was on his mind the whole evening, for he kept on looking at his watch as we played cards. Just as we parted company on the road ...'

'Where exactly?'

'Five hundred yards from the Nauds' house ...'

'The place, then, where he was found dead?'

'More or less ... I had gone half way with him ...'

'And you are sure he went on along the road?'

'Yes ... He squeezed my hands and said with tears in his eyes: "It's all over, Louis, old chap ..."'

'What was all over?'

'It was all over between him and Geneviève … That's what I assumed … He meant he was going to see her for the last time.'

'But did he go?'

'There was a moon that night … It was freezing … I could still see him when he was only about a hundred yards from the house.'

'And the cap?'

Young Louis got up and looked at the others, his mind made up.

'Come with me …'

'Can you trust him, Louis?' asked one of the older men. 'Be careful, son.'

But Louis was at the age when one is prepared to risk all to win all. He looked Maigret in the eye as if to say: 'You're a real blackguard if you let me down!'

'Follow me … I live very near here …'

'Your glass … Yours, Superintendent … And you can believe everything the lad says, I promise … He's as honest as they come, that boy …'

'Your good health, gentlemen …'

Maigret had no choice but to drink a toast with the four men. The large glasses made a tinkling sound as they clinked them together. He then followed Louis out of the room, completely forgetting to pay for his jug of wine.

As they came outside, Maigret saw old Cadaver on the opposite side of the road. He had his briefcase under his arm and was about to go into the Lion d'Or. Was Maigret mistaken? It seemed to him that his former colleague had a sardonic smile on his face, although he only caught a glimpse of him sideways on.

'Come with me … This way …'

They made their way along narrow lanes which were quite unknown to Maigret and which linked up with the three or four streets in the village. They came to a row of cottages, each with its own tiny fenced-in front garden. Louis pushed open a small gate with a bell attached to it and called out:

'It's me!'

He went into a kitchen where four or five children were sitting round the table having their lunch.

'What is it, Louis?' asked his mother, looking uncomfortably at Maigret.

'Wait here ... I'll be back in a minute, Monsieur ...'

Louis rushed up the stairs which led down to the kitchen itself and went into a room. Maigret heard the sound of a drawer being pulled open, of someone walking about and knocking over a chair. Downstairs, meanwhile, Louis's mother shut the kitchen door but did not really know whether or not to make Maigret welcome.

Louis came downstairs, pale and worried-looking.

'Someone's stolen it!' he declared, with a stony expression on his face.

And then, turning to his mother, he said in a harsh voice:

'Someone's been here ... Who was it? ... Who came here this morning?'

'Look, Louis ...'

'Who? Tell me who it was! Who stole the cap?'

'I don't even know what cap you're talking about ...'

'Someone went up to my room ...'

He was in such an excited state that he looked as if he was about to hit his mother.

'Will you please calm down! Can't you see how rude you're being, speaking to me in that tone of voice?'

'Have you been in the house all morning?'

'I went out to the butcher's and the baker's ...'

'And what about the little ones?'

'I took the two youngest boys next door, as usual. The two that are not yet at school.'

'Forgive me, Superintendent. I just don't understand. The cap was in my drawer this morning. I am positive it was. I saw it ...'

'But what cap do you mean? Will you answer me that? Anyone would think you've taken leave of your senses! You'd do better to sit down and have your lunch ... As for this gentleman you've left standing ...'

But Louis gave his mother a pointed look, full of suspicion, and pulled Maigret outside.

'Come with me ... I have something else to say ... I swear, over my father's dead body, that the cap ...'

4

The Theft of the Cap

The impatient youngster walked quickly up the street, his neck taut and his body bent forward as he pulled the reluctant Maigret along with him. Here he was, being guided almost by force towards unknown delights by a glib and persuasive younger man, and the situation made him extremely uneasy. Such equivocal circumstances reminded him of a common enough scene in Montmartre, where one would see the doormen of dubious-looking clubs push an intimidated gentleman through the doors, against his will.

Louis's mother stood on the doorstep and shouted as they were going round the corner of the little street:

'Aren't you going to have your lunch, Louis?'

Was Maigret the only one who heard? He was spurred on by strong feelings. He had promised this gentleman from Paris he would do something and now he was unable to keep his word because an unexpected occurrence had complicated matters. Would he not be taken for an impostor? Was he not endangering the cause he had all too hastily championed?

'I want Désiré to tell you himself. The cap was in my bedroom. I wonder if my mother was telling the truth.'

Maigret was wondering the same thing and at the same time thought of Inspector Cavre whom he could picture vividly wheedling information out of the woman with six children.

'What time is it?'

'Ten past twelve.'

'Désiré will still be at the dairy. Let's go this way. It's quicker.'

Again, Louis led Maigret through little alley-ways, past small, shabby houses which the Superintendent had never seen before; once, a sow covered in mud rushed at their legs.

'One evening, the evening of the funeral, in fact, old Désiré came

52

into the Lion d'Or and threw a cap on the table. Speaking in *patois*, he asked whose it was. I recognized it straightaway as I was with Albert when he bought it in Niort. I remembered having a discussion with him about what colour he should get.'

'What is your trade?' asked Maigret.

'I'm a carpenter. The largest of the men you saw just now in the Trois Mules is my boss. Well, Désiré was drunk that evening. There were at least six people in the café. I asked him where he found the cap. Désiré collects the milk from the little farms in the marshland, you see, and as you can't get to them by road in a lorry, he does his rounds by boat ...

'"I found it in the reeds," he said, "very near the dead poplar."

'I repeat, there were at least six people who heard him say this. Everyone here knows that the dead poplar is between the Nauds' house and the spot where Albert's body was found ...

'This way ... We're going to the dairy. You can see the chimney-stack over there, on the left.'

They had left the village behind them. Dark hedges enclosed tiny gardens. A little further on, the dairy came into view. The low buildings were painted white and the tall chimney-stack stood straight up against the sky.

'I don't know why I decided to shove the cap into my pocket ... I already had the feeling that too many people were keen to hush up this whole affair ...

'"It's young Retailleau's cap," someone said.

'And Désiré, drunk as he was, frowned, for he suddenly realized that he was not supposed to have found it where he did.

'"Désiré, are you sure it was near the dead poplar?"

'Well, Superintendent, the very next day, he didn't want to admit to anything. When he was asked exactly where he had found it, he would say:

'"Over there ... I don't really know exactly! Just leave me alone, will you! I'm sick of this cap business ..."'

Flat-bottomed boats filled with pitchers of milk were tied up beside the dairy.

'I say, Philippe ... Has old Désiré gone home?'

'He can't have gone home, seeing as he never set out ... He must have got plastered yesterday as he didn't do his round this morning.'

An idea flashed through Maigret's mind.

'Would the manager be around at this time of day, do you think?' he asked his companion.

'He'll probably be in his office ... The little door at the side ...'

'Wait here a minute ...'

Oscar Drouhet, the manager of the dairy, was in fact on the telephone when Maigret walked in. The Superintendent introduced himself. Drouhet had the serious, steadfast manner of any local craftsman turned small businessman. Pulling on his pipe with short, sharp puffs, he observed Maigret and let him speak, trying all the while to size him up.

'Albert Retailleau's father was once in your employ, I believe? I've been told he was the victim of an accident at the dairy ...'

'One of the boilers exploded.'

'I understand his widow receives a considerable income from you?'

He was an intelligent man, for he realized immediately that Maigret's question was loaded with innuendoes.

'What do you mean?'

'Did his widow take you to court, or did you yourself ...'

'Don't try to complicate the issue. It was my fault the accident happened. Retailleau had been saying for at least two months that the boiler needed a complete overhaul and even that it should be replaced. It was the busiest time of the year and I kept putting it off.'

'Were your workmen insured?'

'Nowhere near adequately ...'

'Forgive me. Let me ask you whether you were the one who didn't think they were adequately insured, or if ...'

Once more, they both understood each other perfectly, and Maigret did not have to finish his sentence.

'His widow lodged a complaint against us, as she was entitled to do,' Oscar Drouhet admitted.

'I am sure,' the Superintendent went on, smiling slightly, 'she did not approach you merely to ask you to go into the question of compensation pay. She sent lawyers to investigate ...'

'Is that so unusual? A woman knows nothing of these things, would you not agree? I acknowledged the validity of her claim and in addition to the pension she received from the insurance company,

54

I elected to give her a further sum which I pay out of my own pocket. On top of this, I paid for her son's education and took him on here as soon as he was old enough to work. My kindness was rewarded, what's more, for he was a hard-working, honest lad. Albert was a clever boy and quite capable of running the dairy in my absence ...'

'Thank you ... Or rather, just one more question: Albert's mother hasn't called on you since the death of her son, has she?'

Drouhet managed not to smile, but his brown eyes flickered briefly.

'No,' he said, 'she hasn't come to see me *yet*.'

Maigret had been right, then, in this respect. Madame Retailleau was indeed a woman who knew how to defend herself and attack, if need be. She was undoubtedly the sort of person who would never lose sight of her interests.

'It seems that Désiré, your milk collector, did not come to work this morning?'

'That often happens ... On the days he is more drunk than usual ...'

Maigret went back to the pock-marked youth who was terrified he would no longer be taken seriously.

'What did he say? He's a good sort, but he's really on the other side ...'

'Whose side?'

'Monsieur Naud's, the doctor's, the mayor's ... He couldn't have said anything against me ...'

'Of course not ...'

'We've got to find old Désiré ... We could go round to his house, if you like ... It's not far ...'

They set off again, both forgetting it was lunchtime, and eventually came to a house on the fringe of the little town. Louis knocked on a glass door, pushed it open and shouted into the semi-darkness:

'Désiré! Hey! Désiré!'

But only a cat emerged and rubbed itself against the boy's legs. Meanwhile, Maigret came upon a kind of den which consisted of a bed without a cover or a pillow where Désiré obviously slept with all his clothes on, a small, cracked iron stove, a bundle of rags, empty bottles and old bones.

'He must have gone off drinking somewhere. Come on ...'

Still the same concern he would not be taken seriously.

'He worked on Etienne Naud's farm, you see . . . He's still on good terms with them, even though he was sacked. He's the sort of person who wants to be on good terms with everyone, and that is why he put on an act when people started asking him questions about the cap the day after he found it.

'"What cap? Ah, yes! The tattered one I picked up somewhere or other, I've forgotten where . . . I've no idea what's happened to it . . ."'

'Well, Monsieur, I for one can tell you that there were blood stains on the cap. And I wrote and told the Director of Prosecutions . . .'

'So it was you who wrote the anonymous letters?'

'I wrote three, so if there were more, someone else must have written them. I wrote about the cap and then about Albert's relationship with Geneviève Naud . . . Wait, perhaps Désiré is in here . . .'

Louis had darted into a grocer's shop, but through the windows Maigret could see there were bottles at the end of the counter and two tables at the back of the shop for customers' use. The youngster looked crestfallen as he came out again.

'He was here early this morning. He must have done the rounds . . .'

Maigret had only been into two cafés: the Lion d'Or and the Trois Mules. In less than half an hour, he came to know a dozen or more, not cafés in the true sense of the word, but premises the average passer-by would not have suspected were licensed. The harness-maker had a kind of bar next to his workshop and the farrier had a similar arrangement. Old Désiré had been seen in almost every bar they visited.

'How was he?'

'He was well enough.'

And they knew what that meant.

'He was in a hurry when he left, as he had to go to the post-office . . .'

'The post-office is shut,' Louis said. 'But I know the post-mistress, and she'll open up if I tap on her window.'

'Especially when she knows I've a call to make,' said Maigret.

And sure enough, as soon as the boy tapped on the pane, the window opened.

'Is that you, Louis? What do you want?'

'It's the gentleman from Paris. He wants to make a call.'

'I'll open up right away . . .'

Maigret asked to be put through to the Nauds.

'Hello! Who is it speaking?'

He did not recognize the voice, a man's voice.

'Hello! Who did you say? Ah! Forgive me . . . Alban, yes . . . I hadn't realized . . . Maigret, here . . . Could you tell Madame Naud I shan't be coming back for lunch? Give her my apologies. No, it's nothing important . . . I don't know when I'll be back . . .'

As he left the booth, he saw from the look on his young companion's face that he had something interesting to tell him.

'How much do I owe you, Mademoiselle? . . . Thank you . . . I'm sorry to have bothered you.'

Back in the street once more, Louis informed Maigret excitedly:

'I *told* you something was afoot. Old Désiré came in on the dot of eleven. Do you know what he posted? He sent a money-order for five hundred francs to his son in Morocco . . . His son's up to no good. He left home without any warning. He and his father used to quarrel and fight every day . . . Désiré's never been known to be anything other than drunk, as it were . . . And now his son writes to him from time to time, either complaining or asking for money . . . But all his money goes on drink, you see . . . The old man never has a sou . . . Sometimes he sends a money-order for ten or twenty francs at the beginning of the month . . . I wonder . . . Wait a minute . . . If you still have time, we'll go and see his stepsister . . .'

The streets, the houses they had been walking past all morning, were now becoming familiar to the Superintendent. He was beginning to recognize people's faces and the names painted above the shops. Rather than brighten up, the sky had clouded over again and the air was heavy with moisture. Soon there would be fog.

'His stepsister knits for a living. She's an old spinster and used to work for our last priest. This is her house . . .'

He went up three steps to the blue-painted front door, knocked and then opened it.

'Désiré's not here, is he?'

He then beckoned Maigret to come inside.

'Hello, Désiré . . . I'm sorry to barge in like this, Mademoiselle

Jeanne ... There's a gentleman from Paris who'd like to have a few words with your stepbrother ...'

The tiny room was very clean. The table stood near a mahogany bed covered with an enormous red eiderdown. Maigret glanced round and saw a crucifix with a sprig of boxwood behind it, a figure of the Virgin Mary in a glass case on the chest of drawers, and two cutlets on a plate with writing round the picture on it.

Désiré tried to stand up but knew he was in danger of falling off his chair. He maintained a dignified pose and muttering thickly, his tongue not being able to articulate the words, he said:

'What can I do for you?'

For he was polite. He was always anxious to make that clear.

'I may have drunk too much ... Yes, maybe I've had a good few drinks, but I *am* polite, Monsieur ... Everyone'll tell you that Désiré is polite to one and all ...'

'Look, Désiré, the gentleman wants to know exactly where you found the cap ... You know, Albert's cap ...'

These few words were enough. The drunkard's face hardened and assumed a totally blank expression. His watery eyes became even more glaucous.

'Don't play the fool, Désiré ... I've got the cap ... You remember, when you threw it on the table at François's place, that evening, and said you'd found it by the dead poplar ...'

The old monkey was not satisfied with a simple denial. He smirked with delight and went on with more gusto than was necessary:

'Do you understand what he's saying, M'sieur? Why should I have thrown a cap on the table, I'd like to know? I've never worn a cap ... Jeanne! Where's my hat? Show this gentleman my hat ... These youngsters have no respect for their elders ...'

'Désiré ...'

'Désiré, indeed? ... Désiré may be drunk, but he's polite and would be obliged if you'd call him Monsieur Désiré ... Do you hear, you scalliwag, you bastard!'

'Have you heard from your son recently?' interrupted Maigret suddenly.

'So, it's my son, now, eh? You want to know what my son's been up to? Well, just let me tell you, he's a soldier! He's a brave fellow, my son!'

'That's what I thought. He'll certainly be pleased with the money-order.'

'Soon I won't be allowed to send my son a money-order, is that it? Hey, Jeanne! Do you hear? And maybe I won't be allowed to come and have a bite to eat with my stepsister either!'

At the beginning, he had probably been frightened, but now he was really enjoying himself. He made himself a laughing-stock in the end, and when Maigret got up to go he followed him out to the front doorstep, staggering all the way, and would have followed him into the street if Jeanne had not stopped him.

'Désiré's polite ... Do you hear, you rascal? And if anyone tells you, Monsieur Parisian, that Désiré's son is not a fine fellow ...'

Doors opened. Maigret wanted to get away.

With tears in his eyes and his teeth clenched, Louis said emphatically:

'I swear to you, Superintendent ...'

'It's all right, lad, I believe you ...'

'It's that man staying at the Lion d'Or, isn't it?'

'I think so. I'd like to have proof, though. Do you know anyone who was at the Lion d'Or last night?'

'I'm sure Liboureau's son was there. He goes in every evening.'

'Right! I'll wait at the Trois Mules while you go and ask him if he saw Désiré. Find out if the old man got into conversation with our visitor from Paris ... Wait ... We can eat at the Trois Mules, can't we? We'll have a bite of something together ... Off you go, be quick ...'

There was no tablecloth. The table was set with metal knives and forks. All that was offered at midday was a beetroot salad, rabbit and a piece of cheese with some bad white wine. When Louis returned, however, he felt very uncomfortable sitting at the Super-intendent's table.

'Well?'

'Désiré went to the Lion d'Or.'

'Did he talk to old Cadaver?'

'To who?'

'Never mind. It's a nickname we gave him. Did Désiré talk to him?'

'It didn't happen like that. The man you call Cadav ... It sounds really odd to me ...'

'His name is Justin Cavre ...'

'Monsieur Cavre, according to Liboureau, spent a good part of the evening watching the card players and saying nothing. Désiré was drinking in his usual corner. He left at about ten o'clock and a few minutes later Liboureau noticed that the Parisian had disappeared too. But he doesn't know if he left the inn or just went upstairs ...'

'He left.'

'What are you going to do?'

He was so proud to be working with the Superintendent that he could not wait to get started.

'Who was it that reported seeing a considerable sum of money in Madame Retailleau's house?'

'The postman ... Josaphat ... Another drunkard ... He's called Josaphat because when his wife died he had more to drink than usual and kept on saying through his tears: "Good-bye, Céline ... We'll meet again in the valley of Josaphat ... Count on me ..."'

'What would you like for dessert?' asked the *patronne*, who obviously had one of her children in her arms all day and worked with her one free hand. 'I've biscuits or apples.'

'Have which ever you like,' said Maigret.

And the youngster replied, blushing:

'I don't mind ... Some biscuits, please ... This is what happened ... about ten or twelve days after Albert's funeral, the postman went to collect some money from Madame Retailleau ... She was busy doing the housework ... She looked in her purse but she needed fifty francs more ... So she walked over to the dresser, where the soup-tureen is ... You must have noticed it ... It's got blue flowers on it ... She stood in front of it so that Josaphat couldn't see what she was doing, but that evening, he swore he had seen some thousand-franc notes, at least ten, he said, maybe more ... Now, everybody knows that Madame Retailleau has never had as much money as that at one time ... Albert spent all he earned ...'

'What on?'

'He was rather vain ... There's nothing wrong with that ... He liked to be well-dressed and he had his suits made in Niort ... He would often pay for a round of drinks, too ... He would tell his mother that as long as she had her pension ...'

'They quarrelled, then?'

'Sometimes ... Albert was an independent chap, you see ... His mother would have liked to treat him like a little boy. If he had listened to her he would not have gone out at night and he'd never have set foot in the café ... My mother's just the opposite ... She's only too anxious to get me out of the house ...'

'Where can we find Josaphat?'

'He'll probably be at home now, or else about to finish his first round. In half an hour he'll be at the station to collect the sacks with the second post ...'

'Will you bring us some liqueurs please, Madame?'

Through the curtains, Maigret stared at the windows on the other side of the street, imagined old Cadaver eating his lunch just as he was, and watching him likewise. It was not long before he realized his mistake, for a car ground noisily to a halt opposite the Lion d'Or and Cavre got out, his briefcase under his arm. Maigret watched him lean over towards the driver to find out how much he owed.

'Whose car is that?'

'It belongs to the man who owns the garage. We went past it a little while ago. He acts as a taxi-driver every now and again, if someone's ill and needs to be taken to hospital, or if someone wants something urgently ...'

The car made a half turn and judging by the noise did not go far.

'You see. He's gone back to his garage.'

'Do you get on well with him?'

'He's a friend of my boss.'

'Go and ask him where he took his client this morning.'

Less than five minutes later, Louis came running back.

'He went to Fontenay-le-Comte. It's exactly twenty-two kilometres from here ...'

'Didn't you ask him where they went in Fontenay?'

'He was told to stop at the Café du Commerce, in the Rue de la République. The Parisian went in, came out with another man and told the driver to wait ...'

'You don't know who this man was?'

'The garage-man didn't know him ... They were gone about half an hour ... Then the man you call Cavre was driven back. He only gave a five franc tip ...'

Had not Etienne Naud also gone to Fontenay-le-Comte?

'Let's go and see Josaphat . . .'

He had already left his house. They met up with him at the station where he was waiting for the train. When he saw young Louis with Maigret from the other end of the platform, he looked annoyed and went hurriedly into the station-master's office, as if he had some business to attend to.

But Louis and Maigret waited for him to come out.

'Josaphat!' called out Louis.

'What do you want? I'm in a hurry . . .'

'There's a gentleman here who'd like a word with you.'

'Who? I'm on duty and when I'm on duty . . .'

Maigret had the utmost difficulty in steering him towards an empty spot between the lamp-room and the urinals.

'I just want an answer to a simple question . . .'

The postman was on his guard, that was obvious. He pretended he heard the train and was ready to rush off to the carriage carrying the post sacks. At the same time, he could not help glowering briefly at Louis for putting him in this position.

Maigret already knew he would get nothing out of him, that his colleague Cavre had already questioned him.

'Hurry up, I can hear the train . . .'

'About ten days ago, you called at Madame Retailleau's house to collect some money.'

'I'm not allowed to discuss my work . . .'

'But you discussed it that very evening . . .'

'In front of me!' interjected the youngster. 'Avrard was there, and so was Lhériteau and little Croman . . .'

The postman stood on one leg and then the other, with a stupid, insolent look on his face.

'What right have you to interrogate me?'

'We can ask you a question, can't we? You're not the Pope, are you?'

'And what if I asked him to show me his papers? He's been snooping round the neighbourhood all morning!'

Maigret had already begun to walk away, knowing that it was pointless trying to discuss the matter further. Louis, however, lost his temper in the face of such blatant hostility.

'Do you mean you've the nerve to say you didn't tell everyone about the thousand franc notes you saw in the soup tureen?'

'I can say what I like, can't I? Or are you going to try and stop me?'

'You told everyone what you saw. I'll get the others to back me up, I'll get them to repeat what you said. You even said the notes were held together by a pin . . .'

The postman shrugged his shoulders and walked away. This time the train really was coming into the station and he walked down the platform to where the mail-coach usually came to a halt.

'The swine!' growled Louis under his breath. 'You heard what he said, didn't you? But you can take my word for it. Why should I lie? I knew perfectly well this would happen . . .'

'Why?'

'Because it's always the same with them . . .'

'With who?'

'With the lot of them . . . I can't really explain . . . They stick together . . . They're rich . . . They're either related to or else friends of magistrates, *préfets* and generals . . . I don't know whether you understand what I'm trying to say . . . So the townspeople are afraid . . . They often gossip at night when they've had a bit too much to drink and then regret it the next day . . .'

'What are you going to do now? You're not going back to Paris, are you?'

'Of course not, son. Why do you ask?'

'I don't know. The other man looks . . .'

The youngster stopped himself just in time. He was probably about to say something like:

'The other man looks so much stronger than you!'

And it was true. Through the mist that was beginning to come down, as if it were dusk, Maigret thought he saw Cavre's face, his thin lips spreading into a sardonic smile.

'Isn't your boss going to be cross if you don't get back to your work?'

'Oh! No . . . He's not one of them . . . If he could help us prove poor Albert was murdered, he would, I promise you . . .'

Maigret jumped when a voice behind him asked:

'Could you tell me the way to the Lion d'Or, please?'

The railwayman on duty near the small gate pointed to the street which opened up about a hundred yards away.

'Go straight on ... It's on your left, you'll see ...'

A small, plump little man, faultlessly dressed and carrying a suitcase almost as large as himself, looked around for a non-existent porter. The Superintendent examined him from head to foot, but his efforts were in vain. He had absolutely no idea who the stranger was.

5

Three Women in a Drawing-Room

Louis dived into the fog with his head bowed and before it enveloped him completely, he said to Maigret:

'If you want to get hold of me, I'll be at the Trois Mules all evening.'

It was five o'clock. A thick fog had descended over the town and darkness fell at the same time. Maigret had to walk the length of the main street in Saint-Aubin in order to reach the station, where he would take the road leading to Etienne Naud's house. Louis had offered to go with him, but there is a limit to everything and Maigret had had enough. He was beginning to get tired of being pulled along by this excited and restless youngster.

As they parted company, Louis had said with a note of reproach in his voice, almost sentimentally:

'They'll butter you up and you'll start believing everything they tell you.' He was referring to the Nauds, of course.

With his hands in his pockets and the collar of his overcoat turned up, Maigret walked cautiously towards the light in the distance, for any lamp which shone through the fog was a kind of lighthouse. Because of the intense brightness of this halo which looked as if it was still a long way off, the Superintendent felt he was walking towards an important goal. And then, all of a sudden, he almost bumped into the cold window of the Vendée Cooperative which he had walked past twenty times that day. The narrow shop had been painted green fairly recently and there were free offers of glassware and earthenware displayed in the window.

Further on, in total darkness, he came up against something hard and groped about in confusion for some time before he realized he had landed in the middle of the carts standing outside the wheel-wright's house with their shafts in the air.

The bells loomed into view immediately above his head. He was walking past the church. The post-office was on the right, with its doll-size counter; opposite, on the other side of the road, stood the doctor's house.

The Lion d'Or was on one side of the street, the Trois Mules on the other. It was extraordinary to think that inside each lighted house people were living in a tiny circle of warmth, like incrustations in the icy infinity of the universe.

Saint-Aubin was not a large town. The lights in the dairy made one think of a brightly-lit factory at night. A railway-engine in the station was sending out sparks.

Albert Retailleau had grown up in this microcosm of a world. His mother had spent all her life in Saint-Aubin. Apart from holidays in Sables d'Olonne, someone like Geneviève Naud would to all intents and purposes never leave the town.

As the train slowed down a little before arriving at Niort station, Maigret had noticed empty streets in the rain, rows of gaslights and shuttered houses. He had thought to himself: 'There are people who spend their whole lives in that street.'

Testing the ground with his feet, he made his way along the canal towards another lighthouse which was in fact the lantern outside Naud's house. On various train journeys, whether on cold nights or in slashing rain, Maigret had seen many such isolated houses, a rectangle of yellow light being the only sign of their existence. The imagination then sets to work and pictures all manner of things.

And so it was that Maigret came into the orbit of one of these welcoming lights. He walked up the stone steps, looked for the bell and then saw that the door was ajar. He went into the hall, deliberately shuffling his feet to make his presence known, but this did not deter whoever was in the drawing-room from continuing to hold forth in monotonous tones. Maigret took off his wet overcoat, his hat, wiped his feet on the straw mat and knocked on the door.

'Come in . . . Geneviève, open the door . . .'

He had already opened it; only one of the lamps in the drawing-room was lit. Madame Naud was sewing by the hearth and a very old woman was sitting opposite her. A young girl walked over to the door as Maigret came into the room.

'I'm sorry to disturb you . . .'

The girl looked at him anxiously, unable to decide whether or not he would betray her. Maigret merely bowed.

'This is my daughter Geneviève, Superintendent ... She so wanted to meet you. She is quite recovered now ... Allow me to introduce you to my mother ...'

So this was Clémentine Bréjon, a La Noue before she married and commonly known as Tine. This small, sprightly old lady with a wry expression on her face reminiscent of that on the busts of Voltaire, rose to her feet and asked in a curious falsetto voice:

'Well, Superintendent, do you feel you have caused enough havoc in our poor Saint-Aubin? Upon my word, I've seen you go up and down ten times or more this morning, and this afternoon I have it on good authority that you found yourself a young recruit ... Do you know, Louise, who acted as elephant-driver to the Superintendent?'

Had she deliberately chosen the word 'elephant-driver' to emphasize the difference in size between the lanky youth and the elephantesque Maigret?

Louise Naud, who was far from having her mother's vivacity and whose face was much longer and paler, did not look up from her work but just nodded her head and smiled faintly to show she was listening.

'Fillou's son ... It was bound to happen ... The boy must have lain in wait for him ... No doubt he has regaled you with some fine stories, Superintendent?'

'He has done nothing of the kind, Madame ... He merely directed me to the various people I wanted to see. I'd have found it difficult to find their houses on my own as the locals aren't exactly talkative on the whole ...'

Geneviève had sat down and was staring at Maigret as if she was hypnotized by him. Madame Naud looked up occasionally from her work and glanced furtively at her daughter.

The drawing-room looked exactly as it had done the previous evening for everything was in its usual place. An oppressive stillness hung over the room and it was really only the grandmother who conveyed any sense of normality.

'I am an old woman, Superintendent. Let me tell you that, some time ago, something much more serious happened which nearly destroyed Saint-Aubin. There used to be a clog factory which employed fifty people, men and women. It was at a time when there were endless strikes in France and workers walked out at the slightest provocation.'

Madame Naud had looked up from her work to listen and Maigret saw that she found it difficult to conceal her anxiety. Her thin face bore a striking resemblance to that of Bréjon the magistrate.

'One of the workmen in the clog factory was called Fillou. He wasn't a bad sort, but he was inclined to drink too much and when he was tipsy he thought he was a real orator. What happened exactly? One day, he went into the manager's office to lodge a complaint of some sort. Shortly afterwards the door opened. Fillou catapulted out, staggering backwards for several yards, and then fell into the canal.'

'And he was the father of my young companion with the pock-marked face?' inquired Maigret.

'His father, yes. He is dead, now. At the time, the town was divided into two factions. One side thought that the drunken Fillou had behaved abominably and that the manager had been forced to take violent action to get rid of him. The other side felt that the manager was completely in the wrong and that he had provoked Fillou, taunting him when referring to the large families of his employees with remarks like:

'"I can't help it if they breed on Saturday nights when they're pissed . . ."'

'Fillou is dead, you said?'

'He died two years ago of cancer of the stomach.'

'Did many people support him at the time of the incident?'

'The majority of people did not support him, but those who did were really committed to their cause. Every morning various people used to find threats written in chalk on their doors.'

'Are you implying, Madame, that the case is similar to the one we are dealing with now?'

'I am not implying anything, Superintendent. Old people love rambling on, you know. There is always some scandal or other to discuss in small towns. Life would be very dull, otherwise. And there will always be a few people willing to fan the flames . . .'

'What was the end of the Fillou affair?'

'Silence, of course ...'

'Yes, silence just about sums it up,' thought Maigret to himself. For despite the efforts of a few fanatics to stir things up, silence is always the most effective form of action. And he had been confronted with silence all day long.

Moreover, ever since he had come into the drawing-room, a strange feeling had taken hold of him, a feeling which made him somewhat uneasy. He had trailed through the streets from morning till night, sullenly and obstinately following Louis who had passed on to him something of his own eagerness.

'She's one of them ...' Louis would say.

And 'them' in Louis's mind meant a number of people who had conspired not to talk, and who did not want any trouble, people who wanted to let sleeping dogs lie.

In one sense, one could say that Maigret had sided with the small group of rebels. He had had a drink with them at the Trois Mules. He had disowned the Nauds when he declared he was not working for them and whenever Louis doubted his word, he was sorely tempted to give him proof of his loyalty.

And yet Louis had been right to look at the Superintendent suspiciously when he left him, for he had an inkling what would happen when his companion became the enemy's guest once again. That was why he had tried his best to escort Maigret all the way to the Nauds' front door, to bolster him up and caution him not to give in.

'I'll be at the Trois Mules all evening, if you need me ...'

He would wait in vain. Now that he was back in this cosy, bourgeois drawing-room, Maigret felt almost ashamed of himself for having wandered through the streets with a youngster and for having been snubbed by everyone he had persisted in questioning.

There was a portrait on the wall which Maigret had not noticed the night before, a portrait of Bréjon the examining magistrate, who seemed to be staring down at the Superintendent as if to say: 'Don't forget the purpose of your visit.'

He looked at Louise Naud's fingers as she sewed and was hypnotized by their nervousness. Her face remained almost serene, but her fingers revealed a fear which bordered on panic.

'What do you think of our doctor?' asked the talkative old lady.

'He's a real character, isn't he? You Parisians are wrong in thinking no one of interest lives in the country. If you were to stay here for two months, no more ... Louise, isn't your husband coming back?'

'He telephoned a short while ago to say he will be late. He's been called to La Roche-sur-Yon. He asked me to apologize on his behalf, Superintendent ...'

'I owe you an apology, too, for not having come back for lunch.'

'Geneviève! Would you give the Superintendent an *apéritif* ...'

'Well, children, I must be going.'

'Stay to dinner, *Maman*. Etienne will take you home in the car when he gets back.'

'I won't hear of it, my child. I don't need anyone to drive me home.'

Her daughter helped her tie the ribbons of a small black bonnet which sat jauntily on her head and gave her galoshes to wear over her shoes.

'Would you like me to have the horse harnessed for you?'

'Time enough for that the day of my funeral. Good-bye, Superintendent. If you're passing my house again, come in and see me. Good-night, Louise. Good-night, Vièvre ...'

And suddenly the door was closed once more and a great feeling of emptiness prevailed. Maigret now understood why they tried to make old Tine stay. Now that she had gone, an oppressive, uneasy silence fell over the room and one sensed an aura of fear. Louise Naud's fingers ran increasingly rapidly over her work, while the young girl desperately tried to find an excuse to leave the room but did not dare.

Was it not an incredible thought that although Albert Retailleau was dead, although he had been discovered one morning, cut to pieces on the railway-line, his son was living in this room at this very moment, in the form of a creature that would come into the world in a few months' time?

When Maigret turned towards the young girl, she did not look away. On the contrary, she stood up straight and looked Maigret squarely in the eye, as if to say:

'No, you did not dream it. I came into your bedroom last night and I wasn't sleepwalking. What I told you then is the truth. You see I am not ashamed of it. I am not mad. Albert was my lover and I am expecting his child ...'

Albert, the son of Madame Retailleau, a woman who had stood up for her rights so bravely after her husband's death, Albert, Louis's young and faithful friend, used to creep into this house at night without anyone knowing. And Geneviève would take him into her room, the one at the end of the right wing of the house.

'Will you excuse me, ladies. I should like to go for a short walk round the stableyards, if you have no objection, that is . . .'

'May I come with you?'

'You'll catch cold, Geneviève.'

'No, I won't *Maman*. I'll wrap up warmly.'

She went into the kitchen to fetch a hurricane lamp which she brought back lit. In the hall, Maigret helped her on with her cape.

'What would you like to see?' she asked in a low voice.

'Let's go into the yard.'

'We can go out this way. There's no point in going right round the house . . . Mind the steps . . .'

Lights were on in the stables whose doors were open, but the fog was so thick that one could not see anything.

'Your room is the one directly above us, isn't it?'

'Yes . . . I know what you are getting at . . . He didn't come in through the door, naturally . . . Come with me . . . You see this ladder . . . It's always left here . . . He just had to push it a few yards . . .'

'Which is your parents' room?'

'Three windows along.'

'And the other two windows?'

'One is the spare bedroom, where Alban slept last night. The other is a room which hasn't been used since my little sister died, and *Maman* has the key.'

She was cold; she tried not to show it in order not to look as if she wanted to end the conversation.

'Your mother and father never suspected anything?'

'No.'

'Had this affair been going on for some time?'

She answered at once.

'Three and a half months.'

'Was Retailleau aware of the consequences of these meetings?'

'Yes.'

'What did he intend to do?'

'He was going to tell my parents everything and marry me.'

'Why was he angry, that last evening?'

Maigret looked at her closely, trying his best to glimpse the expression on her face through the fog. The ensuing silence betrayed the young girl's amazement.

'I asked you ...'

'I heard what you said.'

'Well!'

'I don't understand. Why do you say he was angry ...'

And her hands trembled like her mother's, thereby causing the lantern to shake.

'Nothing out of the ordinary happened between you that night?'

'No, nothing.'

'Did Albert leave by the window as usual?'

'Yes ... There was a moon ... I saw him go over to the back of the yard where he could jump over the little wall onto the road.'

'What time was it?'

'Roundabout half past twelve.'

'Did he usually stay for such a short time?'

'What do you mean?'

She was playing for time. Behind a window, not far from where they were standing, they could see the old cook moving about.

'He arrived at about midnight. I imagine he usually stayed longer ... You didn't have a row?'

'Why should we have had a row?'

'I don't know ... I'm just asking ...'

'No ...'

'When was he to speak to your parents?'

'Soon ... We were waiting for a suitable moment ...'

'Try to remember accurately ... Are you sure there were no lights on in the house that night? You heard no noise? There was no one skulking in the yard?'

'I didn't see anything ... I swear to you, Superintendent, I know nothing ... Maybe you don't believe me, but it's the truth ... I'll never, do you hear, never tell my father what I told you last night ... I shall leave. I don't yet know what I'll do ...'

'Why did you tell me?'

'I don't know ... I was frightened ... I thought you would find out everything and tell my parents ...'

'Shall we go back? You're shivering.'

'You won't say anything?'

He did not know what to say. He did not want to be bound by a promise. He muttered:

'Trust me.'

Was he, too, 'one of them', to use Louis's phrase? Oh! Now he understood perfectly what the youngster meant. Albert Retailleau was dead and buried. A certain number of people in Saint-Aubin, the majority in fact, thought that since it was impossible to bring the young man back to life, the wisest course of action was to treat the subject as closed.

To be 'one of them' was to belong to that tribe. Even Albert's mother was 'one of them' since she had not appeared to understand why anyone should wish to investigate her son's death.

And those who had not subscribed to this view at the outset had been brought to heel one after the other. Désiré wished he had never found the cap. What cap? He now had money to drink his fill and could send a money-order for five hundred francs to his good-for-nothing son.

Josaphat, the postman, could not remember having seen a wad of thousand franc notes in the soup tureen.

Etienne Naud was embarrassed that his brother-in-law should have thought of sending someone like Maigret, a man bent on discovering the truth.

But what was the truth? And who stood to gain by discovering the truth? What good would it do?

The small group of men in the Trois Mules, a carpenter, a ploughman and a youngster called Louis Fillou whose father had already proved to be strong-willed, were the only ones to weave stories round the affair.

'Aren't you hungry, Superintendent?' asked Madame Naud, as Maigret came into the drawing-room. 'Where is my daughter?'

'She was in the hall just now. I expect she has gone up to her room for a minute.'

The atmosphere for the next quarter of an hour was gloomy indeed. Maigret and Louise Naud were now alone in the old-fashioned, stuffy drawing-room. From time to time a log toppled over and sent sparks flying into the grate. The single lamp with its pink shade shed a soft glow over the furniture. Familiar sounds coming from the kitchen occasionally broke the silence. They could hear the stove being filled with coal, a saucepan being moved, an earthenware plate being put on the table.

Maigret sensed that Louise Naud would have liked to talk. She was possessed by a demon who was pushing her to say ... To say what? She was in considerable difficulty. Sometimes she would open her mouth, as if she had decided to speak, and Maigret would be afraid of what she was going to say.

She said nothing. Her chest tightened in a nervous spasm and her shoulders shook for a second. She went on with her embroidery, making tiny stitches, as if weighed down by this cloak of silence and stillness which formed such a barrier between them.

Did she know that Retailleau and her daughter ...

'Do you mind if I smoke, Madame?'

She gave a start. Perhaps she had been afraid he was going to say something else. She stammered:

'Please do ... Make yourself at home ...'

Then she sat up straight and listened for a sound.

'Oh, my goodness ...'

Oh, my goodness what? She was merely waiting for her husband to return, waiting for someone to come and end the torment of this *tête à tête*.

And then Maigret began to feel sorry for her. What was to stop him getting up and saying:

'I think your brother made a mistake in asking me to come here. There is nothing I can do. This whole affair is none of my business and, if you don't mind, I'll take the next train back to Paris. I am most grateful to you for your hospitality.'

He recalled Louis's pale face, his fiery eyes, the rueful smile on his lips. Above all, he pictured Cavre with his briefcase under his arm, Cavre who after all these years had suddenly been given the chance to get the better of his loathsome ex-boss. For Cavre hated him, there was no doubt about that. Admittedly, he hated everyone, but he hated Maigret in particular, for Maigret was his *alter ego*, a successful version of his own self.

Cavre had doubtless been up to all sorts of shady tricks ever since he got off the train the night before and was nearly mistaken by Naud for Maigret himself.

Where was the clock which was going tick-tock? Maigret looked round for it. He felt really uncomfortable and said to himself:

'Another five minutes and this poor woman's nerves will get the better of her ... She'll make a clean breast of it ... She can't stand it any longer ... She's at the end of her tether ...'

All he had to do was ask her one specific question. Hardly that! He would go up to her and look at her searchingly. Would she be able to restrain herself then?

But instead, he remained silent and even timidly picked up a magazine which was lying on a small round table to put her at her ease. It was a women's magazine full of embroidery patterns.

Just as in a dentist's waiting-room one reads things one would never read anywhere else, Maigret turned the pages and looked carefully at the pink and blue pictures, but the invisible chain which bound him to his hostess remained as tight as ever.

They were saved by the entry of the maid. She was rather a rough-looking country girl whose black dress and white apron merely accentuated her rugged, irregular features.

'Oh! *Pardon* ... I didn't know there was someone ...'

'What is it, Marthe?'

'I wanted to know if I should lay the table or wait for Monsieur ...'

'Lay the table!'

'Will Monsieur Alban be here for dinner?'

'I don't know. But lay his place as usual ...'

What a relief to talk of everyday things, they were so simple and reassuring! She latched on to Alban as a topic of conversation.

'He came to lunch here today. It was he who answered the telephone when you rang ... He leads such a lonely life! We consider him one of the family now ...'

The maid's appearance had given her a golden opportunity to escape and she made the most of it.

'Will you excuse me for a moment? You know what it's like to be mistress of the house. There is always something to see to in the kitchen ... I'll ask the maid to tell my daughter to come down and keep you company ...'

75

'Please don't bother . . .'

'Besides . . .' She listened carefully to see if she could hear anything. 'Yes . . . That must be my husband . . .'

A car drew up in front of the steps, but the engine went on running. They heard voices and Maigret wondered whether his host had brought someone back with him, but he was only giving instructions to a servant who had rushed outside on hearing the car.

Naud came into the drawing-room still wearing his suede coat. There was an anxious look in his eyes as he surveyed Maigret and his wife, astonished to find them alone together.

'Ah! You're . . .'

'I was just saying to the Superintendent, Etienne, that I would have to leave him for a minute and see to things in the kitchen . . .'

'Forgive me, Superintendent . . . I am on the board of the regional agricultural authority and I had forgotten we had an important meeting today.'

He sneezed and poured himself a glass of *porto*, trying all the while to gauge what could have happened in his absence.

'Well, have you had a good day? I was told on the telephone you were too busy to come back for lunch . . .'

He, too, was afraid of being alone with the Superintendent. He looked round at the armchairs in the drawing-room, as if to reproach them for being empty.

'Alban's not here yet?' he said with a forced smile, turning towards the dining-room door which was still open.

And his wife answered from the kitchen:

'He came to lunch. He didn't say whether he'd be here for dinner . . .'

'Where's Geneviève?'

'She went up to her room.'

He did not dare sit down and settle himself in a chair. Maigret understood how he felt and almost came to share his anxiety. In order to feel strong, or in order not to tremble visibly, the three of them needed to be together, side by side, in an unbroken family circle.

Only then would the Superintendent be able to sense the spirit of the house in normal times. The two men helped each other, for they talked of seemingly trivial things and the sound of their chatter reassured them both.

'Will you have a glass of *porto*?'

'I have just had one.'

'Well, have another ... Now ... Tell me what you've been doing ... Or rather ... For perhaps I am being indiscreet ...'

'The cap has disappeared,' declared Maigret, his eyes on the carpet.

'Has it really? This famous cap was to be proof ... And where was it ... Mind you, I have always had my doubts as to whether it really existed ...'

'A young lad called Louis Fillou claims it was in one of the drawers in his bedroom ...'

'In Louis's house? And you mean it was stolen this morning? Don't you think that is rather odd?'

He stood there laughing, a tall, strong, sturdy figure of a man with a ruddy complexion. He was the owner of this house, the head of the family, and he had just taken part in administrative debates in La Roche-sur-Yon. He was Etienne Naud, Squire Naud as the locals would have said, the son of Sébastien Naud who was known and respected by everyone in the *département*.

But his laughter sounded shaky as he took a glass of *porto* and looked round in vain for a member of his family to appear. At a time like this, he needed the support they always gave him. He would have liked them to be present, his wife, his daughter and even Alban who had decided to stay away today of all days.

'Will you have a cigar? ... No, are you sure?'

He walked round and round the room, as though to sit down would have been to fall into a trap, to play right into the hands of the formidable Superintendent whom that idiotic brother-in-law of his had foisted on him. Etienne Naud felt doomed.

6

Alban Groult-Cotelle's Alibi

Before dinner that evening, an incident occurred which, though insignificant in itself, none the less gave Maigret food for thought. Etienne Naud had still not sat down, as though afraid of being even more at the mercy of the Superintendent if he were once to remain still. They could hear voices in the dining-room. Madame Naud was reprimanding the maid for not cleaning the silver properly. Geneviève had just come downstairs.

Maigret saw the look her father gave her as she came into the drawing-room. There was a trace of anxiety in his expression. Naud had not seen his daughter since she had retired to her room the day before, saying she did not feel well. It was perfectly natural, too, that Geneviève should reassure him with a smile.

Just at that moment the telephone rang and Naud went into the hall to answer it. He left the drawing-room door open.

'What?' he said, in an astonished tone of voice. 'Of course he's here, damn it. What did you say?... Yes, hurry up, we're expecting you...'

When he came back into the drawing-room he shrugged his shoulders once again.

'I wonder what has got into our friend Alban. There's been a place for him at our table for years. Then he rings up this evening to find out if you're here and when I say you are he asks if he can come to dinner and says he must talk to you...'

By chance, Maigret happened to be looking, not at Naud but at his daughter, and he was surprised to see such a fierce expression on her face.

'He did more or less the same thing earlier on,' she said crossly. 'He came here to lunch and looked very peeved when he realized the Superintendent hadn't come back. I thought he was going to leave. He muttered: "What a pity. I had something to show him."

'He took his leave as soon as he had gulped down his dessert. You must have met him in the town, then, Superintendent?'

Whatever it was was so subtle that Maigret could not pinpoint it. A hint of something in the young girl's voice. And yet it was not really the voice. What is it, for example, that makes an experienced man suddenly realize that a young girl has become a woman?

Maigret noticed something of this sort. It seemed to him that Geneviève's peevish words displayed something more than plain ill-temper, and he decided to watch young Mademoiselle Naud more closely.

Madame Naud came in, apologizing for her absence. Her daughter availed herself of the opportunity to repeat:

'Alban has just rung to say he's coming to dinner. But first of all he asked whether the Superintendent was here. He's not coming to see *us* ...'

'He'll be here in a minute,' said her father who had finally sat down, now that his family was round him. 'It will take him three minutes by bicycle.'

Maigret dutifully remained seated, looking rather dejected. His large eyes were expressionless as they always were whenever he found himself in an awkward situation. He watched them in turn, smiling slightly when spoken to, and all the while thinking to himself:

'They must be cursing their idiot of a brother-in-law and me, too. They all know what happened, including their friend Alban. That's why they are jittery the minute they are on their own. They feel reassured when they are together and gang up ...'

What had happened, in fact? Had Etienne Naud discovered the young Retailleau in his daughter's bedroom? Had they quarrelled? Had they had a fight? Or had Naud quite simply shot him down like he would a rabbit?

What a night to have lived through! Geneviève's mother must have been in a terrible state and the servants who probably heard the noise must have been petrified.

Someone was scraping his feet at the front door. Geneviève made a move, as if to go and open the door, but then decided to remain seated and Naud himself, somewhat surprised, as if his daughter's behaviour constituted a serious breach of habit, got up and went into the hall. Maigret heard him talking about the fog and then the two men came into the drawing-room.

This was the first time, in fact, that Maigret had seen Geneviève and Alban together. She held out her hand rather stiffly. Alban bowed, kissed the back of her hand and then turned towards Maigret, obviously anxious to tell him or show him something.

'Would you believe, Superintendent, that after you left this morning I came across this quite by chance ...'

And he held out a small sheet of paper which had been attached to some others with a pin, for there were two tiny prick-marks in it.

'What is it?' asked Naud quite naturally, whilst his daughter looked distrustfully at Alban.

'You have all made fun of my mania for hoarding the smallest scrap of paper. I could produce the tiniest laundry bill dated three or eight years back!'

The piece of paper that Maigret kept twirling between his fat fingers was a bill from the Hôtel de l'Europe in La Roche-sur-Yon. Room: 30 francs. Breakfast: 6 francs. Service ... The date: 7 January.

'Of course,' said Alban, as though he were apologizing, 'it's not important. However, I remembered the police like alibis. Look at the date. Quite by chance, I was in La Roche, do you see, on the night the person you know met his death ...'

Naud and his wife reacted as well-bred people do when confronted with a breach of manners. Unable to believe her ears, Madame Naud looked first at Alban, as though she would not have expected such behaviour from him, and then looked down with a sigh at the logs in the grate. Her husband frowned. He was slower on the up-take. Perhaps he was hunting for some deeper meaning to his friend's ploy?

As for Geneviève, she had turned pale with anger. She had obviously had a real shock, and the pupils of her eyes glistened. Maigret had been so intrigued by her behaviour a few moments before that he tried not to look at anyone else.

Alban, with his thin, lanky physique and balding forehead, stood sheepishly in the middle of the drawing-room.

'At any rate, you're making quite sure you are in the clear before you are accused,' said Naud when he finally spoke, having had time to weigh his words.

'What do you mean by that, Etienne? I think you have all mis-interpreted me. I came across this hotel bill quite by chance when I was sorting out some papers a short while ago. I was eager to show it to the Superintendent as it was such a strange coincidence it had the same date on it as the day . . .'

Madame Naud even chipped in, something that rarely happened.

'So you've already said,' she retorted. 'I think dinner is ready now . . .'

The atmosphere was still strained. Although the meal was as elab-orate and well-cooked as it had been on the previous evening, their efforts to create a friendly ambience or at any rate an outward show of relaxation failed dismally. Geneviève was the most agitated. For a long time afterwards Maigret could still picture her, her chest heaving with emotion: a woman's anger but also a mistress's rage, Maigret was sure. She pecked at her food, disdainfully. Not once did she look at Alban who, for his part, made sure he caught no one's eye.

Alban was just the sort of man to keep the smallest scraps of paper and file them away, pinning them together in bundles as if they were bank-notes. It was also just like him to get himself out of difficulty if he had the chance and with a clear conscience leave his friends in hot water.

All this made itself felt. There was something scandalous afoot. Madame Naud looked even more anxious. Naud, on the other hand, endeavoured to reassure his family, although quite probably with another objective in mind.

'By the way, I happened to meet the Director of Prosecutions in Fontenay this morning. In fact, Alban, he is almost a relative of yours through the female side, as he married a Deharme, from Cholet.'

'The Cholet Deharmes aren't related to the general's family. They originally came from Nantes and their . . .'

Naud went on:

'He was most reassuring, you know, Superintendent. Admittedly, he has told my brother-in-law Bréjon that there is bound to be an official inquiry, but it will just be a formality, at any rate as far as we are concerned. I told him you were here . . .'

81

Well! He immediately regretted making this thoughtless comment. He blushed slightly, and hurriedly put a large piece of lobster *à la crème* into his mouth.

'What did he have to say about that?'

'He admires you greatly and has followed most of your cases in the newspapers. It is precisely because he admires you ...'

The poor man did not know how to extricate himself.

'He is amazed that my brother-in-law deemed it necessary to involve a man like you in such a trivial matter ...'

'I understand ...'

'You're not angry, I hope? He only said this because of his admiration for ...'

'Are you sure he didn't also say that my appearance here may well make the case seem more important than it actually is?'

'How did you know? Have you seen him?'

Maigret smiled. What else could he do? For was he not a guest in their house? The Nauds had entertained him as well as they could. And again, that night, the dinner they served was a small but consummate example of traditional provincial cooking.

In a pleasant, very polite way, his hosts now began to make him feel that his presence in their midst was a threat, a potentially harmful factor.

There was silence, as there had been a short while before, after the Alban episode. It was Madame Naud who tried to put things right and she made a bigger blunder than her husband had done.

'At any rate, I hope you'll stay a few more days with us? I expect there will be a frost after the fog has gone and you will be able to go on some walks with my husband ... Don't you think, Etienne?'

How relieved they all would have been if Maigret had replied as they assumed he would, in the manner of a well-bred man:

'I would gladly stay, and greatly appreciate your hospitality, but alas I must return to my duties in Paris. I may pass this way in the holidays ... But I have enjoyed myself enormously ...'

He said nothing of the kind. He went on eating and did not reply. Inwardly, he felt a brute. These people had behaved well towards him from the outset. Perhaps Albert Retailleau's death weighed heavily on their conscience? But had not the young man robbed their daughter of her honour, as the saying goes in their circles? And had

Albert's mother, Madame Retailleau, made a fuss? Or had she been the first to realize that it was far better to let sleeping dogs lie?

Three or four people, perhaps more, were trying to keep their secret, desperately trying to prevent anyone from discovering the truth, and for someone like Madame Naud, Maigret's presence alone must have been an intolerable strain. Had she not been on the point of crying out in anguish a short while ago, at the end of quarter of an hour alone with the Superintendent?

It was so simple! He would leave the following morning with the whole family's blessing and, back in Paris, Bréjon the examining magistrate would thank him with tears in his eyes!

And if Maigret did not take this course of action, was it his passion for justice alone which prompted him to do otherwise? He would not have dared look someone in the eye and say this was so. For there was Cavre. There were the successive rebuttals Cavre had inflicted on him ever since their arrival the night before, without so much as a glance in the direction of his former boss. He came and went as if Maigret did not exist, or as if he were a totally innocuous opponent.

Whenever Maigret passed by, as though by magic, evidence melted away, witnesses could remember nothing or refused to speak, and items of unmistakable proof, like the cap, vanished into thin air.

At last, after so many years, the wretched, unlucky, grudging Cavre had his moment of triumph!

'What are you thinking about, Superintendent?'

He gave a start.

'Nothing ... I'm so sorry. My mind wanders sometimes ...'

He had helped himself to a huge plateful of food without realizing what he was doing and was now ashamed of himself. To put him at his ease, Madame Naud said quietly:

'Nothing gives more pleasure to the mistress of the house than to see her cooking appreciated. Alban eats like a wolf so it doesn't count, as he'd eat anything put in front of him. Everything tastes good to him. He's not a gourmet. He's a glutton.'

She was joking, of course, but none the less there was a trace of spite in her voice and expression.

A few glasses of wine had made Etienne Naud's face even rosier. Playing with his knife, he ventured forth:

'So what do you make of it all, Superintendent, now that you've seen something of the neighbourhood and have asked a few questions?'

'He has met young Fillou ...' his wife informed him, as though in warning.

And Maigret, whom each of them was watching like a hawk, said slowly and clearly:

'I think Albert Retailleau was very unlucky ...'

The remark did not really imply anything and yet Geneviève grew pale, indeed seemed so taken aback by these few insignificant words that for a moment she looked as if she would get up and leave the room. Her father looked puzzled, unsure of what Maigret meant. Alban sneered:

'I reckon that's a statement worthy of the ancient oracles! I'd certainly be very uneasy if I hadn't miraculously found proof that I was sleeping peacefully in a room in the Hôtel de l'Europe eighty kilometres from here, on that very night ...'

'Don't you know,' retorted Maigret, 'that there is a saying in the police force that he who has the best alibi is all the more suspect?'

Alban was annoyed. Taking Maigret's little joke seriously, he answered:

'Then in that case, you will have to hold the *préfet*'s private secretary suspect too, as he spent the evening with me. He is a childhood friend of mine whom I see from time to time and whenever we spend an evening together we don't usually get to bed until two or three in the morning ...'

What made Maigret decide to carry on the pretence to the end? Was it the blatant cowardice of this trumped-up aristocrat which spurred him to act thus? He took a large notebook with an elastic band round it out of his pocket and asked with all seriousness:

'What is his name?'

'Do you really want it? As you wish ... Musellier ... Pierre Musellier ... He has remained a bachelor ... He has a flat in the Place Napoléon, above the Murs garages ... About fifty yards from the Hôtel de l'Europe ...'

'Shall we have coffee in the drawing-room?' suggested Madame

Naud. 'Will you serve the coffee, Geneviève? You're not too tired? You look pale to me. Do you think you had better go upstairs to bed?'

'No.'

She was not tired. She was tense. It was as if she had various accounts to settle with Alban, for she did not take her eyes off him.

'Did you return to Saint-Aubin the following morning?' asked Maigret, with a pencil in his hand.

'The very next morning, yes. A friend gave me a lift in his car to Fontenay-le-Comte, where I had lunch with some other friends, and just as I was leaving I bumped into Etienne who brought me back.'

'You go from friend to friend, in effect ...'

He could not have made it clearer that he thought Alban was a sponger and it was true. Everyone understood perfectly the implications of Maigret's words. Geneviève blushed and looked away.

'Are you sure you won't change your mind and have one of my cigars, Superintendent?'

'Would you be so kind as to tell me if you have finished questioning me? If you have, I would like to take my leave ... I want to get home early tonight.'

'That's absolutely fine. In fact, I'd like to walk as far as the town so if it's all right with you, we can go together ...'

'I came by bicycle ...'

'That doesn't matter ... A bicycle can be pushed by hand, can't it? And anyway, you might bicycle into the canal in this fog ...'

What *was* going on? For one thing, when Maigret had talked of leaving with Alban Groult-Cotelle, Etienne Naud had frowned and appeared to be on the point of accompanying them.

Did he fear that Alban, who was far too nervous that night, might be tempted to confess all? He had given him a long look, as if to say: 'For heavens's sake, be careful! Look how het-up you are. He is tougher than you ...'

Geneviève gave Alban an even sterner, more contemptuous look which said: 'At least try and control yourself!'

Madame Naud did not look at anyone. She was weary. She no longer understood what was going on. It would not be long before she gave way under such nervous tension.

But the person who behaved most strangely of all was Alban

himself. He would not make up his mind to go but walked round the drawing-room, his intention in all probability being to have a private talk with Naud.

'Did you not want a word with me in your study about that insurance matter?'

'What insurance matter?' said Naud stupidly.

'Not to worry. We'll talk about it tomorrow.'

What did he want to tell Naud that was so important?

'Are you coming, my dear fellow?' persisted the Superintendent.

'Are you sure you don't want me to take you in the car? If you would like to have the car and drive yourself . . .'

'No thank you. We'll have a good chat as we walk . . .'

The fog swirled round them. Alban pushed his bicycle with one hand and walked quickly along, constantly having to stop because Maigret would not walk more briskly.

'They are such good sorts! Such a united family . . . But it must be rather a dull life for a young girl, mustn't it? Has she many friends?'

'I don't know of any in the neighbourhood . . . Every now and then she goes off to spend a week or so with her cousins and they come down here in the summer, but apart from that . . .'

'I imagine she also goes and stays with the Bréjons in Paris?'

'Yes, indeed, she stayed with them this winter.'

Maigret changed the subject, playing the innocent. The two men could scarcely see each other in the icy white mist that enveloped them. The electric light in the station acted as a lighthouse and, further on, two more lights which could have been boats out to sea, shone through the haze.

'So apart from staying in La Roche-sur-Yon from time to time, you hardly ever leave Saint-Aubin?'

'I sometimes go to Nantes as I have friends there, and also to Bordeaux where my cousin from Chièvre lives. Her husband is a ship-owner.'

'Do you ever go to Paris?'

'I was there a month ago.'

'At the same time as Mademoiselle Naud?'

'Perhaps. I really don't know . . .'

They walked past the two inns opposite each other. Maigret stopped and suggested:

'What about having a drink in the Lion d'Or? It would be most interesting to see my old colleague Cavre. I saw a young fellow at the station just now and I suspect he has been asked to come to the rescue.'

'I'll take my leave, then ...' said Alban quickly.

'No, no ... If you don't want to stop, I'll keep you company on your way home. You can't object to that, now, can you?'

'I am in a hurry to get back and go to bed. I'll be quite open with you ... I am prone to the most dreadful migraines and I am in the throes of one now.'

'All the more reason to escort you home. Does your maid sleep in the house?'

'Of course.'

'Some people don't like their servants to be under the same roof at night ... Look! There's a light ...'

'It's the maid ...'

'Is she in the sitting-room? Of course, the room is heated ... Does she do odd sewing jobs for you when you are out?'

They stopped outside the front door and Alban, instead of knocking, hunted in his pocket for the key.

'See you tomorrow, Superintendent! No doubt we will meet at my friends the Nauds ...'

'Tell me ...'

Alban took care not to open the door lest Maigret would think he was inviting him inside.

'It's stupid ... Please forgive me ... But I am afraid I've been taken short, and since we're here ... We men can be honest with each other, can't we?'

'Come in ... I'll show you the way ...'

The light was not on in the corridor but the sitting-room door on the left was half-open and revealed a rectangle of light. Alban tried to lead Maigret down the corridor but the Superintendent, in an almost instinctive gesture, pushed the door wide-open, whereupon he stopped in his tracks and cried out:

'Well I never! It's my old friend Cavre! What are you doing here, my dear chap?'

The ex-Inspector had risen to his feet, looking as pale and sullen as ever. He glowered at Groult-Cotelle whom he deemed responsible for this disastrous meeting.

87

Alban was completely out of his depth. He tried hard to think of an explanation but, unable to do so, merely asked:

'Where is the maid?'

Old Cadaverous was the first to regain his composure and bowing, said:

'Monsieur Groult-Cotelle, I think?'

Alban was slow to understand the Inspector's game.

'I am sorry to disturb you at such an hour, but I just wanted a few words with you. Since your maid told me you would not be back late . . .'

'All right!' growled Maigret.

'What?' said Alban with a start.

'I said: All right!'

'What do you mean?'

'I don't mean anything. Cavre, where is this maid who showed you in? There is no other light on in the house. In other words, she was in bed.'

'She told me . . .'

'All right! I'll try once more, and this time I don't want any clap-trap. You can sit down, Cavre. Now! You made yourself comfortable. You took off your overcoat and left your hat on the coat-stand. What were you in the middle of reading?'

Maigret's eyes opened wide when he inspected the book lying on the table near Cavre's chair.

'*Sexual Perversions*! Look at that, now! And you found this charming book in the library of our friend Groult-Cotelle . . . Tell me, gentlemen, why don't you sit down? Does my presence disturb you? Don't forget your migraine, Monsieur Groult-Cotelle . . . You should take an aspirin.'

In spite of everything, Alban still had enough presence of mind to retort:

'I thought you needed to relieve yourself?'

'Well, I don't any more . . . Now, my dear Cavre, what is this investigation of yours all about? You must have been really put out when you realized I was involved in this too, eh?'

'Ah! You're involved? How do you mean, involved?'

'So Groult-Cotelle availed himself of your expertise, did he? Far be it for me to underrate it, by the way . . .'

'I had never even heard of Monsieur Groult-Cotelle until this morning.'

'It was Etienne Naud who told you about him when you met in Fontenay-le-Comte, wasn't it?'

'Superintendent, if you wish to submit me to a formal interrogation, I would like my lawyer to be present when I answer your questions.'

'In the event of your being accused of stealing a cap, for instance?'

'In that event, yes.'

The electric light-bulb cast a grey light over the sitting-room for apart from the fact it was of insufficient strength for the size of the room, it was also coated in dust.

'May I perhaps be permitted to offer you something to drink?'

'Why not?' answered Maigret. 'Seeing as fate has brought us together ... By the way, Cavre, was it one of your men I saw just now at the station?'

'He works for me, yes.'

'Renfort?'

'As you wish.'

'Did you have important matters to settle with Monsieur Groult-Cotelle tonight?'

'I wanted to ask him one or two questions.'

'If you wanted to see him about his alibi, you can rest assured. He thought of everything. He even kept his bill from the Hôtel de l'Europe.'

Cavre, however, kept his nerve. He had sat down in the chair he had occupied before and, with his legs crossed and his morocco-leather briefcase on his lap, seemed to be biding his time, determined, one might have said, to have the last word. Groult-Cotelle, who had filled three glasses with armagnac, offered him one which he refused.

'No, thank you. I only drink water.'

He had been teased a great deal about this at the Police Head-quarters, an unintentionally cruel thing to do, since Cavre was not teetotal by choice but because he suffered from a severe disorder of the liver.

'And what about you, Superintendent?'

'Gladly!'

They fell silent. All three men appeared to be playing a strange kind of game, such as trying to see who could remain silent the longest without giving way. Alban had emptied his glass in one go and had poured himself another. He remained standing and from time to time pushed one of the books in his library back into place if it was out of line.

'Are you aware, Monsieur,' Cavre said to him at last in a quiet voice, icy calm, 'that you are in your own house?'

'What do you mean?'

'That as master of the house you are at liberty to entertain whomever you think fit. I should have liked to talk to you alone, not in front of the Superintendent. If you prefer his company to mine, I will be glad to take my leave and arrange a meeting for some other time.'

'In short, the Inspector is politely asking you to show one of us to the door forthwith.'

'Gentlemen, I don't understand what this discussion is all about. Indeed this whole affair has nothing to do with me. I was in La Roche, as you know, when the boy died. Granted, I am a friend of the Nauds. I have been to their house a great deal. In a small town like ours, one's choice of friends is limited.'

'Remember Saint Peter!'

'What do you mean?'

'That if you go on like this, you will have thrice denied your friends the Nauds before sunrise, assuming, of course, the fog allows the sun to rise.'

'It is all very well for you to joke. My position is a delicate one, all the same. The Nauds frequently invite me to their house. Etienne is my friend, I don't deny the fact. But if you ask me what happened at the Nauds' that night, I don't know and what is more, I don't want to know. So I am the wrong person to question, that's all.'

'Perhaps Mademoiselle Naud would be the best person to question, then? Incidentally, I wonder if you were aware that she was looking at you far from lovingly this evening. I got the distinct impression that she had a bone to pick with you.'

'With me?'

'Especially when you handed me your hotel bill and tried with such style to save your own skin. She didn't think that was very nice, not nice at all. I would be on your guard she doesn't get her own back, if I were you ...'

Alban forced a laugh.

'You are joking. Geneviève is a charming child who ...'

What made Maigret suddenly decide to play his last card?

'... who is three months pregnant,' he let drop, moving closer to Alban.

'What ... What did you say?'

As for Cavre, he was stunned. For the first time that day he no longer looked his confident self and stared at his former boss in spontaneous admiration.

'Were you unaware of the fact, Monsieur Groult-Cotelle?'

'Just what are you getting at?'

'Nothing ... I am looking for ... You want to know the truth, too, don't you? ... Then we will try and find it together ... Cavre has already laid his hands on the blood-stained cap which is proof enough of the crime ... Where is that cap, Cavre?'

The Inspector sunk deeper into his armchair and did not reply.

'I had better warn you that you will pay dearly for it if you've destroyed it ... And now, I have the feeling that my presence is disturbing you ... I will therefore take leave of you both ... I presume I will see you for lunch tomorrow at your friends the Nauds, Monsieur Groult-Cotelle?'

He went out of the room. As soon as he had banged the front door shut he saw a thin figure standing close by.

'Is that you, Superintendent?'

It was young Louis. Lying in wait behind the windows of the Trois Mules, he had doubtless seen the shadowy figures of Maigret and Alban as they went past. He had followed them.

'Do you know what they are saying, what everyone is saying in the town?'

His voice was trembling with anxiety and indignation.

'People are saying that *they* have got the better of you and that you are leaving on the three o'clock train tomorrow ...'

And this had very nearly been the truth.

7

The Old Postmistress

An important contributing factor must have made Maigret more sensitive than usual at that particular moment. Scarcely had he walked out of Groult-Cotelle's front door and taken a few steps in the darkness, the fog clinging to his skin like a cold compress, when he suddenly stopped. Young Louis, who was walking beside him, asked:

'What's the matter, Superintendent?'

Something had just occurred to Maigret and he was trying to follow the thought through. He was still mindful of the sound of voices, blurred but noisy, coming to him from behind the shutters of the house. At the same time, he understood why the youngster was alarmed: Maigret had stopped dead for no apparent reason in the middle of the pavement, like a cardiac who is immobilized by a sudden attack wherever he happens to be.

But this had nothing to do with Maigret's current pre-occupations. He did, however, make a mental note:

'Ah! So there's a cardiac in Saint-Aubin . . .'

He was later to learn, in fact, that the old doctor had died of angina pectoris. For years people had become accustomed to seeing him suddenly stop thus in the middle of the street, rooted to the spot with his hand on his heart.

There was a violent argument going on inside the house, or at least the sound of angry voices gave this impression, but Maigret paid no attention. The pock-marked Louis, who thought he had discovered the cause of the Superintendent's sudden halt, listened conscientiously. The louder the voices, the harder it was to make out the words. The noise sounded exactly like a record whirling round off-centre, due to a second hole having been bored, and blaring out unintelligible sounds.

It was not because of this row between Inspector Cavre and Alban Groult-Cotelle that Maigret stopped like this and looked round rather uncertainly, staring at nothing in particular.

The minute he left the house, an idea had occurred to him. It was not even an idea, but something vaguer, so vague that he was now striving to recapture the memory of it. Every now and then, an insignificant occurrence, usually a whiff of something barely caught, reminds us in the space of a second of a particular moment in our life. It is such a vivid sensation that we are gripped by it and want to cling to this living reminder of that moment. It disappears almost at once and with it all recollection of the experience. Try as we might, we end up wondering, for want of an answer to our questions, if it was not an unconscious evocation of a dream, or, who knows, of some pre-existent world?

Something struck Maigret the moment he banged the front door shut. He knew he was leaving behind two embarrassed and angry men. Brought together by fate that night, the two of them had one thing in common, although there was no rational explanation for this. Cavre made one think not of a bachelor, but of a husband who has been subjected to ridicule and looks woeful and abashed. Envy oozed out of every pore and envy can make one behave just as equivocally as certain hidden vices.

Deep down, Maigret did not bear him a grudge. He felt sorry for him. While relentlessly pursuing him, determined to get the better of his rival, Maigret none the less felt a kind of pity for this man who, after all, was nothing but a failure.

What was the connection between Cavre and Alban? The connection which exists between two completely different but equally sordid things. It was almost a question of colour. Both men had something of the grey, greenish quality of moral and material dust.

Cavre exuded hatred. Alban Groult-Cotelle exuded panic and cowardice. His whole life had been run on the principle of cowardice. His wife had left him and taken the children with her. He had made no effort either to join them or bring them back. He probably had not suffered. He had selfishly reorganized his existence. A man of humble means, he lived in other people's homes, like the cuckoo. And if some misfortune befell his friends, he was the first to let them down.

And now Maigret suddenly recalled the trifling matter that had triggered off this train of thought: it was the book he had caught Cavre holding when they came into the room, one of those disgusting, erotic books that are sold under the counter in certain backrooms in the Faubourg Saint-Martin.

Groult-Cotelle kept books like this in his country library; Cavre came upon one of them seemingly quite by chance!

But there had been something else, and it was this something else that the Superintendent was struggling to put his finger on. For a tenth of a second, perhaps, his mind had been lit up, as it were, by a glaring truth, but no sooner had he realized this than the thought vanished and all that remained was a vague impression. In reality, this was why he stood motionless like a cardiac trying to outwit his heart.

Maigret was trying to outwit his memory. He was hoping ...

'What is that light?' he asked, however.

They were both standing still in the fog. A little way off, Maigret could see a large halo of white, diffuse light. He concentrated his thoughts on this material thing in order to give his intuition time to revive. He now knew the town. So where, then, was this light almost opposite Groult-Cotelle's house coming from?

'It isn't the post-office, is it?'

'It's the window next door,' replied Louis. 'The postmistress's window. She sleeps badly and reads novels well into the night. Hers is always the last light to be switched off in Saint-Aubin ...'

Now, he was still aware of the sound of angry voices. Groult-Cotelle was shouting the loudest, as if he point-blank refused to listen to reason. Cavre's voice was more ponderous, more imperious.

Why was Maigret strongly tempted to cross the street and press his face against the postmistress's window? She was doubtless sitting reading in her kitchen. Was it intuition? A moment afterwards, the thought had gone from his mind. He knew that Louis was looking at him anxiously and impatiently as he wondered what on earth was going on in his hero's head.

What was it he had sensed as he went out of the front door? ... Well ... First of all, Paris had come to mind ... The books, the shops in the Faubourg Saint-Martin which sell those kind of books had made him think of Paris ... Groult-Cotelle had gone to Paris ... and Geneviève Naud must have been there at the same time ...

Maigret could remember the look on Geneviève's face when Alban had produced his alibi in so unpleasant a manner. It had contained more than mere scorn. This time, a naked woman, not a young girl, stood before Alban ... A mistress, suddenly aware of the baseness of ...

He had just got to this point in his thoughts when an inkling of something else had flashed through his mind only to vanish again, leaving a vague memory of something rather nasty.

Yes, the whole affair was very different from what Maigret had initially envisaged. Up until now, he had only seen the bourgeois view of things, had witnessed a thoroughly bourgeois family's indignation upon discovering that a penniless youth with no prospects was making love to their daughter.

Had Naud shot him in a fit of anger? It was possible. Maigret almost pitied Naud, and especially his wife, who knew what had happened. She was desperately trying to control herself and overcome her terror. For her, every minute spent alone with the Superintendent was a terrible ordeal.

But now, Etienne Naud and his wife ceased to be foremost in his mind.

What was the missing link between these thoughts? The dull, balding Alban had an alibi. Was this really just a fluke? Was it also just a fluke that he had suddenly come across that bill from the Hôtel de l'Europe?

No doubt he really had spent the night there. The Superintendent was convinced of this, although he decided to check the fact all the same.

But why had he gone to La Roche-sur-Yon on that particular night? Had the *préfet*'s private secretary been expecting him?

'I must find out!' grumbled Maigret to himself.

He went on looking at the dim light in the house next door to the post-office; he still had his tobacco-pouch in one hand and his pipe, which he was too preoccupied to fill, in the other.

Albert Retailleau was angry ...

Who had said that? None other but his young companion Louis, Albert's friend.

'Was he really angry?' the Superintendent suddenly asked.

'Who?'

'Your friend Albert ... You said that when he left you that last evening ...'

'He was very het-up. He drank several brandies before going off to meet Geneviève ...'

'He didn't tell you anything?'

'Wait ... He said he probably wouldn't stay very long in this godforsaken neighbourhood ...'

'How long had he been Mademoiselle Naud's lover?'

'I don't know ... Wait though ... They weren't lovers in mid-summer. They must have started sleeping together roundabout the month of October ...'

'He wasn't in love with her before that?'

'Well, if he was, he didn't talk to her ...'

'Ssh ...'

Maigret stood quite still and listened carefully. The sound of voices had died away and now, to his astonishment, the Superintendent heard a different sound.

'It's the telephone!' he exclaimed.

He had recognized the familiar sound of country telephones. Someone was turning a handle to call the woman in the post-office.

'Run and have a look through the postmistress's window ... You'll get there quicker than I will ...'

He was right. A second light went on, in the window next to the first. The postmistress had gone through a door which was slightly ajar into the post-office.

Maigret took his time. He loathed running anywhere. Strangely enough, it was young Louis's presence that bothered him. He wanted to maintain a certain dignity in front of the youngster. He at last filled his pipe, lit it and walked slowly across the street.

'Well?'

'I knew she would listen in to the call,' whispered Louis. 'The old shrew always listens. The doctor even complained to La Roche about it once, but she still goes on doing it ...'

They could see her through the window, a small woman dressed in black with dark hair and an ageless face. She had one hand on an earphone and held a plug in the other. The call must have come to an end at that very moment, for she moved the plugs into different holes and walked across the room to switch off the light.

'Do you think she would let us in?'

'If you knock on the little door at the back ... This way ... We'll go through the yard ...'

They groped about in pitch darkness for a moment, edging their way past various tubs filled with washing. A cat jumped out of a dustbin.

'Mademoiselle Rinquet!' the youngster called out. 'Will you open up for a minute ...'

'What is it?'

'It's me, Louis ... Will you open up for a minute, please ...'

As soon as she had unbolted the door, Maigret stepped hurriedly inside for fear she might shut it again.

'There is nothing to be afraid of, Mademoiselle ...'

He was too tall and too bulky for the tiny postmistress's tiny kitchen which was littered with embroidered tray-cloths and knick-knacks made of cheap china or spun glass she had bought at various fairs.

'Groult-Cotelle has just made a call.'

'How do you know?'

'He rang up his friend Naud ... You listened in to their conversation.'

Caught at fault, she defended herself awkwardly.

'But the post-office is shut, Monsieur. I'm not supposed to give anyone a line after nine o'clock. I sometimes do, though, as I'm here and like to be helpful ...'

'What did he say?'

'Who?'

'Look, if you're not going to answer my questions with a good grace, I will have to come back tomorrow, officially this time, and draw up a written report which will go through the proper channels. Now, what did he say?'

'There were two of them on the line.'

'At the same time?'

'Pretty well. They spoke together sometimes. It turned into a shouting match between the two of them and in the end I couldn't catch what they were saying ... They must both have had an

97

earpiece and were obviously pushing each other out of the way in front of the telephone.'

'What did they say?'

'Monsieur Groult said first of all:

'"Listen, Etienne, this can't go on. The Superintendent has just left. He came face to face with your man. I'm sure he knows everything and if you go on . . ."'

'Well?' said Maigret.

'Wait . . . The other man butted in.

'"Hello . . . Monsieur Naud? . . . Cavre speaking . . . Of course it's a great pity you didn't manage to detain him and prevent him from finding me here, but . . ."'

'"But I'm the one who is compromised," yelled Monsieur Groult. "I've had enough, do you hear, Etienne? Put an end to all this! Telephone your idiotic brother-in-law and tell him never to meddle in our affairs again. He's this wretched Superintendent's superior in some respects and since he's the one who sent him down here, he must set about calling him back to Paris . . . So I'm warning you . . . if he is at your house the next time I come round, I'll . . ."'

'"Hello! Hello!" shouted Monsieur Etienne, in a real state at the other end of the line. "Are you still there, Monsieur Cavre? . . . Alban's got me all worried . . . Are you sure . . ."'

'"Hello! . . . Cavre here . . . Will you be quiet, Monsieur Groult . . . Let me get a word in . . . Stop pushing me . . . Is that you, Monsieur Naud? . . . Yes . . . Well! There is nothing to worry about provided your friend Groult-Cotelle doesn't panic and . . . What? . . . Should you ring your brother-in-law? . . . I'd have advised you not to a moment ago . . . No, I'm not afraid of him . . ."'

The postmistress, thoroughly enjoying reporting the telephone conversation, pointed a finger at Maigret and declared:

'He meant you, didn't he? . . . So he said he wasn't afraid of you, but that because of Groult-Cotelle who was thoroughly unreliable . . . Ssh . . .'

The bell rang in the post-office. The little old lady rushed next door and switched on the light.

'Hello! . . . What? . . . Galvani 17.98? I don't know . . . No, there shouldn't be any delay at this time of night . . . I'll call you back.'

Galvani 17.98 was Bréjon's home telephone number and Maigret recognized it at once.

He looked at his watch to see what time it was. Ten minutes to eleven. Unless he had gone to the cinema or the theatre with his family, the examining magistrate was bound to be in bed, for everyone at the Palais de Justice knew that he got up at six in the morning and studied his briefs as day broke.

The plugs went into different holes.

'Is that Niort? Can you get me Galvani 17.98? Line 3 is free? Will you connect me, please? Line 2 was awful just now ... How are you? ... You're on duty all night? ... What? ... No, you know perfectly well I never go to bed before one in the morning ... Yes, there's fog here too ... You can't see more than a couple of yards in front of you ... It'll be icy on the roads tomorrow morning ... Hello! Paris? ... Paris? ... Hello! Paris? ... Galvani 17.98? ... Come on, dear ... Speak more clearly ... I want Galvani 17.98 ... What? ... It's ringing? ... I can't hear anything ... Let it go on ringing ... It's urgent ... Yes, now there's someone ...'

She turned round, terrified, for Maigret's bulky frame towered behind her as he stretched out a hand, ready to take the headset at the appropriate moment.

'Monsieur Naud? ... Hello! ... Monsieur Naud? ... Yes, I'm putting you through ... One moment, it's ringing ... Hold on ... Galvani 17.98? Saint-Aubin, here ... Here's line 3 ... Go ahead, 3 ...'

She did not dare protest when the Superintendent took the headset authoritatively from her and put it on his head. She put the plug firmly in the hole.

'Hello! Is that you, Victor? ... What? ...'

There was interference on the line and Maigret had the feeling that the examining magistrate was taking the call in bed. A moment later, he heard him say for the second time, having heard his brother-in-law's name:

'It's Etienne ...'

He was probably speaking to his wife who was lying in bed beside him.

'What? ... There has been a new development? ... No? ... Yes? ... You're speaking too loudly ... It's making the line buzz ...'

For Etienne Naud was one of those men who yell down the telephone as if they are afraid of not being heard.

'Hello! ... Listen, Victor ... There's nothing new to report really, no ... Believe me ... I'll write to you, anyhow ... Maybe I'll come and see you in Paris in two or three days' time ...'

'Please talk more slowly ... Move over a bit, Marthe ...'

'What did you say?'

'I was telling Marthe to move over ... Well? ... What's going on? The Superintendent arrived safely, didn't he? ... What's your view?'

'Yes ... Never mind ... In fact it's because of him that I am ringing ...'

'Doesn't he want to investigate the case?'

'Yes ... But he's investigating it too thoroughly ... Listen, Victor, you've simply got to find a way of getting him back to Paris ... No, I can't talk now ... I know the postmistress and ...'

Maigret smiled as he watched the tiny postmistress. She was bubbling over with curiosity.

'You'll find a way, I'm sure ... What? It will be difficult? ... But you must be able to, somehow ... It is absolutely vital, I promise you ...'

It was not hard to picture the examining magistrate frowning anxiously as waves of suspicion with regard to his brother-in-law began to creep into his mind.

'It is not what you are thinking ... But he's poking his nose here and there, talking to everyone and doing far more harm than good ... Do you see? ... If he goes on much longer, the whole town will be in an uproar and my position will become untenable ...'

'I don't know what to do ...'

'Aren't you on good terms with his boss?'

'Yes, I am ... Of course, I could ask the head of the Police Judiciaire ... It's a delicate matter ... The Superintendent will find out sooner or later. It was a pure favour to me that he agreed to go ... Do you understand?'

'Do you or don't you want to cause trouble for your niece? And she's your god-daughter, may I remind you ...'

'It really is a serious matter, then?'

'I have already told you ...'

One had the impression that Etienne Naud was stamping his feet with impatience. Alban's own panic had rubbed off on him and the fact that Cavre had not been against his calling Bréjon to get him to summon Maigret back to Paris had not exactly reassured him.

'Can I not have a word with my sister?'

'Your sister has gone to bed ... I'm the only one downstairs ...'

'What does Geneviève say?'

The examining magistrate was obviously beginning to falter, and fell back on commonplace remarks.

'Is it raining in your part of the world, too?'

'I don't know!' yelled back Naud. 'I don't care a damn! Do you hear? Just get that confounded Superintendent of yours out of here ...'

'What on earth has got into you?'

'What has got into me? If this goes on, we won't be able to stay here, that's all. He is poking his nose into everything. He says nothing. He ... he ...'

'Now calm down. I'll do my best.'

'When?'

'Tomorrow morning ... I'll go and see the head of the Police Judiciaire as soon as the offices are open, but it goes against the grain, let me tell you. It's the first time in my career that ...'

'But you will do it, won't you?'

'I've told you I will ...'

'The telegram will probably arrive at about noon ... He'll be able to take the three o'clock train ... Make sure the telegram arrives in time ...'

'Is Louise all right?'

'Yes, she's all right ... Good-night ... Don't forget ... I'll explain later ... And don't start imagining things, please ... Say good-night to your wife for me ...'

The postmistress realized from the look on Maigret's face that the conversation was over and she took the headset from him and moved the plugs once more.

'Hello! ... Have you finished? ... Hello Paris ... How many calls? ... Two? ... Thank you ... Good-night, my dear.'

And then she turned to the Superintendent who was putting his hat on again and relighting his pipe:

'I could be sacked for this ... Do you think it is true, then?'

'What?'

'What people are saying ... can't think that a man like Monsieur Etienne who has everything he could possibly want to make him happy ...'

'Good-night, Mademoiselle. Don't worry. I'll be very discreet ...'

'What did they say?'

'Nothing much. Just family news ...'

'Are you going back to Paris?'

'Maybe ... My goodness, yes ... It is quite possible I'll take the train tomorrow afternoon ...'

Maigret was calm, now. He felt himself again. He was almost surprised to find Louis waiting for him in the kitchen and the youngster was equally surprised when he sensed his hero's mood had changed. The Superintendent paid virtually no attention to the lad. His attitude towards him was flippant, scornful even, or so thought young Louis who was cut to the quick.

Once more, they began to make their way through the fog which seemed to reduce the world to absurdly small proportions. As before, an occasional light shone through the gloom.

'He did it, didn't he?'

'Who? ... Did what?'

'Naud ... He's the one who killed Albert ...'

'I honestly don't know, my boy ... It ... '

Maigret stopped himself in time. He was going to say:

'It doesn't matter ...'

For that was what he thought, or rather what he felt. But he realized that a statement such as this would only startle the youngster.

'What did he say?'

'Nothing much ... Incidentally, speaking of Groult-Cotelle ...'

They were approaching the two inns. The lights were still on, and on one side of the street faces could be seen through the window like silhouettes in a Chinese shadow-play.

'Well?'

'Has he always been a close friend of the Nauds?'

'Wait a minute ... Not always, no ... I was a small boy at the time, you see ... The house has been in his family for a long time, but when I was a kid we used to go there to play ... It was empty then ... I remember because we got into the cellar quite a few times ... One of the airholes didn't shut properly. Monsieur Groult-Cotelle was living with some relations of his, then. They have a castle in Brittany, I think ... When he came back here, he was married ... You should ask some of the older inhabitants ... I must have been six or seven at the time ... I remember his wife had a lovely little yellow car which she drove herself and she often used to go off in it alone ...'

'Did the two of them visit the Nauds?'

'No ... I am sure they didn't ... I say that because I remember Monsieur Groult was always in a huddle with the old doctor, a widower ... I often used to see them sitting by the window playing chess ... Unless I'm mistaken, it was because of his wife he didn't see the Nauds ... He was friendly with them before as he and Naud went to the same school ... They used to say hello to each other in the street ... I used to see them chatting on the pavement, but that's all ...'

'So it was after Madame Groult-Cotelle left ...'

'Yes ... About three years ago ... Mademoiselle Naud was sixteen or seventeen years old ... She was back from school – she was at a boarding-school in Niort for a long time and only used to appear every fourth Sunday ... I remember that, too, because whenever you saw her during term-time you knew it was the third Sunday in the month ... They became friends ... Monsieur Groult used to spend half his time at the Nauds' ...'

'Do they go off on holiday together?'

'Yes, to Les Sables d'Olonne ... The Nauds had a villa built there ... Are you going back? ... Don't you want to know if the detective ...'

The young lad looked back at Groult-Cotelle's house and could still see a glimmer of light filtering through the shutters. Although he dared not show it, he was somewhat disillusioned with the unorthodox way Maïgret seemed to be conducting this inquiry, for he had certainly thought in terms of a very different approach.

'What did he say when you went in?'

'Cavre? Nothing ... No, he didn't say anything ... It's not important, anyway ...'

The fact of the matter was, that at that particular moment,

Maigret was living in a world of his own and not in the present at all, and he answered the boy half-heartedly without really knowing what the question was.

Many a time at the Police Judiciaire, his colleagues had joked about his going off into one of these reveries, and he also knew that people used to talk about this habit of his behind his back.

At such moments, Maigret seemed to puff himself up out of all proportion and become slow-witted and stodgy, like someone blind and dumb who is unaware of what is going on around him. Indeed, if anyone not forewarned was to walk past or talk to Maigret when he was in one of these moods, he would more than likely take him for a fat idiot or a fat sleepy-head.

'So, you're concentrating your thoughts?' said someone who prided himself on his psychological perception.

And Maigret had replied with comic sincerity:

'I never think.'

And it was almost true. For Maigret was not thinking now, as he stood in the damp, cold street. He was not following through an idea. One might say he was rather like a sponge.

It was Sergeant Lucas who had described him thus, and he had worked constantly with Maigret and knew him better than anyone.

'There comes a time in the course of an investigation,' Lucas had said, 'when the *patron* suddenly swells up like a sponge. You'd think he was filling up.'

But filling up with what? At present, for instance, he was absorbing the fog and the darkness. The village round him was not just any old village. And he was not merely someone who had been cast into these surroundings by chance.

He was rather like God the Father. He knew this village like the back of his hand. It was as if he had always lived here, or better still, as if he had created the little town. He knew what went on inside all those small, low houses nestling in the darkness. He could see men and women turning in the moist warmth of their beds and he followed the thread of their dreams. A dim light in a window enabled him to see a mother, half-asleep, giving a bottle of warm milk to her infant. He felt the shooting pain of the sick woman in the corner and imagined the drowsy grocer's wife waking up with a start.

He was in the café. Men holding grubby cards and totting up red and yellow counters were seated at the brown, polished tables.

He was in Geneviève's bedroom. He was suffering with her, feeling for her pride as a woman. Doubtless, she had just lived through the most painful day of her life and was perhaps anxiously awaiting Maigret's return so that she could slip into his room once more.

Madame Naud was wide awake. She had gone to bed, but could not get to sleep and in the darkness of her room, she lay listening for the slightest sound in the house. She wondered why Maigret had not come back, pictured her husband cooling his heels in the drawing-room, torn between hope after his telephone call to Bréjon and anxiety at the Superintendent's absence.

Maigret felt the warmth of the cattle in the stables, heard the mare kicking, visualized the old cook in her camisole ... And in Groult-Cotelle's house ... Look now! A door was opening. Alban was leading his visitor out. How he hated him. What had he and Cavre said to each other in the dusty, stale-smelling sitting-room after the telephone call to Naud?

The door closed again. Cavre walked quickly along, his briefcase under his arm. He was pleased, yet displeased. After all, he had almost won the game. He had beaten Maigret. Tomorrow the Superintendent would be summoned back to Paris. But none the less, he felt a little humiliated that he had not brought this about single-handed. Furthermore, he felt thoroughly ruffled by the Super-intendent's menacing tone with regard to the whereabouts of Albert Retailleau's cap ...

Cavre's employee would be waiting for him at the Lion d'Or, drinking brandy to while away the time.

'Are you going back straightaway?' asked Louis.

'Yes, lad ... What else can I do?'

'You're not going to give up?'

'Give up what?'

Maigret knew them all so well! He had come across so many lads like Louis in his life, youngsters who were just as enthusiastic, just as naive and crafty, who plunged straight into every difficulty in their desire to solve the case come what may!

'You'll get over it, my lad,' he thought. 'In a few years time you will bow respectfully to a Naud or a Groult-Cotelle because you'll have understood that it's the wisest course of action when you're Fillou's son ...'

And what about Madame Retailleau, all alone in her house? She was sure to have carefully removed all the notes from the soup-tureen. She had understood long ago. She had doubtless been as good a wife and as good a mother as anyone else. It was probably not that she lacked feelings, but that she had realized that feelings are of no use. She had resigned herself to this truth.

But she was determined to defend herself with other arms! She was determined to turn all life's misfortunes into bank notes. Her husband's death had secured her her house and an income which allowed her to bring up and educate her son.

The death of Albert ...

'I bet,' he muttered to himself in a low voice, 'she wants a little house in Niort, not in Saint-Aubin ... A brand-new little house, spotlessly clean, with pictures of her husband and son on the wall ... somewhere she can live comfortably and securely in her old age.'

As for Groult-Cotelle and his *Sexual Perversions* ...

'You're walking awfully quickly, Superintendent ...'

'Are you coming back with me?'

'Do you mind?'

'Won't your mother be worried?'

'Oh! She doesn't take any notice of me ...'

He said these words with a mixture of pride and regret in his voice.

Off they went, past the station, along the water-logged path bordering the canal. Old Désiré would be sleeping off his wine on his dirty straw mattress. Josaphat the postman was proud of himself and was no doubt reckoning what he had gained from his cleverness and cunning ...

Ahead of them, at the end of the path, there was a circle of light like the moon seen through the veil of a cloud. A large, warm and peaceful-looking house pierced the mist, one of those houses that passers-by look at enviously and think how nice it must be to live there.

'Off you go, son ... We're here now ...'

'When will I see you again? Promise me you won't leave without . . .'

'I promise . . .'

'You're sure you're not giving up?'

'Sure . . .'

Alas! For Maigret was not exactly thrilled at the thought of what remained to be done and walked up to the steps of the house with his shoulders down. The front door was ajar. They had left it like this so that he could get in. There was a light on in the drawing-room.

He sighed as he took off his heavy overcoat which the fog had made even heavier, then stood for a moment on the doormat to light his pipe.

'In we go!'

Poor Etienne had sat up waiting for him, torn between hope and a deadly anxiety. That very afternoon, Madame Naud had tormented herself in similar fashion, in the same armchair as her husband was sitting in now.

A bottle of armagnac on a small round table looked as if it had served its purpose well.

8

Maigret Plays Maigret

There was nothing affected about Maigret's stance. If his shoulders were hunched and his head slightly to one side, as if he were frozen to the marrow and bent on warming himself by the stove, it was because he was cold. He had been out in the fog for some time and had paid no attention to the temperature outside. He shivered now as he took off his overcoat and suddenly seemed aware of the icy dampness that chilled his bones.

He felt irritable, as one does when one is about to go down with flu. He also felt uneasy, since he disliked the task which faced him. And he was hesitant. As he was about to go into the drawing-room, he suddenly thought of two diametrically opposed methods of tackling the situation, just when he had to make up his mind one way or the other.

It was this, rather than an attempt to live up to his reputation, that made him walk into the room, swerving to and fro like a bear, with a churlish expression on his face and large eyes that did not appear to be focusing on anything.

He looked at nothing, yet saw everything: the glass and the bottle of armagnac, the overly smooth hair of Etienne Naud who said with a false cheerfulness:

'Did you have a good evening, Superintendent?'

He had obviously just run a comb through his hair. He always kept one in his pocket for he liked to be admired. But before, while he was gloomily waiting for Maigret to come back, he had probably run his shaking fingers through his hair.

Instead of replying, Maigret went over to the wall on the left and adjusted a picture which was not hanging straight. Nor was this affectation. He could not abide seeing a picture hang crooked on a wall. It quite simply irritated him and he had no wish to be irritated for such a stupid reason just when he was all set to play the detective.

It was stuffy. The smell of food still lingered in the room and mingled with the bouquet from the armagnac to which the Superintendent finally helped himself.

'There!' he sighed.

Naud jumped in surprise and anxiety at that resounding 'There!' for it was as if Maigret, having debated the situation in his mind, had reached a conclusion.

If the Superintendent had been at Police Headquarters or had even been officially investigating the case, he would have felt obliged, in order to make the odds in his favour, to use traditional methods. Now, traditional methods in this case tended to break down Naud's resistance, to scare him and shatter his nerves by making him oscillate between hope and fear.

It was easy. Just let him get entangled in his own lies first. Then vaguely bring up the subject of the two telephone calls. And then (why not, after all?) say point-blank:

'Your friend Alban will be arrested tomorrow morning . . .'

Not a bit of it, however! Maigret quite simply stood with his elbows resting on the mantelpiece. The flames in the fireplace scorched his legs. Naud was sitting near him presumably going on hoping . . .

'I shall leave tomorrow at three o'clock as you wish,' sighed the Superintendent at last, having puffed at his pipe two or three times in quick succession.

He pitied Naud. He felt uncomfortable before this man who was about the same age as himself and who up until now had lived a comfortable, peaceful, upright life. Now, threatened as he was by the thought of being shut behind prison walls for the rest of his days, he was playing his last cards.

Was he going to carry on the struggle and go on lying? Maigret hoped not, just as, out of compassion, one hopes that a wounded animal, clumsily shot, will die quickly. He avoided looking at him and fixed his eyes on the carpet.

'Why do you say that, Superintendent? You know you are welcome here and that my family not only likes but respects you, as I do . . .'

'I overheard your telephone conversation with your brother-in-law, Monsieur Naud.'

He put himself in the other man's shoes. Afterwards, he preferred to forget such moments as these. He therefore hurried on:

'Furthermore, you are mistaken about me. Your brother-in-law Bréjon asked me as a favour to come and help you with a delicate matter. I realized straightaway, believe me, that he had wrongly interpreted your wishes and that it was not help of this kind that you wanted from him. You wrote to him in a moment of panic to ask his advice. You told him about the rumours circulating but you did not admit, of course, that they were true. And he, poor man, being an honest, conscientious magistrate who works to rule, sent you a detective to sort out the mess.'

Naud struggled slowly to his feet, walked over to the small, round table and poured himself a generous glass of armagnac. His hand was shaking. There were probably beads of sweat on his forehead, although Maigret could not see. No doubt out of consideration for Naud's feelings, the Superintendent had looked the other way at this crucial moment, for he pitied the man.

'If you had not called in Justin Cavre, I would have left the district immediately after our initial meeting, but his presence somehow goaded me into staying.'

Naud said not a word in protest, but fiddled with his watch-chain and stared at the portrait of his mother-in-law.

'Of course, since I am not here on official business, I am not accountable to anyone. So you have nothing to fear from me, Monsieur Naud, and I am in a position to talk to you all the more freely. You have just been through a hellish few weeks, haven't you? And so has your wife, for I am sure she knows all about it . . .'

The other man still did not respond. It had got to the point where a nod of the head, a whisper or a flutter of the eyelids was all that was required to put an end to the suspense. After that, peace would come. He could relax. He would have nothing more to hide, no game to play.

Upstairs, his wife was probably awake, listening carefully and fretting because there was no sign of the two men coming up to bed. And what of his daughter? Had she managed to get to sleep?

'Now, Monsieur Naud, I am going to tell you what I really think, and you will understand why I have not left without saying any-thing, which strange though it may seem, I was on the point of doing. Listen carefully, and don't be too ready to misconstrue what I say. I have the distinct impression, the near certitude, that however guilty you may be of the death of Albert Retailleau, you are also a victim of his death. I will go further. If you have been the instrument of death, you are not primarily responsible for it.'

And Maigret helped himself to a drink, in turn, in order to give the other man time to weigh up his words. As Naud remained silent, he finally looked him in the eye and forced him to look back. He asked:

'Don't you trust me?'

The result was as distressing as it was unexpected, for Naud, a man in the prime of his life, capitulated by bursting into tears. His swollen eyelids brimmed with tears and he pouted his lips like a child. He fought back the tears for a moment, standing awkwardly in the middle of the room, and then rushed over and leaned against the wall. Burying his face in his arms, he started to sob violently, his shoulders moving jerkily up and down.

There was nothing else to do but wait. Twice, he tried to speak, but it was too soon, for he had not regained sufficient composure. As if out of discretion, Maigret had sat down in front of the fire and, not being able to poke the fire as he was accustomed to doing in his own home, he arranged the logs with a pair of tongs.

'You can tell me in your own words what happened in a little while, if you like, although it won't serve much purpose as it is a simple matter to reconstruct the events of the night in question. But what followed is another matter altogether . . .'

'What do you mean?'

Naud looked just as tall and strong, but he seemed to have lost his grip. He had the air of a child who has shot up too quickly and who at the age of twelve is as tall and well-filled out as a fully-grown man.

'Did you not suspect there was something going on between your daughter and that young man?'

'But I didn't even know him, Superintendent! I mean I knew of his existence because I know more or less everyone in the village, but I could not have put a name to his face. I still wonder how on earth Geneviève managed to meet him as she virtually never left the house . . .'

'On the night in question, you and your wife were in bed, were you not?'

'Yes . . . And another thing . . . It's ridiculous, but we'd had goose for dinner . . .'

He clung to facts of this kind, as though investing the truth with such intimate details somehow made it less tragic.

'I love goose, but I find it difficult to digest . . . At about one in the morning, I got up to take some bicarbonate of soda . . . You know the lay-out of the rooms upstairs, more or less . . . Our bathroom is next to our bedroom, then there's a spare room and next to that a room we never go into because . . .'

'I know . . . In memory of a child . . .'

'My daughter's room is at the far end of the corridor and so it is rather isolated from the rest of the house. The two maids sleep on the floor above . . . So I was in our bathroom groping about in the dark, as I didn't want to wake up my wife, as she'd have scolded me for being greedy . . . I heard the sound of voices . . . There was an argument going on . . . It did not cross my mind that the noise could be coming from my daughter's room . . .

'However, when I went into the corridor to see for myself, I realized this was so. There was a light beneath her door, too . . . I heard a man's voice . . .

'I don't know what you would have done in my place, Super-intendent . . . I don't know if you have a daughter . . . We're still rather behind the times here in Saint-Aubin . . . Perhaps I am particu-larly naive . . . Geneviève is twenty . . . But it had never occurred to me she might hide something like this from her mother and me . . . To think that a man . . . No! You know, even now . . .'

He wiped his eyes and mechanically took his packet of cigarettes out of his pocket.

'I almost rushed into the room in my nightshirt . . . I'm rather old-fashioned in that respect, too, as I still wear nightshirts and not pyjamas . . . But at the last moment I realized how ridiculous I looked and went back into the bathroom. I got dressed in the dark and just as I was putting on my socks, I heard another noise, this time from outside . . . As the bathroom shutters had not been closed I drew back the curtain ... There was a moon and I could see a man climbing down a ladder into the courtyard ...

'I got my shoes on somehow ... I rushed downstairs ... I am not sure, but I think I heard my wife calling:

'"Etienne ..."

'Have you already thought of looking at the key to the door which opens onto the courtyard? ... It's an old key, a huge one, a real hammer ... I would not be prepared to swear I took it off its hook without thinking, but it wasn't a premeditated action either for it had not occurred to me to kill and if anyone had said then ...'

He spoke softly but in a shaky voice. To calm himself down he lit his cigarette and puffed slowly at it several times, like condemned men must do.

'The man went round the house and jumped over the low wall by the road. I jumped over it behind him, not thinking to stifle the sound of my footsteps. He must have heard me but he went on walking at the same pace. When I had almost caught up with him he turned round, and although I could not see his face, for some reason or other I got the impression he was jeering at me.

'"What do you want of me?" he asked in an aggressive, scornful tone of voice.

'I swear to you, Superintendent, there are moments I wish with all my heart I had never lived through. I recognized him. He was just a youngster to me, but he had just left my daughter's bedroom and now he was sneering at me. I didn't know what to do. This kind of thing doesn't happen the way you imagine. I shook him by the shoulders but couldn't find the words to express what I wanted to say.

'"So you're annoyed I am jilting your daughter, are you! The hussy! ... You were hand in glove, weren't you?" he flung at me.'

Naud passed his hand over his face.

'I am not sure of anything, any more, Superintendent. With the best will in the world, I could not give you an exact account of what happened. He was every bit as angry as I was but more in control of himself. He was insulting me, insulting my daughter ... Instead of falling on his knees at my feet, as I had stupidly half-imagined he would do, he was making fun of me, my wife, my whole family. He said things like:

'"A fine family, indeed!"'

'He used the most obscene language when referring to my daughter, words I cannot bring myself to repeat, and then I began to hit him. I don't know how it happened. I had the key in my hand. The youth suddenly punched me hard in the stomach and the pain was such that I hit him more violently than ever . . .

'He fell . . .

'And then I ran away. All I wanted to do was to get back to the house . . .

'I swear to you this is the truth . . . My idea was to telephone the *gendarmerie* in Benet . . . When I got closer to the house I saw a light on in my daughter's room . . . I suddenly thought that if I told the truth . . . But you must understand . . . I went back to where I had left him . . . He was dead. . .'

'You carried him to the railway-line,' Maigret interceded, to help him bring this sorry story more quickly to an end.

'That's right . . .'

'All by yourself?'

'Yes . . .'

'And you returned home?'

'My wife was standing behind the door that opens onto the road. She asked in a whisper:

'"What have you done?"'

'I tried to deny it all, but she knew. There was terror and pity in the look she gave me. I went to bed feeling somewhat feverish and she went through my clothes in turn in the bathroom to make sure that . . .'

'I understand.'

'You may or may not believe it, but neither my wife nor I have had the courage to broach the subject with our daughter. We've never talked about it or even referred to it together. That's probably the hardest thing of all. It is sometimes unnerving. Our household routine is exactly the same as it was in the past and yet all three of us know . . .'

'And Alban?'

'I don't know how to tell you. At first, I did not give him a thought. Then the next day I was surprised he didn't turn up as usual as we were about to eat. I started to talk about him for the sake of something to say . . . I said: "I must give Alban a ring."

'I did so, and his maid told me he wasn't in . . However, I was certain I heard his voice when the maid answered the phone . . .

'It became an obsession with me . . . Why doesn't Alban come? Does Alban suspect something? . . . Stupid as it may seem, I convinced myself that he constituted the only real threat, and four days later, when he still hadn't looked near us, I went over to his house.

'I wanted to know the reason for his silence. I had no intention of confiding in him, but somehow I ended up telling him everything . . .

'I needed him . . . You would understand why if you had been in my position. He used to tell me the local gossip . . . He also described the funeral.

'I was well aware of what people were thinking from the outset and another idea took root in my mind. I felt I had to atone for what I had done and this thought never left me . . . Don't laugh at me, I beg of you . . .'

'I have seen so many men like you, Monsieur Naud!'

'And did they behave as stupidly as I did? Did they, one fine day, go and see the victim's mother like I did? In melodramatic fashion, I waited until it was dark one evening, and then paid her a visit after Groult had made sure there was no one on the road . . . I did not tell her the brutal truth . . . I said that it was a terrible misfortune to have befallen her, that as a widow she had lost her only source of support . . .

'I am not sure whether it was a devil or an angel that prompted me, Superintendent. I can still see her, white-faced and motionless, standing by the hearth with a shawl round her shoulders. I had twenty thousand-franc notes in two bundles in my pocket. I didn't know how to go about putting them on the table. I was ashamed of myself. I was . . . yes, I was ashamed of her too . . .

'And yet the notes passed from my pocket to the table.

'"Each year, Madame, I will make it my duty to . . ."

'And as she frowned, I hurriedly added: "Unless you would rather I give you a lump sum in your name which . . ."'

He could not go on and had such difficulty in breathing that he had to pour himself another glass of armagnac.

'There it is . . . I was wrong not to confess to everything at the beginning . . . It was too late afterwards . . . Nothing had changed at home, at least superficially ... I don't know how Geneviève has had the courage to go on living as if nothing had happened. There have been times when I have wondered if my imagination hasn't been playing tricks on me ...

'When I realized that people in the village suspected me, when I began receiving anonymous letters and found out that more had been sent to the Department of Public Prosecutions, I wrote to my brother-in-law. It was stupid of me, for what could he do as I had not told him the truth? One so often hears it said that magistrates have the power to cover up a scandal that I vaguely imagined Bréjon would use his authority in the same way ...

'Instead, however, he sent you down here just when I had written to a private detective agency in Paris ... Yes! I did that too! I picked an address at random from the newspaper advertisements! Unable to bring myself to confide in my brother-in-law, I told a total stranger everything that had happened. I simply had to be reassured ...

'He knew you were on your way, for when my brother-in-law told me you were arriving I immediately sent a telegram to Cavre's agency ... We arranged to meet in Fontenay the following day ...

'What else do you want to know, Superintendent? ... How you must despise me! ... Yes, you do! ... And I despise myself too, I assure you ... Of all the criminals you have known, I bet you haven't come across one as stupid, as ...'

Maigret smiled for the first time. Etienne Naud was sincere. There was nothing artificial about his despair. And yet, as with all criminals, to use the word he himself had just used, his attitude revealed a certain pride.

It was annoying and humiliating to have bungled being a criminal!

For a few seconds, or even a few minutes, Maigret sat quite still and stared down at the flames curling round the blackened logs. Etienne Naud was so disconcerted by this unexpected reaction on the part of the Superintendent that he was at a loss what to do and stood hesitantly in the middle of the room, unsure of his next move.

The fact of the matter was, that since he had confessed to everything, since he had chosen to abase himself, he had naturally supposed that the Superintendent would show him more consideration and come morally to his assistance.

Had he not sunk lower than the low? Had he not painted a pathetic picture of his own and his family's plight?

Earlier on, before confessing, Naud had sensed that Maigret was already sympathetic to his case and prepared to be more so. He had counted on this.

And now, all trace of sympathy had vanished. The game was over and the Superintendent was calmly smoking his pipe, his expression one of deep thought devoid of any sentimentality.

'What would you do in my position?' ventured Naud once more.

One look made him wonder if he had gone too far. Perhaps he had overstepped the mark like a child who is forgiven for misbehaving and as a result of such lenient treatment becomes more demanding and tiresome than ever.

What was Maigret thinking? Naud began to suspect that his manner had merely been part of a trap. He expected him to rise to his feet, take a pair of handcuffs out of his pocket and say the sacred words:

'In the name of the law ...'

'I am wondering ...'

It was Maigret who hesitated, still puffing at his pipe as he crossed and uncrossed his legs.

'I am wondering ... yes ... I am wondering if we couldn't telephone your friend, Alban ... What time is it? ... Ten minutes past midnight ... The postmistress will probably still be up and will put us through ... Yes, indeed ... If you're not too tired, Monsieur Naud, I think it would be best if we got everything over with tonight so that I can catch my train tomorrow ...'

'But ...'

He could not find the right words, or rather dared not say what was on the tip of his tongue:

'But isn't it all over?'

'Will you excuse me?'

Maigret walked across the drawing-room into the hall and turned the handle of the telephone.

'Hello ... I am sorry to bother you, dear Mademoiselle ... Yes, it's me ... Did you recognize my voice? ... Of course not ... No problem at all ... Could you very kindly put me through to Monsieur Groult-Cotelle, please? ... Let it ring loud and clear in case he's a heavy sleeper.'

Through the half-open door, he saw a bewildered Etienne Naud take a large gulp of armagnac, as though resigned to his fate. The poor man was in a terrible state and seemed to have lost all his strength and nerve.

'Monsieur Groult-Cotelle? ... How are you? ... You had gone to bed ... What's that? ... You were reading in bed? ... Yes, Superintendent Maigret here ... Yes, I'm with your friend ... We've been having a chat ... What? ... You've got a cold? ... That's most unfortunate ... Anyone would think you have guessed what I was going to say ... We would like you to pop over here ... Yes, I know it is foggy ... You haven't any clothes on? ... Well, in that case we'll come to you ... We'll be round in a jiffy if we take the car ... What? ... You'd rather come over here? ... No ... Nothing in particular ... I am leaving tomorrow ... I have important business to see to in Paris ...'

Poor Naud understood less and less what was in Maigret's mind and stared up at the ceiling, thinking to himself no doubt that his wife could hear everything and must be thoroughly alarmed. Should he go upstairs to reassure her? But was he really in a position to do so? Maigret's behaviour now made him uneasy and he was beginning to regret having admitted to the crime.

'What did you say? ... A quarter of an hour? ... That's too long ... Be as quick as you can ... See you in a minute ... Thank you ...'

Perhaps the Superintendent was play-acting to a certain extent. Perhaps he was not really angry? Perhaps he did not want to be alone with Etienne Naud and have to wait ten minutes or a quarter of an hour in the drawing-room with him?

'He is coming over,' he announced. 'He's very worried. You cannot imagine what a state my telephone call has put him in ...'

'But he's got no reason to ...'

'Is that what you think?' asked Maigret simply.

Naud was more and more perplexed.

'Do you mind if I go and get a bite to eat in the kitchen ... Stay where you are ... I'll find the light switch ... I know where the fridge is ...'

He switched on the light in the kitchen. The stove had gone out. He found a chicken leg glazed with sauce. He cut and buttered a thick slice of bread.

'Tell me ...'

He came back into the drawing-room smiling.

'Have you got any beer?'

'Wouldn't you rather have a glass of burgundy?'

'I'd prefer beer, but if you haven't got any ...'

'There must be some in the cellar ... I always have one or two crates brought in but as we don't drink beer very often, I don't know if ...'

Just as, during the saddest of deathbed scenes, the family will cease weeping for a moment in the middle of the night and have a little something to eat, so the two men, after an hour of high drama, went matter-of-factly down to the cellar.

'No ... This is lemonade ... Wait a minute ... The beer must be underneath the stairs ...'

He was right. They went back upstairs with bottles of beer under their arms and then set about finding two large glasses. Maigret went on munching the chicken leg which he held between his fingers and got the sauce all over his chin.

'I wonder,' he said casually, 'if your friend Alban will come alone.'

'What do you mean?'

'Nothing. I'm willing to bet that...'

There was no time to finish the wager, for someone was tapping on the front door. Etienne Naud rushed to open it. Maigret meanwhile stood calmly waiting in the middle of the drawing-room with his glass of beer in one hand and the chicken and bread in the other.

He heard low voices:

'I have taken the liberty of bringing this gentleman with me. I met him on the way over here and he ...'

For a second, Maigret's eyes hardened and then, with no warning, they suddenly flickered mischievously as he shouted to the man outside:

'Come in Cavre! I was expecting you ...'

9

Noise Behind the Door

An impression of a dream can remain within us for a long time, sometimes all our lives, whereas the dream itself, so we are told, only lasts a few seconds. Thus, for a moment, the three men entering the room seemed to Maigret to bear no resemblance to the kind of men they actually were, or at any rate considered themselves to be, and it was this new image of them that was to remain so vividly in his mind in the years to come.

They were all more or less the same age, Maigret included. And as he observed them each in turn he felt rather as if he was looking on at a gathering of schoolboys in their last year.

Etienne Naud was probably just as plump and podgy when he took his *bachot* as he was now. He would have had the same sturdy physique, the same soft look about him, and would undoubtedly have been very well-brought-up and rather shy.

The Superintendent had met Cavre not long after he had left school and even then he had been a loner, and an ill-tempered one at that. However hard he tried – for he took a pride in his appearance then – clothes simply did not sit as well on him as on other people. He always looked shabby and badly dressed. He was a sad figure. When he was a little boy his mother must have been forever saying to him:

'Run along and play with the others, Justin.'

And no doubt she would confide to her neighbours:

'My son never plays. It worries me a bit from the health point of view. He's too clever. He never stops thinking . . .'

As for Alban, his looks had changed remarkably little since he was a young man: the long, thin legs, the elongated, rather aristocratic-looking face, the long, pale hands covered with reddish hairs, the upper-class elegance . . . He would have copied his friends' compositions, borrowed cigarettes from them and told them dirty jokes in corners!

And now they were struggling with utmost seriousness over an affair which could send one of them to jail for life. They were mature men. Two children somewhere bore the name of Groult-Cotelle, children who had perhaps already inherited some of their father's vices. In the house were a wife and daughter who would probably not sleep that night. As for Cavre, he was doubtless fuming at the thought his wife might be making the most of his absence.

Something rather curious was happening. Whereas, shortly before, Etienne had confessed his crime to Maigret without a trace of shame and had laid bare, man to man, his innermost fears, now he blushed to the very roots of his hair as he ushered the visitors into the drawing-room, trying in vain to look unconcerned.

Was it not, in fact, rather a childish fancy that caused him to blush so violently? For a few seconds, Maigret became the headmaster or teacher. Naud had remained behind with him to be questioned about some misdeed and be given a wigging. His friends were now coming back into the classroom and looking at him searchingly as if to say:

'How did you get on?'

Well, he had not got on at all well. He had not defended himself. He had wept. He wondered if there were still traces of tears on his cheeks and eyelids.

He would like to have boasted and made them think that everything had gone smoothly. Instead, he bustled about, went into the dining-room to get some glasses out of the sideboard and then poured out the armagnac.

Did these glimpses of a time of life when our actions and conduct are as yet unimportant inspire the Superintendent? He waited until everyone was seated, then positioned himself in the middle of the room and, looking at Cavre and Alban in turn, said squarely:

'Well, gentlemen, the game's up!'

Only at this point, and for the first time since he had become involved in this case, did he play Maigret, as was said of inspectors at the Police Judiciaire who tried to imitate the great man. With his pipe between his teeth, his hands in his pockets and his back to the fire, he talked, growled, poked at the logs with the end of the tongs and moved with bear-like gait from one suspect to the other, either firing questions at them or suddenly breaking off so that a disturbing silence fell over the room.

'Monsieur Naud and I have just had a long and friendly chat. I announced my intention of returning to Paris tomorrow. It was far better, was it not, before taking leave of each other, to come out with the truth, and this is what we did. Why do you jump, Monsieur Groult-Cotelle? In fact, Cavre, I must apologize for having made you come out just when you were going to bed. Yes indeed! I am the guilty one. I knew perfectly well when I rang our friend Alban that he wouldn't have the guts to come here alone. I wonder why he considered my invitation to come round for a chat a threat ... He had a detective to hand and as there was no lawyer around, he brought along the detective ... Isn't that right, Groult?'

'It wasn't me who sent to Paris for him!' replied the bogus country gentleman, now stripped of his importance.

'I know. It wasn't you who beat the unfortunate Retailleau to death, as you just happened to be in La Roche for the night. It wasn't you who left your wife as she was the one who left you ... It wasn't you who ... In fact you're a somewhat negative character altogether, aren't you ... You have never done a good deed in your life ...'

Alarmed at being reprimanded like this, Groult-Cotelle called Cavre to his aid, but the detective, his leather briefcase on his lap, was looking at Maigret in a somewhat anxious fashion.

He was sufficiently well-acquainted with the police, and with the *patron* in particular, to know that this little scene was being staged for a definite purpose and that when the meeting was over, the case would be closed.

Etienne Naud had not protested when the Superintendent had declared:

'The game's up!'

What more did Maigret want? He walked up and down, stood in front of one of the portraits, went from one door to the other, all the time keeping up a steady flow of words. It was almost as if he were improvising and now and again Cavre began to wonder if he might not be playing for time and waiting for something to happen which he knew would happen but was taking a long time to do so.

'I am leaving tomorrow, then, as you all wish me to do, and while

I am about it, I could reproach you, especially you, Cavre, as you know me, for not having had more confidence in me. You knew quite well, damn it, that I was just a guest and treated as well as ever a guest could be.

'What happened in this house before I arrived does not concern me. At most you could have asked my advice. After all, what is Naud's position? He did something most unfortunate, very unfortunate, even. But did anyone come forward and complain?

'No! The young man's mother declares herself satisfied. If I may say so ...'

And Maigret deliberately made light of his next, ominous statement, a tactic which misled all three men.

'The drama in question was enacted by gentlemen, all well-bred people. There were rumours abroad, admittedly. Two or three unpleasant pieces of evidence gave cause for concern but the diplomacy of our friend Cavre and Naud's money, combined with the liking of certain individuals for liquor, averted any possible danger. And as for the cap, which in any case would not have constituted sufficient proof, I presume Cavre took the precaution of destroying it. Isn't that right, Justin?'

Cavre jumped on hearing himself addressed by his Christian name. Everybody turned to look at him but he said nothing.

'That, in a nutshell, is the position at present, or rather our host's position. Anonymous letters are in circulation. The Director of Prosecutions and the *gendarmerie* have received some of them. There may be an official inquiry into the case. What have you advised your client, Cavre?'

'I am not a barrister.'

'How modest you are! If you want to know what I think, and this is my own personal view and not a professional opinion, for I am not a barrister either, in a few days' time, Naud will feel the need to depart with his family. He is rich enough to sell his estate and retire elsewhere, possibly abroad ...'

Naud let out a sigh in the form of a sob at the thought of leaving what had been his whole life up until now.

'That leaves our friend Alban ... What do you propose to do, Monsieur Alban Groult-Cotelle?'

'You don't have to answer,' Cavre hurriedly interjected on seeing him open his mouth. 'I would also like to say that we are under no obligation to put up with this interrogation, which in any case is phoney. If you knew the Superintendent as well as I do, you would realize he is taking us for a real ride, as they would say at the Quai des Orfèvres. I don't know whether you have confessed, Monsieur Naud, or how the Superintendent got the truth out of you, but of one thing I am sure, and that is that my former colleague has a purpose in mind. I do not know what that purpose is, but I am telling you to be on your guard.'

'Well said, Justin!'

'I did not ask for your opinion.'

'Well, I am giving it all the same.'

And suddenly his tone changed. For the past quarter of an hour he had been waiting for something and had been forced into all this play-acting as a result, but now that something had finally happened. It was not without good reason that he had kept on pacing up and down, going from the hall door to the door opening into the dining-room.

Nor was it hunger or greed earlier on that had caused him to go into the kitchen for some bread and a hunk of chicken. He needed to know if there was another staircase besides the one leading down into the hall. And indeed there was a second staircase for the staff near the kitchen.

When he telephoned Groult-Cotelle he had talked in a very loud voice, as though unaware of the fact that two women were supposed to be sleeping in the house.

Now, there was someone behind the half-open dining-room door.

'You are right, Cavre. You are no fool, even though you are rather a sad character ... I have one purpose in mind and that is, let me declare it immediately, to prove that Naud is not the real culprit ...'

This statement by the Superintendent stupefied Etienne Naud more than anyone else, for he had to restrain himself from crying out. As for Alban, he had turned deadly pale and small red blotches which Maigret had not noticed before appeared on his forehead, as if he were prey to a sudden attack of urticaria – a clear proof of his inner collapse.

When he saw the rash, the Superintendent remembered how a certain, more or less notorious murderer, after a twenty-eight hour interrogation during which he had defended himself step by step, had suddenly wet his pants like a frightened child. Maigret and Lucas had been conducting the interrogation and they had sniffed, looked at each other and realized they had the upper hand.

Alban Groult-Cotelle's nettle-rash was a similar symptom of guilt and the Superintendent had difficulty in suppressing a smile.

'Tell me, Monsieur Groult, would you rather tell us the truth yourself, or would you like me to do it for you? Take your time before answering. Naturally, you have my permission to consult your lawyer . . . I mean Justin Cavre. Go off into a corner, if you like, and work something out between you . . .'

'I have nothing to say . . .'

'So it is my job to tell Monsieur Naud, who still does not know, why Albert Retailleau was killed, is it? For, strange as it might seem, even though Etienne Naud knows the young man was killed, he has absolutely no idea *why* . . . What were you going to say, Alban?'

'You're a liar!'

'How can you say I am a liar when I haven't said anything yet? Come now! I will put the question a different way and it will still come to the same thing. Will you tell us why, on a certain, carefully chosen day, you suddenly felt the need to go to La Roche-sur-Yon and bring back your hotel bill with meticulous care?'

Etienne Naud still did not understand and looked anxiously at Maigret, convinced that this line of attack would prove the Superintendent's undoing. At first he had been impressed by Maigret's manner but now he was rapidly going down in Naud's estimation. His animosity towards Groult-Cotelle was pointless and beginning to be thoroughly obnoxious.

It had reached the point when Naud felt he had to intervene. He was an honest fellow who disliked seeing an innocent man accused, and as host of the house, he would not allow one of his guests to be hauled over the coals.

'I assure you, Superintendent, you are barking up the wrong tree . . .'

'My dear fellow, I am sorry to have to disillusion you, and even sorrier that what you are about to learn is extremely unpleasant. Isn't that so, Groult?'

Groult-Cotelle had shot to his feet and for a moment looked as if he was going to rush at his tormentor. He had the greatest possible difficulty in restraining himself. He clenched his fists and his whole body quivered. Finally, he made as if for the door, but Maigret stopped him in his tracks by simply asking in the most natural tone:

'Are you going upstairs?'

Who would have thought, on seeing the stubborn and stolid Maigret, that he was as warm as his victim? His shirt was sticking to his back. He was listening carefully. And the truth of the matter was, he was frightened.

A few minutes before, he'd become convinced that Geneviève was behind the door, as he hoped. He had been thinking of her when he had telephoned Groult-Cotelle earlier on and had consequently talked in a loud voice in the hall.

'If I am right,' he was thinking then, 'she'll come down . . .'

And she had come down. At all events, he had heard a faint rustling sound behind the double doors into the dining-room and one side of them had moved.

It was on Geneviève's account, too, that he had addressed Groult-Cotelle in such a way a moment ago. Now he was wondering if she was still there, for he could not hear a sound. It had crossed his mind that she might have fainted, but presumably he would have heard her fall.

He was longing to look behind the half-open door and began thinking of how he could do so.

'Are you going upstairs?' he had flung at Alban.

And Alban, who seemed no longer to care, retraced his steps and positioned himself a few inches away from his enemy.

'Just what are you insinuating? Out with it! What other slanders have you got up your sleeve? There's not a word of truth in what you are going to say, do you hear?'

'Take a look at your lawyer.'

Cavre looked pitiful, indeed, for he realized that Maigret was on the right track and that his client was caught in his own web of lies.

'I don't need anyone to advise me. I don't know what you might have been told or who could have fabricated such stories, but before you say anything, I would like to state that they are untrue. If a few bright sparks have succeeded in . . .'

'You are vile, Groult.'

'What?'

'I say that you are a repugnant character. I say and I repeat that you are the real cause of Albert Retailleau's death, and that if the laws created by men were perfect, life imprisonment would not be a harsh enough punishment for you. In fact it would give me great personal pleasure, though I don't often feel like this, to accompany you to the foot of the guillotine ...'

'Gentlemen, I call you to witness ...'

'Not only did you kill Retailleau, but others too ...'

'I killed Retailleau? ... I? ... You're mad, Superintendent! ... He's mad! ... He's stark-staring mad, I swear to you! ... Where are these people I've killed? ... Show them to me, then, if you please ... Well, we're waiting, Monsieur Sherlock Holmes ...'

He was sneering. His agitation had reached its peak.

'There is one of them ...' Maigret calmly replied, pointing to Etienne Naud who was looking increasingly bewildered.

'It seems to me he's a dead man in very good health, as the saying goes, and if all my victims ...'

Alban had moved closer to Maigret in such an arrogant manner that the Superintendent's hand automatically jerked up and came down on Alban's pale cheek with a thud.

Perhaps they were going to come to blows, grip each other by the waist and roll about on the carpet as befitted the schoolboys the Superintendent had visualized a short while before. But the sound of a hysterical voice shrieking from the top of the stairs stopped them in their tracks.

'Etienne! ... Etienne! ... Superintendent! ... Quick! ... Geneviève ...'

Madame Naud came down a few more steps, amazed no one appeared to have heard her, for she had already been shouting for a good few seconds.

'Hurry ...' Maigret said to Naud. 'Go up to your daughter ...'

And he turned to face Cavre and said in a tone which invited no reply:

'Just make sure he doesn't escape ... Do you hear?'

He followed Etienne Naud up the stairs and went with him into the young girl's bedroom.

'Look ...' moaned Madame Naud, distraught.

Geneviève was lying across her bed with her clothes on. Her eyes were half-open but had the glazed look of a sleepwalker. A phial of veronal lay broken on the carpet where she had dropped it.

'Help me, Madame . . .'

The opiate was only now beginning to take effect and the young girl was still half-conscious. She drew back, terrified, as the Superintendent bent down and, gripping her hard, forced open her mouth.

'Bring me some water, a lot of water, warm if possible . . .'

'You go, Etienne . . . In the boiler . . .'

Poor Etienne bumped his way down the corridor and backstairs like a giddy goose.

'Don't be afraid, Madame . . . We are acting in time . . . It's my fault . . . I didn't think she would react like this . . . Get me a handkerchief, a towel, anything will do . . .'

Less than two minutes later, the young girl had vomited violently. She sat dejectedly on the edge of her bed obediently drinking down all the water the Superintendent gave her which made her sick all over again.

'You can telephone the doctor. He won't do much more, but to be on the safe side . . .'

Geneviève suddenly broke down and began to cry, softly, but with such weariness that the tears seemed to lull her to sleep.

'I'll leave you to look after her, Madame . . . I think it is best if she rests before the doctor comes . . . In my opinion – and unfortunately I've seen rather a lot of cases like this, believe me – the danger is over . . .'

They could hear Naud on the telephone downstairs:

'Immediately, yes . . . It's my daughter . . . I'll explain when you get here . . . No . . . Come as you are, in your dressing-gown if you like, it doesn't matter . . .'

As he passed Naud in the hall, Maigret took the letter he was holding in his hand. He had noticed it lying on Geneviève's bedside table but had not had a moment to pick it up.

Naud tried to get the letter back as soon as he had put down the receiver.

'What are you doing?' he exclaimed in astonishment. 'It's for her mother and me . . .'

'I will give it back to you in a moment . . . Go upstairs and sit with her . . .'

'But . . .'

'It's the best place for you to be, I promise you.'

And Maigret went back into the drawing-room, carefully closing the door behind him. He held the letter in his hand and was obviously reluctant to open it.

'Well? Groult?'

'You have no right to arrest me.'

'I know . . .'

'I have done nothing illegal . . .'

This momentous word almost made Maigret think he deserved to be slapped again, but he would have had to cross the room to do so and he did not feel up to it.

He toyed with the letter and hesitated before finally slitting open the mauve envelope.

'Is that letter addressed to you?' protested Groult-Cotelle.

'No, and it's not addressed to you either . . . Geneviève wrote it before taking the overdose . . . Would you like me to return it to her parents?'

Dear Mummy, dear Daddy,
I love you dearly. I beg you to believe me. But I must put an end to my life. I cannot go on living any longer. Do not try to find out why, and above all, don't ask Alban to the house anymore. He . . .

'Tell me, Cavre, did he tell you the whole story while we were upstairs?'

Maigret was convinced that in his agitated state, Alban had confessed because of a desperate need to cling to someone, a man who could defend him, whose job it was to do so provided he was paid for his services.

As Cavre lowered his head, Maigret added:

'Well, what have you got to say?'

And Groult-Cotelle, whose cowardice knew no limits, chipped in:

'She began it . . .'

'And she, no doubt, gave you nasty little pornographic books to read?'

'I never gave her any . . .'

'And you never showed her certain pictures I saw in your library?'

'She came across them when my back was turned ...'

'And no doubt you felt the need to explain them to her?'

'I am not the first man of my age to take a young girl for a mistress ... I didn't force her ... She was very much in love ...'

Maigret laughed abusively as he looked Alban up and down.

'And it was her idea, too, to call in Retailleau?'

'If she took another lover, that is certainly no affair of mine, you must admit. I think you have got an absolute nerve to blame me! Me! In front of my friend Naud, just now ...'

'What was that?'

'In front of Naud, then. I didn't dare answer and you had the upper hand ...'

A car pulled up in front of the steps. Maigret went out of the room to open the front door and said, just as if he were master of the house:

'Go straight up to Geneviève's room. Hurry ...'

Then he went back into the drawing-room, still holding Geneviève's letter in his hand.

'It was you, Groult, who panicked when she told you she was pregnant. You're a coward and always have been. You are so afraid of life that you dare not live by your own effort and so you clutch at other people's lives ...

'He was going to foist that child on some poor idiot who would then become its father ...

'It was such a practical solution! ... Geneviève was to ensnare a young man who would think he was sincerely loved ... He would be told one fine day that his ardour had resulted in a pregnancy ... He only had to go to her father, ask to be forgiven on bended knees and declare himself willing to make amends ...

'And you would have gone on being her lover, wouldn't you! You bastard!'

It was young Louis who had put him on the trail when he had said:

'*Albert was angry ... He had several brandies before going off to meet her ...*'

And Albert's behaviour towards Geneviève's father? He had been insolent. He had used the most foul language when speaking of Geneviève.

130

'How did he find out?' demanded Maigret.

'I don't know.'

'Would you rather I go and ask Geneviève?'

Groult-Cotelle shrugged his shoulders. What difference did it make, after all? Maigret could not pin a charge on him.

'Every morning Retailleau used to go to the post-office to collect his employers' post as it was being sorted . . . He would go behind the counter and sometimes helped to sort the letters . . . He recognized Geneviève's handwriting on an envelope which was addressed to me. She had not been able to see me alone for several days and so . . .'

'I see . . .'

'If that hadn't happened, everything would have gone according to plan . . . And if you hadn't meddled . . .'

Of course Albert had been angry that night, when for the last time he went to see the girl who had used him so shamefully with the incriminating letter in his pocket! Moreover, everyone had conspired to make a fool of him, her parents included, why should he think otherwise?

He had been led a fine dance, and they were still deceiving him. The father was even pretending to have caught him in the act in order to make him marry his daughter . . .

'How did you know he had intercepted the letter?'

'I went to the post office shortly afterwards . . . The postmistress said: "Wait a minute! I thought there was a letter for you . . ."

'She hunted high and low . . . I rang Geneviève . . . I asked the postmistress who had been there when they were sorting the post and then I realized, I . . .'

'You realized that things had taken a turn for the worse and you decided to go and see your friend, the *préfet*'s private secretary, in La Roche . . .'

'That's my affair . . .'

'What do you think, Justin?'

But Cavre shelved replying. Heavy footsteps were heard on the stairs. The door opened. Etienne Naud came in looking downcast and dejected, his large eyes full of questions he sought in vain to answer. At that very moment, Maigret dropped the letter he was holding in his hand in so clumsy a fashion that it fell on top of the logs and flared up immediately

'What have you done?'

'I'm so sorry . . . It doesn't really matter, as your daughter is saved and she will be able to tell you herself what she put in her letter . . .'

Was Naud taken in? Or was his attitude the same as that of certain patients who suspect they are not being told the truth, who only half believe or don't believe at all the doctor's optimistic words, but who none the less long to hear these very words and so be reassured at whatever price?

'She is much better now, isn't she?'

'She is asleep . . . The danger is over, it seems, thanks to your swift action . . . I thank you from the bottom of my heart, Superintendent . . .'

The poor fellow seemed to be swimming about in the drawing-room, as if it had suddenly become too large for him, like an article of clothing that has stretched and swamps the wearer. He looked at the bottle of armagnac, almost poured himself a glass, but a sense of modesty held him back and in the end Maigret had to do it for him. He helped himself to a glass at the same time.

'Here's to your daughter and the end of all these misunderstandings . . .'

Naud looked up at him in wide-eyed astonishment, for 'misunderstanding' was the very last word he had expected to hear.

'We have been chatting while you were upstairs . . . I think your friend Groult has something very important to say to you . . . Believe it or not, he is in the process of getting a divorce, though he hasn't told a soul . . .'

Naud looked more and more at sea.

'Yes . . . And he has other plans . . . All this probably won't make you jump for joy . . . Two wrongs don't make a right, I know, but it's a start, anyway . . . Well! I'm asleep on my feet . . . Didn't someone say just now there was a morning train?'

'It leaves at 6.11,' said Cavre. 'I think I'll take it, what's more . . .'

'We'll travel together, then . . . and in the meantime, I am going to try and snatch a few hours' sleep . . .'

He could not help saying to Alban as he went out:

'What a dirty trick!'

It was still foggy. Maigret point-blank refused to let anyone take him to the station and Etienne Naud had bowed before his wish.

'I don't know how to thank you, Superintendent. I haven't behaved towards you as I should have ...'

'You have treated me extremely well and I've shared some excellent meals with you.'

'Will you tell my brother-in-law ...'

'Of course I will! Oh! One piece of advice, if I may be so bold ... Don't be too hard on your daughter ...'

A fatherly flicker of a smile made Maigret realize that Naud understood perhaps far more than one might suppose.

'You're a good sort, Superintendent ... You really are! ... I am so grateful ...'

'You'll be grateful for the rest of your days, as a friend of mine used to say ... Good-bye! ... Send me a note from time to time ...'

He walked away from the house which now seemed stilled, leaving the light behind him. Smoke rose from but two or three chimneys in the village, only to disappear into the fog. The dairy was working at full capacity and looked like a factory from a distance. Meanwhile, old Désiré was steering his boat laden with pitchers of milk along the canal.

Madame Retailleau would undoubtedly be asleep now, and the tiny postmistress too ... Josaphat would be sleeping off his wine, and ...

Right up to the last minute, Maigret was terrified he would bump into Louis. The lad had put so much faith in him and on discovering the Superintendent had left would doubtless think to himself bitterly:

'*He was one of them, too!*'

Or else:

'*They got the better of him!*'

If they *had* got the better of him, they hadn't done so with money or fine words, at any rate.

And as he stood at the end of the platform waiting for the train and keeping an eye on his suitcase beside him, he mumbled to himself:

'Look here, son, I wish the world could be clean and beautiful, just like you ... And I get upset and angry when ...'

Surprise, surprise! Cavre walked onto the platform and stood about fifty yards away from the Superintendent.

'That fellow, there, for instance ... He's a blackguard ... He is capable of all number of dirty tricks ... I know this for a fact ... And yet I feel rather sorry for him ... I've worked with him ... I know his kind and what torments he goes through ... What would have been the point of condemning Etienne Naud? And would he have been found guilty, anyway? ... There is no concrete proof ... The whole case would have stirred up a lot of dirt ... Geneviève would have been called to the witness box ... And Alban would not just have been worried. He would probably have been really pleased to be rid of his responsibilities ...'

There was no sign of Louis, which was just as well, for in spite of everything Maigret was not proud of himself. This early morning departure of his smacked too much of an escape.

'You will understand later on ... They *are* strong, as you say ... They stick together ...'

Having noticed Maigret, Justin Cavre came over to where he was standing but did not dare open a conversation.

'Do you hear, Cavre? I've been talking to myself, like an old ...'

'Have you any news?'

'What sort of news? The girl is all right now. The father and mother ... I don't like you, Cavre ... I pity you, but I don't like you ... It cannot be helped ... There are some people you warm to and others you don't ... But I am going to tell you something ... There is one expression in common parlance that I hate more than any other. It makes me wince and grind my teeth whenever I hear it ... Do you know what it is?'

'No.'

'It will be all right in the end!'

The train came into the station and in the growing din Maigret shouted:

'But it *will* be all right in the end, you'll see ...'

Two years later, in fact, he discovered by chance that Alban Groult-Cotelle had married Mademoiselle Geneviève Naud in Argentina, where her father had started a huge cattle-rearing concern.

'Tough luck on our friend Albert, wasn't it, Louis? But some poor devil had to be the scapegoat!'

Saint-Mesmin-Le-Vieux, 3 March 1943

THE NIGHT-CLUB

Translated by
Jean Stewart

1

A steam-boat coming down the Loire sounded its hooter twice to warn that it was veering to starboard, and a distant cargo boat coming upstream hooted twice in response. At the same moment the fishmonger's cry was heard as he passed along the street pushing his barrow over the uneven paving-stones.

Before opening his eyes, Jean Cholet experienced yet another sensation: something was lacking, something had changed. What he was missing was the patter of rain on the zinc roof next door, which had gone on for most of the night while he slept. Now the sun was shining; he could feel it through his closed lids.

It was late, half-past eight at least, since the fishmonger had already gone by. Cholet used only to hear him from his bed when he was lying ill and had not gone to the newspaper office.

He sat up suddenly and opened his eyes. Partial memories came back to him. This morning was unlike other mornings, and there were some unpleasant moments in prospect for him, in spite of the sunshine that flooded in obliquely and flushed the roses on the wallpaper.

The mere motion of getting out of bed made him feel sick, and when he stood up on the mat he wanted to lie down again because he felt so light-headed.

He had been drunk, and it had left him with a mingled sense of unsteadiness and nausea, together with an unexpected touch of exhilaration.

He didn't feel up to shaving, which he did every day although he was only nineteen. His gingery beard was sparse and irregular, but when he let it grow it gave him an unhealthy and slovenly look.

The bedroom door was open. The smell of coffee had pervaded the house for some time already. He could hear the shuffle of slippers on the kitchen floor and the rhythmical grating sound of a knife scraping carrots.

The water in his jug was cold. It was November. Cholet picked up off the floor a tie that was twisted like a piece of string and a collar splashed with mud. That reminded him that he had seen a lot of mud from very close up. But where?

Monsieur Dehourceau, the editor of the *Gazette de Nantes*, had sent him for the first time to cover a banquet, the one which concluded the Congress of Footwear Manufacturers. There had been five reporters sitting at the end of the high table and the rain had been beating down on the glass roof of the dining hall.

And then suddenly Cholet had lost his temper and gone out. Why? and what had he said? and hadn't something pleasant happened afterwards? For in spite of everything there still lingered in his heart a kind of incomplete delight which he was trying to identify. Amid the chaos of his recollections, he could picture something black and white: very black and very white. He muttered:

'The man in evening dress!'

But he was incapable of connecting the words with anything definite. What man in evening dress?

He left his room and on the staircase he was seized with slight dizziness. His temples and his upper lip were damp. He wanted to vomit.

'Morning, mother.'

She was in the kitchen, bending over her carrots, and she did not turn round, did not answer while he went to sit down in his place after taking the coffee pot from the stove. He was barely able to swallow two sips of coffee, and he kept a single piece of bread in his mouth for a long time.

'Is it nine o'clock already?'

His father had gone off. The dairywoman had passed. When his mother half turned to put the carrots into the soup pot he saw that her eyes were red and he realized why she kept on sniffing.

He would have liked to ask her at what time he had come home and in what state. But that would only set her weeping more than ever, and his courage failed him at the thought of comforting her. He'd rather go away. He went towards the coat-rack in the passage.

'Jean!'

'Yes, what?'

'Last night I saw your father weep for the first time.' Thereupon she started sobbing herself. He fled. He had just picked up, not his own raincoat, but a yellow one which belonged to nobody in the house. He felt that something very serious was going to happen. Out in the street he put on the mackintosh, which was too big for him. In its pockets, among shreds of tobacco, he found two gloves with holes in them and a key.

He had begun to panic. He was following his usual route, across the bridges over the Loire and then the level crossing. The traffic in the streets was unfamiliar to him; a different set of people were going about. It was because he was late. The market was over. The municipal dust carts were sweeping up cabbage leaves and refuse. One could look at the sun directly, because it was veiled by a haze that made it seem redder and colder.

Where had that raincoat come from? The banquet had taken place at two in the afternoon. Cholet had left before the speeches, and he would have to ring up a colleague, Bourceau for instance, to get the substance of his report.

Then he halted with a sudden shudder. Where had he met his boss the day before? And how, why, had he had that close-up view of his boss's beard?

He hurried on. He was impatient to find out. He felt unwell, and yet this vague sense of euphoria still clung to him, just as when after dreaming of a woman he would sometimes remain conscious of an extravagant gush of feeling, his soul pervaded by an emotionalism of which he was ashamed.

There had been a tail-coat and a white waistcoat and an odour of Oriental cigarettes ...

Jean Cholet hurried down the passage which led him, by way of a narrow staircase, to the editorial offices of the newspaper. From the landing he could hear the voice of Mademoiselle Berthe taking down messages from the Havas agency over the telephone. Léglise had been at his post since seven that morning, absorbedly studying telegrams and newspapers, scissors in hand, suppressing paragraphs, inserting headlines, his upper lip stained yellow by the cigarettes which he smoked continuously down to the very tip.

'Here you are!'

He dragged Cholet into the next room because Mademoiselle Berthe, who was finding it hard to hear Paris on the line, was showing signs of impatience.

'The boss asked for you half an hour ago.'

Léglise could not restrain a smile on seeing Cholet's haggard face.

'Well, you've gone and done it!'

'Did I come up here?'

That was what he was most afraid of.

'You stood there at the end of the table and you grabbed the telephone. The porter tried to make you drink some hot tea, and you threw the cup into that corner.'

Fragments of china were scattered on the grey floor-boards.

'When the boss appeared you leaned over and called him a swine, a hypocrite, a . . .'

That was enough! Cholet remembered! He could picture Monsieur Dehourceau's bearded face and his strawberry-red nose. What right had he, who put away two bottles of burgundy a day all by himself, to lecture one on the dangers of drink? Well, Cholet had given him a piece of his mind!

'You were a sight! Covered with mud! You must have been rolling in the gutter . . .'

But the man in evening dress? And that feeling of lightness, of frivolity, of eroticism? For there had been a feeling of eroticism!

'Who took you to the Trianon?'

Cholet's gaze softened. A tune came into his mind, something from a musical comedy. Red plush, lights, ballet girls in their tutus screaming with laughter . . .

'You went back stage and ran after all the girls to kiss them. The manager had to take you out . . .'

'Speelman!' Cholet suddenly declared.

He remembered! Speelman! The man in evening dress! The manager of the theatrical company. They had drunk something together, some liqueur. Cholet had *tutoyéd* him. They had been very friendly.

'Is that all?'

'Run off to see the boss and try to get round him.'

Now everything had become clearer. There had been the general meeting of the Congress of Footwear Manufacturers, then the banquet at the Hôtel de l'Europe. And it was all Bourceau's fault. He had said:

'Try mixing white Bordeaux and red Burgundy. It's smashing!'

Cholet had declared that it was indeed smashing; then he had lost his temper because Bourceau and the others had refused to drink the same mixture. He had gone off in a rage.

How he'd got into the Trianon he had no idea. He had shown his press card; he had spoken self-confidently; he had wandered about in the wings. Somewhere or other there had been a long narrow room lined with a whole string of mirrors, where a dozen dancing-girls were getting dressed amid a cloud of face-powder.

And then Speelman ... The mud had come later, after they'd dropped him. And after the mud, the *Gazette de Nantes*?

'You slept here until eleven o'clock at night. Then you rough-housed the porter because he didn't want to let you leave, and you went off home ...'

He had been sick under his desk and in the street, he had been sick everywhere. There were traces of vomit on the mackintosh which did not belong to him.

The sub-editor and Gillon had not turned up yet. The page-setter was clamouring for copy, and glanced knowingly at Léglise, indicating Cholet.

'I'll go and see the boss.'

At this time of the morning, as he had done for the past twenty years, the editor sat writing his daily article in his Gothic office on the other side of the courtyard.

'Come in!'

The Catholic newspaper of Nantes had originally been owned by his grandfather, who had signed similar leading articles. The pictures of Father and Grandfather Dehourceau hung on the wall, with identical beards and strawberry-red noses.

'Have you recovered?'

On the desk lay sheets of paper covered with minute handwriting. A mirror behind Monsieur Dehourceau showed Cholet his own reflection, with its reddened eyelids and the incipient gingery beard, more noticeable than ever, smudging his whole face.

'Just look at yourself!'

There was a brief moment of near-disaster; Cholet came very

close to tears. His head was reeling. The mouthful of coffee he had drunk that morning was rising back in his throat.

'Have you had a good look at yourself?'

And like a small boy he replied, with the ghost of a voice:

'Yes, sir.'

'That's all I had to say to you. If it ever occurs again I shall be obliged to dismiss you. You can go now!'

He picked up the top sheet of paper, and as Cholet was opening the door he called him back to say:

'I've told Gillon to write that report.'

Cholet sat down at his desk, a couple of yards away from Gillon, who had just come in and was writing with exaggerated assiduity. Mademoiselle Berthe, as she walked through the office, inquired:

'Feeling better?'

Cholet, dejected and queasy, stared at the window, which had ugly panels of stained glass. It was 10 a.m. At eleven, and not before, he would go to the central police station to collect news items. Debras, the page-setter, asked him through the hatch:

'Your gossip column?'

Cholet wrote a daily note on local events which he had christened thus.

'Just print what I gave you in advance.'

He scowled, because his glance had fallen on the mackintosh hanging on the coat-rack. It was the first time he had ever been drunk, and the first time he had ever been sent to cover a banquet.

But beside his resentment he was still vaguely conscious of that questionable light-heartedness which he was trying to pin down. He had been sitting with Speelman, who was in evening dress, on a red settee, drinking something through straws. They had addressed one another as *tu*. Speelman had dark hair and a smooth pale skin. Some kind of scent hung around him; there were diamond studs in his waistcoat.

The clock behind Jean Cholet gave a click; it was a quarter to eleven. He went off without the raincoat, and made for the police station where the day's reports consisted merely of a brawl between Scandinavian sailors, two cases of insults to the police and one of shop-lifting.

The streets were still cool from last night's rain. In the shade, the pavements retained traces of moisture, and the semi-transparent haze that floated up in the sunlight seemed to intensify all noises, especially those of the trams and the harbour cranes.

On his way back from the police station Cholet hesitated at a crossroads and suddenly turned left, towards the Trianon. All the doors were open, showing the inside of the theatre in a semi-darkness that glowed crimson because of the velvet upholstery. Cleaning women were at work with their brooms, sending clouds of dust into the sunlight that flooded the peristyle. Green and yellow billboards proclaimed the performance of *La Mascotte* by Speelman's company.

Nobody prevented Cholet from going in. They must have assumed he belonged to the place. He went through between the rows of seats, shrouded in dust-covers, and caught sight of a private door. It had been through there! He remembered. He prowled round it shamefacedly. Finally he approached one of the cleaners.

'Monsieur Speelman ...'

'Who?'

'The manager of the touring company.'

'That's all over, for the last performance was last night. The lorry left this morning with the props and costumes.'

The night before, he had been on the other side of the curtain. He could even have stated specifically that there was an iron spiral staircase and that the corridors were painted grey.

He went out. He didn't want to return to the newspaper office. His head was throbbing, perhaps because he was feeling cold without an overcoat, or else because his stomach was empty.

He went round the theatre. Even the doors at the back were wide open, letting in the chilly morning air. On the other side of the street stood a row of small cafés, bars in which he had never set foot, particularly in the lane at the far end, where electric signs shone at night. Now, all the lights were out. He noticed one sign, the Âne Rouge, and thought he recognized its well-worn door-handle which was made of horn.

The red settee, Speelman, the liqueur they had drunk through straws: this was the place!

The local news column had to be handed in to the compositors before noon, but he allowed himself a few minutes' grace.

'Heads or tails! If the door's open I go in, and if it's shut . . .'

It was open. A fat blonde woman, who had only just got out of bed, was collecting the brimming ashtrays and the glasses scattered about the tables. She greeted Cholet without surprise.

'So you're feeling better?'

He remembered her, or rather her smile, which was as soft and limp as her figure.

'Isn't Speelman here?'

'Don't you even remember what you said yesterday? When he told you the company was leaving this morning, you promised to take him to the station . . .'

He flushed. The woman was laughing.

'Not too much of a hangover?'

'No.'

'Just a little something to pull you round?'

Without waiting for his consent, she selected a bottle of green peppermint brandy and poured out a glass. She was naked underneath her dress, that was obvious from the way her breasts shook and the material clung between her thighs every time she bent over.

'Were you able to finish your report? I've still got a bit of it for you, for you began it at this table. If you can manage to read any of it . . .'

What on earth could he have said? And what had he told them about the *Gazette de Nantes*?

'The company left at nine o'clock. They were almost all of them sleeping up above here . . .'

She was wiping the mahogany tables. The room was a small one, with a piano on a platform, an American bar, twenty chairs at most and some settees. On the walls hung a profusion of pictures framed and unframed, caricatures and watercolours, and also of heterogeneous objects, an old wooden crucifix, a Negro mask, a set of Madagascan weapons, some pewter jugs and a Jewish ritual lamp.

'Didn't you bring back the raincoat?'

'Where's my own?'

'The pianist had to wear it to go home in. Don't you remember wanting to buy that crucifix because the figure reminded you of an uncle of yours who died last year?'

Jean Cholet dared not look at her. He felt ill at ease and yet he could not bring himself to go away. A woman's voice called from the staircase: 'Mélanie!'

'What d'you want?'

The footsteps. The kitchen door opened and a young woman came in, her feet bare in down-at-heel slippers; she was carrying a jug.

'Sorry . . . You've got company . . .'

'No, no! Come in, Lulu. You need some more hot water?'

The girl was in a dressing-gown. She was small and slender, with delicate irregular features and untidy hair; she stared at Cholet with curiosity.

'Don't you recognize him?'

'Was it him?'

And then Lulu inquired kindly: 'Not feeling too bad?'

'Not at all!'

'Take some out of the kettle, Lulu. But leave me a little, because I'm going to get dressed.'

The girl's dressing-gown was salmon pink and the hem was dirty, presumably from having dragged about on the stairs.

'Are you coming this evening?' the *patronne* asked him. 'You were too tight to listen to the artistes. You'll see Lulu and tell me what you think of her. She used to sing at La Cigale . . .'

'I'll bring back the raincoat,' he said.

'That's right. A drop more peppermint?'

In the street he felt agitated, with a mixture of humiliation, embarrassment and an unaccountable secret delight.

'I saw your father weep for the first time . . .'

His mother had wept too, but that wasn't the same thing. She wept as freely as other people might laugh or sing, on the least provocation, just for the pleasure of weeping. She enjoyed being unhappy; she was always complaining, about everything, about her inadequate means, about people's unkindness, the ingratitude of her sister-in-law and the irrational obstinacy of her neighbour, who wanted to build on to his house and thus rob her courtyard of its sunlight.

It was after twelve when he went into the newspaper offices, which were deserted. Only Léglise was still busy with scissors and paste, eating his sandwiches meanwhile; a blue enamel coffee pot was purring on the stove.

'Hurry up, Debras is waiting for you.'

Cholet wrote up his gossip column in the composing room, a couple of metres away from the rattling linotypes.

Like Léglise, his father took his lunch in the office of the insurance firm where he worked as book-keeper. It was at the other end of the town, towards Saint-Nazaire. Cholet was on the point of going there; then his courage failed him.

'Gillon wasn't half mad,' Léglise said, 'when the boss told him to write up your report!'

For Gillon was in charge of important reports, meetings of the Chamber of Commerce and economic questions. Jean Cholet smiled. It was such a strange smile that it puzzled honest Léglise; it was unaccountably detached and carefree. A man who is deeply in love must smile thus when he is spoken to in all seriousness about matters unconnected with his love.

Because Cholet was thinking about Speelman, about his black evening coat and white waistcoat and the three diamonds sparkling on it; he was thinking about red velvet upholstery, about sucking liqueurs through a straw, about the women who were sweeping out the theatre and the one called Lulu who had asked for hot water.

His mother was waiting for him for lunch; their two places were laid on the kitchen table. At this time of day the sun came over the courtyard wall and shone directly on to the table.

Jean was not hungry. He didn't want to talk, he didn't want, above all, to give any explanations or to get emotional. The silence lasted for a long while.

'So you've lost your new raincoat!'

'I shall get it back tonight.'

Madame Cholet laid down her fork; she had begun sniffling again. The small china clock above the stove was ticking away the seconds frantically. The kettle sent out an oblique jet of steam. The cutlets were overcooked.

'If Monsieur Dehourceau finds out!'

He had to rush out of the room to vomit. It tasted of green peppermint. The time must have been one o'clock, for the cranes were all blowing their whistles at once.

2

Three lights were enough to give the lane its questionable character. The first was a white globe of frosted glass inscribed with the word Hotel. Further on was the sign of the Âne Rouge: a luminous donkey showing its teeth and kicking out its four feet. And at the far end of the cul-de-sac Cholet thought he saw a red lamp over a door that stood permanently ajar.

It was half past nine. Shadows were moving behind the curtains of the night-club, and the piano was rattling out snatches of noisy music to create an impression of busy gaiety. But someone inside must have been on the watch for footsteps on the pavement for, as soon as Jean Cholet grasped the handle of the door, it was flung open, and a voice called out from somewhere in the background:

'A table for our guests!'

Then, in a different tone: 'Oh, so it's you?'

Cholet did not remember the proprietor of the Âne Rouge. He was a lean dark man with a loud voice and tired eyes, wearing a velvet suit and a flowing bow tie.

'This way, old man. Feeling better?'

From the platform, the pianist watched with an air of indifference as his mackintosh came towards him. The *patronne* was behind the bar. Lulu was sitting at a table with her back to the wall, busily writing, and next to her a man of about sixty, dressed in a frock coat, was reading a newspaper.

There were only a couple of customers; the young man had his arms round the girl's shoulders and they were looking at one another and smiling.

'Hello,' said Lulu, holding out a moist hand.

And the man in the frock coat greeted him in a deep bass voice:
'Hello, Johnny!'

Cholet knew none of them, and yet they all called him by his first name. Layard, the proprietor, hurried to the door, for he had heard someone coming down the street. People came in, three men this time who had obviously just been dining well.

'Ladies and gents, you are going to have the pleasure of listening to our good friend Doyen, a star from the leading Montmartre cabarets, in some of his sensational numbers.'

The old man sang in a sepulchral voice. Jean Cholet had sat down at the table where Lulu was sticking down the envelope of her letter and glancing at him with furtive curiosity.

'A green peppermint?' asked the *patronne*.

'I'd rather have something else.'

'A drop of cherry brandy?'

It was very warm. Customers came in, and Layard shepherded each of them to a table with teasing gibes; when he returned to his place he would give Cholet a knowing glance. And so the young man who had never set foot in the Âne Rouge before the previous night was already considered an old friend of the house. He sat at the artistes' table. They called him by his first name. After Doyen had sung, the pianist came up in his turn and held out his hand.

'How are you? I've brought back the raincoat.'

His face was pallid, his eyes deeply shadowed, his lips colourless; from his stool on the platform, while his fingers ran over the keys, he looked down at the customers with haughty indifference.

'A quarter of Vichy water!' he ordered.

In barely half an hour the room had filled. People were talking loudly. Women were laughing. The piano had started up again.

'Our charming star Lulu d'Artois is now going to give us ... by the way, what are you going to give us, honey?'

She was not pretty, but she had a shy, somewhat sullen attractiveness. Against all expectation the cherry brandy had banished the last trace of Cholet's queasiness, and he ordered another in an effort to rediscover what he had come here in search of, for he felt disappointed. The atmosphere was the same as on the previous night. The lights were dimmed with pink silk shades and a soft semidarkness pervaded the room. The cherry brandy stood on the table, with its pale yellow straws. Lulu left the platform amid applause and came back to sit beside him.

'Do you know Speelman?' he asked her.

'Of course! I worked with him for two years.'

He wanted to put other questions to her but did not dare, and confined himself to scrutinizing her closely. If she had stayed all that time with Speelman hadn't she probably slept with him?

'Will you have a drink?'

'If you like.'

Old Doyen, smoking his pipe, watched them. He was waiting for his turn to sing again, and had his back to the room where Layard was walking up and down rattling off quips and puns.

Cholet did not know what to say. He felt empty and unsteady; and he ordered a third glass and then a fourth. A hot flush rose to his cheeks and soon, as though a key had turned, reality altered: faces became more mysterious in the dim light, and the music more seductive.

'Is he coming back soon?'

'Who?'

'Speelman.'

Cholet longed to be wearing evening dress and a broad white shirt-front, like Speelman. He went on questioning Lulu.

'How long have you been in Nantes?'

'Three weeks.'

'Are you lodging here?'

'It's cheaper than a hotel, and Layard is very decent.'

Doyen lodged in the house too; he spoke familiarly to Lulu, called her 'baby' and 'my lovely'; did she sleep with him? And with Layard?

Cholet tried hard to understand the bohemian familiarity of this set-up. Doyen, Layard's wife and Lulu all discussed their most intimate concerns in front of him. Doyen in his mournful voice explained that one of these days he would have to have an operation on his bladder, because he found it difficult to urinate, and he made this confidential remark with the same expression as when he was singing '*Le pantalon réséda*'.

'Like when I had my first miscarriage!' said Lulu.

Cholet blushed. It shocked him and yet excited him. He felt the same uneasy satisfaction that one gets from fingering an aching tooth.

He now saw the customers only as a vaguely moving background, but on the other hand he was conscious of being there among the artistes as the centre of interest of the whole room.

'What'll you have, my dears? On me this time!' Layard said, as the crowd began to thin out.

And he sat down beside Cholet.

'So you didn't have any trouble with your rag? No sparks flying?'

'None at all! My private life doesn't concern them.'

He was obviously beginning to be tipsy; his voice had risen a whole tone and people three tables away could hear everything he was saying.

'I say, you must be on good terms with the police, aren't you?'

'I know all the superintendents.'

'When we have a spot of bother I'll contact you. They're a darned nuisance; it's about the music, chiefly. If we're unlucky enough to go on playing a few minutes after hours they raise hell.'

'I'll speak to the Chief Superintendent about it.'

And he drained his glass. He felt bigger, more alive. He almost fancied he was Speelman in person.

'Is he the manager of the touring company?'

'And of a whole lot of other things, laddie!'

Layard laughed and nudged Doyen, who sat unsmiling, his eyelids flickering assent.

'Such as?'

'We'll tell you later. Lulu, you look sleepy . . .'

She gave a start, for she had not been following the conversation.

'Me?'

'Yes, you,' said Cholet, emphasizing the *tutoiement*. 'And you're not drinking!'

Images and sounds had become muffled. It's true that there was a great deal of smoke in the room. Only five customers were left and the pianist was now merely strumming with two fingers, looking down on them with haughty contempt.

Somebody went out. At any rate, there was the sound of a door opening and a gust of cooler air swept through the night-club. This was a sort of turning-point. Before that sensation of coolness Cholet had been fairly well aware of what was happening. After it, he talked a great deal, with self-confidence. Around him, faces were distorted with laughter. The pianist must have left his platform because his face was a pale blur a couple of feet away from Jean. The last customers seemed to have left.

'Madame Layard! ... Another round! ... And come and join us ...'

He was a prey to a sort of feverish excitement that urged him on, speeding up everything he did, everything he said.

He was happy, he was magnificent. He was cock of the walk. He said amazing things. He talked about the *Gazette de Nantes* and Monsieur Dehourceau's strawberry nose without ever losing his awareness of Lulu's presence on the settee beside him. At one point, he said to her:

'Give us a kiss!'

And she kissed him on the lips, an unexpected kiss, warm and moist. Doyen, from time to time, glanced up at the clock, which now showed after 1 a.m. Madame Layard had come to sit at the table; her husband was watching the young man ceaselessly with those baggy eyes that gave him a depraved look.

'I'll be back in a minute ...' Lulu excused herself; she slipped behind the bar and started up the stairs.

'Where's she going?' Cholet asked.

Then he rose too; with a knowing smile and a wink to the assembled company he turned on his heel and followed Lulu behind the bar. The staircase was dark and he nearly fell. It was an old house; there was no banister, but a rope held by eye-bolts.

Hearing sounds overhead, Cholet went upstairs laughing to himself. He saw a door standing ajar. In the unlighted room something was moving.

'What are you doing?' he asked, stretching out his arms in empty space.

A voice said breathlessly: 'You frightened me!'

He had caught her! It was Lulu; she had taken off her dress already.

'You little cheat!'

'I was dropping with sleep ...'

He held her tight. She did not try to free herself, but there was a certain tensing of the thin back, with its prominent spine. He touched a small limp breast, and bent over her neck; its female odour was curiously mixed with the scent of toilet water.

'You're hurting me,' she whispered. 'Not tonight!'

'Why not?'

Her figure was a blur of milky whiteness. He sought her mouth and she kissed him, but it was not so warm and moist as the first kiss she had given him downstairs.

'Tomorrow ...'

She was gently pushing him towards the door.

'Promise?'

'I promise! ... And don't drink any more tonight ...'

'I'm not tight!'

'Of course not! Good-night now ...'

He bumped into a wall, then found himself back in a lighted room and saw faces turned towards him without a trace of gaiety or curiosity. Doyen was yawning, poking the ash from his pipe with his forefinger. Madame Layard was tidying away glasses. Layard, alone, had the enterprise to wink at him and ask:

'Back already?'

The pianist had put on his raincoat. Cholet went up to the bar counter and embarked on a complicated reckoning, of which he only took in two words: 'Artistes' rate ...'

He held out notes; he was given back others and some small change.

'Good-night ... Good-night ...'

'Are you going towards the embankment?' the pianist asked him.

The streets were deserted. The pianist was silent. Cholet walked with little skipping steps and tried hard to keep up a conversation. At one point he noticed a light.

'Let's have one more drink!'

'My wife's expecting me.'

That was all. They shook hands at a street corner. He went home. Going past his parents' bedroom he heard slight sounds there.

The fishmonger had already gone by when he woke up. His mother was not in the kitchen; this was the time when she did her shopping. Jean's blue china bowl was in its usual place on the tablecloth. The coffee was keeping warm on the corner of the stove.

It felt funny to be all alone in the house which had already been cleaned from top to bottom and the smell of stew mingled with that of detergent. Cholet felt sad, but it was a philosophical sort of sadness such as he had never felt before.

'Poor woman!' he muttered, thinking of his mother who at that very moment was running round the shops carrying her string bag.

And poor man, too, thinking of his father, who, ill though he was, had left for his office at half past eight. For he had suffered from angina pectoris for the past two years; he was liable to have to stop short, every day, wherever he happened to be in the street, and wait with his hand on his heart until the spasm was over. People stared at him; embarrassed, he would pretend to be looking at something, to stop in front of a shop window for instance or to watch children coming out of school. In fact some kind soul had come along to report:

'Did you know, Madame Cholet, that your husband ogles little girls?'

Poor man! Poor mankind! Jean felt like pitying everyone. When he reached the newspaper office he pitied Léglise, who earned less than any of the reporters because he had begun as an office boy.

Léglise had yellow teeth. He was badly dressed. His wife, who had three children already, sometimes came to fetch him to go with her to the doctor's, for she had some internal complaint nowadays. And Léglise was always good-humoured! He went on cutting out and pasting and providing headlines for articles. He could quite well have produced the paper all by himself!

'You O.K., Cholet?'

'I'm O.K.'

And Cholet said to himself: 'He knows nothing about it . . .'

Nor did Mademoiselle Berthe who, at twenty-eight, had never known love, and who, maybe on that account, was liable to fits of morbid ill-humour!

Cholet was smiling, a slight melancholy little smile which he could picture without needing to see himself in the glass. On his desk he found a note: '*Report on fire at No. 6 dock.*'

His head was aching, but not too unpleasantly. Hands in pockets, he went towards the harbour in the chilly morning sunlight. Shop windows were being washed; girl assistants were arranging their displays. Messengers on carrier-tricycles were threading their way between trucks and trams.

'Poor people! Poor things!'

He was comparing them with another image which was vividly alive within him: that of a man in evening dress, with diamond studs, a smooth skin, scented hair, who travelled over the world with actresses and dancing girls.

'And he's something else besides ...' Cholet had been told the night before.

Of course! he must be something else besides! What? Cholet had no idea. But so much the better; the image, veiled in mystery, was all the more attractive.

The fire had been under control since six o'clock that morning. A fireman who had been left on guard in front of the half-destroyed shed gave Jean the necessary information. Around them, cranes were unloading a boat flying the Latvian flag, whose cargo of timber was stacked half-way up the funnel.

Suppose he were to go and pay a brief visit to the Âne Rouge? Lulu must still be in bed. He recalled her flaccid breast. There was something touching about it just because it was so soft and limp and because in spite of that Lulu had let him hold it.

From the harbour he went to the police station, where the secretary received him with his customary good humour.

'Nothing interesting. Two cases of theft by employees; one abortion, but you'd better not mention that because there's nothing specific as yet.'

Hadn't Lulu talked about her miscarriage?

'By the way ... Layard, of the Âne Rouge, was saying yesterday that you often bother him about his music ...'

'Do you know him?'

'He's a friend of mine. It would be very kind of you to ...'

'See here, Cholet. A piece of advice: be careful, old man!'

'Why?'

'Oh, nothing. Be careful.'

'Is there anything against Layard?'

'I'm just telling you that you'd better be careful in that place. Particularly as you're working for a Catholic paper!'

'Do you know Speelman too?'

'The theatre manager? I know him. Watch your step!'

Five minutes later, Cholet went down the lane and stopped in front of the door of the Âne Rouge. He found the latch wedged.

Presumably nobody was up yet, or else they were still in their bedrooms. An old woman was washing the doorstep of the lodging-house next door. Beyond the cul-de-sac lay a main thoroughfare, bright and noisy.

In his heart of hearts Cholet felt an anxiety of which he pretended not to be aware, but at midday, when he had written up his copy, he resigned himself to facing it: in a couple of days, he had spent his whole month's salary. It made him furious. It was ridiculous, humiliating, and he made up his mind to go back to the Âne Rouge that very evening.

He suddenly took a decision and went to the office where his father was always alone between twelve and two o'clock. When he came out again, he felt an urge to walk very fast and for a long time he did not look at anything about him. He had money in his pocket: two hundred francs!

But he had to forget the details of the interview. His father, sitting at his desk close to the guichet, was eating sandwiches and reading the newspaper. The room was dark, and even gloomier than Léglise's office. Jean had talked volubly.

His colleagues had taken advantage of the banquet to get him drunk. They had made him spend money ... now he owed two hundred francs, which had to be paid ...

His father hadn't a beard like Monsieur Dehourceau, nor a strawberry nose. He went on quietly eating his sandwich, and contrary to expectations, as had been the case with the editor, he did not raise his voice.

'Careful, son!'

He had added: 'You're sure there's not a woman in the picture somewhere?'

And Jean, blushing as he remembered Lulu's breast, had declared: 'No!'

'You should be very kind to your mother. She was unhappy on Sunday, when some people we didn't know rang at the door and you were sprawling across the threshold ...'

The scene described thus, quite simply, in the neutral atmosphere of the office, made a solemn impression on Cholet, like that of a cathedral seen in a dream. His father's voice went on, muffled by a piece of bread:

'I was very frightened too. You looked at one point as if you were dead ...'

He took two hundred-franc notes from his wallet.

'Be nice to your mother. Last night when you came back I told her it was twelve o'clock ...'

Cholet had shed no tears. He had put an awkward kiss on his father's stiff moustache, which smelt of tobacco. Now he was walking fast and the pavements, which frost was beginning to harden, rang under his feet.

'But I've got the two hundred francs!' he kept telling himself.

He walked for a whole quarter of an hour with lowered head, then he hummed a little tune and finally caught himself saying with a sigh:

'Poor people!'

3

'One minute. I'll get him . . .'

Turning to Gillon, Cholet pushed the telephone towards him.

'It's your fiancée!'

They shared a long table between them, and each had a lamp hanging at eye-level, so that at night each lived within his individual ring of light. On Cholet's right was the baize door leading into the office where Léglise and Mademoiselle Berthe worked. It was time, now, for the Stock Exchange reports; the stenographer, earphones on her head, was rapidly scribbling down figures on ready-prepared sheets of paper and Debras, the page-setter, picked them up one at a time and rushed off with them like a thief.

'I'm not sure,' Gillon was saying down the telephone. 'I've got an interview with the Prefect first.'

Even when telephoning he maintained his formal manner, wearing the vague solemn smile of a man who knows the right thing to think. His cuffs lay in front of him on the table. For the past month he had been wearing a green eye-shade for working.

It was half past four. Rain was falling. Outside, the crowd was splashing through mud, and the reflected lights of shop-windows stretched out endlessly over the wet pavements. Just below Cholet's seat, the rotary press was working at top speed, and for two hours more the entire building would be shaking to the rhythm of the machine.

People who came here for the first time could not, to begin with, understand why the walls and floors seemed to be alive, why the pens on the table and even the keys of the typewriter vibrated so. They listened apprehensively to the monotonous purring: 'What's that?'

One got used to it. In winter it began at about lighting-up time.

On the other side of the courtyard you could see the lights go on in the editor's office. Down below, the news-vendors were shouting, sitting in the doorway or perched on window ledges. Debras, in his long blue overall, ran to and fro, picking up the Stock Exchange reports one after the other.

It was hot. The general throbbing that pervaded the place left one dazed because it blurred the rhythm of one's own heart-beats.

'If the boss asks for me,' said Gillon, pulling on his cuffs, 'tell him I've gone to see the Prefect.'

Cholet replied with a grunt. He felt limp. In front of him was a whole pile of books in unusual formats, with uncut pages. They were the sort of works ignored by literary critics, published for the most part at author's cost: the Memoirs of an ex-Army major, travel diaries of a doctor in Norway, verse – a great deal of verse – and also treatises on gardening or child welfare.

On each of these he had to write a few lines. Beside them were spread out readers' letters, all with differing demands: a short article on a display of gymnastics, a well-earned distinction, a centenary or the urgent need to shift some lamp-post.

This was Cholet's job, but he hadn't the heart to get down to it. When the apprentice came through the rooms handing everyone a copy of the paper, still damp from the press, he did not even glance at it.

He felt feverish. His head rang with all the din of the rotary and each time Debras crossed the room with his Stock Exchange reports he gave an uneasy start.

Who could understand what he was feeling? Nobody, so that he was reduced to thinking about it all alone, fiercely, in his little ring of light.

It had happened very differently from how he had expected; and better; and better! But nobody would admit that it was better.

For the past week he had been going to the Âne Rouge every night. He had his regular place on the settee beside Lulu, opposite old Doyen. He had formed certain habits, such as drinking cherry brandy; he paid, on an average, for two rounds to Layard's one. Then he would go off with the pianist, who never talked but who always parted from him at exactly the same spot, as though a certain paving stone in the pavement had been set aside for that purpose.

Every day, Doyen informed them of the state of his bladder. He spoke in the same funereal voice that delighted his audience when he used it for his songs. It seemed like a gimmick to make people laugh, like the baggy frock coat, but it was not. This was his normal appearance, and his normal voice. The coat was too big because since his illness he had lost eighteen kilos. And it was not his fault, either, if his eyes under their grey bushy brows were always watering.

Lulu wrote a great many letters and Cholet had not yet dared ask her to whom she was writing.

When there were not many people there, on certain weekdays, there was an atmosphere of quiet intimacy and sometimes, even, the pianist would leave his platform and come to sit at the table.

Only Layard kept pacing about the room and then anxiously opening the door, letting in the cold night air. Jean Cholet could not get used to him, chiefly because of those eyes with deep pouches under them which gave him such a strange expression. He seemed to look at everyone with fierce contempt and hatred, in spite of his loud-voiced good humour.

When, for instance, he looked at Lulu, then at Cholet, then at Lulu again, Jean felt as uncomfortable as at some obscene remark.

While Doyen was performing, Cholet spoke to the girl in a low voice.

'Can't I see you outside here?'

'I don't go out.'

'Where, then?'

'I don't know.'

And yet she was sweet to him. She kissed him when he arrived and when he left. She let him fondle her stealthily. She even asked him about his family and his job on the newspaper.

'What would they say if they knew you spent all your evenings here?'

He saw another member of the group, the singing star Lola, as the posters proclaimed her. She was a tall dark girl with a slight squint. She made a little money on the side by reading people's palms and she spent hours playing patience.

'Can't I come up to your room?'

Sometimes Cholet addressed Lulu as *tu* and sometimes as *vous*, according to his mood and the time of night.

'Do you really want to very much?'

Layard, meanwhile, would watch them with his small glittering, deeply shadowed eyes. And then, the night before, it had happened quite unexpectedly. Jean and Lulu had been whispering together at greater length than usual. Cholet had ordered a third round. The pianist had gone home at midnight because his wife was unwell.

Jean could not bring himself to leave. Layard walked back and forth crossly, shifting the chairs around. Doyen was dozing.

Suddenly Layard switched off half the lights and growled:

'Off to bed now, everybody!'

As though taking for granted that Cholet would stay, he had locked the front door. Lulu's eyes were misty.

'Good-night!'

'Good-night!'

She had gone up first, with Cholet at her heels. There was no electric light on the landing, but the bedroom was faintly lit by the glow from a gas lamp in the street.

Doyen's heavy footsteps sounded, then the singer could be heard going into her room, humming a little tune as she sat down on the bed to take off her shoes.

Lulu turned down the bed. Cholet dared not undress. The Layards passed along the passage and went into their room; for an hour longer they were to be heard muttering, while Doyen, who slept only two or three hours a night, paced about his room.

Lulu, still fully dressed, had sat down on the edge of the bed and her face, in the darkness, was the colour of moonlight.

'Come and sit here . . .'

He had done so. It was strange. It wasn't happening the way one expected these things to happen. She was very gentle, very tender. She had taken his hand between her own.

'Listen to me . . .'

He had thought at first that he ought to put his arms round her and clasp her tight. But she had freed herself resolutely from his embrace. The rain could be heard pattering on the uneven paving-stones in the street. The singer had turned in; the Layards, in their bed, were talking business, in a low continuous whisper.

'No . . . Let me explain . . . You mustn't . . . Well, what you'd like to . . .'

She spoke in a low voice because of the thinness of the surrounding walls. She kept Cholet's hand between her own, against her knee; he could feel its warmth.

'You're much too nice . . . You can stay here . . . We'll just be good friends . . . but you mustn't insist . . .'

He was so moved by this that he had a lump in his throat, he couldn't tell why. Lulu seemed a different person. The whole house was pervaded by a sort of mysterious grandeur. In the darkness she went on talking, slowly, in a low voice.

'I may as well tell you right away, mayn't I? . . . I'm sick! . . . not what you think . . . it's not as bad as that . . . But still . . . D'you understand?'

And he had nearly burst into tears: tears of emotion, pity, bewilderment! Just at that moment she had pressed her lips to his in a long kiss, deep and moist as the first had been.

'You're not too vexed with me?'

In the darkness, he sensed her meek, embarrassed smile.

'You can stay here all the same . . . There's no risk . . .'

From time to time he could hear the steps of a policeman on the beat, at the end of the lane.

'Let's lie down, shall we?'

She had kept on only a thin chemise. Her body was warm; she twined her legs round his and hid her face against his breast.

His emotion, instead of dissolving, grew tenser. From where he lay by the wall Cholet could see the window and the streaks of rain in the shaft of light from the street lamp. He heard the floorboards creak under Doyen's footsteps, even though the old man had taken off his shoes. And Lulu was there in his arms, alive, her hair against his cheek. He was steeped in an indefinable odour in which a lingering sourness underlay the sweetish perfume.

'Does Layard know?' he asked abruptly, opening his eyes wide.

'Yes.'

'And Doyen?'

'Of course. You're not too vexed with me?'

Lulu's hand was stroking his bare chest and it was at this point that his emotion reached its peak, he didn't know why. Everything was transfigured: the lane, the house, Lulu herself and her thin body pressed against his own. He rolled his face in her hair, breathing in the smell of it and saying: 'My poor darling . . .'

He had been drinking, but he was not drunk, or rather his intoxication was not due to alcohol. They were there together in a dark room in that badly-paved back street, and all around them lay the whole world, with its millions of people, machines and streets and ships, bosses and parents . . .

He held her tight as though he were afraid of having her stolen from him, and yet she was a stranger to him, he did not know where she came from nor what she was thinking. He went on saying words that intensified his excitement still further.

'My poor love . . . My poor little love . . .'

Then the singer with the squint banged on the wall to make him shut up, and he had said nothing more.

About seven next morning, when a little daylight filtered through the window, Cholet had the taste of another mouth on his lips. Feeling drained, he had got out of bed noiselessly, climbing across Lulu, who had turned over and muttered something in her sleep.

He had pulled on his clothes but had not bothered to wash, to save time. In the passage he had tried to avoid making any noise, but a voice – it was Layard's – had called out from the bedroom, so loud that the whole house could hear:

'The key's hanging on a nail behind the bar. Just put it back through the letterbox.'

He was in such a state of agitation that it took him quite a while to find the key. Out in the street he felt like running, wild with excitement and panic.

He had gone too far to retreat now. He went home, and from the doorway he could see the lighted kitchen at the end of the passage; his mother was in there preparing breakfast. His father must be upstairs getting dressed.

Very pale, he first took off his raincoat, then ran a comb through his hair in front of the hall-stand mirror. Then he went slowly towards the smell of coffee with which, every morning, the house came to life.

'Morning, mother.'

She stood speechless for a moment, appalled by his brazen coolness. She was a small, thin, wiry woman. Suddenly she struck him in the face, with her nails rather than with her fingers, screaming hysterically:

'Aren't you ashamed? Aren't you ashamed? Aren't you . . .'

The cloth was laid, the places set, the bread cut. But Madame Cholet collapsed on to a chair, hiding her face on the table, and she sobbed and howled, her thin frame shuddering spasmodically.

'Mother . . . Please . . . Listen to me . . .'

He felt he was liable to break down himself. He couldn't stand seeing her weep thus, as though he were the most unnatural son in all creation.

'I'm old enough to . . .'

His ears were tingling. His mother's hair had come undone and was straggling down her back.

'Please, mother . . . listen to me!'

Back in the office, amid the din of the rotary press, he still blushed when he recalled the details of the scene. Some of them had been ridiculous and hateful. At the time it had all seemed tragic. Terrible words had been spoken: *'die of shame . . . kill me . . . you'll be weeping on my grave . . .'*

Madame Cholet had been gasping and hiccoughing wildly, and tearing at her apron. Jean had been weeping too. They were both in tears, there in the kitchen; they had not thought of switching off the electric light, although it was broad daylight.

'I'd sooner be dead and gone than see my son become . . .'

He remembered picking up a knife from the table and calling out something absurd, like threatening to commit suicide on the spot. She had flown at him, cursing him; she had vowed never to see him again.

Monsieur Cholet had come in, newly shaved, ready to set off for his office. He had quietly grasped his wife's shoulders, and she had shouted:

'I know you're going to take your son's side!'

His father had been sad and grave, but there was no harshness towards either of them in his gaze. He had signalled to Jean to leave off and go away.

Probably the scene between husband and wife had gone on for a long time. Jean had got to the office too early, his eyelids aching, and had washed at the tap on the landing. He had not gone home to lunch, but had eaten a couple of croissants at the office. As the day passed, he felt increasingly drained, but that morning's scene no longer affected him in the same way. It seemed to him less dramatic, indeed somewhat undignified. He shrugged his shoulders on recalling that he had threatened to kill himself and that he had seriously spoken of leaving home for good.

He felt hot, and broke into a feverish sweat when he made the least movement or thought about certain things. At noon, in the neutral light of a rainy day, in the deserted office where he was alone with Léglise, he had suddenly felt very far away from the Âne Rouge and from Lulu.

But since the lamps had been lit and the walls were shuddering with the regular thump of the rotary press, his fever revived. He could picture certain scenes, certain figures with nightmarish clarity. Layard, for instance – and he suddenly felt afraid of Layard – with his stentorian voice, his mercenary gaiety, his endlessly repeated jokes. Well, Layard's eyes never smiled; when everything else about him smiled, his eyes didn't; they shone, but it was with malice. And his wife, that plump motherly creature, was really only concerned with serving drinks and collecting tips!

Where had they come from? What sort of people were they really? By what concourse of circumstances, with what object had they ensconced themselves in this town, which could not assimilate them?

Next to them, Cholet recalled the pianist, so pale as to be colourless, with his lashless, eyebrowless, lipless face, staring at people with his dull eyes until it was time to go home to his sick wife.

'You will now have the pleasure of hearing Maestro Duvigan perform his own works ...'

He had never talked to Cholet. Perhaps he had never even looked at him.

Now Debras crossed the room for the last time; the Stock Exchange had closed down. Mademoiselle Berthe got up and went to the mirror to put on her ridiculous velvet hat.

'Are you ill?' she asked.

'Me? No. Why do you ask?'

'I don't know.'

A few weeks earlier everybody had thought something might be going on between the two of them. Nothing definite. Several times,

Cholet had arrived early at the office so as to be alone with her in the back room. On another occasion, as she happened to be tired he had taken down the messages from Havas on the telephone for her. That was all. They had not said anything to one another.

'Till tomorrow, then.'

'Till tomorrow.'

So she was feeling resentful already! A hunchbacked fellow, who acted as a sort of book-keeper in the newspaper office, now came into the room. He handed Cholet an open notebook.

'What's that?'

'Read it and sign it.'

This was something new. Never yet had a notebook been used to convey instructions to the staff. Under the heading: 'Notice to Staff' it said:

The editorial staff are reminded that they must not absent themselves during working hours without informing the sub-editor. Furthermore, that all copy must be handed in to the sub-editor, who alone is entitled to pass it on to the printers.

'Is that for my benefit?' sneered Cholet, scrawling his initials on the page.

'I couldn't say.'

Obviously, it was for his benefit! For the past few days he had been bringing in the local news items late, when the sub-editor had already gone out to lunch. Nothing had been said to him. His intoxication and the sensational scene at the banquet had barely been mentioned. But they must have decided to keep an eye on him. Even Léglise betrayed a certain unease when he looked at him.

Well, it couldn't be helped. They could never understand; nobody could understand! Only he had to find a hundred francs by that evening. He put on his hat and coat and stopped at the cashier's desk.

'I have to dine in town because of a press conference. I haven't any money with me. Would you advance me a hundred francs?'

He averted his eyes and assumed a detached air.

'Thank you. Don't forget to remind me.'

Outside, he walked fast. At this time of day the streets were full of people. At home he found his parents already seated at table. The kitchen had never seemed so quiet. Monsieur Cholet was sitting in his wicker armchair. Madame Cholet, opposite him, had an empty plate in front of her; she was eating nothing, and her eyes were still red, her face puffy. Obviously they had barely spoken to one another since the beginning of the meal. Jean kissed his father's forehead as usual.

'Hullo, son.'

He tried to kiss his mother, but she turned her head away and his lips only touched her hair. She served him none the less. Nothing more was heard but the sound of spoons and forks. When Jean had eaten his soup, his mother got up and fetched the plate of beans that was keeping warm by the fire. The stove was purring, the rain pattered down on the zinc roof of the kitchen.

Jean ate his meal in less than ten minutes, refused dessert, and stood up, while his mother slowly turned to him as though to say something. But it was his father who spoke.

'Are you going out?'

'I've got a conference.'

'And are you letting him get away with it?'

He heard nothing more. He was out in the passage already, grabbing his coat and hat. He could still hear the voices through the glazed door, but he could not make out the words. The street was empty and the pavements were wet. He walked as far as the third lamp post before putting on his coat and hat. He looked as though he were trying to run away.

4

It was the first time he had seen her in a hat, with her brown coat wrapped about her so tightly that the play of her thigh muscles was visible. She was standing on the edge of the pavement, a tiny creature, looking straight in front of her patiently, as though her thoughts were far away.

Cholet went up to her quickly, and she gave a start and then smiled.

'Oh, it's you . . .'

It was five o'clock. Jean had been trying for a long time to persuade Lulu to meet him in town, and he had got his way at last. On their left was the light-studded darkness of the quays and harbour; on their right the bright lights of the town streets.

'Where would you like to go?'

'I don't mind . . .'

He was surprised to find her looking so schoolgirlish. At the Âne Rouge she wore a green silk dress of daring cut; but here she thrust ungloved hands into the pockets of a drab shapeless coat. Her black shoes were down at heel, and stray locks of reddish hair escaped from her little felt hat. Standing there on the pavement she seemed to be some creature without identity, about to drift like flotsam down the street.

'I've got to buy some stockings,' she said, as he put his arm round her shoulders.

She was really tiny, so that he had to stoop as he walked. But that didn't matter, nor the fact that she was so shabbily dressed. On the contrary, he was touched by this, as he was by her submissiveness. At the risk of meeting people from the *Gazette de Nantes*, he made his way towards the town centre, and when he saw Lulu turning to look into some shop window he would stop.

'We've agreed about what I told you, haven't we, Jean? I've got things to buy but that's my business. We're pals, and I don't want you to be giving me presents.'

He had never before been through the town with a woman on his arm, and he felt very excited. He went into a shop with Lulu and watched her examining stockings and arguing about the price.

'Twenty francs is too dear.'

She went from one counter to the next, and paused longingly in front of some silk pyjamas.

'I'll give her some for a New Year's present!'

When they set off again she was carrying a little parcel dangling from her finger by a red string.

'Shall we go and have a drink?'

It was all unfamiliar and delightful and a little bewildering. They sat down in the Café de la Paix, where the band, at this time of day, was playing light music. The windows were misty with steam. Lulu drank a cup of chocolate and ate two cakes, after asking him: 'May I?'

She had told him that Layard paid her twenty-five francs a day and kept back twenty-two for her board and lodging, so that she had three francs left. Jean had been back to her room several times, but had always left about three in the morning on account of his parents.

'Does Layard go to bed with his artistes?'

'It depends.'

The air was like a warm bath, throbbing with music, and there was a cheerful clink of glasses and plates.

'And with you?'

'I've told him I'm sick.'

'And Speelman?'

'Why do you keep asking me that?'

He pressed her, flushing with impatience. Every time he mentioned Speelman she changed the subject or replied evasively.

'Tell me the truth. Did you sleep with Speelman?'

'I can't remember. Let's talk about something else.'

'Where did you meet him?'

'In Constantinople. He was on tour, and he engaged me to sing in Alexandria and Cairo.'

'Why do Layard and the rest call him the boss?'

'Don't bother about that. Six o'clock already! I'm going to be late for dinner . . .'

Out in the street, they walked faster.

'Are you coming tonight?' she asked.

'Yes.'

'I'm glad! When you're not there I'm so bored! I'll show you a new dress I've just made . . .'

She stopped at the corner of the street. He could have gone into the Âne Rouge with her; they had no need of concealment. Yet he preferred this furtive parting. She stood on tiptoe to kiss him and then tripped off towards the electric sign, which had just lit up.

Why did Cholet, as he watched her move away, feel so convinced that he would always remember the walk they had just taken? He had such experiences from time to time; for no apparent reason his heart would swell with emotion, tears would rise to his eyes and he would feel he was living through unforgettable moments.

As he went home, he saw nothing all the way but lights and moving shadows. His thoughts were on the little parcel tied with red string, on Lulu staring dreamily at the ground as she waited for him, on Constantinople and Cairo, on that shabby coat.

The street he lived in was deserted, but something peculiar struck him and for a moment he could not say definitely what it was. In his home the light was on upstairs, on the first floor, and also on the ground floor, in the front parlour which was never used. He felt uneasy, opened the door, and saw at a glance that there was nobody in the kitchen.

'Mother!' he called out, with a stab of anxiety.

Somebody moved upstairs. A shadowy figure leaned over the banisters. 'Hush!'

He rushed upstairs. His mother was on the landing, with his Aunt Léopoldine, whom he disliked and who kissed him as people kiss you when something dreadful has happened.

'The doctor's in there . . . Your father . . .'

Madame Cholet was sniffling, dabbing her nose with a screwed-up handkerchief, but Jean could scarcely see her because the landing was in darkness. There was just a streak of light showing under the bedroom door, and a bright spot where the keyhole was.

Seized with panic, he wanted to go in; he grasped his mother's arm.

'What's happened?'

'I don't know. They brought him back in an ambulance. It seems he was taken ill in the Place de la République . . .'

And Jean pictured the ambulance stopping in front of the house, in the quiet street. He imagined his father in the crowd, people running hither and thither and gathering round him; and the policeman. It had happened quite close to the Café de la Paix, where he had been eating cakes with Lulu.

Eventually the door opened and Dr Matray beckoned them to go in quietly. The smell of ether was choking. A cardboard shield had been fastened to the lamp to prevent the light falling straight on to the bed.

Monsieur Cholet was smiling. His face was slightly puffy, under the eyes particularly. His hands lay still and limp on the blanket. But he was smiling at Jean, at his wife, particularly at Jean, with a weary apologetic smile.

'It's nothing,' he breathed.

Then Jean, suddenly, burst into tears, flung himself violently against his father's breast and pressed his head to it. His distress was intolerable. He couldn't bear to see his father lying there motionless; there was something monstrous and inhuman about it.

'Son! . . . son! . . . son! . . .' his father sought to quieten him.

And the doctor pulled him by the sleeve so as to release the invalid. Madame Cholet was weeping too, as she stood by the foot of the bed, while Aunt Léopoldine tried to tidy up the room.

Jean straightened up again, his face bathed in tears and his nose wet. His eyes were close to his father's rough cheeks, and he could see that tears were welling in the sick man's eyes too.

'Son . . .' Monsieur Cholet repeated, smiling.

He must have been very frightened. How horrible it had been for him there in the Place de la République, when he had felt his strength give way and had collapsed on the pavement, among the legs of the passers-by!

That was why he was smiling! Now, he was at home! He had not died in the street! Jean was there!

'Don't tire him,' the doctor said. 'He'll be all right. The attack's over. But he needs absolute rest . . .'

'Come, Jean ...' muttered Madame Cholet. 'You can come up again when you've had your dinner. Coming, Poldine?'

Jean wanted to stay with his father, if only for a moment, he didn't know why. He had nothing to say to him. The doctor was drying his hands and taking leave of his patient.

'Five drops every hour, not more,' he ordered.

The door closed behind him. Jean had stopped crying and now he was smiling too, a smile that resembled his father's, a smile of deliverance. They had both been badly frightened; now they were saved!

'It was a shock for your mother ...'

Cholet was surely speaking without thinking of what he was saying. He kept his eyes on Jean with joyful eagerness, and his Adam's apple swelled, his eyes grew misty again. His lips twisted oddly as he said:

'I'd given up hope ...'

He said no more; he had to clench his jaws not to break into sobs. Then gradually he recovered his composure and his smile.

'Go and have something to eat now. Your mother's waiting for you.'

'I'm not hungry.'

'Go along. I've got to rest.'

The two women were at table, in the kitchen. Aunt Poldine was describing the death of her first husband.

'Has the doctor talked to you?' Jean asked his mother.

'He's only just left. He says the attack might have been fatal. It's over now, but there may be another in a fortnight or a year ...'

'Does father know?'

'Dr Matray wanted to make him believe he could live for another ten years, and he didn't say anything, but I'm sure he realizes his condition.'

Madame Cholet, her mouth full, started weeping again.

'And you take advantage of it to distress me as much as you can!' she added.

'It's true, Jean!' put in his aunt. 'Your mother's told me all about it. I can't understand how a boy like you ...'

'That's enough!' he said sharply, glaring at her.

'You hear, Poldine? That's how he talks to me too, to me, his mother! He comes home at four in the morning. His father lets him, and even prevents me from scolding him. And this is the son I should have to rely on if I were to be left a widow.'

It was all a hateful mixture of tears and kitchen smells and a hushed atmosphere pervaded by whiffs of ether. Jean pretended not to listen, and ate sullenly, with his elbows on the table. When he stood up his mother said: 'I hope you're not going out tonight?'

He left the room with a growl by way of answer. His father, alone in his bedroom, was lying awake, looking up at the ceiling.

'Have you finished eating already?' he said in some surprise. 'Your mother's crying, isn't she? Yes, she is, I can hear her from here. And Aunt Poldine must be taking the opportunity to cry too ...'

He was speaking in his normal voice, only a little weaker. He was breathing regularly, as though this were an important exercise, and avoiding the least movement.

'You can smoke,' he said.

And, seeing Jean hesitate: 'The doctor's forbidden me to, but if you smoke I can enjoy the smell. There are some cigarettes in my jacket pocket.'

Jean found the jacket, which was stained with dust, and from which one button had been wrenched off in his rescuers' efforts to give him some air. Half the cigarettes in the packet were broken.

'Haven't you got a conference tonight?'

'No.' And Jean blushed, for he realized that his father was trying to help him. He was supposed to report on the conferences that took place at least once a week, but for the past month he had not been to any of them. He had taken to ringing up his colleagues on the *Ouest-Eclair* to get the information, or even to making up a report based on the title.

The smell of tobacco mingled with that of ether. Jean was sitting on a chair beside the bed, and he could hear the two women putting away the dishes.

'Have you got money?'

'Why?'

'I don't know. It's at least a week since you've been to see me at the office.'

Jean averted his eyes, because he felt humiliated by his father's indulgent smile. It was true! He had been several days without borrowing money from his father, but that didn't mean that he had spent any the less. At the end of last month the journalists had been given a rise of a hundred francs, and Jean had kept this extra money without mentioning it at home.

'You ought to think of your mother more. She can't understand. She worries over nothing.'

Monsieur Cholet had a high balding forehead and, under his moustache, the same sinuous lips as his son. He looked far handsomer lying there than in everyday life, in his usual drab clothes, stiff collar and ready-made tie.

'Will you give me my drops? Five in half a glass of water.'

Their relation was one of simple familiarity, of undemonstrative affection. Jean would sometimes go three days without seeing his father, who left before him in the morning and did not come home for the midday meal. When he kissed his father it was on the forehead, almost absentmindedly.

'Evening, father.'

'Evening, son.'

And that was all. Since the business about the banquet they had not talked about anything, and yet they understood one another.

Jean counted the drops, which clouded the water like pernod. He helped his father to sit up, and felt the damp warmth of his neck.

'Matray says that in a couple of days I can get up and go out. With these attacks, it's all or nothing. Once they're over they leave no after-effects.'

The women were coming upstairs; the door opened. Aunt Poldine had brought her needlework.

'Why are you smoking?'

'I told him to.'

'Oh, of course! Poldine, fetch the easy chair from the next room.'

The spell was broken, the sense of intimacy had vanished. While Monsieur Cholet lay down again after having drunk his medicine, he exchanged a glance with Jean, a glance which was not particularly meaningful but which implied a sense of mutual understanding and complicity. Aunt Léopoldine started talking:

'If I were in your husband's place I know I'd go for a month's rest to the South of France.'

'What about the money?' retorted Madame Cholet.

For Aunt Léopoldine owned three houses and went to Lourdes every year!

'You can always find money when your health's at stake.'

Jean was standing up now, leaning against the wall, his head empty of thoughts, and looking blankly in front of him. His emotion had died away. The drama was over and done with. He scarcely remembered that he had wept.

He noticed details which had never struck him, such as the tastelessness of the wallpaper and the shabbiness of the curtains, which had been widened with strips of material when the family had moved house five years earlier.

'Are you feeling better? Does it tire you to hear us talking?'

'No.'

'You don't sound very sure. Is there anything you want? A hot bottle for your feet? There's some hot water in the kitchen.'

'No, thank you.'

And Aunt Léopoldine, who had put on her spectacles, commented:

'The dreadful thing about men is that they won't look after themselves. Though actually, in any household, it's better the husband should be ill than the wife, for when the wife's in bed, it's the end!'

'I never stopped in bed,' her sister remarked, 'except when Jean was born ...'

Jean was staring at the floor. He could hear his father's careful breathing, and gradually the mental images of that afternoon's experiences recurred to him, particularly that of Lulu patiently waiting and day-dreaming at the edge of the pavement.

She had bought two pairs of stockings at thirteen francs fifty. The expedition had raised her spirits, and she had started skipping as she walked beside him through the town. And she had said in such a comical way:

'Tonight I'll show you the dress I've made myself!'

There was an alarm clock on the bedside table, beside the medicine bottles and the empty glass. It showed half past nine. That was the time Lulu would be putting on her make-up, because Layard was about to announce:

'Now for a song from our delightful star Lulu d'Artois, from the leading cabarets of Montmartre!'

And Doyen, who wore the same steel spectacles as Aunt Léopoldine, would take advantage of this brief respite to read the *Intransigeant*, which had just come on the latest train. What would Lulu think if Jean failed to appear?

'Don't stand there like that,' said Madame Cholet.

Perhaps she would think he'd been disappointed when he saw her out of her usual setting. For she was sensitive to shades of feeling; several times she had surprised him by guessing at his thoughts when he had not admitted them to himself. His mother did, too; but his mother exaggerated, and always for the worse.

'Sit down. Take a book. If you think I don't know what you're after ...'

He sighed, and sat down to avoid a scene; then he noticed that his father was trying to catch his eye.

'Why do you want Jean to stop here?'

'Why?' Madame Cholet was choking with indignation. 'Why, because you're ill! It would be the limit if he were to go off after his dreadful women when his father nearly ...'

She stopped. Aunt Poldine put in, biting off her thread:

'My son, who's a barrister now, never went out at night until he was twenty-one!'

'He wasn't a journalist!' Jean retorted irritably.

He was vexed with himself for that. It only worsened the atmosphere, which was gloomy enough already. This was the first time that Lulu had insisted on seeing him, and maybe she had her reasons. Who knows? She might have thought he was trying to break with her out of jealousy, on account of Speelman!

'You're not cold?' Madame Cholet asked her husband.

She was sewing too. The two sisters sat there in the lamplight, Aunt Léopoldine with her white hair and Madame Cholet who looked barely forty. They had the same delicate features, the same thick hair, the same flat chests, but above all they had in common a latent sadness that seemed organic, as though fate was too much for them.

'Jean,' called out Monsieur Cholet, unclasping his hands as they lay on the coverlet.

'Yes, father?'

'Why don't you go to the meeting you told me about yesterday?'

He kept his eyes averted. Madame Cholet's needle was poised in mid-air.

'What meeting?' she asked.

'The meeting of the Journalists' Union,' Jean replied quickly, at random.

'For all the good you get out of them!'

She made three stitches in the hem she was holding between two fingers.

'At what time is it?'

'At ten o'clock. Some people aren't free before then.'

And Monsieur Cholet said firmly: 'It's time you went.'

Jean dared not stand up yet. He was less afraid of his mother's wrath than of seeming weak in his father's eyes and in his own.

'Anyhow, I want to sleep. I'd like the light turned out.'

It was twenty minutes to ten! Lulu would be singing, but there would still be only five or six people in the room, and the applause and enthusiastic exclamations to be heard from outside would come mainly from Layard. People passing by would pause, under the impression that something amusing was happening inside, and would then go in.

'Now a hand for our good friend and colleague, who's jolly well deserved it! ... One! ... Two! ... Three! ...'

'Good-night, father.'

He had gone up to the bedside, humbly, and kissed his father's damp brow. He would have liked to say something to him, but he didn't know what. He touched his hand shyly, as he might have done with a woman. It was only a furtive contact. The sick man's hand was moist.

'Good-night, son; don't be too late back.'

'I should hope not,' echoed a voice. 'He surely wouldn't have the face, today ...'

Jean laid a kiss on the hair that covered his mother's temples.

'Good-night.'

He did not kiss his aunt. He could not bring himself to do that. Out in the street, where his steps resounded, he walked slowly at first, then faster. The luminous church clock, which he had seen ever since his childhood, having always lived in the same district, showed 10 p.m.

Then he suddenly broke into a run, for Lulu must be thinking he was not coming. He crossed the bridges and turned right, pausing briefly to take breath at the corner of the lane where she had parted from him. He could see shadows behind the window, hear the insistent beat of the piano and the sepulchral voice of Doyen singing 'Le pantalon réséda'.

Nearer by, the word 'Hotel' stood out on the globe of frosted glass, and beyond the Âne Rouge was the winking light, the shameful lamp towards which he had never ventured.

Behind him, less than a hundred metres away, lay the Place de la République, almost silent now; but at about half past five there had been a disturbance there amid the crowd ...

He felt a moment's dizziness and recoiled instinctively; then he grasped the familiar, greasy horn door-handle.

'Come in, old man! Slip in as quietly as a breath of air!' called out Layard, who repeated the same phrase twenty times a night.

On the platform, lugubrious Doyen was waiting for Jean to be seated to begin his next song, and the pianist's long fingers were poised above the keys.

'Excuse me ... excuse me, monsieur ...'

His temples throbbing, Jean threaded his way between the tables. Lulu watched him coming. Beside her, in the place that was usually his own, there was a man with a crooked nose whom Cholet had never seen before, who was speaking in a low tone without paying attention to what was going on around him. Jean himself was oblivious of the moment, and yet he clearly overheard Lulu's whispered remark to her companion:

'That's him!'

5

It was shortly after ten o'clock when they noticed that the overcoat of a guest who had just come in was almost white; the damp and the cold had furred every shred of wool.

At frequent intervals, moreover, Layard would pause to listen intently, for there was something unusual about the noise from the town. Every motor-horn in the place seemed to be sounding, together with the shrill hooting of ancient cars and the clang of tram bells. At half past ten the harbour siren filled the background with its wail.

More customers came in, a couple this time; the woman was laughing excitedly, looking back at the street. The guests at the nearest table got up to have a look.

The town was submerged in the thickest fog anyone could remember. The street was no longer a street; there were no pavements, no houses on the opposite side, not even any street lamps, nothing but an opaque substance out of which, suddenly, voices sounded or ghostly figures emerged.

'It's ice,' somebody said, showing a sleeve covered with white droplets.

It was strange and somewhat frightening. Less than a hundred metres away, on the now invisible square, fifty cars were hooting simultaneously, moving forward blindly at a snail's pace. Even Doyen came to stand in the doorway. Layard resumed his jokes. At 11 p.m. a newcomer announced that all the trams had stopped and the taxis had given up trying to drive.

As a result of this phenomenon, the Âne Rouge assumed a peculiar aspect. There was an increased liveliness; the fog was an excuse for people to call to each other from one table to another. Men assured their women companions that they would have to stay there until morning, and made an endless series of jokes on this theme.

178

Jean Cholet had gone like the rest to look out into the milky opacity of the street, and then had taken his seat again opposite Lulu and her companion.

'This is Gybal, a friend of Speelman's,' she had told him.

Cholet was ill at ease, and repeatedly wondered why it all felt so strange. The air was overheated as usual, but when the door opened an icy breath ran down one's neck.

There was something else, something in addition to the presence of Gybal, perhaps the fact that the crowd was so noisy, excited by the thought of being present at an unusual and memorable happening. Nobody was listening to the singers, and Layard frowned as he walked about between the tables.

Jean felt anxious, and shivered from time to time as though at the onset of a fever. Lulu noticed his sullenness, and looked at him with some surprise.

'You've not put on your new dress.'

He clearly remembered the last few minutes of their conversation at the street corner. She had asked him to come so as to see her dress, and this had touched him so much that he had recalled it in his father's sickroom.

'I hadn't time. Gybal was here.'

This Gybal was a tall, strong fellow, well dressed, with the fresh healthy complexion of an athlete. Jean recognized an indefinable quality that had struck him earlier in Speelman. For instance, he himself, however carefully he shaved, could never acquire those smooth even cheeks! He looked at his own big bony hands, and then at those of Lulu's companion, with their long fingers and manicured nails, and they put him to shame, as did the man's silk shirt and neatly knotted tie, because he felt himself incapable of attaining such refinement. The details mattered little in themselves; beside this man, he felt awkward and shabby.

'What'll you have?' Gybal asked him.

Gybal took no interest in the crowd milling about in the room. He was smoking a cigar, rolling the damp end of it between his lips every now and then.

'Yesterday I had supper with Speelman, who spoke of you. He sends his kind regards.'

Jean could see the pallid profile of the pianist, who alone had not gone to peer out into the fog. Layard laid a hand on Cholet's shoulder.

'You've been introduced? He's a good sort, you'll see!'

And the time passed slowly, more slowly than usual. Doyen came to sit with them, sighing:

'In weather like this they'll still be here at two in the morning!'

For in fact people showed no signs of leaving. They were waiting for the fog to clear. In spite of the piano, the wail of the siren could be heard filling the heavens.

'Lulu tells me you're a journalist.'

Gybal was trying to be friendly, but Cholet could not bring himself to look kindly at him. The hand was moving jerkily over the clock face: twelve o'clock, five minutes past twelve.

He was on the point of leaving, for at home they must be lying awake. He had promised himself just to pay a brief visit to the Âne Rouge to give Lulu a kiss, and he hadn't even kissed her, he hadn't even spoken to her.

'Another drink? *Patronne*, the same again!'

'Nothing for me,' Lulu said.

His elbows on the table, his face close to Cholet's, Gybal was talking, showing his fine teeth.

'You've got a swell job! Particularly as you must make so many contacts. I expect you know everybody in Nantes ...'

'Everybody.'

They were trying to flatter him. They were urging him to drink. There seemed to be a sort of plot, and the proof was that Layard never stopped watching them, from one or another corner of the room. He came periodically to lay a hand on Cholet's shoulder.

'All right?'

And Gybal's eyelids flickered as though to say:

'All right! I'll deal with this ...'

After the third glass Jean reflected:

'You think you're going to make me tight and that then you'll do whatever you like with me. But I've got my eye on you! I can see what you're up to!'

He affected not to look at Lulu, whom he considered responsible. She, too was not her usual self. It looked as if she'd been given a scolding! When a fourth round was brought, she actually stretched out her arm and said:

'No, Jean! Be careful!'

'Give it me!'

'You'll be ill again.'

'Can't be helped.'

'Women are all the same,' joked Gybal.

What did they want from him? For they clearly wanted something. It was becoming more and more evident. Everybody seemed in collusion. Old Doyen was watching Cholet curiously with his sharp little eyes. Layard even forgot to press his customers to drink. The pianist himself was casting furtive glances towards their table.

'Shut the door,' came a shout from time to time. For as soon as the door was opened the violent contrast between heat and cold became unbearable. The big window was as white as frosted glass.

'Do you often go to Paris?'

'Very seldom.'

'Next time, we'll arrange to have dinner together, the three of us, you and me and Speelman. He'll be delighted! Oh, he's a card!'

If only Speelman had been there himself! But Cholet did not trust Speelman's friend; he detested him. As he drank, he said to himself:

'We'll see who's the cleverest!'

He was furious with Lulu, who was gazing at him with sad, reproachful eyes. At one point he could not restrain himself from making a spiteful remark:

'You needn't look at me like that! If I hadn't been drunk I'd never have come in here!'

She almost burst into tears. Gybal laughed noisily.

'My round, Madame Layard!'

'The same again?'

Twenty past twelve. He ought to go. His mother must be furious, and she was quite capable of taking it out on his father in spite of his illness. 'It's your fault! You insisted on his going off and now his meeting's lasting half the night!'

It was so hot that his jacket felt uncomfortable round the arm-holes and his skin was tingling. Inevitably, on the slightest provocation, his blood would rush to the surface of his skin in red patches and it would start itching.

'I need a good breath of air.'

'You'll catch cold,' said Lulu.

With a shrug, he went to the door. On the edge of the pavement he felt a glow of excitement as he looked out into the fog, which made the town infinitely more mysterious. Behind him was the Âne Rouge with its music, laughter and talk. At the same time he could picture the harbour, the siren, the boats gliding through the unseen water, the people groping their way along the streets. Lulu appeared beside him and took him by the arm.

'Coming, Jean? You're going to catch cold.'

'Why haven't you kissed me?'

She had never seemed so tiny. She scarcely came up to his shoulder. She stood on tiptoe and put her mouth to his, but it gave him no pleasure.

'I had to ask you for it,' he grumbled.

Unconsciously, he had begun to assume Gybal's intonations and his cavalier manners.

'What does that fellow want from me?'

'I don't know. Why do you ask that?

He laughed silently and pushed open the door. Layard was leaning over Gybal's shoulder. On seeing the couple they separated. Some guests were standing in the doorway, as though at the water's edge, reluctant to plunge into the fog.

However, they were beginning to disperse. It was one in the morning. The air was still as stuffy. Only one group of commercial travellers showed no sign of leaving, and the pianist went on strumming unconcernedly for their benefit.

'Shall we have a bottle of champagne?' Gybal suggested.

'I don't mind.'

Doyen was still there. He would stay there until everybody went to bed, out of habit. But he was not talking. Probably he was not listening. He merely waited.

Lulu had not resumed her place on the settee, but had pulled up a chair close to Jean. As for Layard, who had nothing to do now that the visitors were enjoying themselves without his help, he went on walking about none the less, and only occasionally turned up at the table.

'I suppose you're on good terms with them at the town hall?'

'Sure!' Cholet sniggered. 'You won't find anyone in Nantes who's on better terms with them than me . . .'

Lulu was growing impatient and shuffling her feet for no reason. It irritated him. He told her: 'Keep still, can't you?'

His voice betrayed his tipsiness. He was self-confident, full of contempt and pity for the rest of mankind.

'I suppose you often go there?'

'Every day. I pick up information here and there in various offices. All the staff know me; they're afraid of me.'

'Really?' Gybal's smile expressed wonder and encouragement.

'Because of my daily column, where I don't mince words. I've already obliged one councillor to resign . . .'

'Splendid!'

'Your good health! Drink up, Lulu.'

Half past one. Deep down, he was quaking with anxiety because he knew his mother was waiting for him. He drained his glass three times in quick succession.

'I must be off.'

'Oh no! Layard has promised to stand us a bottle too.'

'Tomorrow.'

'Nothing of the sort! Tonight . . .'

Lulu had laid her hand on his knee. Gybal noticed, and she promptly took it away. The pianist left the platform and came to sit with them as usual, saying nothing, his eyelids as red as ever, his lips contemptuous.

'A glass of champagne?'

'A quarter of Vichy.'

He seemed to be waiting for something. Everybody was waiting. Madame Layard herself stayed behind her bar instead of coming to sit with the rest.

'You live with your parents?'

Cholet was ashamed of admitting this simple fact to Gybal.

'How much do they pay at the newspaper?'

'A thousand francs.'

He was lying. He only got eight hundred francs a month.

'That's nice!'

Layard's shadow was visible, aimlessly roaming.

Cholet, without glancing at Lulu, was aware that she was making signs to Gybal as though to say: 'No, no, you mustn't . . .'

Then she yawned and stood up.

'I'm dropping with sleep.'

'Go to bed,' he snapped.

She did not move. Doyen's eyes were half closed. Was he listening? Was he, too, waiting for something?

'*À votre santé!*'

'*À la tienne!*' And Cholet laughed, because he had been the first to say *tu*. After all, he had *tutoyéd* Speelman!

'You know the chief registrar?' Gybal offered him a cigar.

'Very well.'

'Is he intelligent?'

'He's an idiot, the father of a colleague of mine on the *Petit Nantais*, and he's interested in nothing but theosophy . . .'

Jean smiled, for drunk though he was he guessed that his companions did not know what the word meant.

'What d'you think of this champagne?' Layard came up to ask him. 'This isn't the stuff I give my customers!'

'It's all right.'

And Layard went off. What a long business; twenty to two already! All the same, Cholet wanted to know what it was all about, for he was tired of waiting.

'They're all idiots . . .' sighed Gybal. 'A set of old fools who get rich at other people's expense. You must know something about that.'

'Sit down,' Jean said to Lulu, who was standing beside him. 'Or else go to bed!'

Gybal resumed the *tutoiement* which he had unconsciously dropped.

'Would you have the guts to play a good trick on them?'

A minute earlier Cholet had felt himself flushing, and now he was suddenly aware of turning pale and cold. His whole being seemed to shrink, and yet at the same time his brain became abnormally lucid.

'I'm listening,' he said, narrowing his eyes, as though he were a very cunning man watching another getting caught in his own trap.

'What I'm trying to say is . . . It might have been better to see Speelman, since it's his concern. Yesterday we were a bit worried. Suddenly he exclaimed: "There's a young friend of mine who's a journalist at Nantes. If I had the time . . . But you might go and see him for me."'

Lulu had moved away. She was leaning on the bar and had started

184

talking to Madame Layard, who was not listening to her but trying to hear what was going on at the table. The commercial travellers were making a noise. The *patron* was strumming on the piano with one finger.

And the tension increased. Cholet's temples were throbbing. He was holding his ice-cold glass and watching the bubbles rise.

'I didn't know you, and so I said it wasn't worth bothering. There are so many idiots about!'

Now he was nearly at the top of the hill. Just one more tiny ridge to be got over!

'Well now, I see that you're a man. It'll mean two thousand francs for a few minutes' work, if you can call it work!'

Jean was frightened, painfully frightened. His features were frozen stiff; he could not even move his eyes, and he made a heroic effort to break free of the drunken stupor that was paralysing him. The voice went on, speaking lower.

'They're sure not to distrust you. They're used to seeing you about the place . . . I don't know where they keep the birth certificates, but it's probably close to the guichet. And the stamp is on the desk! You pick up a dozen or so, quite casually. Maybe they're already stamped? . . .'

Cholet drank, to keep himself in countenance. In the mirror behind the bar he saw Lulu's face saying No, no!

And then he saw, not the reflection but the flesh and blood figure of Madame Layard, who had noticed Lulu's gesture and was roughly pushing a glass towards the girl so as to have an opportunity to nudge her hand.

'What d'you say to it? Two thousand for you, plus expenses . . .'

Doyen had not moved a fraction of a millimetre. The pianist gave a sigh. He, too, earned twenty francs a night, but twice a week he played in a teashop for a fee of fifty francs.

'Did Speelman really say? . . .' muttered Cholet suspiciously.

'As sure as we're sitting here drinking Layard's bubbly! We were having supper in the Rue du Faubourg Montmartre. He's leaving for Spain in a few days' time.'

The clock showed ten minutes to two, and Jean's panic intensified. If it had been possible he'd have dashed off home. The siren was wailing. The pianist was waiting to leave with him.

'What d'you say to it?'

The answer was no, of course! But he cast his eyes round, without daring to say so. And he noticed the meaningful glance with which Layard called out to his wife:

'Another bottle of the same!'

'It's as easy as anything. At least, it's easy for a chap in your position. For us, of course ...'

'I won't drink any more,' Jean declared as the bottle was uncorked.

'Really? Then Speelman was telling lies? He said he'd seldom seen a fellow hold his drink as well as you ...'

They were trying to catch him! They were flattering him! Cholet was perfectly well aware of it. Lulu no longer dared to look at him. The commercial travellers were now leaving, uttering exclamations as they ventured into the fog. The glasses were refilled.

'Cheers!'

'No,' Jean retorted.

And he turned round because he felt someone standing behind him, Layard, who picked up a glass from the table and drank from it. He was quite calm, and seemed annoyed with Gybal for persisting:

'So you refuse to drink Speelman's health?'

'Leave him alone,' growled Layard. 'Can't you see he's sleepy?'

'Me?'

'Yes, you, Jeannot. You go off to bye-byes at home with your mum and dad ...'

His eyes were more deeply shadowed than usual, perhaps because of the cold, which was particularly noticeable now that the room was empty. Lulu made for the stairs, saying:

'I'm all in ... Good-night ...'

'Buzz off,' called out Layard with a laugh.

Gybal was worried. He had let his third cigar go out.

'We should get him to realize that there's no danger,' he began, 'and that ...'

'All right! That's understood!' Layard said, leaning over to set down his glass, and brushing up against Cholet's shoulder. 'Leave him alone! Let him go off to bed. Tomorrow he'll do what he's got to.'

'Me?'

'Don't you worry about that tonight, sonny! And now to bed with you ... No, no, you can pay tomorrow ...'

Jean's legs were like cotton wool, and he didn't know who put his coat on his back. On the other hand, he overheard Gybal whispering:

'We've got to be sure, though ...'

'You don't need to worry,' Layard sighed wearily. 'Let him alone!'

Chairs stood about higgledy-piggledy, blocking the way. The hoar-frost from people's overcoats had left damp marks on the floor.

'Good-night, Jeannot ...'

If Layard had not grasped his hand peremptorily, Cholet would not have offered it. He proved as much by going off without saying good-bye to anyone else. He plunged into the mist and heard a footstep beside him. It was the pianist, silent as usual. Somewhere, however, he heard a voice say:

'No ... This way ... Mind the parapet ...'

But there was no water to be seen, no street, no pavement. Only the wail of the siren, now close and now distant.

Why did the pianist walk with him as far as his front door? Jean entered the warm hall and went silently up to the first floor; he noticed that no light was showing under the door of his parents' room. He stopped to listen for a moment, and heard loud breathing that was almost a snore.

He felt furious, disgusted, sick. In his bed, alone, his feet frozen and his head burning, he began to cry. But the sobs would not come; they stopped short like the backfiring of an engine short of petrol. The sheets gradually grew warmer; the pillow was damp with sweat.

The last clear picture in his mind was that of the chief registrar, who had a look of Doyen – perhaps they suffered from the same bladder trouble? – and who had a theosophical journal hidden in his desk pad.

6

Chance and the elements combined, as though deliberately, to bring calm. It was five minutes to ten when Cholet awoke, and the last few moments of his sleep had been pleasurable. Although he did not remember his dreams they had left a cheerful after-taste. He was further encouraged by a strange, unexpected sky. Last night's fog had only partially dispersed. It no longer lay at ground level but hung over the roof-tops in an even canopy. The sun was behind it, invisible, tingeing earth and sky with a diffused rosy glow, so that the town seemed to be covered with a huge lampshade.

The rosy glow was not confined to out-of-doors; it filtered into houses. There were scattered gleams of it in Cholet's bedroom, but his father's, in particular, was pervaded by it.

As Jean pushed open the door he knew that his father was lying in bed, and yet it was distressing to see him there, a newspaper in his hand. On the bedside table stood a bowl containing the remains of some cold chocolate.

'Morning, son.'

'Is mother downstairs?'

'She's gone out shopping.'

It was the sort of day when everything seems easy. Jean was not even conscious of his last night's intoxication. His head was not aching, and on his way to work it never once occurred to him that he would be over an hour late at the office. He didn't care. The air was as fresh and pungent as sparkling wine or some savoury titbit. The Loire was unbelievably munificent: in the middle of the velvet-soft water there floated a cargo boat in ballast, whose hull, stained with red lead, sent shimmering patches of colour as far as the horizon. The creaking of cranes, the thump of steam-hammers, the hooters, the whistle of an engine, were all organized into a vast symphony to the music of which Jean walked along the pavements.

Monsieur Dehourceau might have asked for him before ten o'clock. He might, as he often did, go through the editorial offices on his way to the press. And in fact he had not even arrived yet! He had rung up to ask for his copy to be fetched from his home, because his daughter had measles.

Gillon, who had a cold, was writing with one hand, and with the other holding his handkerchief to his nose, which made Cholet laugh. His own light-heartedness surprised him. He wrote a piece about the fog in poetic vein, and then it was time to call at the police station: seven motor accidents and a boat stranded at the mouth of the Loire. On the police superintendent's desk tiny rings of sunlight quivered, narrowing and widening like laughing eyes, and Cholet, as he made his notes, laughed back at them.

He had never been so conscious of the benevolent pointlessness of things. His father had nearly died. There had been a sickening, agitating family argument. Jean had wept; his mother and Aunt Poldine had wailed.

And now Monsieur Cholet was reading the paper in bed while his wife went from shop to shop exactly as on any other day!

Jean knew that he was going to turn left when he reached the crossroads and that he would stand motionless for a moment at the corner of the lane. All the doors of the theatre were wide open. In the half-light he could make out figures wielding brooms. The door of the Âne Rouge stood open too, and Layard, wearing a cap, was taking money out of the till.

'Hullo, there you are . . .'

He finished pinning a bundle of notes together before holding out his hand in friendly greeting.

'What'll you have? A little export-cassis?'

He showed no curiosity; he did not even look at his visitor. It was a lovely day. The door stood open. There was a delightful tingle in the air and it was apéritif time.

'Cheers! I was just going out . . .'

He refilled the glasses, closed the till and glanced upward.

'Lulu's still asleep. It's quite a business getting her out of bed in the morning.'

The room had already been cleaned and tidied. Cholet yawned, stretching his arms, and followed his companion outside. They had to step over a pail of water in the doorway of the hotel. Layard did not ask Jean to accompany him, but walked calmly on as though by some long-standing agreement.

'Things all right at your office?'

'All right . . .'

'It's not a bad job you've got.'

Only then did Cholet realize that they had reached the town hall. Layard went up the stairs to the entrance and he followed him.

'By the way, I wanted to tell you . . . Don't let Gybal cheat you! . . . It's worth three thousand or nothing, you get me?'

They were standing together in the dimly lit vestibule. Layard held out his hand, then vanished up the staircase on the right. The first door, close to this staircase, was that of the registry office. Cars were drawing up in the square outside, and Jean glimpsed top hats and flowers and a white dress. Interested spectators were lining up alongside the steps.

Cholet pushed open the door and shook hands with the thin clerk, who was an old acquaintance.

'How goes it?'

'Too much work. The boss has got flu!' replied the other, indicating an office that stood empty.

'It's the day for it,' said Jean. 'So has mine.'

'Have you come for the statistics? I don't know where they've been put . . .'

And he went into his boss's office; Jean, meanwhile, bent over his desk. His voice could be heard next door, saying:

'He's got such a mania for tidiness that you can never find anything! Everything's classified, sure enough! But where? that's a different question.'

Borough of Nantes. Birth certificate . . .

There was a whole pile of forms already stamped. The clerk went on talking in the next room.

'Did you know he's published a book on spiritualism, at his own expense? . . . Ah, here's the file! I might have gone on looking for it all day!'

The job was done; he could come back now. Jean had a little

bundle of papers in the pocket of his raincoat. Footsteps sounded in the vestibule, and the clerk opened the door to watch the wedding procession pass. Jean watched too. Two children dressed in white silk were holding the train of the bride.

Cholet walked quickly through the crowd of people darting about in the sunshine like minnows in a swift stream.

Everything was so easy! On one condition: that you didn't take things too seriously. The clerk wouldn't even notice that the papers had disappeared. In any case, they were just common or garden forms!

In the office, Léglise was eating a cold veal sandwich. Mademoiselle Berthe was typing out that morning's latest messages.

Debras was clamouring for the local news items. Jean produced a whole column in a few minutes. The ink ran smoothly from his fountain pen; the nib glided over the paper. Cholet added, just to amuse himself:

'A lovely wedding took place this morning; it was between ...'

A distant knock sounded at the door of the main office; somebody came in, walked hesitantly through the first room, then the second.

Jean opened the baize door. Gybal stood before him, too tall and broad for the poky room. He held out his hand with a smile, looking splendid in his well-cut striped suit, neatly shod and sleek-haired. He was smoking a cigarette, and a spicy scent hung about him.

'Hello there! Is this your office?'

He perched on the edge of the table, after laying down his hat and gloves, and fiddled with the pens and papers scattered there. He was close-shaven and there was a trace of talcum powder under his ear.

'Have you seen Layard this morning?'

'Yes,' Jean replied.

'I haven't seen him myself. Actually I've been staying at the Hôtel d'Angleterre. Layard is a nice fellow, but his rooms are squalid and they reek of toilet water.'

He was lying. He had seen Layard, who was quite likely waiting for him outside the door. The noise of the typewriter in Léglise's room accompanied their conversation. Gybal's gaze dwelt on Jean's jacket, where the papers made a bulge.

'I've brought you ...'

He did not pull out his wallet; in his coat pocket there was a whole bundle of thousand-franc notes.

'Two?' he murmured, dropping two notes on to the desk, with his eyes fixed on Cholet.

The young man did not move. His mind was a blank.

'Two and a half? Well, since I've got no change, I'll leave the three . . .'

The rest of the bundle went back into Gybal's pocket. He held out his hand. In the next room, Léglise was getting up, preparing to come through the office. Jean thrust the notes under his blotting paper and quickly passed the forms over to his companion, who had now stood up and was talking in a loud voice.

'I'd have liked to be a journalist myself! Actually, I wrote two or three articles a long time ago . . . By the way, shall we be seeing you presently?'

When he went out he left a trail of scent behind him in the room. Léglise, opening the baize door, inquired: 'Who was that?'

'A friend of mine.'

'Any news from Saint-Nazaire?'

'I'll try to get them on the line again.'

And he chattered more volubly than he need have done.

'Hello! yes, mademoiselle . . . Publicity department, please . . . What did you say? The harbour office? . . . Good morning, monsieur . . . It's about the steamer that . . . Hello! *Gazette de Nantes* speaking . . . What did you say?'

As he spoke, he was doodling on his blotter, a tangle of curved lines. Then, still holding the receiver, he thrust the three notes into his pocket.

'Hello! The moorings? yes, I hear you . . . broke three times? . . . Next tide? . . . Thanks . . . No, no serious accidents here . . . Motor cars, as you say! . . .'

By four o'clock the fog, which had hung at roof-top level all day, had crept down into the streets again, bringing cold air with it. The pavements were a ghostly white. Every noise was intensified, and some, the sound of footsteps for instance, were so altered as to be unrecognizable.

For a moment Cholet wished he could be ill like his father, like

Monsieur Dehourceau or like the chief clerk in the registry office. He had certainly caught a cold; he felt that with a very slight effort he could be feverish. Everybody else was. Gillon left at three o'clock to go home to bed. Mademoiselle Berthe was coughing. Only Léglise, though he had the flushed prominent cheekbones of a consumptive, was never ill.

'The two of us are going to have to set up the paper by ourselves!'

Léglise was happy. He was capable of staying put on his chair for nine or ten hours at a stretch, in a room littered with crumpled papers. That evening the reduction in the staff made the office look more than ever like a guardroom. Léglise, Cholet and Mademoiselle Berthe were eating on the premises. They had sent out for glasses of beer from a neighbouring café; half-eaten sandwiches were lying about on the tables. At nine o'clock a telephone call informed them that two steamers had just collided less than a mile from Nantes and that one of them was sinking.

'You'll have to go there,' said Léglise.

Cholet took the office motor-cycle and rode along the quayside without seeing anything ahead except blurred lights in the dense fog. He might have called at the harbour office, but he had ridden past it unawares, and then he decided it was unnecessary. He knew exactly where the collision had taken place. He rode slowly along a bad road outside the town, with the Loire on his left and fields on his right, his headlamp barely lighting up a metre of ground ahead. The grass was white and stiff. His skin was taut with the cold and his fingers frozen inside his gloves.

He found it so exciting that he wanted to shout aloud. The whole world, moreover, was full of chaotic noise, for on the scene of the accident all the boats seemed to have arranged to blow their hooters and whistles simultaneously.

Sometimes one glimpsed a headlight, but it was only a luminous blur that dissolved immediately. There were signs of intense activity on the water; the tugs signalled to one another with brief, vicious little hoots.

Cholet halted to look for the bollards. Somewhere he came across an isolated house and heard voices. Someone came out of the shadow close by to stop him.

'Careful!'

A cable had been stretched across the road; figures were bending over at the water's edge, two women, two men, a child. The head-lamp of his motor-bike shone on a meagre garden and cabbages beaded with whiteness.

'Switch off your engine! We can't hear anything! ...'

Once the motor-cycle was silenced, sounds of oars and voices could be heard. On the left, the fog was vaguely luminous.

'The German boat ...' somebody said to Jean.

'Is she sinking?'

'It's the other one that's sinking, the British collier. They're all round her trying to save her, but it's too late. So they're hunting for the three missing men ...'

That was why there were dinghies moving to and fro in the fog, and voices, and ghostly lights.

'You can't hear the lifeboat. Perhaps they've picked up one of them?'

From time to time a thud was heard, or the whistle of a steamship. Cholet climbed back on to his machine and turned towards the town. At the harbour office they gave him the names of the ships, and the latest information.

'They're still looking for the three missing men. The telegraphist is one of them. But in this fog ...'

Jean had hidden the three thousand-franc notes on top of the wardrobe in his room. He felt horribly restless; he needed to keep on the go. Still on his motor-cycle, he stopped in front of the Âne Rouge and heard the piano, and Layard's voice announcing:

'Ladies and gents, here's our good friend ...'

He went in, bringing with him a gust of icy air. Cold clung to his clothes, his face and hands exuded cold. Lulu, up on the platform, was waiting for him to sit down.

'Now I shall have the pleasure of singing to you ...'

Layard shook hands with him silently.

'Gybal not here?'

'He took the four o'clock train. Didn't you see him?'

'Of course I did!' said Cholet furiously.

'Aren't you going to take your coat off?' And Layard turned round to applaud, for Lulu had just finished a verse of her song.

'I say, what's he going to do with those papers?'

'Which papers?'

Jean shrugged impatiently. 'I want to know what he's going to use them for.'

'What's that to do with me? I don't even know what it's all about. He comes here from time to time. Yesterday I heard you whispering together, and that's all!'

'Of course!' Cholet sneered. He was still feeling frozen. Lulu cast timorous glances at him as, in her shrill thin voice, she concluded her song. He stood up.

'Are you going? What has . . .'

Nothing! He was leaving! He was furious! He kicked at the self-starter of his motor-bike, his foot slipped and the pedal knocked his shin. He tried again three times. The roar of his engine drowned the sounds from the Âne Rouge, even the piano. Just as the motor-cycle started off, Lulu opened the door, but Cholet did not stop.

He went back to the harbour office. A body had just been brought in and an official was turning the pages of a sodden notebook which had been found in its pocket.

7

'You smell as if you'd been with a woman!' his mother had said disgustedly, while he was drinking his breakfast coffee.

And that was enough, now, to set him yearning after the Âne Rouge. Rain was falling. On the river the funnel of the cargo boat that had sunk could be seen emerging from the grey lapping water.

'I'm going to get the latest news,' he told Léglise.

Only one body out of the three had been recovered, but Cholet did not even go towards the harbour. It was true that a smell of woman hung about him, even though he had not kissed Lulu the night before. His clothes, his underwear, his hair were all pervaded by a sexual odour mingled with a stale reek of alcohol, and as he walked, hands in pockets, he tried to breathe in that pungent smell.

Madame Layard, her hair in curlers, was swabbing the zinc counter, and her coarse linen apron was soaked.

'You didn't stay long last night,' she observed.

'Is Lulu up?'

'Not yet.'

He went up the stairs without another word. He was as limp and depressed as the weather; he felt a general discomfort, an uneasy yearning. Upstairs, he knew, he would see the untidy room, the crude whiteness of the sheets, and Lulu asleep with one leg outside the blanket as usual.

A door was open at the near end of the passage, the door of a room which was generally unoccupied. Jean was aware that a new artiste was expected, and he stopped to peer into the room.

A woman was sitting on the edge of the bed, wearing only a chemise; she had one leg raised and was filing her toe-nails. Sensing that somebody was there, she looked round towards the door and called out: 'Don't mind me!'

But she did not alter her posture, whose erotic character was emphasized by her broad thighs, her strong belly, her full breasts. Her body was immersed in exactly the same dull, flat light as that in pornographic photographs, and the dark triangle of pubic hair stood out as crudely. Even the setting was the same: the quilt at the foot of the bed, the floral pattern on the wallpaper, and a framed portrait standing on the bedside table.

'You're Nelly Brémont?'

'And you're Lulu's boyfriend, I bet! Come in or stay out, but shut the door . . .'

And as she grasped the other foot he could see the play of muscles in her thighs and pelvis.

'Hand me the buffer that's on the table, will you?'

He took the opportunity to cup her heavy breast, while she looked him up and down with curiosity.

'Make yourself at home!'

'Sure!' he retorted with a snigger.

He felt a sudden hot flush and he slid his fingers down her body till they touched the plump curve of the pubis.

'What about Lulu? You're knocking me over, you idiot!'

She was laughing. He held on to the pillow, and suddenly stopped motionless with his head five centimetres from the woman's face; she looked at him in astonishment. It was over already. He couldn't even have said how he set about it. He did not get up again immediately, but lay crushing her with all his weight, and the woman, who was still clutching her nail-buffer, said reflectively:

'You're a fast worker, you are! Careful, you're smothering me!'

She kept her eyes on him with the same untroubled interest, and saw him go up to the wall, listening intently. He could hear a strange noise in Lulu's room.

'I'm coming right away . . .' he stammered. And he noiselessly opened the door into the next room.

Lulu was standing against the wall, her face hidden in her bent arm, her shoulders shaking rhythmically. He wasn't sure that he didn't hate her, but he was vexed.

'Lulu!'

She did not move, and he touched her, laid a cold kiss on the back of her neck.

'What's the matter? Why don't you speak?'

He was growing impatient. He couldn't be sure, yet, that she had overheard it all.

'Lulu, dear ...'

He spoke without tenderness, while she revealed a flushed face, wet with tears, and glistening eyes. It struck him that she was looking at him with the same curiosity as the other woman had done, as though he were a stranger.

'Don't mind me. I'm silly ...'

And she shrugged her shoulders, with a faint resigned smile.

'You're entitled to, aren't you? There's no reason why ...'

She was too calm, too resigned, and at that point Cholet lost his own self-possession.

'Lulu, please! You must understand ... I don't know myself how it happened ... I don't care about that woman in the least, and I didn't even look at her ...'

She stared at him, perhaps to find out if he were sincere, and suddenly she flung herself on her bed and started weeping again, her head buried in the pillow, till her breath failed her. She was gasping spasmodically like a sick child, then a fit of coughing seized her.

'Lulu, love ...'

'Yes ... Leave me alone ... I'm a fool ... It's time you went to your paper ...'

'I don't give a damn for the paper!'

It was quite true. He was feeling feverish and yet clear-headed. He was conscious of a sharp split in his mind and feelings.

It was like the effect of alcohol, only with a more intense and insidious glow. The setting affected him: the sordid room, the rain-streaked window-panes, the coarse sheets, and the smell too. And also Lulu's tears, her unselfconscious half-nakedness, the hollows in her neck, the artificial red of her cheeks.

He felt like crying too, but not for any definite reason. It was complex: the whole atmosphere of hopelessness, the drowned man of the previous night, the insulting attitude of Gybal and Layard, the newspaper, his mother, and furthermore, the impossibility of doing something, he wasn't sure what.

He felt a burning in his breast. His eyelids were tingling. He held Lulu in his arms and felt her wet cheek against his own.

198

'My poor kid ... You mustn't ...'

But Lulu was only a pretext. He was really thinking about himself and about his vain efforts to achieve something of which he only had a vague, dreamlike presentiment.

'Don't cry ... I'm very fond of you ... That other doesn't count ...'

And as he said this he was trying to visualize clearly certain features, a man's face above a white waistcoat and tailcoat, to recover a different atmosphere, a smell, an elusive impression.

Lulu was wiping her eyes and trying to smile; she put her hands up to Cholet's chin and looked at him with timorous affection.

'Really and truly?'

He didn't know why, but a tear suddenly ran down his cheek. Lulu, in distress, kissed the tear away.

'Forgive me, Jean! I've been horrid, I've been selfish! I shouldn't have cried, nor even let you see I minded. You're in your rights, of course ... But when I saw ... I was going down the passage ... You'd left the door ajar ...'

She nearly started weeping again, but she controlled herself in time and it all ended with wet kisses mingled with tears.

Out in the street, Cholet walked quickly, for he was late for his visit to the police station. His head felt empty, his breast felt empty, his whole being felt empty to the point of dizziness. He was becoming feverish, but he greedily breathed in the female smell that pervaded his clothes, his skin, his hands.

'Two women!' he thought.

And his face, for all its tragic expression, betrayed a ghost of a smile.

At the newspaper office he did not look at anyone, but people looked at him, for his features were distorted, his eyes shining, and his breath came in jerks. He handed in his copy through the hatch that gave on to the printing works.

Unconsciously he grew calmer. He tried to stay feverish, for it was exciting to feel so intensely alive, to be aware of his own sensitivity and to know that later on he would think back nostalgically about the present moment.

Gillon was watching him with a suspicion that was tinged with instinctive respect, and Cholet self-consciously brushed off a trace of face-powder that lingered on his lapel.

'H'm, h'm!' Gillon coughed, with an arch smile.

'How's your fiancée?'

'Very well . . .'

And Jean in his turn gave a smile, a smile which might mean nothing or a great deal.

'So you're at it in the morning nowadays!' muttered Gillon.

Jean's eyes were sparkling. He no longer tried to recall the image of the man in evening dress but felt it within him, he had that free-and-easy manner, those blasé sceptical eyes, and by his mere presence created around him an atmosphere of sensuality.

Twice, Mademoiselle Berthe passed through the room and each time she avoided looking at him.

'What's the matter with her?' he asked with sham naivety.

'Can't you guess? . . . Hm! . . . Poor girl!'

Gillon went off. Léglise's wife was waiting for her husband on the landing, for they were going to use the lunch break for a visit to the doctor. The typist was taking down the latest messages on the telephone, and her voice was heard saying every few seconds: 'Yes . . . yes . . . yes . . .'

The window in front of Cholet was unrelievedly grey. Rain was still falling; the roofs were glistening. People gradually deserted the office. Léglise went past behind him.

'Not gone yet?'

No! Jean stayed on there, with his elbows on the table, but he really couldn't tell why. When he was alone he felt a bitter taste in his mouth and a sense of vague disquiet, a sort of instability and rootlessness, the fear of some possibly non-existent danger.

The room was empty. He heard the regular purr of the stove, the gurgle of water in a gutter, and Mademoiselle Berthe's voice saying over the telephone:

'Till tonight, then, Monsieur Tomasi. Enjoy your lunch . . .'

And then she got up and moved over to type out her messages. She had sensed immediately, when he came in, that he had just been in bed with a woman. With two women, in fact! But of that she could have no suspicion. What sort of thing could a virgin like that imagine?

He rose and pushed open the baize door that separated them.

'You dictate and I'll type . . .'

This had happened on two or three previous occasions when they had been very busy, at election time for instance. She gave up her place to him in surprise, and sat down beside him with her shorthand pad in her hand.

'". . . and these frauds can only have been perpetrated with the connivance of some official, whom the investigators will inevitably identify . . ."'

'"From Berlin. The Wolff Agency informs us . . ."'

He could see her rather indistinctly out of the corner of his eye, and he noticed chiefly the swell of her breasts under the black woollen dress. He looked down, and seeing the strap shoes and black stockings, imagined the contrast between the blackness and the bare flesh, just above the knees.

'". . . That the Government is determined not to be influenced by these demonstrations . . . by these demonstrations . . ." New para.'

It was the darkest room in the office. Through the window, across the narrow courtyard, another window could be seen, which gave on to a landing and a staircase.

'Would you like me to take over?'

'No, no! You dictate . . .'

He was aware that her mind was no more on the messages than his own. As the time passed, her voice stumbled increasingly over certain syllables, and she found it more difficult to read her own shorthand.

'Do you hate me?' he asked suddenly, still typing.

'Me?'

The clock showed 1 p.m. Debras came in to cut the typed-out messages level with the machine roller. As soon as he had left again Cholet resumed:

'I can guess what people must be saying . . .'

'". . . The Chamber of Deputies will resume its sessions on January 7th and it is believed, in well-informed circles, that the Government's intention is to . . ."'

He put his right hand on Mademoiselle Berthe's knee, and her breathing grew louder.

'They're incapable of understanding!' he said. 'Some people are born to spend their lives in sordid mediocrity ...'

His heart was thumping. He knew there was still time to stop. He would not have liked to see himself in a mirror, for he was aware that his face must have worn a strange expression.

Close beside him, Mademoiselle Berthe sat motionless, as though frozen, and she too must have known that in a few moments it would be too late to stop. He was still grasping her knee through the rough material of her dress. He could see her black stockings. He felt her pulse throbbing.

And he remembered the naked woman on the bed, her muscular belly, the automatic final act. He remembered Lulu and her tears and her blue-veined, goose-pimpled legs.

'Do you really hate me?'

He would not have liked to hear himself, either! Something was urging him on, a kind of despair, of disgust, of anxiety. He wanted to see Mademoiselle Berthe's thighs above those black stockings.

She gave no answer. She averted her head. She was ridiculous in love, with her hard awkward profile and her virginal timorousness.

He leaned over and with a slight effort laid his lips on hers, while her neck, which had momentarily stiffened, relaxed. She didn't even know how to kiss! Her lips barely parted, and his kiss met her large, widely spaced teeth.

To come close to her he had to tilt his chair, which creaked on the floorboards.

'Careful ...' she whispered, as he released her mouth for a moment.

And he saw her mild eyes, eyes that confessed that she had been waiting for a long time but which were pervaded by an innate melancholy.

There was something melancholy about her flesh, too. He had slipped his hand down the front of her dress, and under the heavy garments the skin he touched was damp with sweat. His other hand ran up her leg and under her skirt.

She never stirred. As she sat there, her eyes staring into a private world of her own and her mouth half open, she looked at times like someone dead.

He was reluctant to kiss her again. He did so, to give his hand time to climb higher, to reach the moist thighs which suddenly jerked convulsively.

'Jean ...'

She lay slackly now, increasingly inert, so that he took fright. He was incapable of calling her by her first name. He merely carried on his systematic assault on her most private being, vindictively, and without any physical enjoyment. He tore something, a ribbon or some fabric. When he broke off his kiss, she thrust her head forward a little, blindly seeking him.

And he looked over her forehead and her dark hair to stare at the window. He could see the other window over the way, the drab grey staircase and the head, and then the body, of the hunchbacked book-keeper going up the stairs.

She was unaware of anything. Her whole nervous system was shaken by unexpected spasms. On the other side of the courtyard the book-keeper, as grey as the window and the staircase, had halted and was looking at them. Jean looked at him too; their eyes met. Nobody could have told what the hunchback was thinking.

Then suddenly Jean sat up, knocking over his chair.

'I think someone's coming ...'

She almost lost her balance. Her eyes could not yet adjust to reality. Cholet concealed the window from her, pretending to listen to sounds.

'Quick, dictate the end of the message ...'

He was able to type away quite calmly, but she could scarcely see her shorthand signs. She dared not speak. She hung her head.

'"... and that an imminent ministerial crisis can only be averted by the union of the parties which ... parties which ..."'

She passed her hand over her forehead, repeating the words without taking in their meaning:

'"parties which ..."'

Debras came in and Cholet, with relief, called out:

'Here you are! Just another couple of lines ... "the union of the parties ..."'

The hunchback had moved away from the window.

Jean Cholet did not return to the newspaper office until five o'clock, by which time the whole building was shaking with the pulsating movement of the rotary press. When he appeared, Gillon glanced at him with silent curiosity.

In spite of the noise and vibration, the atmosphere was oppressively quiet. Everyone was reading the newspapers which the boy had brought in, the ink scarcely dry upon them. Léglise offered his hand in silence, as did Gillon. And Mademoiselle Berthe sat crouching in her dark corner.

Cholet knew at once that she had been weeping, that she was still weeping, without tears or sobs, very slowly, as his mother would sometimes weep for days at a time. He said nothing to her, for fear of letting loose the flood of her despair, and he took his seat and switched on his lamp, which cast a circle of light on the newspaper.

'... *and these frauds can only have been perpetrated with the connivance ...*'

Over the way, the round-shouldered, bearded figure of Monsieur Dehourceau was silhouetted against the window-panes. The newsvendors were standing about the courtyard, gossiping. The bookkeeper passed silently by; he always went about in slippers, because he had trouble with his feet. He said nothing, he did not smile, but he might just as well have smiled. Gillon cast a knowing glance at him. Debras crossed the room with a taunting swagger.

Behind the baize door, in her corner which was more dimly lit than the rest because she had put a parchment shade on her lamp, Mademoiselle Berthe must be seeing the printed characters through an unsteady haze.

Cholet had probed the most secret places of her body! He deliberately let his thoughts dwell on it, trying to recall details; details, too, about that morning's encounter with the singer Nelly; and details about Lulu.

He felt steeped in his intimate contact with these women, with their femaleness; he sought for traces of it on and within himself.

Gillon, who was reading a few feet away from his desk, was casting furtive glances at him; after all, Gillon was after the same thing.

It was on Gillon's table that Gybal had sat when he laid down the bank-notes. And when Cholet, dead drunk, had collapsed under that same table, he had just been seeing Speelman.

'*The Chamber of Deputies will resume ...*'

Thousands of people were reading that without suspecting that the man who had written those lines and the woman who had dictated them . . .

The baize door opened. Mademoiselle Berthe, without a word, paused for a moment in front of the mirror on the coat-rack, and then went off, without saying good-bye. When the door closed after her, Gillon half turned his head and remarked pointedly: 'Ahem!'

This time Cholet looked back at him and winked. Gillon winked too.

'You're a brute!'

A second wink, less sincere because of a thought that had just occurred to Jean.

'I bet that won't stop you, this evening . . .'

'By the way, I say . . . you couldn't lend me a hundred francs, could you?'

For he dared not go home to take some of the money from the top of the wardrobe. He thrust the hundred francs in his pocket with a casual air.

'You've got a nerve!'

And then, because the loan required some response, he gave a meaningful glance that implied all that was expected of him. Jean felt he was wearing a starched shirt-front with three diamond studs on his chest.

'If the boss wants me . . .'

He hadn't the patience to wait till the evening to visit the Âne Rouge.

8

Usually, Jean did not carry a key with him, but when he got home would announce his arrival by rattling the flap of the letter-box. He had retained from his schooldays, quite automatically, the habit of bending down to peer through the keyhole. In winter the glazed door into the kitchen, at the end of the passage, was left ajar, so as to let the heat spread through the house.

This time, however, it was closed. Madame Cholet failed to appear. He knocked again, then rang, feeling rather worried because it was after twelve o'clock and his mother had never yet been absent at meal-times.

A window opened in the house next door. Madame Jamar looked out, her head bristling with curlers.

'She went out, Jean.'

'How long ago?'

'About half an hour.'

He thought of going off to lunch in town, but then he caught sight of the bank clerk who lived three houses further down on his way home. The year before, when a key had been lost, they had discovered that the two doors had identical locks.

It was a clear, bright February day, the sort of precocious springtime weather that made tufts of grass shoot up between the paving stones. Jean exchanged a few words with his neighbour and returned the key after opening the door.

He was all alone in the house, and the sounds had an unfamiliar ring. In the kitchen the table was not laid. Nothing was prepared for lunch, and only the lid of the kettle was jerking about under the pressure of the steam. He called, on the off-chance:

'Mother! ... Mother! ...'

He was puzzled. He went upstairs and saw that his parents' room had not been done, which had never happened before. He opened the wardrobe and noticed that his mother must have put on her best clothes.

There was something ominous about all this, and he went down again to make sure that no explanatory note had been left for him.

'Mother!' he kept repeating anxiously.

He went out and made his way hurriedly into the town centre, and then to his father's office. He was sure that something was wrong and that he was in for trouble. What had happened? What had they discovered? He could hardly restrain himself from running.

The office was in a street that was more prosperous and even quieter than the one where the Cholets lived. Jean pushed open the door, which set the bell ringing, and announced himself as usual:

'It's me!'

He went past the guichets. In his father's room the coffee-pot was on the stove, but Monsieur Cholet was nowhere to be seen.

'Isn't he here?' Jean asked a young clerk who was sitting at a typewriter beside the window.

The clerk pointed to the door that led into the boss's room, and Jean sat down on the edge of a table, so impatient that his knees were shaking.

'Your mother's been here a little while ago.'

'How long ago?'

'She's been gone twenty minutes.'

Jean knew the clerk, because he had seen him two or three times at the Âne Rouge with some other young men. The clerk must have remembered too, for he looked with a certain respect at Cholet, who always sat at the artistes' table.

'Are you still having a good time at the Âne?' he ventured.

Jean felt somewhat encouraged. It was nothing, really; an insignificant young man admired him. But it restored his self-confidence. He lit a cigarette, and happened to look over at the house opposite, a fine new house with a gleaming loggia. Behind the glass of this loggia he saw a woman in a light blue housecoat, who seemed to be looking pointedly at him.

The clerk followed the direction of his glance. He got up, blushing, and the woman held up her hand with five fingers outspread, then two fingers of the other hand, which she finally laid on her lips with a smile.

'I understand,' Jean murmured.

His companion smiled. Like Jean, he had an irresolute young face that betrayed the slightest trace of emotion.

'You mustn't tell your father. She's a kept woman.'

Jean could see her, looking relaxed and comfortable as she arranged flowers in a vase, while a ray of sunshine gleamed on one bare shoulder.

'It's a lodging house for women,' the clerk explained in great excitement. 'I got to know this one by signalling across the street and . . .'

The door opened. The manager walked through, wearing his hat; he did not notice Jean. Then Monsieur Cholet came in, carrying a bundle of files.

'Oh, it's you!' he simply said. 'You can go now, Bourgoin, but be back by two o'clock . . .'

While Bourgoin prepared to leave, and his father spread out his lunch on a sheet of newspaper, Jean kept his eyes fixed on the loggia over the way, and the woman in the housecoat that must have been of quilted silk, with her clear well-tended skin and her pleasant smile.

'Have you seen your mother?'

'No. But . . .'

'She's just gone.'

He was watching Bourgoin, and waited to go on speaking till the clerk had left the room. They saw him walk past the windows, and in the loggia the woman in blue leaned forward. Monsieur Cholet got up to pour himself some coffee and then resumed his seat. Jean dared not look at him. He waited tensely, and was aware that his father was opening a drawer and laying something on the desk.

'Jean . . .'

With a single glance, he recognized his watch, and his ears crimsoned. He had bought it a month previously with part of the three thousand francs. He had always longed for a gold precision watch. He had not shown it to his parents, and his mother had probably found it in one of his pockets.

His father, with averted eyes, slowly embarked on a sandwich.

'Your mother's in a fearful state. She declares you'll end up in jail. She wanted to go and see Monsieur Dehourceau.'

'What for?'

'How do I know? I promised her I'd ask you for the truth.'

What was Jean to say? He racked his brains. For weeks now he had been living a lie, or rather an inextricable network of lies. He had to think of something right away, and his glance fell on the loggia opposite, which was now deserted.

'Somebody gave it me,' he said.

His father was eating without appetite, in order to keep himself in countenance and to avoid embarrassing Jean by his immobility.

'Who gave it you?'

'A friend . . . My girl friend . . .'

And with sudden loquacity: 'It's a watch she's always owned. As she no longer has any relatives, it seemed natural to her to make me a present of it . . .'

'You can't tell your mother that. She's convinced you stole it. The other day she found two hundred-franc notes in your pocket . . .'

Monsieur Cholet gazed at his son almost imploringly.

'You're sure you're not doing anything wrong, Jean?'

Jean did not give way to tears. And yet he had never been so close to a passionate confession. Elsewhere, perhaps, he might have made it; but the office was too huge, too cold. The two of them could not bring all that space to life. Outside, people went past from time to time in the bright sunlight.

'Don't you trust me?' he retorted.

It needed only the merest trifle, a word, a gesture; or perhaps if he'd been closer to his father, not three metres away! And if there hadn't been that pleasant loggia over the way, in which the blue figure had reappeared!

'Mother can't understand. She thinks a young man ought to stay virtuous until he's married.'

He knew this had been the case with his father, whose only recreation until the age of twenty-five had been amateur theatricals in a church club.

'I try not to distress her, but she distresses herself, she goes out of her way to do so, like Aunt Poldine who never stops weeping . . .'

He began talking volubly. He was afraid of silence.

'I'm old enough to have a girl friend, and I'm intelligent enough not to let myself get caught.'

'Is she young?' asked Monsieur Cholet, trying to help him out.

'I don't know. About twenty-five, I suppose.'

'She's not trying to get you to marry her?'

Putting on an indignant tone, he replied: 'I should hope not!'

He was getting so excited that he had practically stopped being afraid.

'I feel uneasy myself sometimes,' Monsieur Cholet admitted, as he sipped his coffee. 'You've got a fine career ahead of you, every-body tells me so. I know, of course, that at your age you need to have some fun . . .'

As though to apologize for so long a sermon and to counteract its effect, he inquired with a kindly smile:

'Is she pretty?'

No, Lulu was not pretty. But for Monsieur Cholet's benefit she had to be.

'Very pretty! She's an actress. She just happens to be here at Nantes, for most of the time she's on the Paris stage.'

'Is she nice to you?'

Jean went on lying now, not to deceive himself but to impress his father, and also to prolong the conversation which created a re-assuring atmosphere.

'She does whatever I want. She's more my slave than my mistress.'

'Take care, all the same!'

'Oh, I could easily leave her tomorrow. It amuses me, that's all!'

He was aglow. He no longer wanted to go away. He realized that his father was looking at him with admiring fondness, and he acted his part as he did everywhere, at the office, at the police station, at the night-club. But here he acted it better because he met with neither opposition nor scepticism. His impetus was halted, however, when he glanced at the watch.

'If I let her, she'd be giving me presents every day.'

'What are you going to tell your mother?'

'I don't know yet. I'd like to spare her distress.'

'By the way, you've had no lunch. Would you like to . . .'

Monsieur Cholet indicated the newspaper spread out by way of tablecloth, the remaining sandwich, the cup half full of coffee. Jean had to turn away his face, for his eyes were glistening.

'No, I've got a lunch date in town at half-past one . . .'

He told lies to give pleasure or to get money, to excuse his absence from work or simply to make an impression. He lied profusely; one lie entailed another, and sometimes he felt overwhelmed by so many imaginary things.

'You'll have to think of an explanation. Your mother's suspicious . . .'

Jean suddenly felt weary. But it was no longer possible to check the movement which was sweeping him away, heaven knows where.

'I know! I'll tell her that on January 1st we got an extra month's salary by way of a New Year bonus . . .'

'Do you think she'll believe you?'

His father was rolling a cigarette and tilting his chair a little backward. 'She's capable of going to see Monsieur Dehourceau.'

Jean gave a helpless shrug.

'Take back your watch.'

They no longer had anything to say to one another. And yet it was obvious that Monsieur Cholet would have liked to detain his son a little longer. He was always alone in the office when it was empty between twelve and two.

'Don't you need any money?'

Jean did need money. Only the night before, the fancy had taken him to treat them all to a bottle of champagne, because old Doyen was leaving for Paris. But he said no. He promptly regretted it, because he would have to invent another story elsewhere, and touch somebody from the *Gazette*.

'You're off, then? Good-bye, son!'

Monsieur Cholet dared not say: 'Be careful!' But there was anxiety in his gaze.

'Good-bye, father.'

Walking down the street, however, he burst into tears, perhaps because his nerves were on edge, perhaps also at the thought of the two hundred francs he must at all costs find before that evening. It was an odd sort of weeping. He kept talking to himself in little disjointed sentences. He had had no lunch, but he went straight back to the office, where he found Léglise sweeping up his breadcrumbs.

Mademoiselle Berthe did not speak to him; she avoided looking at him. Her face was even more severe than usual, and this made her look ugly. Even when telephoning her voice was surly.

'Yes . . . yes . . . yes . . .'

She was covering her pad with shorthand signs.

'Have you had lunch already?' Why did Léglise look at him so suspiciously? Everybody looked at him like that, with a mixture of amused curiosity and mistrust. Even Debras watched him through narrowed eyelids.

'You're early!'

'Go to hell!' he replied. And he pulled up a pile of books which had to be reviewed in a few lines. He owed the cashier four hundred francs, and small sums to everyone else. Monsieur Dehourceau was the only person who did not know that he had stopped attending conferences and that he wrote up his reports out of his head. The day before, he had learned at the last minute that the speaker whose speech he was supposed to summarize had been prevented from coming to Nantes.

None the less, at half past nine he would push open the door of the Âne Rouge and go to sit beside Lulu, under the ironical gaze of the singer with the brawny thighs. Some evenings he did not even say a word when Layard teased him, and the pianist had taken to asking, as he put on his shabby raincoat:

'Are you coming, or are you going upstairs?'

In the office mail he found an envelope which they had forgotten to open. It contained a hundred-franc note for a charity appeal, and a letter asking for a few lines about a wedding held the day before. He made sure that there was nobody behind the guichet, slipped the note in his pocket and wrote the paragraph.

On the other side of the courtyard, Monsieur Dehourceau's back was silhouetted in black against the lighted windows.

Mademoiselle Berthe went up to the mirror as though to put on her hat, but then left without a word, her hat in her hand.

9

He went straight up to the bar-counter without looking around him and ordered a marc. It was in a workman's *buvette* at the corner of the street.

'Same again!'

His face was streaming with rain, his features drawn, his eyes staring fixedly. He spoke and moved with exaggerated decisiveness. He paid for his drinks and then plunged into the dark street, towards his home, dizzily, as though the weight of his head were carrying him forward. He saw nothing of what was to right or left of him; all he remembered of that last bistro was a feeling of warmth and a smell of marc.

Then he was at home, in the passage, hanging his raincoat on the bamboo hall-stand. He moved towards the glazed kitchen door, sat down at the table and heard himself greeting his parents:

'Hullo.'

His father and mother had finished eating. Monsieur Cholet was sitting in his wicker armchair near the stove, reading the paper. Madame Cholet got up to serve her son. Jean was aware of all this without paying attention to it, without looking, almost intuitively.

The blood was circulating through his veins so fast that his wrists were throbbing painfully. He could scarcely see, for his pupils were dilated with nervous tension. But above all he had the sensation of hurrying through time, through space, through life, at a terrifying pace, without being able to brake.

It was ended! Ended! Ended!

It had all been ended an hour ago. He had been expecting this for so long that it was a relief. Perhaps, however, it had been a mistake to go into four or five bars and drink two glasses of spirits in each of them. It was all happening too fast! His sensations were too acute!

He saw things that he didn't want to look at, such as, for instance, on the pale green wall, to the right of the window, a calendar bearing the date in large letters: March 23rd.

And immediately opposite it was the china clock which had been going since before he was born: ten minutes past nine! The angle between the hands was widening. The most hateful thing about it was its ticking, which was unlike the ticking of any other clock. He used to hear it when he was very small and spent hours playing trains with an upturned chair. The chair still stood on the other side of the table, but it was never used now because it was broken.

March 23rd; ten minutes past nine!

He ate greedily, breathing hard and looking straight in front of him, and he stuffed his mouth so full that he nearly choked.

'You've been drinking,' his mother said as she sat down.

He gave a sneering laugh; there was no point in answering now. What difference did it make if he'd been drinking or not? His father looked up over the top of his newspaper, then turned over the page, which rustled.

March 23rd!

And they neither of them suspected anything! For them, this was just a slowly-passing evening like any other. The stove purred; from time to time the wicker armchair creaked. And the clock . . .

Jean's hair, wet with rain, clung to his temples. He dared not glance at his father for fear of losing his self-control, of bursting into tears maybe, of breaking down completely.

9.20; still an hour to go!

He had made up his mind. It had to be. But the lump in his throat got bigger. His eyes fell on the chair which used to turn into a train, and he remembered one spring morning when his mother had climbed on to the table, leaving him on the ground amidst his toys, because a mouse was running across the kitchen floor.

Nobody spoke to him. For some time past Madame Cholet had only talked to him when it was absolutely indispensable. She must have wondered at seeing him stay there with his elbows on the table, once he had finished eating.

'I hope you're not going out?'

He merely smiled in reply. No, he wasn't going out! He would spend a quarter of an hour with them, his last quarter of an hour, in the kitchen, by the fireside, and then ...

'You're looking tired,' observed his father, who was reading the local news.

'I'm all right.'

Monsieur Cholet said no more. He did not know that for him, too, this was the last quarter of an hour, the last in which he'd have a son. Perhaps they would never see one another again? Jean dared not look at him. He stared at the wall in front of him, but in spite of that he could see his father's profile and the smoke rising gently from his cigarette. Too gently! He himself filled a pipe, but he forgot to light it and he soon took it out of his mouth because it made the chattering of his teeth too obvious.

March 23rd! 9.25!

The figures on the calendar were horrible, thick, black and shiny. On the mantelpiece there was a coffee tin which had a coloured picture of Robinson Crusoe on each of it sides. Jean got up and held it in his hands. He knew every detail of the four pictures. He had made the scratches in the paint himself, when he was four or five.

Standing behind his father, he could see his almost bald crown with a dent in the middle like a scar.

'I'm going to bed,' he said.

He was at the end of his tether. He bent forward with his eyes closed and put his lips to his father's forehead.

'Good-night, son.'

He felt so unsure of himself that he hardly dared kiss his mother. He bent over, however, and held out his cheek; she touched it lightly.

He ran upstairs; he did not switch on the light. In spite of the cold, he opened the window wide and looked down at the little walled gardens half-hidden in the wet darkness.

His feet were soaking, for his shoes leaked.

March 23rd! Quick! ... Quick! ...

At last his parents came upstairs and went into the next room. High time, too! He listened attentively. His father got into bed first. His mother said:

'He was drunk again.'

'I don't think so.'

'I could tell from hearing him breathe.'

Actually, he was not drunk. Today, no matter how much he drank, he would stay sober.

Lying side by side, his parents went on talking, but it was just a murmur now. They spoke in lowered tones and had turned out the light.

Jean could wait no longer. He took his fibre suitcase from under the wardrobe, opened a cupboard and flung in, at random, underclothes and a suit. Even if they heard him go out they would not worry more than on any other day. He opened the door. In the room on his left, his father was lying on his back waiting for the attack that he had every night at about eleven.

The staircase. The hallway. He grabbed his raincoat from the hall-stand and went out without putting it on. He hurried, half running, skirting the edge of the pavement.

A great shudder shook him, as though danger threatened, when he heard footsteps behind him. It was a neighbour setting out for a game of cards. Apart from the two of them the street was empty, even emptier than all the other streets because of the endless wall of the school.

Cholet had slowed down. His feverishness had abated so much that he stopped for a moment at the end of the bridge, listless, looking at the town and its rows of street lamps. What was he doing there with his little case and his raincoat over his arm, in the pouring rain?

March 23rd.

He no longer felt tearful or emotional. His legs were limp. At the corner of the street he heard the piano in the Âne Rouge and Nelly's shrill voice. He lacked the courage to go in, to speak to them and explain things. In a few minutes Lulu would come out, since the train left at 11.27. The light was on in her room; she must be fastening her suitcase. He set his own down in a doorway while he put on his raincoat, which made his wet jacket cling even more closely to his body.

The lane was empty. The crossroads at the end of it was empty. The whole town was empty, its emptiness lit by thousands of lights. The piano sounded like an instrument being played in an empty room.

Jean stepped back a little and hid in the shadow, so that Lulu should not see him when she came out. She knew nothing; she thought she was leaving alone. They had wept together in one another's arms, the night before.

Layard was sacking her because Nelly, who was livelier and more welcoming to his customers, had imperceptibly taken her place.

'You see, there's something depressing about you,' Layard had told her.

But she did not know that Jean would be going off with her. He hadn't known it himself two hours earlier, and yet the previous evening he had the feeling that he was not really saying good-bye to her.

Whereas this evening, with his father . . .

He felt like running home to kiss his father, and above all to urge him to cling to his son in a long, tight embrace. For his father had said such a casual good-night! He had not thought of living this last evening more intensely than any other.

The door opened. Layard came to fling out his cigarette-end on the pavement. There was hardly anyone inside. Cholet started walking. He went twice to the square outside the theatre, and as he was turning for the third time he saw a woman's figure run across the lane, carrying a suitcase, like an ant bearing a burden bigger than itself.

Jean had only a few steps to take, and they could have walked together, helping one another. But he chose instead to follow Lulu from a distance, as though he had not yet made up his mind. On account of the rain she had put on her oldest coat, a shapeless greenish garment. Her case bumped against her knees at every step. She lurched along with one shoulder higher than the other.

They turned right, then left . . . Here were taxis, stationary trams, a yellow clock: the station . . .

He dashed forward to reach the ticket office at the same time as Lulu. She was saying: 'Third single to Paris.'

'The same for me!'

She gazed at him in astonishment, almost terrified. He was smiling in an odd way, betraying self-conscious pride and a slightly manic elation.

'It's me!'

She thought he was leaving solely on her account. This worried her, and fear mingled with her pleasure.

'You mustn't, Jean!'

But they had to hurry, get their tickets punched, cross the lines and run down the train to find the third class carriages.

'Think it over, do!' she shouted to him without stopping, while her heavy case knocked against her knees; he hadn't thought of relieving her of it.

There were four of them in the compartment, the floor of which was streaked with trickles of water. On the seat opposite, two soldiers kept closing and opening their eyes, each time casting lustful glances at Lulu.

Jean was huddled in a corner, his neck pillowed on his folded raincoat. He had made Lulu lie at full length, with her head on his knees, and she was sleeping or pretending to sleep. It was too hot, in spite of the draughts that suddenly froze one's neck or one's ears. They had tried in vain to dim the light, and its crude glare flooded the compartment. Lulu had taken Jean's hand and laid it against her aching eyes, while the soldiers stared at her exposed legs.

Jean was neither asleep nor awake. The rhythm of the train had taken possession of him and had become the rhythm of his thoughts, the very pulse of his blood. After sitting motionless for some minutes he was forced to move and Lulu's head slipped against his thighs. The first few times she had asked him:

'Aren't you comfortable?'

'Yes, yes!'

'You should lie down too.'

Jean did not even answer. She hadn't understood anything. He shut his eyes and a picture beset him, not always the same picture but always depressing.

For the past month this had often happened, though less forcibly, when he went to bed. He would, for instance, visualize Léglise's little office with its floor strewn with papers, and the journalist's honest face, and himself saying with a falsely casual air:

'Listen ... Just between ourselves ... Yesterday a woman pinched a five-hundred-franc note from me ...'

He didn't want to remember the rest, but it came back by itself: how he'd promised Léglise to return the money at the end of the month, explaining that his parents couldn't understand him ...

It grated painfully on his nerves, just as when his mother scraped the bottom of a saucepan with a knife.

He opened his eyes. One of the soldiers promptly closed his own, to conceal the fact that he had been staring at Lulu's knees. Her cheeks were crimson, her hair was dishevelled. Her scalp, pale as ivory, was visible between her locks.

And then when he'd spoken to the Superintendent in charge of the Vice Squad! It was idiotic! What had impelled him to take the man aside and say to him with a swagger:

'You know the Âne Rouge? I've got a girl friend there, Lulu. Would you be kind enough to let me see her file?'

It wasn't even boastfulness, but a crazy impulse to self-destruction.

Lulu's head was rolling about on his knees. He had to support it with his hand. He felt hot and cold, and his shoulders were damp with rain.

He tried desperately to drive away these pictures, to evade their hold by withdrawing into himself, but then others, cruder and sharper, recurred, such as the feel of Mademoiselle Berthe's cotton knickers and the insipid taste of her half-open mouth.

One soldier was snoring. The other had his eyes half closed and his head was swaying from one shoulder to the other. Lulu's shoes were on the floor.

Jean wanted to think of something else, or rather not to think at all. But then he visualized himself at the office pay-desk, chattering away for a quarter of an hour and finally blurting out:

'By the way, would you advance me two hundred francs on my expense account?'

He owed money to everybody: to his colleague on the *Ouest-Eclair*, to the sub-editor, to Gillon. He could not have said how he spent it. Not on Lulu; rather on endless rounds of drinks at the Âne Rouge, which nobody had asked him to pay for.

The train stopped at a station. They saw a platform, doors, people running.

'Where are we?' Lulu asked, in a voice distorted by her parched lips.

'I don't know.'

'I'm thirsty.'

There was nothing to drink. He was thirsty too. His tongue was coated and his throat burning.

'Can't you sleep?'

'Yes.'

He missed the noise of the train; the stillness threw him off balance, and when they started off again he sank back into his corner with his eyes closed.

He did not want to recall his father. He strove to keep all thought of him at bay. But the whole thing came back to his mind, all the lies he had told, all his exaggerations, all his tricks!

He'd known how to get round his father when he visited his office at midday, telling spicy stories, talking of transitory love affairs and the need to enjoy one's youth. And his father, who had had no youth, had been touched and even vicariously excited.

Lulu had not been glamorous enough, so Cholet had invented a married woman, then a musical comedy star, with all relevant details, the telling of which with a disillusioned air could earn him a couple of hundred francs!

Just at this moment, his father would probably be having one of his attacks, getting out of bed to stand quite still in the dark until the pain in his chest had died down.

Jean had felt for a long time that he couldn't go on living like this. He detested everyone: Monsieur Dehourceau, solemn and weakly good-natured, Léglise who worked twelve hours a day for nine hundred francs a month, and Gillon, particularly Gillon, who was always so spick and span in his striped trousers and braided jacket, self-confident, correct and staid although he was not yet thirty, engaged to the daughter of one of the wealthiest doctors in the town.

Towards five o'clock, when the paper was ready for printing and the walls rattled with the vibration of the rotary press, they all forgathered in the office, and then Jean used to attack his colleague with the gibes that sent Léglise and the typist into fits of laughter.

He worked himself up, he was almost inspired on occasion, giving a marvellous imitation of Gillon's way of walking and talking, sitting or writing.

'You must realize that what interests *me* is the application of this formula to political economy! . . .'

The louder they laughed the more spiteful Jean became, and this very day he had ...

He'd have given anything, everything in the world, half his own life to stop thinking about it!

'What's the matter?' Lulu mumbled sleepily.

'Nothing.'

'You keep wriggling.'

He remembered Gillon standing beside the coat-rack, Léglise putting on his scarf and overcoat, Mademoiselle Berthe bringing in the latest messages. Gillon had just had a telephone call from his fiancée. Jean knew that Lulu was leaving that very night.

'Won't you let us see your lady-love some day?'

Usually Gillon did not reply, letting the flood roll over him with a slight superior smile.

'Is it true that she limps?'

Léglise burst out laughing and that was enough to spur on Cholet.

Gillon looked away. Jean was vaguely aware that the door had opened, but he thought it was Debras, the page-setter, returning with the editor's copy. He was launched now, and couldn't stop.

'Never mind, old man! You mustn't feel ashamed of such a trifle. Her father's a County Councillor, isn't he? That offsets the limp! Limps don't matter when you're as high up as that! As for the squint, there's the hundred thousand franc dowry to ...'

For just a quarter of a second he noticed that Léglise's laughter was more hesitant.

Then someone grabbed him by the ear. Gillon had reacted at last. Cholet could not break free. The hand pulled his head this way and that.

'See here, young fellow! A low-down little bastard who owes money right and left ought to have the decency to keep quiet. Get it?'

There came a more violent shake that nearly threw Jean off his balance. He had time to catch a glimpse of Monsieur Dehourceau standing in the doorway and retreating in some embarrassment.

'Jean, what's the matter with you?'

He was so restless that he kept Lulu awake.

'Nothing. Go to sleep ...'

'You can't keep still.'

'Yes, I can!'

He'd have gone down on his knees to pray to stop thinking about it! His ear still felt hot and sore. Gillon was an idiot, a pompous idiot, as Jean had never ceased telling him, to the great amusement of all their colleagues on the staff. None the less, when he finally stood up again, he had found nothing better to answer Gillon with than a feeble: 'We'll see about that tomorrow.'

He had gone into a bistro and then into another. He had kept on walking in the rain. There wasn't even any need to take a decision; it was already taken! He had been expecting a catastrophe for a long time now; but he would rather it had happened differently. He was breathing hoarsely. Lulu raised herself on one elbow.

'Aren't you feeling well?'

The soldier opposite was looking enviously at them. Lulu smelt of wet hair. She picked up her mud-spattered scarf.

'Go to sleep.'

'Are you wishing you hadn't come?'

'No, no! Please leave me alone.'

He would stop thinking about it. He was aching all over; his toes were stiff with cramp. The train stopped at a big station. Lulu took the opportunity to visit the toilet and came back with powder daubed on her thin cheeks. He looked at her coldly, without the least affection.

'You're not looking well. I did tell you . . .'

She was feeling remorseful. Her brow was furrowed and it made her look like a little old woman.

'Do you think Speelman is in Paris?' he asked.

'I don't know.'

He clung desperately to this thought.

'Lie down again. Put your head here.'

'I must be tiring you.'

The soldier could not go to sleep, nor even take his eyes off the couple who had somehow made the compartment into a bedroom.

'Sleep now!'

He owed fifty francs to Debras, whom he despised. And now he could hear the ticking of the china clock. His father was turning the pages of the newspaper; that would be his last picture of his father, for he would never go back!

He flung out his arm to drive it all away, and he suddenly saw Lulu standing up in front of him.

'Listen, Jean. I don't know what's the matter with you, but ...'

The light hurt his eyes. He looked at the girl without understanding.

'... You ought to get a breath of air ...'

He got up, wearing the same smile as when, a few hours previously, his mother had declared he had been drinking.

For Lulu, too, thought he must be drunk!

10

Jean was waiting underneath the last lamp-post on the right, just at the corner of the Rue Caulaincourt and the Place Constantin-Pecqueur, opposite No. 67, where Lulu lived with her aunt when she was in Paris.

On one side of the door there was a cleaners'; on the other a coal merchant's. Spring was very late. Although it was the end of April, Cholet kept his hands in his pockets so that his fingertips should not be frozen.

It was a quarter past eight. There was no sign of Lulu. Jean had seen most of the tenants come past as they went to empty their dustbins in the courtyard, but he waited patiently, for he was used to it.

When she suddenly appeared she was hatless and coatless, and was carrying an oilcloth shopping bag over her arm. In spite of the buses she ran across the street and took Jean's arm familiarly.

'Come along quickly. I've only a few minutes to spare.'

He was annoyed. Her hair was untidy and her black woollen frock was badly stained.

'Aren't you coming out tonight?'

'No. My aunt's got her pains. I must stay in case she needs a poultice.'

He said nothing. They walked along the pavement as far as the busiest part of the street, beyond the square.

'I've contrived to come out to do some shopping. But what about you? Any good news?'

He shrugged his shoulders; she knew perfectly well that he had no good news.

'What about the *Petit Journal*?'

'I'm to go back there in a few days.'

This was untrue. He had not gone to the *Petit Journal*. He had stayed in his hotel bedroom until three o'clock that afternoon, and since then he had been roaming the streets.

As Lulu was shorter than he was, she hung on to his arm and walked with little skipping steps.

'Wait! I've got to go in here.'

He went in with her. There were five people in front of them, buying butter and eggs, or cooked vegetables which lay, green and yellowish, stagnating in china dishes.

'What about your hotel?' Lulu asked in a low voice, as she felt some artichokes.

'I've had to leave, of course.'

'And the money order you're expecting?'

'It can't be there before tomorrow.'

She cast a brief, sharp glance at him. It was her turn to buy now; she took a couple of cooked artichokes and a quarter of butter, paying with some small change which she counted out on the marble counter.

'Come along.'

Outside, she clasped his arm more tightly. As they drew nearer to No. 67 she slowed down her pace.

'It's quite simple. At eleven o'clock you can come into the house. Mutter some name or other as you go past the concierge's lodge. Go up to the third floor. I'll be waiting behind the door on the left. Eleven o'clock exactly!'

'What about your aunt?'

'She's almost deaf. You'll just have to leave tomorrow morning before she gets up.'

'You really think so?'

'Quick! You'll come? Give me a kiss ...'

And she held out her lips to him, then ran across the street with her shopping bag flapping against her hip.

Jean had not even three francs in his pocket. He turned towards the square and saw that the lights were on already in the Lézard, a night-club something like the Âne Rouge, where he often went with Lulu. In fact, they went there almost every night because Lulu, who used to sing there, did not need to pay for their drinks.

But there was nobody there yet. He chose instead to go down as far as the Place de Clichy, then up the Rue Caulaincourt and down again, to fill in the time until ten o'clock. He was not depressed or desperate; he was less so than in the train which, a month earlier, had brought him from Nantes.

He was drained, that was all! And he hadn't the courage to make the slightest effort. The only step he had taken was to introduce himself to the editor of a leading newspaper. On his card he had written: 'Jean Cholet, of the *Gazette de Nantes.*' He had waited for two hours in a crowded ante-room where the visitors all knew one another, greeted each other with cries of delight and forgathered in corners to whisper. There were a good many elderly gentlemen, well-groomed and well-dressed, decorated with the Legion of Honour, who were shown into the various offices, unless the people from those offices came out to see them.

'By all means, *cher ami*!'

Twice, Cholet had to ask the doorkeeper whether he had been forgotten. The first time he was told:

'The Editor is in conference.'

The second time:

'The Minister is still with him.'

Eventually he was shown into a huge office with red curtains. A hand touched his.

'Please take a seat, my dear *confrère.*'

And Jean talked, blind to his surroundings, saying that he was anxious to make a start in Parisian journalism, that he could do practically anything, including a daily letter.

'That's fine, that's fine! Well, that's understood then. As soon as I see a suitable opening I'll write to you at your newspaper. Please give my kind regards to Monsieur Dehourceau.'

He did not try anywhere else. He felt too alien from everything around him. Everything, even the city! He disliked it. He was frightened of all the people who hurried to work each morning, crowding into greasy bars to gulp down a coffee and a croissant, clinging to the platforms of buses or plunging into the underground.

And even now, as he walked along the almost deserted pavement, he felt a kind of nausea at the thought of the millions of nameless beings swarming around him.

He felt it wasn't worth while making any efforts. The whole thing

226

was temporary. He was waiting for deliverance, but he did not know what form it would take. In any case there was nothing he could do about it, since it could not come from himself.

The third day after his arrival in Paris, after drinking five or six glasses at the Lézard, he had written his parents a long letter which he preferred not to remember. He had been over-excited; in an inflated style, he had talked about escaping from mediocrity, about mastering fate, about making a name for himself in ...

And his father had replied, *poste restante* as requested:

'... if you're in any difficulties, write to me at the office. Better let your mother go on thinking all is well.'

And he had written to him at the office! But not a despairing letter, although he'd had nothing to drink before sitting down in front of a sheet of paper.

'... I'm within reach of my goal ... I've already got a footing in the world of journalism and I've been entrusted with important jobs ... Just now what I urgently need is a dinner jacket, for I'm constantly invited to parties at which one has to wear evening dress ... you can get them for six hundred francs ...'

It was not true! But what did that matter? He had to keep going. He had to wait. Lulu was the one who worried most. The fact was that she was out of a job. She'd tried to see Speelman, but he was on tour somewhere near Bordeaux or Saintes. They had failed to find Gybal either.

'Well, tomorrow I shall have my money order ...'

He had walked three times from the Place Constantin-Pecqueur to the Place de Clichy. It must be nearly ten o'clock now, and he pushed open the door of the night-club, where there were only half a dozen customers. The *patron* came to shake him by the hand.

'How are things? Lulu not here?'

'She's not free tonight.'

Why did he add: 'She's singing at a reception!' He was lying out of habit, or rather for the sake of saying something. Old Doyen had been there for the past week, singing the same gloomy songs.

'Hullo, young man!'

The pianist here was like the one at Nantes. He was as pale and as impassive, with the same contemptuous smile when he looked at his audience.

'A glass of champagne?'

That meant that some customer had left his bottle unfinished. It was the first time Jean had come here alone and, actually, he was only entitled to free drinks when he accompanied Lulu. However, it was warm here, and he sat in his corner of the settee with a whole hour to spend; he had stopped thinking.

'You found anything yet?'

'I've got prospects.'

Neither of them believed that. It didn't matter! Jean was only there, inserted into the life of Montmartre – of the Place Constantin-Pecqueur and the Rue Caulaincourt – as a transient visitor. The surest proof of that was that he didn't even trouble to shave; indeed, he deliberately neglected his appearance.

One of these days he would go away, he didn't know how, but when he was so acutely conscious of something it always happened. At Nantes, too, on that last afternoon, when he went to the office, he'd had a very definite feeling that Lulu would not go away alone. And yet he had not even imagined the possibility of making a complete break, with the paper, with his parents, with the whole town, in order to follow the girl!

Yet it had happened! Everything that had to happen had, in fact, happened! Now, he knew that he was not born to drag out a wretched existence in Paris, nor to be faithful all his life long to a girl like Lulu.

Wasn't this, in fact, why he stared so brazenly at people and took a sort of delight in defying fate? And when he gave way to emotion in Lulu's arms, wasn't there always another Cholet watching Cholet weep?

At this very moment, he could see himself in a big mirror, ensconced in a corner of the settee, one arm stretched out along the top. He had a three days' old beard; his collar was dirty, his tie badly knotted. In the same mirror he could see the pianist sitting upright on his stool, and opposite him a rubicund bourgeois who had come to a Montmartre night-club for the first time with his wife and who was eagerly watching everything.

Cholet must have shocked him, with his feverish eyes, his ravaged face, his faraway look.

Further off, at another table, the *patron* was talking to four people: two men and two women in evening dress. The men were smoking cigars. One of the women pursed her lips to apply her lipstick as though for a kiss, with half-closed eyes. Twice, the *patron* turned towards Cholet and eventually addressed him.

'Hey, old fellow, here's the sub-editor of *Paris-Midi*. Come and be introduced ...'

Jean stood up limply.

'A good friend of ours from Nantes, a very able journalist, who's down on his luck for the moment ...'

'Glad to meet you; do sit down. Will you have something to drink?'

'No, thanks! I only drink water.'

The proprietor couldn't get over this, but he dared not comment. Jean had sat down, and his features were obstinately set.

'You were with Dehourceau?'

'I was.'

'A fine town, Nantes. I remember ...'

'Beastly!'

And he stared insolently at the women. Old Doyen was singing. No one listened to him. Jean spoke louder than anyone else.

'Verrier tells me you're out of a job.'

'In a manner of speaking.'

'What do you mean?'

'I can have a job on the *Petit Journal* whenever I want.'

'And you don't want it?'

'I've my own plans.'

'What's your line?'

'Topics of the day, and foreign affairs.'

He felt an urge to shock them. He had exactly two francs twenty-five in his pocket. He could not be sure the money order would be there next day, nor even that his father would send one at all. He was acting under compulsion from an idea which was not strictly speaking an idea at all, since he could not formulate it clearly to himself. It was more like an impression, almost a superstitious belief: *one had to go right down to the bottom of things!* That was the only way out; once you were at the bottom things couldn't get worse. Now he was not at rock bottom yet, since he still had some money in his pocket and a bed to sleep in tonight!

It was not bravado, and it was not premeditated. There was within him an indefinable hope that impelled him to act thus, that had always impelled him. At Nantes he'd had no need to borrow money from Gillon, and yet he'd done so! He need not have referred to the man's fiancée and her dowry, and yet he'd done so! And now he asked calmly, with his eyes not on the journalist but on the two women:

'Does *Paris-Midi* pay well?'

The man muttered in some embarrassment:

'Better than any other paper.'

'In that case I may go and see the editor.'

He was pleased with himself. He could still see his reflection in the glass, his cheeks flushed as they always were in a heated room, his eyes deeply ringed, his lips colourless.

'You must excuse me. I've an important engagement . . .'

The proprietor, who had not overheard the conversation, caught up with him at the door.

'So what luck?'

'I'm not interested! See you tomorrow . . .'

It was ten to eleven. Lulu had said eleven o'clock. Cholet walked down the pavement between the lamp-posts. He had never walked as much as in Paris. He could hear muffled music sounding from the Lézard, he could see the windows clouded with steam and, through the upper ones, the paintings for sale hanging on the walls.

So the *patron* thought he'd been doing him a good turn by introducing him to the journalist from *Paris-Midi*? And the journalist was convinced he was showing great kindness when he invited Jean to join him at his table! They were fooled, both of them!

And Lulu put on such heroic airs about hiding him in her aunt's flat! Was he supposed to have to thank them all?

He felt cold and stiff in his raincoat, which was torn in two places. He went back to look through the windows of the night-club to see the time: three minutes to eleven!

With a contemptuous laugh, he rang at the door of No. 67. He had to ring twice; then there was a click and he pushed the door open, muttered a name and hurried up the stairs.

Here he felt ill at ease. The floors were not numbered. And he knew now that some houses in Paris count the mezzanine as one floor and others don't. Two ... Three ... It was here, unless the mezzanine counted. The lights went out. He had not discovered where the switch was. Seconds lapsed, and his heart-beats were like the ticking of a clock. He heard a latch lift on the floor below.

He had made a mistake; he should have counted the mezzanine. He went down. The door was ajar and Lulu, in her nightgown, was standing there, frightened, beckoning him in.

It was warm inside. There was a smell of cooking. He bumped into something, probably a hall-stand, but it didn't make as much noise as he had feared. She was holding his hand. A door closed, and Lulu, with her lips close to his ear, whispered almost inaudibly:

'Take your clothes off!'

To reassure himself, he had to make believe it was just a joke, like his introduction to the newspaper sub-editor, and he let his shoes drop on the floor. It was pitch dark. A feeble glimmer came from the courtyard. Very far off, lights could be seen, no bigger than stars.

While he was pulling off his socks, Lulu leaned over to him again. 'My aunt sleeps just behind the wall.'

He smiled. He took off all his clothes and stood there stark naked, since he had no nightwear, thinking of the aunt, whom he pictured as plump and flabby, and knowing that she was less than a yard away from him.

'Mind the springs!' They creaked. Lulu stared apprehensively at the long pallid form of her companion, glimpsed in the darkness.

'Don't move ... Go to sleep ... You've got till seven o'clock, for she never gets up before half-past seven ... No, Jean! Not tonight ...'

But it was just tonight that he wanted to! Sometimes he would go ten days without touching her. Tonight his desire was aroused by the thought of the aunt's closeness on the other side of the wall; there were only sixty centimetres between the three bodies.

Lulu was frozen with fear. She lay unresponsive. And his elbow hit the wall.

'Jean!' she implored. Then, in a whisper: 'Be careful! I can't get up to fix myself ...'

Well, that was her bad luck! Her feet were still cold from waiting for him behind the door. When he collapsed beside her she murmured, controlling her tears:

'You're not kind!'

She lay there quite still. There was a sound of movement from the next room. She would sleep like that, and Cholet was glad of it, for it was the first time. And yet he felt sorry for her too; in fact, his pity was part of his gladness.

He fell asleep with his head on Lulu's thin shoulder, and as he dozed off he felt the closeness of her body, he breathed the odour of the bed, the odour of their two bodies made sharper by the warmth.

Somebody was shaking his shoulder. Lulu stood there in her nightgown, one breast exposed, and her face was distraught. She scarcely dared speak. Her voice was just a breath. Daylight was coming in through the window, beyond which hundreds of roofs were visible.

'Quick! She's up . . .'

Slow, heavy steps sounded somewhere in the apartment.

'Hide under the bed . . . She'll go out at ten o'clock, as she does every morning, and then . . .'

He was dazed. He did not understand at first. But she had already gathered up his scattered garments and was thrusting them under the bed.

'I'll try to bring you some coffee . . .'

The floorboards were cold. Jean was not properly awake. He could see the springs of the mattress coated with dust, and Lulu's feet as she opened the door. He had never yet felt so indifferent, so detached from everything. He was hiding under a bed in a house he did not know, introduced there secretly by a woman he did not love.

For he did not love her! She was too emotional; she had a skinny body and flat breasts. When her hair was not done you could see how scanty it was, and under her make-up her skin was coarse and uncared-for, like a peasant's.

He heard them moving about in another room, and talking. He could not catch the words, but he made out the aunt's louder voice, the sound of the stove being poked, the clink of plates or coffee cups.

The door was standing ajar. He could see in the hallway a bamboo coat-rack, like that in his own home, with an oval mirror at eye-level and Lulu's green coat hanging from the right-hand hook.

232

At this moment the Place Constantin-Pecqueur was presumably deserted and the Lézard closed; dogs would be wandering from one dustbin to another, while shivering office workers hurried towards the bus stop to take their tickets.

In the kitchen they had got a blazing fire going; gusts of hot air and the smell of coffee reached him. It was a slow business; the two women were eating unhurriedly. Then Lulu came back, in her dressing-gown, her bare feet in slippers, and began to dress, with an occasional encouraging little wave at random.

'She'll be off soon!' she whispered. 'She has to go to a funeral.'

He could only see the lower part of her body, the thin legs marked with tiny red scars where she had plucked them. He heard the splash of cold water and glimpsed the edge of a darned towel.

'Don't look,' she muttered. 'Turn to the wall.'

The light that pervaded the room was grey as dust. It shone harshly on Lulu's flesh, revealing the small blue veins in her calves, veins which some day would become varicose. She bent down and put her face to the floor to look under the bed.

'You've not turned away . . .'

'That doesn't matter.'

A shrill voice called: 'Lulu! Come and help me on with my bodice.'

'In a minute.'

She flung down the towel and slipped on her dressing-gown. When she came back she told him:

'Nearly ready now!'

And in fact the aunt presently came into the room. Cholet could only see clean shoes, black woollen stockings, the hem of a black dress.

'Take one and a half litres of milk. If the gas man calls, you'll find the money in the drawer.'

The landing door closed.

'You can come out. Just a minute . . .'

Lulu went to listen, as the footsteps died away down the staircase. When she returned, Jean was standing up and had pulled on his trousers.

'You're not angry?'

'What about?'

'I don't know. You must have been cold. Would you like some hot water? She won't be back before noon.'

He had no desire to stay there until noon. Lulu took him into the kitchen and poured him some coffee.

It was a fairly neat, fairly comfortable home, scarcely shabbier than the Cholets' house in Nantes. There were the same enlarged photographs in the dining-room, which was equally unused, and a stew was already cooking on the stove.

'You're very silent.'

He had never seen Lulu busy in a kitchen. And she did her housework as efficiently as Madame Cholet. She served him, put sugar in his coffee.

'Another croissant?'

Did she, too, feel that something was happening? He didn't know what, and she knew even less. Yet he felt at the same time oppressed and light-hearted. He was sad at the thought that he would never come back to this house, and on the other hand he felt his heart leap up inexplicably at the thought of fresh adventures.

'You're sure you've not caught cold?'

'Quite sure!'

'You mustn't be vexed with me because of last night . . .'

He had to search his memory to recall Lulu's unresponsive body.

'Oh, of course. No, I'm not vexed with you at all.'

'I was so frightened!'

If she only knew how little he cared!

'A drop more coffee?'

'No, thanks.'

He did not even wash. He'd do that somewhere else, any-where else! He did not feel at home; he longed to get outside. Lulu was still half-naked under her dressing-gown, and her body was so meagre that he was loath to look at it in the crude morning light.

'You're forgetting your muffler. When shall I see you?'

'Probably this evening as usual.'

She was on the verge of tears and he didn't want to watch. That was why he was in such a hurry. He was not in the mood for weeping with her, for pitying her, above all for comforting her.

'I've made you a little parcel.'

She slipped it into his raincoat pocket and he did not try to see what it was.

'You see, Jean! It's easy. You can come every day until you're fixed up.'

She was appealing for something, for some effusive display of feeling. But he couldn't respond! He was remote from her already. He felt he was being called away outside, that he was in the wrong place here.

'Good-bye, Lulu.'

'How you said that!'

'What d'you mean?

'I don't know. You've got a funny look.'

They kissed awkwardly in the doorway, keeping it half-open and closing it for a few minutes as the fifth-floor tenant came upstairs with a shopping bag full of provisions. They could hear the dull thud of her feet on the stairs and the cabbages brushing against the wall.

'You're not angry with me?'

'Why should I be?'

He had opened the door again.

'See you tonight!'

'Good luck!'

He turned back and saw her face, partly hidden by the door, as she watched him go down the stairs. He might have smiled to her. He hadn't the heart to.

Down below, he raised his head. She was there, half way up the symmetrical coils of the banister, leaning over and waving to him.

Outside there were sudden wintry showers. The pavements were wet from an earlier rainstorm, but the sun was more dazzling than in summer: a yellow brightness that made one's eyeballs ache.

Cholet went along the Rue Caulaincourt, and twice turned to look at some old woman in black shoes, thinking it might be the aunt. He went into the post office, queued up behind a Czech at the *poste restante* counter and showed his Union of Journalists' card. As on previous days, the clerk examined a pile of letters.

'A telegram,' he announced.

'A money order?'

'No, a telegram. Sign here. Thirty centimes . . .'

He read it in the presence of the people who were waiting behind him.

'Father dead. Return immediately.'

It was all over! He stood there, motionless, reading those four words which were not even signed. It was all over! That was all he could understand. He did not even take in the meaning of the telegram; he shed no tears. When he thrust it into his pocket and looked round him, his gaze was firm and determined.

'Excuse me, madame,' he said, passing in front of a woman through the revolving door.

It was chilly outside. The air was keen and the sun bright. At this time of day the Rue Caulaincourt was almost like a street in a provincial town. Unhesitating, he went past No. 67 without a sideways glance, and crossed the Place Constantin-Pecqueur. The door of the Lézard night-club had just been opened, and the sharp April air flooded into the stuffy room.

With exaggerated bluntness he held out the telegram to the landlord, who was still in pyjamas and slippers.

'Read that!'

And while the other man hesitated to reply:

'I need three hundred francs at once to go home. I'll wire you the money order. And will you please tell Lulu when you see her . . .'

11

The street was asleep, with pavements empty and shutters closed. But when Jean rang at the door of his own home it opened immediately in solemn silence. He went up the steps, and moved towards the lighted kitchen as though he were walking through a cathedral, unaware of the ground he was treading on. The passage seemed endless and the walls were like the rows of chairs in a church.

Noiselessly, the front door closed again, and somebody followed him, trotting along like some pious crone or chair-attendant. It was an aunt whom Jean had not seen since a family quarrel ten years previously.

'Give me your coat.'

Tearfully, she helped him off with his raincoat; she squeezed his hand, and her kiss lingered on his cheek. And once more he started walking amid imaginary organ music. The glazed kitchen door opened of its own accord. Aunt Poldine, all in black, got up and turned to address the back of the room:

'It's your son . . .'

And Madame Cholet raised her head, looked at Jean with reddened eyes, and broke into sobs when he laid his hands on her shoulders. Beside her sat a neighbour, an old man smoking a meerschaum pipe. The other aunt came in out of the passage, and Jean noticed that she was wearing his mother's slippers.

'Where is he?'

That was the question everyone had been waiting for with anguished impatience. Aunt Poldine, her hands crossed on her shawl, sighed: 'Come!'

Madame Cholet rose. 'I want to go with him.'

Everything they said seemed prearranged, part of a ceremony. Jean walked down the passage ahead of the others.

'Yes, in there.'

Then he opened the parlour door. His aunt, behind him, switched on the electric light. His mother attempted to go in, but had to lean for support against the door-post.

The three women stood in the doorway and he was alone in the room, reluctant to go forward. No *chapelle ardente* had been set up. His father was lying, pale and smiling, on something white, a bed or a table. Jean stared at him, clutching his throat in both hands, and he heard Aunt Poldine's voice urging him from the doorway:

'Go and kiss him, dear boy. They're coming presently to lay him in his coffin.'

He stared at her wildly and moved forward, in a world that seemed to be giving way, turning to water. He was frightened. He stared at the three women, twice over, to reassure himself, then he bent down and his lips touched his father's dead forehead.

His energy was used up. He stepped back, incapable of weeping or breathing. He needed something to lean on. Around him the furniture was hidden by sheets. He hurried out of the room, and in the passage, leaning his arm against the wall, he stayed for a moment getting his breath back, biting his lower lip and shivering.

The aunts showed no sign of leaving, nor did the old neighbour who, sitting in the dead man's wicker armchair, was slowly puffing at his pipe.

'Don't you recognize him, Jean? This is Monsieur Nicolas, who used to give you bricks to play with when you were little. He's been very kind to us.'

Monsieur Nicolas was nodding his head. Aunt Léopoldine cut some bread.

'Have something to eat. That's the only way to keep going, as I've been telling your mother ...'

The table was laid, but for an indeterminate meal and an indeterminate number of people. They had been eating all day, one after the other, eating all sorts of things: cold meats, chicken, pickled herrings, three kinds of cheese, preserves and tarts. There were also some bottles of old wine and a flask of brandy.

'I think I left the light on,' said Aunt Lucie, trotting down the passage yet again.

Jean ate. Everybody watched him. Aunt Poldine served him, and nobody thought of uttering reproaches.

'Did you travel third class?'

'Second.'

'Have something to drink. What time did you get the telegram?'

'At ten o'clock this morning. There was no train before one.'

They subdued their voices so as to sound more affectionate. But what seemed strangest to Jean was the atmosphere of respect with which he was surrounded. His mother herself watched him to see what he was going to do, since he was now the only man in the household.

'You ought to go to bed, Monsieur Nicolas.'

'Aren't we going to watch over him?'

'What's the point?'

Jean could hear the ticking of the clock, he could see the calendar, but he was thinking of nothing and feeling nothing. It was all too neutral. The kitchen wasn't itself; the words spoken bore no relation to real life. As a car stopped outside the door Aunt Lucie stood up.

'I expect that's the coffin.'

People were numb; the hours were passing limply. They had wept so much that they were inwardly pervaded by a kind of tepid dampness.

There had been no emotional exchanges between Jean and his mother, who looked to him for advice. Aunt Lucie came up to ask him: 'May they?'

And it was to Jean that Madame Cholet now turned. Sounds were heard at the end of the passage.

'Yes, they may! . . .' he said.

It had happened the day before, some time between twelve and two o'clock. Monsieur Cholet had stayed in the office by himself, as usual. When the clerks came back they had found him on the floor, at the foot of his chair, beside the stove. There was some wine left in his glass and he had only eaten half a sandwich.

'The doctor says it was instantaneous.'

The Police Superintendent had been informed, and he had taken the precaution of ringing up the Public Prosecutor's office. Not until four o'clock had one of the office staff come to ring at the door of the house and tell Madame Cholet that her husband was very ill, but the ambulance bringing back the body had been so quick that she could already see it coming.

Monsieur Nicolas, who was sixty-eight, was breathing deeply with his mouth half open. Aunt Poldine was listening attentively to the hammering going on in the parlour. Jean caught himself lighting a cigarette. He felt quite incapable of thinking. He needed to get used to things, and he looked at the objects around him as if he were seeing them for the first time.

'Do you want to come and see? . . .' whispered Aunt Lucie.

Everyone followed her, even Monsieur Nicolas. The undertaker's men were arranging the last flowers on the coffin. The family looked at one another, and felt better.

'All those flowers!' moaned Madame Cholet.

Aunt Poldine leaned over to ask Jean:

'Shall I give the men a tip?'

Until the end, he had the same sense of living in the midst of organ music, of going down an endless straight avenue amidst people who spoke in low respectful tones and bowed their heads. There were some whom nobody knew and who performed useful tasks apologetically, and others who told everybody what to do.

On the Thursday morning the master of ceremonies had stood beside Jean and turned to him every now and then.

'Everyone's there. I think we might go.'

And Jean, thin, feverish and dry-eyed, his hair still damp with toilet water, had nodded assent.

'I assume these gentlemen of the Press may come immediately after the members of the family?'

He had caught sight of Monsieur Dehourceau's black beard, and of Gillon, and Léglise who had said, showing his bad teeth:

'Please excuse me. I must go and make up the paper . . .'

As he came out, hat in hand, and stood alone on the doorstep, while six men carried the coffin, Jean recognized Layard's jaded face in the crowd.

All the best people were there. Everyone looked solemn, and displayed earnest goodwill.

As though death had purified everything! All previous meannesses seemed to have been burnt, and their ashes scattered. They were not even remembered! Jean walked behind the hearse in a dim world through which trams ran, seeming to restrain the clatter of their wheels. On the pavements, men took off their hats.

Jean stared at the feet of the master of ceremonies, who walked in front of him. Paving-stones were followed by asphalt, then more paving-stones and tram rails. He was aware of the smell of incense, the sound of organ music – real, this time – and when at last he found himself in front of a straw-bottomed chair, alone in an empty row while others crowded behind him, he wept gently, hot free-flowing tears. He could hear the shrill ringing of the altar-boy's bell and the rustle of his black cassock.

His mother was on the other side of the catafalque, at the head of the group of women. Monsieur Dehourceau and his father's employer stood side by side just behind him.

Jean had forgotten Paris. Even by making an effort he could not recall the last few weeks with any vividness. It was all a dead blank. Lulu was remote and dim already.

What he was desperately trying to do was to recall his father's face, and he could scarcely do so. He could picture the rather flabby oval, but he failed to put each of the features in its place or to give any life to the whole. On the other hand, he could hear the voice saying so simply: 'Good-night, son!'

He was weeping.

'Good-night, son . . .'

Had his father known that Jean was unhappy in Paris and that only a miracle could save him? That miracle was – death! And that miracle had brought them all around him today, united in boundless indulgence.

The priest moved round the catafalque, sprinkling it with holy water.

– *Et ne nos inducas in tentationem . . .*

The organ had been silent, but now its serene voice sounded anew.

– *Libera me, Domine . . .*

It really meant liberation for him! Jean was gulping and coughing, incapable of recovering his breath. People turned to look at him. A hand was laid on his shoulder.

'Be a man!'

It was Monsieur Dehourceau speaking, and Jean clung to him for support, which was not withheld. He was choking; he could see through his tears the white surplices surrounding the black shape of the catafalque.

'Be brave!'

'You don't know ... He ... he ...'

There were no words to express it! His father had saved him by dying! Nobody had ever understood what went on between Jean and his father. Only the two of them knew!

'This way,' whispered the master of ceremonies.

Jean did not even wipe his eyes. The fresh air outside dried them, and left his skin smarting where the tears had been. More walking, endless walking. He stared at the ground and yet he could see people, cars, houses. He gave a start when he read on a poster: '*Speelman Touring Company*'. It was quite a recent poster. He did not want to think about it and yet, from then on, something went along with him, something as subtle and seductive as a smile or the faint smell of fine tobacco.

He wanted only his father's image. He tried to picture him, reconstructing him in his mind's eye line by line, in patches, but the whole face remained vague and pallid, whereas Speelman's was as clear as a photograph.

Jean turned round to make sure Speelman was not there; he saw his uncles and cousins, journalists, hundreds of people walking at the same pace all down the endless street, along which a tram was crawling.

A bell rang loudly, the cemetery bell, and the procession slowed down, passed through a gate and moved on between lanes of graves.

'Death must have been instantaneous.'

That comforted Madame Cholet. Jean knew, however, that his father must have had the time, even if his death agony had lasted only the hundredth of a second, to think of him, to picture him sitting on the table as when he used to visit the office.

Nobody knew that. Really, Jean was following the hearse alone. The others did not count, apart from that image of Speelman that clung to him like a fog.

They turned left, then right. They passed from the wealthy section of the cemetery into a suburb where crosses stood askew on their mounds.

Jean was not aware that they had stopped and that the bare coffin was being carried on a stretcher. He could see nothing, except one geranium on a square patch of soil. Then something was thrust into his hand, as a spade, and only then did he perceive the open grave and the coffin at the bottom of it; he threw away the spade, leaning over the hole to shout his grief:

'Father! Father!'

Someone bustled up and drew him away. It was Monsieur Dehourceau again, but Jean did not recognize him until they were much further off.

'You must come and see me as soon as possible, Cholet. I'm counting on you. You must remember your responsibilities now. Your mother! . . . We'll have a talk together.'

They were following an avenue of plane trees. People were walking behind them.

'Of course we shall still have a place for you . . .'

Jean was incapable of thanking him. He turned round, not to look at the procession breaking up and people leaving by short cuts, but to try and glimpse, in the distance, the place where his father . . .

The insurance agent made a little sign to him as though to say:

'When you're ready, I'd like to speak to you.'

He did so at the cemetery gate, while anonymous hands were clasping Jean's.

'As soon as possible, I'd be glad to see you for a moment in the office.'

'Yes.'

Everything was dissolving. The group of black figures had almost completely disappeared and Jean was there alone with a cousin who was an artillery officer and who was wearing a mourning-band on his uniform sleeve. The bell was ringing. At the corner of the street a new funeral procession had begun to appear.

12

His mother had insisted on it.

'You must go and see Monsieur Lenoyer, since he's asked you.'

Jean walked through the town, in the mid-morning sunshine, towards his father's office. They had been through their accounts the previous evening, in the presence of Aunt Poldine, who now only left the house to go to bed; they had even opened the wallet found in Monsieur Cholet's pocket. And they had done so in the kitchen, on the tablecloth, before clearing away the meal. After paying the costs of the funeral they had barely two thousand francs left in the house.

'Since Monsieur Lenoyer has asked you to go! ... When I think, Poldine, that my husband had been with the firm for twenty-two years and that I could never persuade him to ask for a rise! ...'

Jean went past the office of the *Gazette de Nantes* and saw in the distance Gillon making his way to the police station, as he himself used to. The harbour was steeped in sunlight. A Finnish boat was unloading planks of pinewood and you could see them, like gigantic matchsticks, dangling from the arms of cranes.

The air was mild. Jean walked like a convalescent, and looked around him with the eyes of a convalescent, surprised to find himself in an unchanged world.

'*Speelman Touring Company ... Speelman Touring Company ...*'

There were posters everywhere, and he deliberately averted his eyes from them and from the Trianon, on his right, with all its doors open into the darkened house. He walked fast. He left the busy streets and soon recognized, facing the office, the house with the loggia, its windows ablaze with sunlight.

'Is Monsieur Lenoyer there?'

'I'll go and see.'

It was the clerk who sat close to the window, in front of the typewriter. Jean stared at the floor, for he was afraid of seeing on the stove the little blue coffee-pot in which his father used to heat up his coffee.

'Will you go in?'

He wanted to close his eyes. He was specially afraid of a certain spot on the ill-washed floor where the body had been found. He went through the doorway into an office whose only window gave on to the courtyard.

'I'd rather not have bothered you . . .'

Monsieur Lenoyer was a timid man. Although he was not yet forty his round baby face was topped by a shiny bald crown. He had stood up.

'Take a seat. Cigarette? I asked you to come because . . .'

He went to make sure the door was closed.

'It must have been a dreadful shock for you in Paris when you heard . . .'

He sat down, then stood up again.

'You're a man now. Your mother has nobody but you . . .' How many times had Jean heard that during the past few hours!

'You've got to know the whole story, for you would inevitably learn the truth one day or another. It's my duty . . .'

Jean looked at him aggressively. He disliked the man's chubby cheeks, his light prominent eyes, even his way of dressing.

'We did all we could. Your father did not die here . . .' He was alarmed when he saw Jean spring up.

'Please! The secret has been well kept, as you'll have realized. The . . . the accident occurred over the way, and that was what appalled us . . .'

Jean was motionless now.

'And then?'

'There could be no question of telling your mother, particularly as it was all quite recent; I heard from the staff that just within the last few weeks your father had formed the habit . . .'

A sky-blue peignoir floated like a banner between Cholet's eyes and the little man in front of him.

'These things happen, don't they? As a matter of fact I've

repeatedly asked the police to prevent an establishment of that sort being set up so near my office. Well, in short, the Superintendent was very kind. He understood. We let it be thought ... But you know that as well as I do.'

He sat down again, and obviously the hardest part was over for him. Now he regained his self-possession.

'Note that I don't want to tarnish the memory of your father, who was an exemplary worker. But this discovery led me to examine certain accounts. I had intended, at the funeral, to hand over an envelope to your mother.'

He leafed through some papers and then concluded, hurriedly:

'Unfortunately there are some three thousand francs missing and ...'

He stood up, a second later than Jean.

'I'm not asking for the money back. It was about the amount I'd intended to put into the envelope. But you must understand ...'

He hurried after Jean, who had already opened the door and was staring at the stove, at the place where his father used to sit, at the young man by the window and at the loggia.

'Listen ...'

Listen to what? The story of the sandwich and the glass of wine was false! So was the story of the body on the dusty floorboards! Jean opened the street door. He had never been in such a state of agitation. It was not emotion, but something else. He was breathing too fast. His pulse was throbbing rapidly and his imagination was in turmoil.

He did not even glance at the house opposite. He walked very fast and when he stopped it was at the door of a bistro.

'A brandy.'

Beside the bar there was a poster: *Speelman Touring Company*. He drained his glass with a sneering laugh.

'Same again!'

He was thinking of nothing; he could not think. His mind was a chaos of half-formed ideas, of grotesque imagined scenes such as that of the policeman surrounded by women in dressing-gowns screaming and weeping and smiling.

He remembered sitting on a table with his legs dangling, while his father ate his lunch, and telling him stories about women.

'Same again!'

He shrugged his shoulders, because the woman serving him was looking at his mourning clothes and apparently attributing his drunkenness to grief.

But it wasn't that at all! It was rage!

The woman in blue, up there, in her sunny loggia . . . And her little pimp, the clerk . . .

'Filthy lot!' he growled.

'What did you say?'

'Nothing!'

He paid and left, jostling a woman on his way.

The pictures were linking up in his mind, the drama was taking shape. He'd a presentiment of it in the cemetery, when he was vainly trying to banish Speelman.

On one side there was his father . . . On the other side there was Speelman . . . That was all!

It was stupid! It was horrible! And now everybody was being nice to him, of course! They were going to put him back on the right path! The past was blotted out!

He went into a second bistro and leaned his elbows on the bar.

'Something to drink.'

'An apéritif?'

'Anything, I don't care what!'

He had been robbed of his father! Someone had to die, someone had to be a victim, and it was his father who, in that cosy house, behind the shiny pitchpine loggia . . .

'Same again!'

'*Speelman Touring Company* . . .'

Speelman had gone into hiding! He had not been seen again. But now he'd come back. It was all over! He had nothing more to fear!

'How much?'

Jean rubbed his hand through his hair till it stood on end, and a couple of building workers who were drinking white wine looked at him anxiously. He was shaking in the way one shakes when, on board ship, one walks over the steel plates covering the engine room. He hurried on, turning to cast hostile glances at passers-by.

'The three thousand francs that . . .'

He turned about suddenly, for he had just passed a gunsmith's window. There was a stuffed owl displayed amid rifles and revolvers. He went in.

'Give me a Browning.'

'A real Herstal Browning?'

He had all the household's money in his pocket, now that he was its head!

'Load it.'

And he smiled at the gunsmith's look of dismay. Out in the street he kept muttering syllables out loud. He passed once again in front of the *Gazette* offices; they must have known the truth there. They had come to the funeral none the less!

Further on, he stopped short on the edge of the pavement, as though his impetus had been interrupted or he'd been short of breath. People seemed to be hurrying past like ants, with no aim, for no reason.

Luckily there was a bistro!

'A double brandy!'

He pictured the Trianon, the posters, Speelman alongside the hearse, Layard who had in fact been there behind it with his velvet jacket, his flowing bow tie, his weary face.

'Same again!'

He coughed, letting fall a bundle of notes, and almost fell down himself as he bent to pick them up.

'Good-night, son!'

He was aching all over. He left the bar he didn't quite know how, and almost straight away found himself in front of the Âne Rouge. He pushed open the door with his foot and his hand. The *patronne*, who was doing her accounts, looked up.

'You! . . .'

She must have understood at a glance, for she took fright.

'What'll you drink? Wait a minute . . .'

He heard voices next door in the kitchen, where a meal was going on. He recognized Speelman's. But to reach him he would have to go round the bar counter, lifting the flap.

Perhaps he looked like a madman. As the *patronne* hurried into the kitchen, he drew his revolver from his pocket, while Layard appeared, trying to smile.

'So it's you? I say, I was there yesterday, and . . .'

'Where's Speelman?'

The staircase was close by, separated from the main hall by a thin wall, and hurried steps were heard going up. Jean lifted the counter flap. Layard dared not intervene, but just called out:

'I say . . .'

The rings round his eyes had never seemed so livid.

The house reeked of cabbage.

In the stairway Jean yelled: 'Speelman!'

He imagined the man wearing evening dress, running away from him, and he laughed silently. A door opened and closed in the dimly-lit passage, and Jean started running.

'Speelman!'

His head seemed on fire. He rattled the door.

'Speelman, damn you!'

He'd got to see him. The coward, he only had to show himself!

'Speelman!'

He rattled the door, and heard the sound of furniture being pulled against it to make a barricade.

Had Speelman still got the same smile, the same smooth skin and sleek hair and all the rest? . . .

A door opened behind Jean. A woman in a state of undress looked out, uttering a shrill scream at the sight of the weapon; when the door closed again, a heavy lavatory smell lingered in the passage.

'Speelman!'

Cholet's call sounded less resolute. He could hear breathing behind the wall. He pictured Layard crouching at the foot of the stairs, he heard him saying to his wife:

'22.32 . . .'

And she began dialling.

22.32: the police!

The woman behind the door was panting too. They were frightened, the swine! Wasn't the woman Nelly Brémont, with her broad belly and her prominent pubis?

'Speelman!'

But he had lost all conviction. He looked round him in disgust. Speelman was opening his window, ready to call passers-by to his assistance.

'Hullo! 22.32 . . .'

Madame Layard was afraid of being heard from the upper floor! Heavy footsteps came down the stairs. She saw Cholet's feet, his hand clutching the revolver and finally his face, pale but calmer now.

Layard retreated, trying to smile while his back collided with the bottles on the bar.

'Look here, he's done nothing to you ...'

Jean stared at them each in turn, the *patron* with his bags under the eyes and the *patronne* who had put down the telephone now and crept behind her husband. A door opened upstairs; Nelly came out and tiptoed softly to the top of the stairs.

Jean had not seen her; why did he picture her henceforward, in his memory, as wearing a blue peignoir?

'Put it back in your pocket. You can never be sure ...'

He flung the revolver on the floor.

'That's right! Now ...'

There was no point in saying anything. Jean went away, perfectly quiet now. He knocked over a chair at the table where he had spent so many evenings. His hand found the door-latch without an effort.

The Layards, behind the bar-counter, watched him leaving, and they saw his silhouette go past behind the curtain.

He turned back, however. A window was open on the first floor. Somebody retreated, and Cholet did not have time to recognize Speelman's figure.

The theatre doors were being closed. The harbour cranes had stopped, and workmen were resting amongst the piles of planks that smelt of resin.

Jean, walking slowly, crossed the bridges.

For one moment he thought of Lulu, but that reminded him of Speelman who had been to bed with her as he himself, one morning, had been to bed with Nelly, in a room smelling of toilet water and urine.

He opened the door of his home with his latchkey. The aunts and Monsieur Nicolas had gone. The table was laid for two. His mother gazed at him with the innate anxiety of a woman looking to the man on whom she is dependent.

'What did he say?'

She had got up to serve his food.

'Nothing. Monsieur Dehourceau expects me this afternoon.'

Beneath him, to his surprise, there sounded a familiar creak; he had unconsciously taken his seat in the wicker armchair.

MAIGRET IN NEW YORK

Translated by
Adrienne Foulke

1

The ship must have reached quarantine around four in the morning and most of the passengers were asleep. Some had stirred drowsily, hearing the anchor's crash, but very few, in spite of their promises, had had the heart to go up on deck to watch the lights of New York.

The last hours of the crossing had been the hardest. Even now, in the estuary, only a few cable lengths from the Statue of Liberty, a strong swell rocked the ship ... It was raining. Or rather, it was drizzling, a chilly dampness settled down, penetrated everything, turned the decks dark and slippery, lacquered the railings and the metal bulkheads.

But Maigret, the moment the engines stopped, had slipped his heavy overcoat over his pyjamas and gone up on deck, where shadowy figures were striding back and forth, zigzagging, seeming now way above, then way below his head because of the ship's roll.

Puffing on his pipe, he had watched the lights and the other ships that lay waiting for the health and customs people to arrive.

He had not seen Jean Maura. He had passed his cabin, where the light was on, but hadn't knocked. What was the point? He had gone on back to his own cabin to shave. He had taken – he was to remember this as one remembers insignificant details – he had taken one swallow from the bottle of brandy Madame Maigret had slipped in his bag.

What had happened then? This was his first crossing – at fifty-six – and he was surprised to find himself not at all curious, quite unmoved by the picturesque scene.

The ship was coming to life. The stewards could be heard dragging luggage along the corridors, the passengers were ringing for service one after another.

Once dressed, he went up on deck again. The dense fog was

turning milky, the lights were beginning to pale in the concrete pyramid Manhattan offered for his view.

'You're not angry with me, Inspector?'

Young Maura had walked up to him without Maigret's having heard him come. He was pale, but everyone, that morning up on deck, had splotchy skin and bleary eyes.

'Why should I be?'

'You know ... I was so jittery, so tense ... Then when those people asked me to have a drink with them ...'

All the passengers had drunk too much. It was the last night. The bar was about to close. The Americans, especially, wanted to take advantage of the last French liqueurs.

But Jean Maura was barely nineteen. He had just gone through a long period of nervous tension and his intoxication had been rapid and unpleasant, for he was tearful and aggressive by turn.

Maigret had finally put him to bed, around two in the morning. He had had to drag him by force to his cabin where the boy protested, upbraided him, flung at him in rage:

'Just because you're the famous Inspector Maigret doesn't mean you can treat me like a child ... Only one man, you hear, only one man in this world has the right to order me around: that's my father ...'

Now, he was ashamed, heart and stomach both upset; Maigret tried to restore his self-possession, resting his heavy hand on the boy's shoulder.

'It happened to me long before it ever happened to you, young fellow ...'

'I was unkind, unfair ... You see, I kept thinking about my father ...'

'Of course ...'

'I'll be so glad to see him, to know that nothing's happened to him ...'

Maigret was puffing on his pipe in the mist, watching a grey boat tossed up and down by the water skilfully manoeuvre to the ship's ladder. Some officials clambered aboard and disappeared into the captain's quarters.

The holds were being opened. The capstans were already turning. More and more passengers appeared on deck and some, despite the half light, persisted in taking photographs. And there were those who exchanged addresses, promised to see each other again, to write soon. Still others, in the salons, were filling out their customs declarations.

The officials left, the grey boat moved off, and then two launches came to the ship's side bringing the police, health, and immigration officials. Simultaneously breakfast was served in the dining-room.

At what moment did Maigret lose sight of Jean Maura? That was what he had the greatest difficulty establishing later. He had gone to have a cup of coffee, then he had distributed his tips. People he scarcely knew had shaken his hand. Afterwards he had stood in line, in the first-class salon, where a doctor had taken his pulse and looked at his tongue while other officials examined his papers.

Out on deck there was a commotion. Somebody explained that the reporters had just come aboard and were photographing a European minister and a film star.

One detail amused him. He overheard one of the reporters, in looking over the passenger list with the purser, say, or probably say, for Maigret's knowledge of English dated back to his college days:

'Hey! That's the same name as the famous inspector of the Police Judiciaire.'

Where was Maura at that moment? The passengers leaned against the rail; the ship, towed by two tugs, was now approaching the Statue of Liberty.

Small dark boats jammed with people, like underground trains in the rush hour, brushed by the big ship continually: suburbanites these, people from Jersey City or Hoboken who were on their way to work.

'Will you come this way, Monsieur Maigret?'

The steamer had been tied up at the French Line quay and the passengers were filing down the gangway, eager to locate their luggage in customs.

Where was Jean Maura? He searched for him. Then he had to disembark, for they were calling him again. He told himself he would find the young man down on the quay with their luggage, since they had the same initial.

There was no atmosphere of impending tragedy, no tension. Yet

Maigret felt heavy, depressed by the bad crossing and a feeling that he had made a mistake ever to leave his house in Meung-sur-Loire.

He was so keenly aware that he did not belong here! At such moments he readily became grumpy, as he had a horror of crowds and formalities. Since he had trouble understanding what was said to him in English, his mood grew irritable.

Where was Maura? They made him look for his keys, for which, foolishly, he always hunted endlessly and in every pocket before finding them in the one place where inevitably they had to be. He had nothing to declare, but he was none the less requested to undo all the little packages carefully tied by Madame Maigret, who had never had occasion to go through customs.

When it was all over, he caught sight of the purser.

'You haven't seen young Maura?'

'He's no longer on board. He isn't here, either. Do you want me to find out?'

This might have been a railway station, only more hectic, with porters banging bags against one's legs. They searched for Maura everywhere.

'He must have gone, Monsieur Maigret. Someone must have come to meet him?'

Who would have met him, since no one had been notified of his arrival?

There was nothing to do but follow the porter who had taken his luggage. He was unfamiliar with the little silver coins the barman had supplied him with and he did not know how much to give for a tip. He was literally shoved into a yellow cab.

'Hotel St Regis,' he repeated four or five times before making himself understood.

It was perfectly silly. He should never have allowed himself to be moved by this boy. For he was, after all, only a boy. As for Monsieur d'Hoquélus, Maigret began to wonder if he were any more reliable than the young man.

It was raining. They were driving through a filthy neighbourhood where the houses were ugly enough to make one sick. Was this New York?

Ten days ... No, nine days ago, exactly, Maigret was still sitting at his usual place in the Café du Cheval Blanc, in Meung. It was raining there too, for that matter. It rains along the banks of the Loire just as well as in America. Maigret was playing *belote*. It was five o'clock in the afternoon.

After all, was he not a retired official? Was he not enjoying his retirement to the full, and the house he had so lovingly furnished? A house such as he had longed for all his life, one of those country houses that smell of ripening fruit, fresh-mown hay, wax, not to mention the simmering stew, and God knows Madame Maigret knew how to simmer a stew!

Some fools, now and then, would ask with a little smile that infuriated him:

'Not too homesick, Maigret?'

Homesick for what? For the vast, icy corridors of the Police Judiciaire, for the endless investigations, for the days and nights spent in pursuit of some rascal or other?

Well! He was happy. He didn't even read the news in brief, or the accounts of crimes, in the papers. And whenever Lucas came to see him, Lucas who for fifteen years had been his favourite sergeant, it was clearly understood that the slightest allusion to 'Headquarters' was forbidden.

He was playing *belote*. Bidding three-high in trump. At just that moment the waiter came to tell him he was wanted on the telephone and he went over, holding his cards in his hand.

'Is that you, Maigret?'

His wife. For his wife never got used to calling him by anything but his surname.

'There's someone here who's come down from Paris to see you . . .'

He went home, naturally. In front of his house a car of ancient vintage was parked, gleaming, with a uniformed chauffeur at the wheel. Maigret glanced inside and thought he saw an elderly man wrapped in a plaid rug.

He went into the house. Madame Maigret, as always in such cases, waited for him by the door.

She whispered:

'It's a young man. I've shown him into the sitting-room. There's an old gentleman out in the car, maybe his father. I wanted to ask him in, but he said not to worry . . .'

And that is how, stupidly, when in the middle of a quiet game of cards, a man lets himself get shipped off to America!

Always the same song and dance to start with, the same nervousness, the hands clenching and unclenching, the little sidelong glances:

'... I'm familiar with most of your investigations ... I know you're the only man who ... and that ... and so on and so forth ...'

People are invariably convinced that the drama they are living is the most extraordinary one in the world.

'I am only a young man ... You will probably laugh at me ...'

All of them are sure, also, that they will be laughed at, that their case is so unique no one will be able to understand it.

'My name is Jean Maura. I am a student at law school. My father is John Maura ...'

So what? The boy said it as if the whole world owed it to itself to know John Maura.

'John Maura, from New York.'

Maigret grunted, pulling on his pipe.

'The papers speak of him often. Excuse me for telling you, but he's a very rich man, very well known in America. You must know it in order to understand ...'

And he launches into an involved story. To a yawning Maigret who is not the slightest bit interested, who keeps thinking of his *belote*, and who mechanically pours himself a glass of brandy. Madame Maigret can be heard moving backwards and forwards in the kitchen. The cat rubs herself against the Inspector's legs. Through the curtains the old gentleman can be seen dozing in the depths of the car.

'My father and I, you see ... well, we're not like other fathers and sons. I am the only person in the world to him. I am the only one who matters. In spite of being so busy, he writes me a long letter every week. And every year, during vacation, we spend two or three months together, in Italy, Greece, Egypt, India. I've brought you his last letters so you'll understand. Don't think because they're typewritten that he's dictated them. My father always writes his personal letters himself on a portable typewriter.'

'My dear ...'

It is almost the tone one would use with a beloved woman. This father in America worries about everything, about his son's health, his sleep, his dates, his moods, yes, even his dreams. He is anticipating the next holiday with joy. Where shall they go this year, the two of them?

It's very tender, at once maternal and loving.

'I'd like to convince you that I am not a jittery boy who dreams up wild ideas. For about the last six months, something serious has been going on. I don't know what, but I am sure there is something. One senses that my father is afraid, that he's no longer himself, that he feels some danger.

'Furthermore, his way of life has suddenly changed. During the last few months, he's travelled constantly, going from Mexico to California, and from California to Canada, at such a headlong pace that to me it's like a nightmare.

'I was sure you wouldn't believe me ... I've underlined the passages in his letters where he talks about the future with a kind of unspoken terror.

'You'll see how certain words turn up again and again, words he never used before:

"If you were to be alone ..."

"If I were to be taken from you ..."

"When you're alone ..."

"When I am no longer here ..."

'These expressions are more and more frequent, they haunt him, and yet I know my father has an iron constitution. I've cabled his doctor for my own peace of mind. I have his reply. He makes fun of me and assures me that short of an unforeseen accident my father has thirty more years ahead of him ...

'Do you understand?'

The question they all ask:

'Do you understand?'

'I went to see my lawyer, Monsieur d'Hoquélus, whom you no doubt know by reputation. He's an old man, as you know, a man of experience. I showed him the recent letters ... I found him almost as disturbed as I.

'And, yesterday, he told me in confidence that my father has instructed him to undertake some inexplicable transactions.

'Monsieur d'Hoquélus is my father's counsel in France, his confidential representative. He is the person authorized to give me all the money I might need ... Now, recently, my father has ordered him to make substantial gifts to several persons.

'Not in order to disinherit me, you can believe me. On the contrary. Because under simple contracts it is agreed that these sums will later be remitted to me ...

'Why? Since I am his sole heir? ...

'Because he is afraid, don't you agree, that his fortune cannot be passed on to me normally?

'I've brought Monsieur d'Hoquélus with me. He's in the car. If you want to talk to him ...'

How could one not be impressed by the gravity of the old lawyer? And he has more or less the same things to say.

'I am convinced,' he says, weighing his words, 'that an important event has taken place in Joachim Maura's life.'

'Why do you call him Joachim?'

'It's his real first name. In the United States, he took the more common name of John. I, too, am convinced that he feels threatened by a serious danger. When Jean confided in me that he intended to go over there, I didn't have the heart to dissuade him, but I advised him to be accompanied by someone of experience ...'

'Why not yourself?'

'Because of my age, in the first place ... then for reasons that you will understand later, perhaps ... I am convinced that what is needed in New York is a man with experience in police matters. I may add that my instructions have always been to give Jean Maura all the money he might ask for and that, in the present circumstances, I can only approve his wish to ...'

The conversation had lasted for two hours, in undertones, and Monsieur d'Hoquélus had not been unappreciative of Maigret's old brandy. From time to time Maigret heard his wife come to listen at the door, not from curiosity, but to find out if she could lay the table.

How amazed she was when, the car gone, her husband, none too proud for having allowed himself to be persuaded, had announced briefly:

'I'm leaving for America.'

'What did you say?'

And now a yellow taxi was carrying him through streets he did not know, under a fine rain that made the setting gloomy.

Why had Jean Maura disappeared the very moment they reached New York? Should one suppose he had met somebody, or that, in his haste to see his father again, he had casually given his companion the slip?

The streets were becoming more elegant. The cab stopped at the corner of an avenue Maigret did not yet know was famous Fifth Avenue, and a doorman rushed up.

A fresh embarrassment to pay the driver with this strange currency. Then the foyer of the St Regis, the reception desk, where he finally found someone who spoke French.

'I would like to see Mr John Maura.'

'One moment, please.'

'Can you tell me if his son has arrived?'

'No one has asked for Mr Maura this morning.'

'Is he in?'

Frostily polite, the clerk replied, lifting the telephone receiver:

'I will ask his secretary.'

Then, into the instrument:

'Hello ... Mr MacGill? This is the desk speaking. There is someone here asking to see Mr Maura ... What did you say? ... I'll ask him ... May I have your name, sir?'

'Maigret ...'

'Hello ... Mr Maigret ... Very well ... One moment.'

And, hanging up:

'Mr MacGill asks me to tell you that Mr Maura sees people only by appointment ... If you want to write to him and give him your address, he will certainly answer your letter.'

'Will you kindly tell this Mr MacGill that I've just come from France expressly to meet Mr Maura and that I have important things to say to him.'

'I'm sorry. The gentlemen would never forgive me for disturbing them again. But if you will take the trouble to write him a word, here, in the lounge, I'll send your note up with a bellboy.'

Maigret was furious, more with this man than with MacGill, whom he did not know but was beginning already to detest. As he detested, *in toto*, and in advance, everything around him, the ornate foyer, the bellboys who watched him ironically, the pretty women who came in and out, the self-assured men who elbowed him without deigning to excuse themselves.

Sir:
I have just arrived from France, entrusted with an important mission by your son and Mr d'Hoquélus. Since my time is as precious as your own, I would be obliged if you received me immediately.

Very truly yours,
Maigret

They let him cool his heels for a good quarter of an hour and, peevishly, he smoked his pipe, although he realized this was not the proper place. A bellboy finally came to look for him and went with him into a lift, piloted him the length of a corridor, knocked on a door, and abandoned him.

'Come in.'

Why had he pictured MacGill as a middle-aged, surly man? Here was a tall young man, well built, and smartly dressed, who came towards him with outstretched hand.

'Forgive me, sir, but Mr Maura is so beset by petitioners of all sorts that we are forced to raise a barrier around him. You say you come from France. Am I to understand that you are the – the ex – that is, the –'

'Ex-Inspector Maigret, yes.'

'Sit down, please . . . A cigar?'

There were several boxes on the table. The room was immense. A drawing-room, modified by a large mahogany desk that did not, however, make it look like an office.

Maigret, disdaining the Havana cigar, had once more filled his pipe and was studying Mr MacGill with no particular warmth.

'Your note said you bring news of Mr Jean?'

'With your permission, I shall speak to Mr Maura personally about that as soon as you are good enough to take me to him.'

MacGill revealed all his teeth, which were very fine, in a smile.

'It's easy to see, sir, that you come from Europe. Otherwise, you would know that John Maura is one of the busiest men in New York, that I myself, at this moment, have no idea where he may be, and finally that I am entrusted with all his affairs, including the most private. So you can talk to me freely and tell me –'

'I will wait until Mr Maura consents to see me.'

'Even so, he would have to know what it is about.'

'I have told you, about his son . . .'

'Am I, given your calling, to suppose that he has done something foolish?'

Maigret did not stir, did not answer, and continued to examine MacGill coldly.

'Forgive my insistence, Inspector. I suppose, although you are retired, according to what I've read in the papers, that people still call you by your rank . . . Forgive me, as I say, if I remind you that we are in the United States and not in France and that John Maura's time is precious . . . Jean is a charming boy, a little too sensitive, perhaps, but I wonder what he could –'

Maigret rose quietly, picked up the hat he had set on the carpet by his chair.

'I am taking a room in this hotel. When Mr Maura has decided to see me . . .'

'He won't be back in New York for two weeks.'

'Can you tell me where he is now?'

'That's difficult. He travels by plane and, the day before yesterday, he was in Panama. Perhaps, today, he has landed at Rio or in Venezuela . . .'

'Thank you.'

'You have friends in New York, Inspector?'

'No one except for a few police officials with whom I've had occasion to work.'

'May I invite you to lunch?'

'I think I will lunch with one of them . . .'

'And if I insisted? I'm sorry for the role which my position obliges me to play and I venture to hope you will not hold it against me . . . I am older than Jean, but not by much, and I am very fond of him. You have not even given me any news of him –'

'Excuse me . . . May I know how long you have been Mr Maura's private secretary?'

'For about six months. I mean that I have been with him for about six months, but I've known him for a long time, if not always.'

Someone was walking about in the next room. Maigret saw MacGill's face change colour. The secretary listened apprehensively to the approaching footsteps, watched the gilded knob on the connecting door turn slowly. Then the door opened.

'Come here a moment, Jos –'

A thin, nervous face, under hair still blond but shot through with white. His glance frowned on Maigret. The secretary moved quickly, but the new arrival had already changed his mind and come into the office, his eyes fastened on Maigret.

'It seems to me . . .' he began, as one does, thinking one recognizes another, and searching for the name.

'Inspector Maigret, of the Police Judiciaire . . . More exactly, ex-Inspector Maigret, since I have been retired for a year.'

John Maura was short, of less than average height, spare, but obviously endowed with uncommon energy.

'You wish to speak to me?'

He turned to MacGill without awaiting a reply.

'What is it, Jos?'

'I don't know, Chief. The Inspector –'.

'If it is all the same to you, Mr Maura, I would like to talk to you alone. It is about your son . . .'

But not one line of the face of the man who wrote such tender letters moved.

'You can speak in front of my secretary.'

'Very well . . . Your son is in New York.'

And Maigret's eyes did not leave either man. Was he mistaken? He had the very distinct impression that MacGill reacted visibly, while Maura remained imperturbable, uttering a noncommittal:

'Ah!'

'It does not surprise you?'

'You no doubt know that my son is absolutely free?'

'It doesn't in the least surprise you that he hasn't come to see you yet?'

'Since I don't know when he may have arrived . . .'

'He arrived this morning, with me . . .'

'In that case, you must know . . .'

'That's just it, I know nothing at all. In the confusion of landing and customs, I lost sight of him. The last time I saw him, and talked to him, the ship was still anchored in quarantine.'

'He may conceivably have met some friends.'

And John Maura slowly lighted a long cigar, stamped with his own initials.

'I am sorry, Inspector, but I don't see how my son's arrival –'

'Has any connection with my visit?'

'That is more or less what I meant. I am extremely busy this morning. With your permission, I shall leave you with my secretary, to whom you can talk with complete freedom. Excuse me, Inspector.'

A rather dry nod. He turned and disappeared by the way he had come. MacGill hesitated a second, murmured:

'Excuse me.'

And he disappeared on the heels of his employer, and closed the door. Maigret was alone in the office, alone and not at all proud of himself. He heard them whispering in the next room. He was going to leave, furious, when the secretary reappeared, alert and smiling.

'You see, sir, you were wrong to be on your guard with me.'

'I thought Mr Maura was in Venezuela or Rio?'

The man laughed.

'At the Quai des Orfèvres, with your heavy responsibilities, didn't you ever use a white lie to get rid of a visitor?'

'Thank you indeed for having done as much to me!'

'Come now. Don't hold it against me. What time is it? Eleven-thirty. If you don't mind, I'll phone the desk to reserve you a room, otherwise you'd have trouble getting one. The St Regis is one of the most sought after hotels in New York. I'll give you time to have a bath and change and, if you like, we'll meet at the bar at one, and afterwards go on to lunch together.'

Maigret was tempted to refuse and, with his gruffest air, to walk out. He would have been quite capable, had there been a ship for Europe that evening, of re-embarking without making any further acquaintance with this city that had given him such a rude welcome.

'Hello. Reservations, please. This is MacGill. Hello, yes. Will you be good enough to reserve a room for a friend of Mr Maura? ... Yes ... Mr Maigret ... Thank you.'

And, turning to the Inspector:

'Do you speak English at all?'

'Like all those who learned it in college and forgot it.'

'In that case, you'll have a little trouble at first. Is this your first trip to the States? ... Please feel that I am at your disposal, as far as I can call my time my own.'

There was someone behind the door, John Maura, no doubt. MacGill knew it too, but it did not seem to disturb him.

'Just follow the bellboy. See you later, Inspector. And no doubt Jean Maura will have reappeared in time to have lunch with us. I'll have your luggage sent up to you.'

A lift once more. A sitting-room, a bedroom, a bath, a porter waiting for his tip, and Maigret staring at him blankly, having rarely been so confused, indeed so humiliated in his life.

To think that, ten days before, he was peacefully playing *belote* with the mayor of Meung, the doctor, and the fertilizer merchant, in the warm and always slightly dusky room of the Cheval Blanc!

2

Surely this redheaded man was a kind of benevolent genie? On 49th Street, two steps from Broadway's lights, its hubbub, he walked down several steps as if he were about to dive into a cellar, and pushed open a door. On the window of the door there was a red and white check curtain. That same democratic checked cloth, which recalled the cafés of Montmartre and the Paris suburbs, was to be found on the tables and here, too, were the zinc-covered bar, the smell of familiar cooking, the plumpish *patronne*, slightly provincial, who came over to ask:

'What are you going to eat, *mes enfants*? There's always steak, of course, but today, I have a *coq au vin* such as ...'

And there was O'Brien, smiling a very sweet, almost shy smile.

'You see,' he said to Maigret, not without a touch of irony, 'New York is not what one thinks.'

And soon there appeared on the table a genuine Beaujolais to accompany the *coq au vin* which steamed in their plates.

'You won't try to tell me, Captain, that Americans are in the habit –'

'Of eating the way we are this evening? Perhaps not every day. Perhaps not everyone. But, actually, there are quite a few of us who don't dislike the cooking of the old countries, and I could find you a hundred restaurants like this in town. You landed this morning. That gives you less than twelve hours and you feel quite at home already, don't you? ... Now, go on with your story.'

'This MacGill, as I told you, was waiting for me at the bar in the St Regis. I sensed immediately that he had decided to change his attitude towards me.'

It had been six o'clock before Maigret, freed of MacGill, who had attached himself to him the whole afternoon, could telephone

Special Agent O'Brien, of the FBI, whom he had known in France, several years before, in the course of an important international case.

Nothing could be more gentle, more calm than this big, woolly-haired, redheaded man, so shy that timidity could still make him blush at the age of forty-six.

He had arranged to meet the Inspector in the St Regis lounge. As soon as the latter had mentioned Maura, he had taken his colleague out to a little bar near Broadway.

'I suppose you don't like whisky or cocktails?'

'I confess that if it is possible to get a beer . . .'

It was a nondescript place. A few men at the bar and lovers at four or five tables drowned in shadows. Wasn't it a strange idea to take him to a place like this?

Wasn't it even stranger to see O'Brien search for a coin in his pocket and gravely slip it in the slot of an automatic record player, which began to play a stickily sentimental tune?

And the redheaded man smiled as he observed his colleague with amused eyes.

'You don't like music?'

Maigret had not yet had time to get rid of all his bad temper and he could not help but let it be felt.

'Well. I won't keep you dangling. You see this machine that grinds out music . . . I've just put a nickel, five cents, in the slot and that gives me the right to about a minute and a half's worth of some tune. There are several thousand machines like this in the bars, the taverns, and the restaurants of New York. There are tens of thousands of them in other cities of the United States all the way to the most remote little villages. Right now, this very minute, while you and I are talking, at least fifty per cent of these instruments that seem barbaric to you are in use; in other words, people are putting five cents in each of them, and that makes thousands and thousands of times five cents, which makes . . . But I'm not very good at arithmetic.

'But do you know to whom these nickels, as we call them, go? To your friend John Maura, better known in the United States as Little John, because he's so short.

'And Little John has installed identical machines, on which he's got some sort of monopoly, in most of the Latin American republics.

'Now do you understand that Little John is a personage of some importance?'

Always this barely perceptible touch of irony, to a point where Maigret, who was not used to it, still wondered whether his companion was naive or if he was making fun of him.

'Now, we can go and have dinner and you'll tell me your story.'

They were having dinner now, warm and comfortable, whilst outside the wind blew in such strong gusts that passers-by bent double as they walked, people chased their hats, and women had to hold their skirts down with both hands. The storm, probably the same one Maigret had suffered at sea, had reached the coast, and New York shook under the blast: from time to time signs ripped loose, or debris came tumbling down from the tops of buildings. Even the yellow cabs seemed to have difficulty ploughing their way through the wind.

It had begun just after lunch, as MacGill and Maigret were leaving the St Regis.

'You know Maura's secretary?' he asked O'Brien now.

'Hardly. You see, my dear Inspector, the police, here, are not quite the same as in France. I regret it, actually, for our job would be much easier. We have a highly developed sense of the freedom of the individual and, if I took the liberty of inquiring, even discreetly, about a man against whom I had no precise charge, I would be putting myself in a very bad spot.

'Now, Little John, I must tell you, is no gangster. He is a big businessman, well established and well thought of, who lives all the year round in a luxurious apartment at the St Regis, one of our best hotels.

'We have no reason, therefore, to concern ourselves with him or his secretary.'

Why this vague and yet mischievous smile that seemed somehow to qualify what he said? It annoyed Maigret a little. He felt foreign and, like every foreigner, he easily got the impression he was being made fun of.

'I am not a reader of detective stories and I don't expect to find America peopled with gangsters,' he replied testily.

'To come back to this MacGill, who, in spite of his name, strikes me as probably being of French origin . . .'

And the other man, again, with his exasperating blandness:

'It's hard, in New York, to unravel people's exact origins!'

'I was saying that, from the *apéritif* on, he put himself out to appear as cordial as he had been otherwise this morning. He informed me that they still had no word from young Maura, that his father was not worried yet, because he supposed there was some woman behind this escapade, and he questioned me about the women passengers . . .'

'Now it's a fact that during the crossing Jean Maura seemed taken with one passenger, a young Chilean woman, who is leaving tomorrow for Latin America on one of the Grace Line ships.'

French was being spoken at most of the tables and the *patronne* went from customer to customer, affable, a little vulgar, inquiring in her savoury Toulouse accent:

'*Ca va, les enfants*? . . . What do you say to this *coq au vin*? . . . Afterwards, if you feel like it, there's mocha cake, homemade . . .'

Lunch had been very different, in the main dining-room of the St Regis, where MacGill greeted people by the dozen. At the same time he was very attentive to Maigret, talking to him volubly. Now what had he had to say? That John Maura was a very busy man, somewhat eccentric, had a horror of new faces, and was suspicious of everybody.

Why shouldn't he have been surprised, this morning, to have a man like Maigret arrive to see him?

'He doesn't like people to concern themselves with his affairs, you see? Particularly family matters. Look! I am sure he adores his son, and yet, he never says a word about him even to me, and I work more closely with him than anyone.'

What was he driving at? It was easy to guess. He was obviously trying to find out why Maigret had travelled across the Atlantic in Jean Maura's company.

MacGill went on:

'I've had a long talk with the Chief. He's instructed me to find out about his son. I have an appointment presently, here in the hotel, with a private detective whom we've hired in the past for some little things, a first-rate man who knows New York almost as well as you know Paris. If it appeals to you, you can come with us, and it would surprise me if, by this evening, we haven't found our young man.'

All this Maigret now recounted to O'Brien, who listened to him while relishing his dinner with a rather exasperating leisureliness.

'In fact, a man was waiting for us in the lounge when we left the dining-room.'

'Do you know his name?'

'We were introduced, but I confess I caught only his first name ... Bill ... Yes, that's right, Bill ... I've seen so many people, today, and MacGill calls them all by their first name, so that I admit I'm a little lost.'

That smile again.

'You'll get used to it. It's an American custom ... What's he like, this Bill of yours?'

'Rather tall, rather heavy-set. About my size. Broken nose and scar down the middle of his chin.'

O'Brien certainly knew him, for his eyelids flickered, but he said nothing.

'We took a cab and went over to the French Line quay.'

The storm had been at its peak. The wind had not yet driven off the rain, which fell on them in sheets every time they got out of the cab. Bill conducted operations, energetically chewing gum, his hat pushed back in the most traditional movie style. In fact, had he taken that hat off once during the whole afternoon? Probably not. But then, maybe he was bald!

He spoke to people, the customs men, stewards, company employees, with equal familiarity, sitting on the edge of a table or desk, tossing out a few casual questions in a slow drawl. If Maigret did not understand everything he said, he understood enough to certify that it was a job well done, the work of a real professional.

First, customs ... Jean Maura's luggage had been claimed ... At what time? ... They leafed through the receipts ... A little before noon ... No, they had not been taken into town by any of the trucking firms that had offices on the pier ... Therefore, they had been taken by taxi or in a private car.

The person who had claimed the luggage had the keys. Was it Jean Maura in person? Impossible to make sure of that. Several hundred passengers had passed through that morning and others were still coming to claim their luggage.

Next, the ship's purser. It gave him a funny feeling to go aboard an empty ship, to find it deserted after having known it bubbling with activity, to watch the gigantic cleaning up and all the preparations for a new crossing.

No possible doubt, Maura had left the ship and handed over his customs forms on leaving ... At what time? ... No one remembered ... Probably among the first passengers, at the height of the rush.

The steward ... He recalled definitely that, around eight in the morning, shortly after the arrival of the immigration and health officers, young Maura had given him his tip ... And the steward, at that moment, had set his overnight case down near the gangway ... No, the young man was not nervous at all ... A bit tired ... He must have had a headache, for he had taken some aspirin. The empty bottle had remained on the shelf in the bathroom.

The imperturbable Bill with the exasperating gum dragged them still further. At the French Line offices, on Fifth Avenue, he leaned against the mahogany counter and carefully studied the passenger list.

Then, from a drugstore, he telephoned the harbour police.

MacGill was getting nervous. Maigret's impression was that he did not want to show it, but, as one step followed another, it was evident that he grew restive.

There was something amiss, something that must not have tallied with what he'd expected, for, from time to time, Bill and he exchanged a quick glance.

And now, as the Inspector told O'Brien about the day's happenings, the latter, also, was becoming more grave and sat sometimes with his fork in mid-air, forgetting to eat.

'They came across the name of the Chilean girl on the passenger list and they managed to find out the name of the hotel where she was staying between boats. It's a hotel on 66th Street ... We went there ... Bill questioned the doorman, the desk clerk, and the lift men, but they knew nothing about Jean Maura.

'Then Bill gave the driver the address of a bar, near Broadway ... On the way he spoke to MacGill so fast I couldn't understand ... I took note of the name of the bar, the Donkey Bar ... What are you smiling for?'

'Nothing,' O'Brien replied. 'Actually, for your first day in New York, you covered a lot of ground ... You've even gotten to know the Donkey Bar, which is not bad at all ... What do you think of it?'

Again this impression that he was being teased, in a friendly way, but teased just the same.

'Straight out of Hollywood,' he grunted.

A long smoke-filled room, an endless bar with the inevitable bar stools and multicoloured bottles, a Negro barman and a Chinese barman, the juke box, and the dispensing machines for cigarettes, gum, and roasted peanuts.

Everybody at the bar knew everybody else, or seemed to. Everybody called each other Bob, or Dick, or Tom, or Tony, and the two or three women appeared as much at home there as the men.

'It seems,' said Maigret, 'that it's a meeting place for newspaper and theatre people ...'

And the other murmured, with a smile:

'More or less.'

'Our detective wanted to see a reporter he knows who covers ship arrivals and who must have come aboard this morning. We did meet him, dead drunk or just about ... He generally is, I was told, after three or four in the afternoon ...'

'You know his name?'

'Vaguely ... Something like Parson ... Jim Parson, if I'm not mistaken ... He has straw-coloured hair and bloodshot eyes, and nicotine stains around the mouth ...'

O'Brien might protest as much as he liked that the American police had no right to concern themselves with people who had nothing on their conscience, but just the same it was rather curious that from each name Maigret mentioned, each new description, the redhead seemed to recognize the fellow perfectly.

So the Inspector could not refrain from observing:

'You are sure that the police in your country are so different from ours?'

'Very! What did Jim have to say?'

'I understood only snatches now and then. Drunk as he was, he seemed very much interested. I must add that the detective had pushed him into a corner and talked to him roughly, giving it to him straight from the shoulder, as they say, and pinning him firmly against the wall. The other fellow was trying to remember something. Then he staggered into a phone booth and through the glass I saw him dial four different numbers.

'During all this, MacGill explained to me:

'"You see, it's still through the reporters on board that we have the best chance of finding out something. Those fellows have the habit of observing things. They know everybody ..."'

'However, Jim Parson came out of the booth puzzled and a minute later ordered a double whisky.

'He's supposed to continue making inquiries. If he's to inquire at bars, he must be stiff by now, for I've never seen anyone down his drinks so fast.'

'You will. In short, if I understand correctly, Jos MacGill seemed to you, this afternoon, very anxious to find his boss's son.'

'Whereas, this morning, he didn't want to be bothered.'

O'Brien was pretty concerned, after all.

'What do you plan to do?'

'I'll tell you frankly, I wouldn't mind finding the boy.'

'You don't seem to be the only one.'

'You have an idea, don't you?'

'I remember, my dear Inspector, something you said to me in Paris, during one of our talks at the Brasserie Dauphine ... Do you remember?'

'Our talks, yes, but not this particular remark ...'

'I was asking you more or less the same question you've just asked me and you puffed on your pipe and replied:

'"Me? I never have any ideas!"'

'And so, my dear Maigret, if you allow me to call you that, I am like you, at least at this moment, which proves that all the police in the world do have some things in common.

'I don't know anything. I have no knowledge, or practically none – just what everybody else knows – of Little John's affairs or of the people around him.

'I didn't even know he had a son.

'And, to top this off, I belong to the FBI, which concerns itself only with certain clearly defined crimes. In other words, if I were

274

so ill-advised as to stick my nose into this business, I would stand every chance of being given a dressing down.

'I imagine that it isn't advice you want from me?'

Lighting his pipe, Maigret growled:

'No.'

'Because, if it were advice you wanted, I would say this:

'"My wife is in Florida at the moment, she can't stand the winter in New York ... So I am alone, for my son is away at college and my daughter got married two years ago ... Consequently, I have a few free evenings ... I am delighted to put them at your disposal to introduce you to New York as you once upon a time introduced me to Paris."

'As for the rest, you see ... How do you put it again? ... Wait ... No, don't tell me ... I've remembered a few expressions of yours and often repeat them to my colleagues ... Oh yes! For the rest, *drop it*.

'I know perfectly well that you won't. So, if you feel like it, you can come chat with me once in a while.

'I can't prevent a man like you from asking me questions, can I?'

'And there are some questions it's very hard not to answer.

'Look! For example, I am sure you would like to see my office ... I remember yours, with the windows looking out over the Seine. Mine looks out more prosaically on a tall blank wall and a parking lot.

'You must admit that the Armagnac is excellent and this little *bistro*, as you people say, is not too bad!'

Just as in some Paris restaurants, they had to compliment the *patronne* and even the chef, promise to come back, drink a last drink, and finally sign a gilt and slightly greasy guest book.

The two men, a little later, found a cab and O'Brien gave an address to the driver.

Each smoked his pipe in his corner, and there was a rather long silence. Each, as if by chance, started to speak at the same moment and they looked at each other, smiling at the coincidence.

'What were you about to say?'

'And you?'

'Probably the same thing.'

'I was going to say,' the American began, 'that MacGill, according to what you've told me, had no wish for you to meet his boss.'

'I was thinking just that. And yet, contrary to what I expected, Little John didn't seem any more eager than his secretary to have news of his son. See what I mean?'

'And it was MacGill, later, who hustled around or pretended to be very busy trying to locate the young man.'

'And who went to a lot of trouble on my account ... He told me he would phone me tomorrow morning to give me any news.'

'He knows we're seeing each other tonight?'

'I didn't mention it to him.'

'He guesses as much. Not that you are seeing me, personally, but someone from the police. Given the connections you've had with the American police, it's inevitable ... And, in that case ...'

'In that case?'

'Nothing ... Here we are.'

They went into a tall building and seconds later the lift deposited them in a corridor lined with numbered doors. O'Brien unlocked one, switched on the light.

'Sit down ... I'll do the honours of the house for you another day because, at this time of night, you wouldn't see it at its best ... Will you excuse me if I leave you to yourself for a few minutes?'

The few minutes were a good quarter of an hour and the whole time Maigret caught himself thinking of nothing but Little John. It was strange: he had seen the man for only a few seconds. Their conversation had been, actually, quite commonplace. And yet the Inspector suddenly realized that Maura had made a strong impression upon him.

He could still see him, short and thin, dressed with an almost excessive correctness. His face was not remarkable. What was it, then, that could have struck Maigret so?

It intrigued him. He forced himself to remember, evoking the slightest gestures of the dry, nervous little man.

And suddenly he remembered his gaze, his first glance especially, when Maura did not know that he himself was being observed, when he had half opened the door to the office.

Little John had cold eyes!

Maigret would have been hard put to explain what he meant by this, but he knew how he meant it. Four or five times in his life, he had met people who had cold eyes, those eyes that can stare at one without establishing any human contact, without one's sensing the need that every human being feels to communicate with his fellow man.

The Inspector had come to talk to him about his son, about this boy to whom he sent letters as tender as to a beloved woman, and Little John observed him without curiosity, without any emotion at all, much as he might have contemplated the chair or a spot on the wall.

'You don't mind my having left you alone for so long?'

'No, because I think I've just discovered something.'

'Ah! . . .'

'I've discovered that Little John has cold eyes.'

Maigret was expecting a fresh smile from his American colleague. He prepared himself, almost aggressively, for that smile. O'Brien, on the contrary, looked at him gravely.

'That's a nuisance . . .' he said slowly.

And it was as if they'd had a long conversation. There was suddenly something between them that resembled a shared disquiet. O'Brien offered him a tin of tobacco.

'I prefer my own, if you don't mind.'

They lighted their pipes and were silent again. The office was ordinary and rather bare. There was only the smoke from the two pipes to confer on it any semblance of intimacy.

'I suppose that after your rough crossing you must be tired and probably want to go to bed?'

'Otherwise you would have suggested some other use for my time?'

'Simply to go and have a nightcap. In French, literally, a *bonnet de nuit* . . . in other words, one last whisky.'

Why had he taken the trouble to bring Maigret to his office, where he had done nothing but leave him alone for a quarter of an hour?

'Don't you find it's rather cold in here?'

'Let's go wherever you like.'

'I'll drop you near your hotel . . . No, I won't go in . . . the people at the desk would worry when they saw me come in. But I know a little bar . . .'

Still another little bar, with a juke box in the corner and a row of men leaning on the bar, each man quite alone, drinking with dreary obstinacy.

'Try a whisky, anyhow, before going to sleep ... You'll see, it's not as bad as you think, and it has the advantage of being good for the kidneys ... By the way ...'

Maigret understood that O'Brien was finally coming to the point of this last nocturnal outing.

'A little while ago, in the corridor, I ran into a colleague of mine ... And, as chance would have it, he spoke to me about Little John.

'Mind you, he's never had any dealings with him officially ... Neither he nor any of us ... you understand? ... I assure you that the respect for individual freedom is a fine thing. When you've understood that, you'll have gone a long way towards understanding America and Americans.

'Look ... A man comes here, a foreigner, an immigrant ... You get indignant, you Europeans, or you make fun of us because we ask him a lot of questions in writing; because we ask him, for example, if he's suffering from any mental disturbances, or if he's come to the United States with the intention of trying to assassinate the President.

'We require his signature to this statement which seems so crazy to you.

'However, after that, we ask him nothing more. The formalities for entering the United States may have been long and fussy, but at least, once they're completed, our man is absolutely free.

'Do you follow me?

'So free that unless he kills somebody, or steals, or commits rape, we have no further right to concern ourselves with him.

'What was I saying?'

There were moments when Maigret could have slapped him for this false candour, for this humour the nuances of which he knew he could not grasp.

'Oh! Yes. Here's an example. The colleague I met when you were in my office was just telling me the story as we were washing our hands. About thirty years ago, two men walked off a ship coming from Europe, just as you did this morning ... At that time, many more were arriving than today, because we needed labour. They came over in the holds, on the decks ... they came mostly from

Central and Eastern Europe ... some were so dirty, so lousy with vermin, that our immigration people had to hose them down ... Shall we have another nightcap?'

Maigret was too interested even to think of refusing and he contented himself with filling a new pipe and moving a little, for his neighbour on the left was digging him in the ribs with his elbow.

'The thing is there were all kinds and descriptions. And they met various fates ... some, among them, are today big Hollywood magnates ... you'll find some in Sing Sing, but there are still others in government offices, in Washington. You must admit that we are really a very great country to assimilate all comers as we do.'

Was it the whisky? Maigret was beginning to see John Maura no longer as a nervous and strong-willed little man, but as a symbol of the American assimilation his companion was talking about in his slow, gentle voice.

'My colleague was telling me ...'

Did he drink three, four whiskies? They had already drunk Armagnac, and before the Armagnac, two bottles of Beaujolais, and before the Beaujolais, several *apéritifs*.

'*J and J*.'

That's what stood out in his memory when he finally fell into bed, in his too sumptuous suite at the St Regis.

Two Frenchmen, in an era when men still wore stiff wing collars, starched cuffs, and patent-leather shoes, two very young Frenchmen, still wet behind the ears, who had not a cent in their pockets as they disembarked, full of hope, one with a violin under his arm, the other with a clarinet.

Which of the two had a clarinet? He simply couldn't remember any more. Yet O'Brien of the curly hair, O'Brien who none the less was as clever as a monkey, had told him.

The violin, that must have been Maura.

And both originally came from Bayonne or its outskirts. And both were about twenty years old.

And they had signed a statement with regard to the President of the United States, whom they swore not to assassinate.

A funny man, that O'Brien, taking him to a little bar just to tell him that tale, so offhandedly, as if he were rambling on about things absolutely remote from his profession.

'One was called Joseph and the other Joachim. That's what my friend told me ... You know, one mustn't believe every tale one hears ... But this is no affair of ours at the FBI ... Those were the Gay Nineties, the days of what, in Paris, you call the *bastringues* ... So, in order to earn a living, and although both of them had graduated from the Conservatory, although they felt they were great musicians, they put on a comedy number under the name of *J and J*. Joseph and Joachim. And both of them hoped one day to make a career as concert artist or composer.

'My friend told me all this. It's of no consequence obviously ... Only, I know that you are interested in the personality of Little John ... I don't think now that he was the clarinet –

'Bartender – another round ...'

Was O'Brien drunk?

'*J and J*,' he repeated. 'Now, my first name's Michael ... You know, you may call me Michael ... That doesn't mean I'll call you Jules. I know it's your first name but that you don't like it ...'

What else did he say that evening?

'You don't know the Bronx, Maigret ... You must get to know the Bronx ... It's a fascinating place ... not beautiful, but fascinating ... I didn't have time to drive you up there – we're very busy, you know. Findlay ... 169th Street ... you'll see ... it's an interesting neighbourhood. Apparently, to this day, there is still a tailor's shop exactly opposite the house. It's only gossip ... gossip from my colleague and I'm still wondering why he told me all that since it's no business of ours, *J and J* ... They did a half-comic, half-musical number in cabarets ... It would be interesting to know which was the comic. Don't you think so?'

Maigret may not have been accustomed to drinking whisky, but he was even less used to being taken for a child and he was furious when a bellboy followed him into the lift at the St Regis and, with much too much solicitude, made quite sure that he needed nothing before retiring.

That was O'Brien's doing, O'Brien of the curly red hair and the terribly ironic smile.

3

Maigret was sleeping at the bottom of a deep well and a redheaded giant was leaning over the well-head, smiling down at him and smoking an enormous cigar – why a cigar? – when a spiteful, angry ringing of a bell chased a few frowns across his face, like the morning breeze riffling a mirror-smooth lake. The whole body rolled over twice, dragging the bedclothes with it, and then an arm stretched out, clutched the water flask before finding the telephone. A voice grunted:

'Hello . . .'

Sitting up in bed, uncomfortable at that, for he had had no time to adjust his pillow and was obliged to hold the cursed telephone, he already knew one sure thing, and a humiliating thing it was: in spite of O'Brien's undoubtedly ironic pronouncements on the diuretic virtues of whisky, he had a headache.

'Maigret, yes . . . Who's speaking? . . . What?'

It was MacGill and there was no pleasure, either, in being awakened by this character whom he did not care for in the least. Especially when the other man could tell from his voice that he was still in bed and allowed himself to quip:

'Late night, I bet? . . . Did you at least have a good time?'

Maigret's eyes sought his watch, which he habitually put on the bedside table and which was not there. He finally noticed an electric clock set in the wall and his eyes flew wide open when he saw that the clock said eleven.

'Tell me, Inspector . . . I'm calling you on behalf of the Chief . . . He would be very glad if you could stop by to see him this morning . . . Any time from now on, yes, I mean as soon as you've dressed. See you later, then . . . You remember the floor, don't you? . . . seventh, at the end of the left corridor . . . See you then.'

He looked everywhere for a service bell, such as there is in France, to call the waiter, the valet, anybody, but he found nothing like it and for one second he felt lost in this ridiculously big suite. He finally thought of the telephone, had to repeat three times, in his approximate English:

'I should wish my little lunch, miss ... my little lunch, yes ... What? ... You do not understand? ... Coffee ...'

She said something to him that he could not catch.

'I am asking for my little lunch!'

He thought she hung up, but it was only to switch him to another connection over which a new voice droned: 'Room Service.'

It was very simple, obviously, but still one had to know, and, at that moment, he was annoyed at the whole of America for not having had the elementary idea of installing service bells in hotel rooms.

By the way of a last straw he was having a bath when someone knocked at the door, and though he bellowed, 'Come in!' they kept on knocking. He was obliged, dripping wet, to put on his dressing-gown and go and open the door, for he had attached the safety chain. What was the waiter standing there for? All right, so he had to sign the bill. But then what? For the man was still waiting and Maigret finally gathered that it was his tip he was after. And his clothes lay in a heap on the floor!

He was in a bad mood when, half an hour later, he knocked at the door of Little John's apartment. MacGill welcomed him, elegant as always, dressed to perfection, but the Inspector had a feeling that he had not slept much either.

'Come in ... sit down for a second ... I'll go and tell the Chief you're here.'

He was evidently preoccupied. He did not bother to put himself out. He paid no attention to Maigret and went out of the room, leaving the door wide open.

The next room was a sitting-room, which he crossed. Then a spacious bedroom. And still MacGill walked on, knocking at the last door he reached. Maigret had no time to see clearly. What struck him, however, after the succession of luxurious rooms, was an impression of poverty. Later when he thought about it, he tried to reconstruct the picture he had had for that one second before his eyes.

He would have sworn that the bedroom the secretary entered last resembled a servant's room rather than a St Regis bedroom. Wasn't Little John sitting at a plain wood table and wasn't that an iron bedstead Maigret glimpsed behind him?

A few words were exchanged in an undertone and the two men came out, one behind the other. Little John was nervous as always, precise in his movements, with, one would have said, a prodigious reserve of energy he seemed forced to contain.

He was no more cordial than MacGill when he came into the office and, this time, it did not occur to him to offer one of his famous cigars to his visitor.

He walked over to the mahogany table and sat down in the chair MacGill had been occupying before, and the latter sat down very casually in an armchair and crossed his legs.

'I am sorry, Inspector, to have disturbed you, but I thought it necessary for us to have a talk.'

He raised his eyes at last to look at Maigret, eyes which expressed nothing, neither sympathy, nor antipathy, nor impatience. His hand, delicate and astonishingly white for a man, played with a tortoise-shell paper-knife.

He was wearing a navy-blue suit of English cut, a dark tie against a white shirt. It enhanced his very delicate, sculptured features, and Maigret noted that it would be hard to tell his age.

'I suppose you have no news of my son?'

He did not wait for a reply, and continued in a neutral voice, the way one addresses a subordinate:

'When you came to see me yesterday, I was not interested in asking you any questions. If I understood correctly, you came from France with Jean and you gave me to understand that my son had requested you to make the trip . . .'

MacGill was smoking a cigarette and quietly watching the smoke rise towards the ceiling. Little John kept playing with the paper-knife, staring at Maigret as if he did not see him.

'I do not believe that, after leaving the Police Judiciaire, you opened a private detective agency. On the other hand, in view of what everyone knows of your character, it is hard for me to believe that you embarked lightly on an adventure of this kind. I imagine, Inspector, that you understand me? We are free men in a free country. Yesterday, you gained entry here to talk to me about my son. That same evening, you contacted an official of the FBI in order to get information about me ...'

In other words, the two men were already informed of his comings and goings and of his meeting with O'Brien. Had they had him followed?

'Allow me to ask you a first question: On what pretext did my son ask your help?'

As Maigret made no reply, and MacGill seemed to be smiling with irony, Little John continued, tense, incisive:

'Retired police inspectors are not in the habit of playing chaperon to young people on their travels. I ask you once again: What did my son tell you to persuade you to leave France and cross the Atlantic with him?'

Wasn't he purposely showing contempt, and didn't he hope in this way to make Maigret lose his temper?

But what happened was this: Maigret grew more calm and more grave as the other man talked on. And more lucid.

So lucid – and it showed so much in his glance – that the hand that held the paper-knife began to finger it jerkily. MacGill, who had turned to look at the Inspector, forgot his cigarette and waited.

'If you will allow me, I will answer your question with another question. Do you know where your son is?'

'I do not and that is not the issue at the moment. My son is free to do as he likes, is that clear?'

'So, you do know where he is.'

It was MacGill who started and turned sharply towards Little John, his eyes hard.

'I repeat, I know nothing of his whereabouts and they do not concern you.'

'In that case we have nothing more to say to each other.'

'One moment ...'

The little man had risen precipitously and, still holding the paper-knife, rushed between Maigret and the door.

'You seem to forget, Inspector, that you are here somewhat at my expense ... My son is a minor ... I don't suppose he allowed you to bear the expenses of a trip that you undertook at his request.'

Why did MacGill seem furious with his employer? It was clear that the turn of the conversation did not please him. And, for that matter, he was not slow to intervene.

'I believe the problem does not lie in that direction and that you are offending the Inspector needlessly.'

The two men exchanged a look that Maigret caught, unable though he was to analyse it on the spot, but promising himself to understand its meaning later.

'It is evident,' continued MacGill, also rising and striding up and down the room with more calm than Little John, 'it is evident that your son, for some reason we do not know, that you perhaps may not be unaware of . . .'

Well! Well! It was to his boss that he tossed such insinuations?

'. . . felt he had to appeal to a person known for his perspicacity in criminal matters . . .'

Maigret remained seated. It was interesting to watch the two of them, each so different. To believe, at times, that the game was being played between the two of them and not with Maigret.

For Little John, so incisive at the outset, allowed his secretary, his junior by thirty years, to talk on. And he did not seem to be doing so gladly. He was humiliated, that was obvious. He yielded his place with regret.

'Given the fact that your son cares about one person and one only, his father, given the fact that he's come running to New York without letting you know . . . at least, so I suppose . . .'

A thrust, no doubt about that.

'. . . there's every reason to believe that he's received disturbing news about you. It remains to be seen who put such thoughts in his head. Don't you think, Inspector, that this is the whole problem? Let's review the question as simply as possible . . . You are alarmed at the rather inexplicable disappearance of a young man disembarking in New York. Without being versed in police matters and using only common sense, I say this:

'When we know who made Jean Maura come to New York, in other words, who cabled him I don't know what about some danger threatening his father – for otherwise, there was no need to bring a policeman with him, please, excuse the word – when that is established, it will, no doubt, not be hard to learn who made him disappear.'

Little John, during this speech, had gone over to plant himself before the window and, drawing back the curtain with one hand, he looked out. His silhouette presented the same sharp lines as his face. And Maigret caught himself thinking: Clarinet? Violin? Which of the two J's was this man in the burlesque skit of long ago?

'Am I to understand, Inspector, that you refuse to answer?'

Then Maigret, on the off-chance:

'I should like to talk with Mr Maura alone.'

The latter started and wheeled about. His first look was for his secretary, who appeared supremely unconcerned.

'I have told you before, I think, that you can talk in front of MacGill.'

'In that case, you will forgive me if I have nothing to say to you.'

Yet MacGill did not offer to leave. He stayed right on, sure of himself, like a man who knows where he belongs.

Was it the little man who was going to lose his composure? There was something in his cold eyes that resembled exasperation, but it resembled something else, too.

'Listen to me, Mr Maigret. We must get to the bottom of this and we will in a very few words ... Talk, or don't talk, it's the same to me, for whatever you could have to tell me interests me only moderately ... A boy, worried for reasons I do not know, went to you and you launched into an adventure where you did not belong. This boy is my son. He is a minor. If he has disappeared, it concerns only me and if I have to call on someone to find him, it will be the police of this country ... I imagine I make myself clear?

'We are not in France and, until further notice, my comings and goings are no one else's business. I will therefore not allow anyone to meddle in my affairs and, if necessary, I will take steps to see that my full and complete freedom is respected.

'I do not know if my son arranged to give you an advance. In the event that he should not have thought to do so, tell me, and my secretary will remit a cheque covering your expenses and your return to France.'

Why did he glance quickly at MacGill as if to see whether the latter approved?

'I am waiting for your answer.'

'About what?'

'About the cheque.'

'Thank you.'

'One last word, if you allow me ... You can't be prevented, obviously, from staying as long as you like in this hotel, where I am only a guest like any other. Let me tell you simply that I should find it extremely disagreeable to meet you constantly in the foyer, the corridors, or in the lift ... I bid you good day, Inspector.'

Maigret, still seated, slowly knocked out his pipe in an ash tray on a side table. Then he took his time filling a fresh pipe, which he pulled from his pocket to light, looking meanwhile from one man to the other.

Finally he rose. In doing so he seemed to unfurl his height, and his breadth, and he appeared taller, broader than usual.

'Good day,' he said simply, in so unexpected a voice that the paper-knife snapped in two between Little John's fingers.

It seemed to him that MacGill meant to speak again, to keep him from leaving immediately, but Maigret turned his back, calmly walked to the door, and disappeared down the corridor.

It was only in the lift that Maigret's headache returned and that the previous night's whisky made itself felt in the form of a queasy stomach.

'Hello ... O'Brien? ... Maigret speaking.'

He was smiling. He was drawing short puffs on his pipe as he looked about him at the rather faded, flowered paper that covered the walls of the room.

'What? ... No, I'm no longer at the St Regis ... Why? ... For several reasons, the most important being that I wasn't very comfortable there. You understand that? So much the better. But of course, I have found a hotel. The Berwick. You don't know it? I don't remember now the number of the street. I've never had a memory for figures and you people are really tiresome with your numbered streets. Why couldn't you say Victor Hugo Street, or Pigalle Street, or President-What's-His-Name Street ...

'Hello ... Just imagine Broadway. I don't know how far up there's a cinema called the Capitol ... Good. Well, it's the first or second street on the left. A little hotel which isn't much to look at and where

I suspect they don't rent rooms at night only ... What did you say? ... Against the law in New York? Well, that's too bad!'

He was in a good mood, even a jovial mood, for no precise reason, perhaps simply because he was once again in a familiar atmosphere.

First of all, he liked this noisy, rather vulgar corner of Broadway that reminded him both of Montmartre and the Grands Boulevards of Paris. The hotel desk was little short of shabby and there was only one lift. And the lift boy a limping little fellow!

Through the window he could see the electric signs flashing on and off.

'Hello! ... O'Brien? Can you imagine? I need you again ... Don't be afraid ... I am scrupulously respecting all the freedoms of this land of the free ... What? ... Of course not. I assure you, I am completely incapable of sarcasm ... Imagine this, I should like – *I* should like – to call on the services of a private detective ...'

The FBI agent, at the other end of the line, wondered if he was joking and, after muttering a syllable or two, decided he'd better burst into laughter.

'Don't laugh. I am completely serious. I do have one detective at my disposal ... I mean that, ever since noon, I've had one on my heels ... My dear friend, of course I'm not blaming the police ... What's the matter with you today, being so touchy? ... I'm talking about the aforementioned Bill ... Yes, that would-be boxer with the cleft chin who accompanied MacGill and me yesterday, on our peregrinations ... Well, he's still around but with one difference, he now walks ten yards behind me, just like a footman in the old days ... If I leaned out of the window now, I'd certainly see him down in front of the hotel ... He doesn't hide, no ... He follows me, that's all ... I even think he's a little uncomfortable and that sometimes he'd like to say hello ...

'What? ... Why do I want a detective? Laugh all you like. I admit it's pretty funny. All the same, in this devilish country of yours, where people do not deign to understand my English unless I've repeated the same thing four or five times complete with gestures, I wouldn't mind having someone's help on a few little inquiries I want to make ...

'Above all, please, may your man speak French! ... You have one on tap? ... You'll telephone? ... Yes indeed, starting this evening

... I'm in fine shape, just fine, in spite of your whiskies ... It's true I inaugurated my new room at the Berwick by treating myself to a two-hour nap ...

'In what circles do I want to make my inquiries? ... I thought you would have guessed ... Of course ... That's right ...

'I'll wait for your call ... Until later, then ...'

He went over to open the window and discovered Bill, as he had foreseen, some thirty yards from the hotel, chewing his gum and not seeming to be enjoying himself at all.

The room was as commonplace as could be, with enough battered furniture and faded carpeting to make one believe one was in a furnished room in any city in the world.

Not ten minutes had passed before the telephone rang. It was O'Brien, informing Maigret he had found him a detective, one Ronald Dexter, and recommending that he should not allow the man to drink too much.

'Because he can't hold his whisky?' inquired the Inspector.

To which O'Brien replied with evangelical sweetness:

'Because he cries ...'

And the curly-haired redhead was not joking. Even when he had not been drinking, Dexter gave the impression of a man who carries through life a burden of infinite sorrow.

He came to the hotel at seven that night. Maigret met him in the foyer just as the detective was inquiring for him at the desk.

'Ronald Dexter?'

'I am ...'

And he seemed to be saying:

'Alas!'

'My friend O'Brien briefed you?'

'Ssshh!'

'I beg your pardon?'

'No names, please. I'm at your service. Where do you want to go?'

'Outside, to begin with ... Do you know that gentleman over there who seems so interested in the passers-by and who chews gum? ... That's Bill ... Bill who? ... I've no idea. I know only his first name, but what I do know is that he's a colleague of yours who's been instructed to tail me. I'm telling you so you won't worry about his comings and goings. It doesn't matter, you see? . . . He can follow us as much as he likes . . .'

Dexter may or may not have understood. In any event, he assumed an air of resignation and seemed to raise his eyes to heaven:

'If it's not one thing, it's another!'

He must have been in his fifties and his grey suit, his worn-out trench coat did not speak well for his prosperity.

The two men walked towards Broadway, which was less than half a block away, and Bill followed imperturbably at their heels.

'Are you acquainted with theatrical circles?'

'A little.'

'More exactly, vaudeville and cabaret entertainers.'

And then Maigret could take the measure of O'Brien's sense of humour as well as of his practical sense, for his companion sighed:

'I was a clown for twenty years.'

A sad clown, no doubt?

'If you like, we can stop in a bar and have a drink.'

'It's okay with me.'

Then, with disarming simplicity:

'I thought you'd been warned?'

'About what?'

'I don't carry my liquor very well. Oh well! Just one drink, okay?'

They sat down in a corner, while Bill came in and took up his position at the bar.

Maigret explained:

'If I were in Paris, I'd immediately find the information I'm after because, around the Porte Saint-Martin, we have a number of shops which date back to another era. Some sell popular songs and you can still buy today songs that were sung on every street corner in 1900 or 1910. In another one I know, a wigmaker's shop, you find every style of beard, moustache, and wig that actors have worn from way, way back. And then, in some very shabby quarters, there are offices where most unlikely impresarios organize tours in small provincial towns.'

As Maigret talked, Ronald Dexter stared at his glass with a profoundly sad eye.

'Do you understand me?'

'Yes, sir.'

'Good. On the walls of these offices, it wouldn't be hard to find posters of vaudeville acts which were popular thirty or forty years ago ... And sitting on the waiting-room benches, a dozen old hams or faded dance-hall queens.'

He stopped short, then said:

'I beg your pardon.'

'Not at all.'

'I mean to say that actors, singers who are seventy years old or more today still come seeking engagements. Those people have prodigious memories, especially for anything related to the heyday of their success. Now, Mr Dexter ...'

'Everyone calls me Ronald.'

'Well, I wonder if in New York there is the equivalent of what I've just described.'

The former clown took time to think, his eyes glued to his glass, which he had still not touched. Then he inquired, with dead seriousness:

'Must they be really very old?'

'What do you mean?'

'Must they be very old troupers? You said seventy or more. For here that's a lot, because, you see, people die quicker.'

His hand reached towards the glass, withdrew, reached out again, and, finally, he downed the whisky in one gulp.

'There are places ... I'll show you ...'

'It's a question of going back only about thirty years. At that time, two Frenchmen, under the name of *J and J*, were doing a musical number in the cabarets.'

'Thirty years ago, you say? I think that's possible. And what do you want to know?'

'Everything you can find out about them. I'd also like to get hold of a photograph. Artists have a lot of photographs made. Their pictures are used on posters and programmes.'

'And you plan to come with me?'

'Not this evening. Not right away.'

'That's better. Because you might scare people. They're very sensitive, you know. If you want, I'll come and see you tomorrow at your hotel, or I'll phone you. Is this very urgent? I can begin this evening. But it would take' – he hesitated, lowered his voice – 'you would have to give me something to pay for several rounds, to get into certain places.'

Maigret pulled out his wallet.

'Oh, ten will be enough. Because, if you give me more, I'll spend it. And when I've finished your job, I won't have anything left. Do you need me any more now?'

The Inspector shook his head. He had fleetingly thought of dining with his clown, but the man turned out to be too hopelessly gloomy.

'It doesn't bother you to have that fellow following you?'

'What would you do if it did?'

'I think if he were offered a little more than his employers pay . . .'

'He doesn't disturb me.'

And it was true. It was almost a diversion for Maigret to feel the former boxer tagging along behind.

He dined that evening in a brilliantly lighted cafeteria on Broadway where he had some excellent sausages but was vexed to get Coca-Cola instead of beer.

Then, around nine o'clock, he hailed a cab.

'Corner of Findlay and 169th Street.'

The driver sighed, lowered his flag with an air of resignation, and Maigret understood his reaction only a little later, when the car left the brightly lighted sections behind to enter a new world.

Soon, along the dead-staight, interminable streets, he saw only coloured people. They were crossing Harlem, with its houses all alike, its blocks of dark brick that iron fire-escapes, zigzagging across the façades, made only uglier.

They crossed a bridge. Later they passed by some warehouses or perhaps factories – it was hard to make out in the darkness – and then, in the Bronx, more desolate avenues, the occasional yellow, red, or purple lights of a local cinema, or the windows of a big store crowded with wax dummies frozen in stiff poses.

They'd been driving for more than half an hour and the streets grew still darker, more deserted, until finally the driver stopped his cab, turned around, uttered one disdainful word:

'Findlay.'

169th Street was there on the right. But a long debate was required to persuade the driver to wait. Even then he was not prepared to wait at the corner but, when Maigret set off down the pavement, he crept along quietly behind him.

And a second taxi followed, also at a crawl, behind the first, with Bill, the detective-boxer, no doubt in it, only he did not bother to get out.

In the darkness, outlined against the sky, was the rectangular shape formed by several shops such as exist in the poor sections of Paris and every other big city.

What had Maigret come here for? Nothing specific. Did he even know what he'd come to New York for? And yet, for the last few hours, in fact since the moment he'd left the St Regis, he no longer felt himself a stranger. The Berwick had already reconciled him to America, perhaps because it smelled of humanity, and now he was imagining all the lives crouching within these brick honeycombs, all the scenes unrolling behind these curtains.

Little John had not impressed him, that was not the word, but, nevertheless, as an individual he was contrived, artificial.

MacGill, too, perhaps even more so.

And even the young man, Jean Maura, with his fears and the approval of Monsieur d'Hoquélus.

And his disappearance the moment the steamer finally reached New York ...

All that, in short, was unimportant. That's the word Maigret would have used if O'Brien had been there at that moment, with that vague smile on his red, pock-marked face.

A passing thought as he walked along, hands in pockets, pipe between his teeth. Why are redheads the most often scarred by smallpox and why, almost invariably, are they likeable people?

He sniffed. He breathed in the air with its musty fumes of petroleum and poverty. Were there new *J and J*'s in some of these cells? Most certainly! Young people, fresh from the ship, who were waiting, with clenched teeth, for the great day of the St Regis.

He was looking for a tailor's shop. Two taxis were following him like a parade. And he was aware of the comical side of the situation.

Two young men, once upon a time, in the days when one still wore stiff collars and cylindrical cuffs – Maigret had had washable ones of rubber or rubberized cloth, he still remembered them – two young men had lived on this street, opposite a tailor's shop.

Now, another young man, a few days ago, had feared for his father's life.

And this young man, with whom Maigret had talked a few minutes earlier on the deck of the ship, had disappeared.

The Inspector was searching for a tailor's shop. He looked at the windows of these houses, so often barred by those wretched fire-escapes that stopped above the ground floor.

A clarinet and a violin ...

Why did he press his nose, the way he used to as a boy, against the window of one of these shops where they sell everything – vegetables, groceries, and sweets? Right next to this shop there was another, which was not lighted, but was without shutters, so that through the windowpane and thanks to a nearby street light could be seen a pressing machine and some suits motionless on their hangers.

Arturo Giacomi.

Still tailing him, the two taxis stopped a few yards behind him. Neither the drivers nor that lumpish clod of a Bill suspected the contact that this man in the heavy overcoat, with the pipe clamped between his teeth, was achieving as he turned towards the house across the street. Contact with two twenty-year-old Frenchmen who had walked off a ship long ago, one with his violin under his arm, the other with his clarinet.

4

It was touch and go that morning whether a man lived or died, whether or not a foul crime was committed, and the result depended on how Maigret spent a few minutes of his time.

Unfortunately he did not know it. During the thirty years spent with the Police Judiciaire he was in the habit, when an investigation did not keep him out at night, of getting up around seven in the morning, and he loved to walk the fairly long distance between Boulevard Richard Lenoir, where he lived, and the Quai des Orfèvres.

At heart, despite his activity, he had always been a dawdler. And, once retired, in his house in Meung-sur-Loire, he got up even earlier, often in the summer, before the sun, which would rise to find him up and about in his garden.

On board ship, he was almost always the first to stride along the deck, while the sailors busily mopped it and polished the brass rails.

But his first morning in New York, because he had drunk too much with O'Brien, he had got up at eleven.

The second day, in his room at the Berwick, he began by waking early, from habit. But, precisely because it was too early, because he sensed the streets were empty, the shutters still closed, he decided to go back to sleep.

And he did fall heavily asleep. When he opened his eyes, it was after ten. Why did he happen to be in the mood of people who have worked the whole week long and for whom the great joy of Sunday is to sleep late?

He dawdled. He spent an eternity over breakfast. Still in his dressing-gown, he went to the window to smoke his first pipe, and was astonished not to see Bill down in the street.

True, the detective-boxer had to sleep too. Had he been replaced for those few hours? Were there two, working in relay, on Maigret's trail?

He shaved with care and devoted still a little more time to putting his things in order.

Yet it was on all those minutes, so banally squandered, that the life of a man depended.

At the moment when Maigret went down into the street, there was, strictly speaking, still time. Bill was definitely not there and the Inspector saw no one seemingly assigned to tail him. A cab went by, empty. He raised his arm mechanically. The driver did not see him and, instead of looking for another taxi, Maigret decided to walk for a while.

That's how he discovered Fifth Avenue with its expensive shops, and he paused to look in the windows. He stood a long time in contemplation of some pipes and he decided to buy one, although ordinarily this was Madame Maigret's gift at each birthday and anniversary.

Another absurd, bizarre detail. The pipe was very expensive. Coming out of the shop, Maigret remembered the fare he had paid the taxi the evening before and he promised himself to economize that morning.

That is why he took the subway, in which he lost a considerable amount of time before finding the corner of Findlay Avenue.

The sky was a steely, luminous grey. The wind was still high but no longer blowing a gale. Maigret turned the corner of 169th Street and immediately he scented disaster.

Down the street, about two hundred yards away, a crowd stood in front of a door and, although he did not know the place well, had seen it only at night, he was almost certain it was the Italian tailor's shop.

For that matter, everything, or almost everything in the street, in the neighbourhood, was Italian. The children seen playing on the doorsteps had the black hair and the knowing faces, those long, bronzed legs of the street urchins of Naples and Florence.

Most of the shops bore Italian names, and their windows were filled with *mortadella*, *pasta*, and the salted meats that come from the shores of the Mediterranean.

He lengthened his stride. Twenty or thirty people were clustered outside the tailor's shop, which a policeman was defending against invasion, and a swarm of more or less ragged youngsters buzzed around the group.

It smelled of accident, of the sordid tragedy that suddenly explodes in a street and furrows the faces of passers-by.

'What happened?' he asked a fat man in a bowler hat who kept to the back and stood on tiptoe.

Although he had spoken in English, the man merely stared at him curiously, then looked away with a shrug.

He caught snatches of talk, some in Italian, some in English.

'... just as he was crossing the street ...'

'... every morning, at the very same time, for years and years, he took a walk ... Fifteen years I've lived in this neighbourhood and I always saw him ...'

'... His chair is still there ...'

Through the shop window they could see the steam press with a suit stretched out over it, and, closer, next to the pane, a low, straw-bottomed chair, which was old Angelino's.

For Maigret was beginning to understand. Patiently, with the agility of the heavy man, he eased himself towards the centre of the crowd, piecing together the snatches of talk he overheard.

It was fifty years ago and probably more that Angelino Giacomi had come from Naples and set himself up in business in this shop, long before steam presses were invented. He was practically the patriarch of the street, of the neighbourhood, and, during city elections, no candidate failed to call on him.

His son, Arturo, had taken over and this son, now almost sixty, was himself father of seven or eight children, most of them married.

In winter old Angelino spent his days sitting on this straw-bottomed chair in the front of the shop, of which he seemed a permanent fixture, smoking from morning till night those badly made, black Italian cigars that give off an acrid smell.

And, in the spring, just as one witnesses the swallows' return, so the whole block watched old Angelino set his chair out on the pavement, by the door.

Now he was dead or dying, Maigret still did not know exactly. Different versions on this point were circulating around him, but soon the characteristic siren of an ambulance was heard and a van with a red cross drew up to the kerb.

The crowd eddied, parted slowly, and the two men in white coats passed through, only to reappear a few minutes later, carrying a stretcher on which nothing could be seen but a blanketed body.

They shut the door at the back of the ambulance. A man wearing no collar, Giacomi's son, no doubt, who had simply slipped a jacket over his work clothes, climbed in beside the driver and they drove off.

'Is he dead?' they asked the policeman, who still stood at his post.

He didn't know. It was all the same to him. It wasn't his job to worry about these details.

A woman was weeping inside the shop, her uncombed grey hair falling over her face, and at times she moaned so loudly that they heard her out in the street.

One person, then two, then three began drifting away. House-wives looked around for their children, wanting to get on with their marketing in the local shops.

The crowd was dispersing, but enough people remained to block the doorway.

It was a barber, now, comb behind his ear, who explained with a strong Genoese accent:

'I saw it all just the way I'm seeing you now, because it's a slack period for me and I was standing at the door of my shop.'

Sure enough, a few houses away stood the blue and red pole that bespeaks a barbershop.

'Almost every morning he'd stop a minute or two in front of my shop to talk. I used to shave him, every Wednesday and Saturday. I always shaved him . . . not my helper, but myself. And I've always known him to be the same as he was this morning. Yet he must have been eighty-two . . . Wait . . . no . . . eighty-three. When Maria, his youngest granddaughter got married four years ago, I remember he told me . . .'

And the barber went into calculations to establish the exact age of old Angelino, who had just been brutally snatched away from the street where he had lived so long.

'There's one thing he would never have admitted for anything in the world: he couldn't see much any more. He always wore his glasses, thick glasses in old silver frames. He was forever polishing them with his big red handkerchief and putting them back on. But to tell the truth, they weren't much use to him. That's the reason – and not because his legs were bad – he still had the legs of a twenty-year-old – why he'd taken to walking with a cane.

'Every morning at half-past ten exactly . . .'

Now, in the logical order of things, Maigret should have been in the shop around that time. He had promised himself so the evening before. It was old Angelino he wanted to see and question.

What would have happened if Maigret had arrived on time, if he had not fallen asleep again, if he had not lingered by the window, if the cab he had hailed had stopped, if he had not bought a pipe on Fifth Avenue?

'They used to tie a heavy knitted scarf around his neck, a red wool scarf. A while ago I saw a kid, the son of the vegetable grocer, bringing it back. He never wore an overcoat, even in the middle of winter . . . he walked with short, very even steps, keeping close to the houses and I, well, I knew his cane helped him feel his way.'

There were only five or six around the barber now and, as Maigret seemed the most serious, the most interested of the group, the man had eventually begun to speak directly to him.

'In front of every shop, or almost, he used to wave a greeting, because he knew everybody. At the corner, he would stop a minute on the kerb before crossing, for his morning walk invariably meant three blocks.

'This morning, he did what he always did . . . I saw him . . . I maintain I saw him take a few steps into the road . . . Why did I turn around just then? I've no idea . . . Maybe my assistant, who was in the shop with the door open, called to me? . . . I must ask him, I'm curious . . .

'I distinctly heard the car coming – it happened less than half a block away from my shop – then a funny noise – a kind of soft noise – it's hard to describe. Anyhow, a noise that spells right off – accident.

'I turned around and I saw the car driving off at top speed. It was already passing my shop. At the same time, I looked towards the body on the ground.

'If I hadn't been busy doing the two things at once, I'd have gotten a better look at the two men in the front. A big grey car – a rather dark grey. I'd almost be tempted to say black, but I think it was grey, or else it was covered with dust.

'People had started to run up. I came here first to tell Arturo. He was pressing a pair of pants. They carried old Angelino back with a trickle of blood running out of his mouth and one arm hanging down, one shoulder of his coat ripped. You couldn't tell anything else at first glance, but I understood that he was dead . . .'

Because of his long legs Special Agent O'Brien had tipped back the chair in his office, and was pulling at his pipe in short puffs, caressing the stem with his lips, watching Maigret from under heavy lids.

'I imagine,' Maigret was saying in conclusion, 'you won't go on claiming that individual freedom prevents you from doing something about those swine?'

Maigret, after more than thirty years of police work, during which he had seen every kind of human baseness, cruelty, and cowardice, could still be as outraged by certain things as on his first day.

It darkened his mood even more to realize that, had he visited old Giacomi as planned, instead of buying a new pipe, he would, no doubt, have saved the tailor's life.

'Unfortunately it's not in the province of the FBI, but, barring further developments, of the New York police.'

'They killed him in a foul, filthy way,' muttered the former Inspector.

And O'Brien murmured thoughtfully:

'The way they killed him doesn't strike me so much as the fact that they killed him just in time.'

Maigret had already thought of that and it was hard to see it as a coincidence.

For years and years no one had bothered about old Angelino, who had been able to spend his days in his chair, in full view of passers-by, and every morning, like a gentle old dog, take his turn around the block.

The evening before, that very night, Maigret had stopped for a few seconds in front of the tailor's shop. He had promised himself, without mentioning it to anyone, to come back in the morning and question the old man.

But, by the time he arrived, someone had taken care to prevent the old man from ever talking again.

'They had to move fast,' he grumbled, looking at O'Brien with involuntary bitterness.

'It doesn't take long to organize an accident of this kind, if the essential details are known in advance. I won't go so far as to say that there are agencies that handle this kind of work, but almost. Actually, it's only a matter of knowing whom to go to, of giving them the necessary information, establishing one's reliability, and paying the price, you understand? . . . They're the so-called professional or hired killers. But the killers couldn't have known that old Angelino used to cross 169th Street every morning at the same hour and the same place.'

'Someone had to tell them that, very likely the person who ordered the job to be done.'

'And that person must have known this for a long time.'

They looked at each other gravely, for both were drawing identical conclusions from the developments.

Someone, over an undetermined period of time, knew that Angelino had something to tell and that this something constituted a threat to his security.

In spite of himself, Maigret kept seeing in his mind's eye Little John's nervous, slender silhouette, and his light, cold eyes in which one could detect no flicker of humanity.

Wasn't he precisely the man capable of hiring killers, without batting an eye, to do the job they carried out this morning?

And Little John had lived on 169th Street, right opposite the tailor's shop!

Furthermore, if one were to believe his letters to his son – and they had a disturbing ring of truth – it was Little John who felt threatened, who no doubt feared for his life!

And it was his son who had disappeared before setting foot on American soil!

'They kill . . .' said Maigret after a long silence, as if this summed up his thoughts.

And it more or less did. He had just thought of Jean Maura, and now that he knew this involved people capable of murder, he was not without remorse.

Shouldn't he have kept closer guard over this young man who had asked for his help? Hadn't he been wrong not to take his fears more seriously, in spite of what Monsieur d'Hoquélus had to say?

'In short,' the FBI agent now said, 'we are dealing here with people who are defending themselves, or, more exactly, who attack in self-defence. I wonder, my dear Maigret, just what you'll be able to do ... The New York police won't want to see you mixed up in their investigation. On what authority, for that matter? This is a crime committed on American territory ... Angelino has long been an American citizen ... The murderers too, no doubt. Maura is a naturalized citizen. MacGill, I've learned, was born in New York ... and, furthermore, you'll see that those two won't be brought into it. As for young Maura, no one has notified the police and his father doesn't seem anxious to do so.'

He got up with a sigh.

'That's all I can tell you.'

'You know my bulldog wasn't at his post this morning?'

The other man understood that he was talking about Bill.

'You hadn't told me so, but I would have bet on it. It was essential, wasn't it, that between last evening and this morning, someone should be informed of your visit to 169th Street.'

'So that, later on, I might go back without endangering anyone.'

'Do you know, if I were you I'd take a few precautions when crossing the streets? ... I think, by George, that I'd avoid deserted places, especially after dark ... It isn't always necessary to run people down ... It's easy, driving by in a car, to shoot them down with a machine gun.'

'I thought gangsters existed only in detective stories and films. Isn't that what you told me?'

'I'm not talking about gangsters. I'm giving you some advice. But aside from that, what have you done with my tearful clown?'

'I've put him to work and he's to phone me or come to see me at the Berwick sometime during the day.'

'Unless he has an accident too.'

'Do you think ... ?'

'I don't know anything. I have no right to intervene in any part

302

of it. I feel like telling you to do as much, but it would obviously do no good.'

'No ...'

'Good luck. Phone me if you have any news. It's possible that – quite by chance – I might run into my colleague on the New York force who's in charge of this business. I don't know yet who's been picked for it. And it's also possible that, in the course of a conversation, he might tell me one or two little things which could interest you. I'm not inviting you to lunch because I have a date with two of my superior officers.'

It was quite different from their first meeting and their genial, even jocular conversation.

Both men had heavy hearts. That street in the Bronx, with its Italian shops, its swarming children, its hearty life, where an old man shuffled along on his morning walk and where a car leaped savagely forward ...

Maigret almost turned into a cafeteria for a bite of lunch, but then, since he was not far from the St Regis, it occurred to him to go into the bar. He was not expecting anything in particular, unless perhaps to see MacGill, who seemed to be in the habit of going there for cocktails.

And he was there, in fact, with an extremely pretty woman. He noticed the Inspector and half rose to bow to him.

Then he must have said something about him to his companion, for she stared curiously at Maigret as she puffed on a lipstick-stained cigarette.

Either MacGill knew nothing or he possessed remarkable composure, for he appeared quite at ease. Since Maigret stayed on alone at the bar, drinking a cocktail, he decided suddenly to get up, excused himself to his friend, and came over to the Inspector with outstretched hand.

'I'm not sorry to meet you because, after what happened yesterday, I intended to speak to you.'

Maigret pretended not to see the proffered hand, which the secretary finally slipped in his pocket.

'Little John behaved towards you in a brutal and clumsy manner. That's what I wanted to say: there's more awkwardness than malice in him. He's long been accustomed to having everybody obey him.

The least obstacle, the least opposition irritate him. And then, where his son is concerned, he has a very special feeling. It is, if you like, the intimate part, the secret part of his life, which he keeps jealously to himself. That's why he got angry when he saw you intervene in this affair.

'I can tell you in confidence that, ever since your arrival, he's been moving heaven and earth to find Jean Maura.

'And he will find him, for he has the means.

'No doubt in France, where you could be of some help to him, he would accept your co-operation. Here, in a city you don't know . . .'

Maigret was motionless, as unmoved in appearance as a stone wall.

'In a word, I ask you . . .'

'. . . to accept your apologies,' he let the words fall.

'. . . and his.'

'He told you to offer them?'

'Well, what I mean is –'

'That you're anxious, both of you, for the same or for different reasons, to see me somewhere else.'

'If you take it like that . . .'

And Maigret, testily, turning back to the bar to pick up his drink:

'I take it any way I please.'

When he looked around the room again, MacGill was sitting beside the blonde girl, who was asking questions that, patently, he had no wish to answer.

He looked gloomy, and as Maigret left he felt MacGill's eyes follow him with a look of mingled anxiety and bitterness.

So much the better!

A cable was waiting for him at the Berwick, forwarded from the St Regis. Ronald Dexter was there too, patiently waiting for him on a bench in the lobby.

The wire read:

Receive by cable excellent news Jean Maura. Stop. Will explain situation your return. Stop. Investigation now pointless. Stop. Count on your return by next boat. Kind regards.

François d'Hoquélus

Maigret folded the yellow sheet and, with a sigh, slipped it into his wallet. Then he turned to the sad clown:

'Have you eaten?' he asked him.

'Sort of, I had a hot dog a little while ago. But if you want me to keep you company ...'

And that allowed the Inspector to discover another unexpected side to his strange detective. Dexter, who was so thin that the skimpiest clothes flapped around his body, had a stomach of vast capacity.

He was no sooner seated at the counter of a cafeteria than his eyes began to shine like those of a man who had gone days without food, and he murmured, pointing to some ham and cheese sandwiches:

'May I?'

He wasn't asking permission to eat one sandwich, but the whole pile, and while he gulped them down, he kept glancing anxiously around him, as if he were afraid someone would try to prevent him from finishing his meal.

He ate without drinking. Enormous mouthfuls followed each other into his amazing elastic mouth and each mouthful pushed down the preceding one without his seeming bothered in the least.

'I've got something already ...' he nevertheless managed to say.

And, with his free hand, he reached into the pocket of his trench coat, which he had not wasted time taking off. He laid a folded piece of paper on the counter. While the Inspector unfolded it, he asked:

'You don't mind if I order something hot? It's not expensive here, you know.'

The paper was a handbill such as actors used to sell in the theatre after their numbers.

Ask for a photograph of the artists.

And Maigret who, in those days, was a devotee of the Petit Casino, at the Porte Saint-Martin, could still hear the everlasting:

Costs me ten centimes.

It was not even a postcard, such as the stars could afford to have printed, but a plain sheet of coarse paper, now a faded yellow.

J and J, the celebrated musical improvisors, who have had the honour of playing before all the crowned heads of Europe and before the Shah of Persia.

'I must ask you not to get any marks on it,' said the clown as he started on some bacon and eggs. 'It wasn't given to me, just loaned.'

That was comic: the idea of lending such a piece of paper which no one would bother to pick up in the street.

'A friend of mine ... well, a man I've known a long time, who used to play Mr Loyal in the circus. It's much harder than people think, you know. He played it for over forty years, and now he never leaves his wheelchair, he's very old. I went to see him last night, because he scarcely sleeps any more.'

He talked on with his mouth full, eyeing the sausages one of his neighbours had just ordered. He would eat some, for sure, and no doubt one of those enormous pieces of cake lacquered with a livid frosting that turned Maigret's stomach.

'My friend didn't know *J and J* personally. He only worked in the circus, see? But he has a unique collection of posters, programmes and newspaper clippings about circus and music-hall families. He can tell you that such and such an acrobat, who is thirty today, is the son of such and such a trapeze artist who married the grand-daughter of the anchor man in a pyramid act who was killed at the Palladium in 1905.'

Maigret was listening absently and studying the photograph on the shiny yellow paper. Could it be called a photograph? The reproduction, in such a thick screen offset, was so bad that the faces could hardly be made out.

Two men, both young, both thin. The biggest difference between them was that one wore his hair very long. He was the violinist, and Maigret was convinced that this one had become Little John.

The other, with thinner hair and already, young as he was, showing signs of baldness, wore glasses and, rolling his eyes, blew on a clarinet.

'But of course, of course, order some sausages,' Maigret said before Ronald Dexter had time to ask.

'You must think I've been hungry all my life, don't you?'

'Why?'

'Because it's so ... I have always been hungry. Even when I earned some money, I never had enough to eat as much as I'd have liked. You must give me back the paper because I promised my friend to return it to him.'

'I'll have it photographed right away.'

'Oh! ... I'll have more information, but not immediately. Just to

306

get the handbill, I had to keep after my friend to look for it. He lives in his wheelchair and rolls himself all around his room, which is piled high with papers. He assured me he knew people who could give us information, but he wouldn't tell me who ... because he doesn't quite remember, I'm sure. He has to rummage around in his stuff. He has no telephone. He can't get out, either, so it doesn't speed things up.

'"Don't worry ... People come to see me ... People come to see me ..." he told me over and over. "There are enough artists who remember old Germain and who are only too glad to come for a chat in this hole in the wall.

'"One of my old friends is a woman who used to be a tightrope dancer, and later a medium in a supernatural number, and finally ended by telling fortunes. She comes every Wednesday.

'"Stop by now and then. When I have something for you, I'll tell you. But you must admit the truth. It's for a book on cabaret and variety acts, isn't it? There's already one about circus people. I had a lot of visitors, who pumped me for all I was worth, walked off with my material, then, when the book came out, my name was not even mentioned ..."'

Maigret understood what kind of man he was dealing with and knew there would be no point in pressing him.

'You go back there once a day ...'

'I have some other places to call on, too. You'll see, I'll get you all the information you're after. Only, I have to ask you again for a little expense money. Yesterday you advanced me ten dollars and I wrote them down on account for you. Look ... go on ... I want you to see ...'

And he displayed a filthy notebook, on one page of which he had written down in pencil:

Received for expenses, J and J investigation: ten dollars.

'Today, I'd rather you gave me only five, because I'd spend the whole thing anyhow and it would go too fast. Then I wouldn't dare ask you for any more and, without money, I couldn't help you. Is five too much? Would you rather make it four?'

Maigret handed him five and, for no reason, as he held out the money, he gave the clown a searching glance.

Stuffed to the gills, the man in the trench coat, wearing an acid-green ribbon as a necktie, looked none the gayer, but his eyes bespoke an infinite gratitude, an infinite submissiveness in which there was some anxiety. Like a dog that at long last has found a kind master and begs for a sign of his satisfaction.

But, at that moment, Maigret was remembering the words of O'Brien. He was also remembering old Angelino, who, that morning, had set out as on every other day to take his walk and who had been killed in such a brutal way.

He asked himself if he had the right . . .

A brief, fleeting emotion. He was employing the old clown in a quiet sector, wasn't he?

'If ever they should kill him . . .' he thought.

And he recalled the office at the St Regis, the paper-knife that had snapped between Little John's nervous fingers, then MacGill, at the bar, busy talking about him to his girl friend.

Never had he begun an investigation in such vague, even lunatic circumstances. In point of fact, he had no investigation to conduct for anyone. Even old Monsieur d'Hoquélus, so insistent at the house in Meung-sur-Loire, was now politely begging him to return to France and mind his own business. Even O'Brien.

'I'll come around to see you tomorrow at about the same time,' Ronald Dexter said, picking up his hat. 'Don't forget I must return the handbill.'

J and J . . .

Maigret found himself alone again, out on the pavement, on an avenue he did not know, and he wandered about for some time, hands in pockets, pipe between his teeth, before catching sight of the lights of a Broadway cinema that he recognized and that put him on the right track.

Suddenly, just like that, for no reason, an impulse to write to Madame Maigret seized him and he went back to his hotel.

5

It was between the second and third floors that Maigret thought, rather inconsequentially, how he would not relish a man like O'Brien, for example, watching him go about his business that morning.

Even people who had worked with him for years and years, like Sergeant Lucas, did not always understand when he was in this state.

And did he know himself exactly what he was looking for? For example, when he stopped without reason halfway up the staircase, staring before him with eyes dilated and drained of all expression, he must have resembled a man whom heart trouble forces to a stop, no matter where, and who tries to look innocent so as to escape the pity of passers-by.

To judge from the number of children under seven he saw on the stairs, the landings, in the kitchens, and the bedrooms, the building after school hours must have been truly crawling with youngsters. And furthermore toys were scattered all over the place, broken scooters, old soap-boxes to which wheels had been somehow attached, collections of assorted odds and ends which made no sense to grown-ups, but which, for their makers, must have been prized possessions.

There was no *concierge*, as in French houses, and this somewhat complicated the Inspector's task. Nothing but letter boxes, in the hall, painted brown, each one numbered, some with a yellowed calling card or a name badly engraved on a metal strip.

It was ten in the morning and the hour, no doubt, when this barrack-like building lived its most characteristic life. One door out of every two or three was open. Women, their hair still uncombed, were busy with their housework, scrubbing their children's faces, shaking faded carpets out of the window.

'Excuse me, madame . . .'

They looked at him distrustfully. Whom could they take him for, with his great height, his heavy overcoat, his hat, which he always took off when he spoke to women, no matter who they were? No doubt for an insurance salesman, or the representative of the makers of the latest model of vacuum cleaner.

Moreover, there was his accent, but it made no impression, for here, it seemed, could be found not only freshly arrived Italians, but Poles and Czechs also.

'Do you know if there are still any tenants in the house who were living here thirty years ago?'

They frowned, for indeed that was the last question they expected. In Paris, in Montmartre, for example, or in the section where he lived, between the République and the Bastille, there was probably not a single building of any size where he would not have immediately found an old woman, an old man, or a couple who had lived in the house for the last thirty or forty years.

Here they answered him:

'We came only six months ago . . .'

Or one year, or two. The maximum was four years.

Instinctively, without realizing it, he lingered in front of the open doors to look in at a shabby kitchen encumbered with a bed, or at a bedroom where four or five people lived.

Rare were those who knew people on another floor. Three children, the eldest a boy who might have been eight – he probably had mumps, for he was wearing a heavy bandage around his head – had started to tag after him. Then the boy had grown bold and, now, hurried on ahead of Maigret.

'The man wants to know if you were here thirty years ago.'

A few old people, in their armchairs, by the windows, often near a cage with a canary, old folks brought over from Europe once a regular job had been found. And, among them, some who did not understand a word of English.

'I would like to know . . .'

The landings were wide and constituted a kind of no-man's-land where everything no longer of any use in the apartments was heaped; on the second-floor landing a thin woman, with yellow hair, was doing her washing.

Here, in one of these cells, *J and J* had come to live on their arrival in New York; here Little John, who now occupied a sumptuous apartment at the St Regis, spent months, perhaps years.

It was hard to pack more human lives into such little space, and yet one felt no warmth; here more than anywhere else one sensed a feeling of irremediable loneliness.

The milk bottles proved it. On the third floor Maigret froze like a pointer in front of one door because, on the straw mat, eight bottles of milk sat untouched, in a row.

He was about to question his friendly young guide when a man of about forty came out of the next room.

'Do you know who lives here?'

The man shrugged without answering, as if to say it was no business of his.

'You don't know if anyone's at home?'

'How would I know?'

'Is it a man, a woman?'

'A man, I think.'

'Old?'

'That depends on what you mean by old. My age, maybe ... I don't know. He only came about a month ago.'

What his nationality was, where he came from nobody cared, and his next-door neighbour, not intrigued by the milk bottles, went on down the stairs, turned around, frowning, to look at this strange visitor who asked absurd questions, and went off about his own business.

Had the tenant of this room gone away on a trip, forgetting to let the milkman know? Possibly. But people who live in a barracks such as this are poor people for whom a penny is a penny. Was he behind this door, perhaps? Alive or dead, sick or dying, he could stay there a long time before it occurred to anyone to worry about him.

Even if he had cried out, called for help, would anyone have troubled to answer?

A little boy, somewhere, was learning to play the violin. It was agony to hear the same stumbling phrase endlessly repeated, to visualize the clumsy bow that could do no better than drag a dismal sound from the instrument.

Top floor.

'Excuse me, madame, do you know anyone in the house who . . .'

He was told about an old woman whom no one knew, who was said to have lived in the building for a long time, and who had died two months before as she climbed the stairs with her shopping bag. But maybe she hadn't been there for thirty years?

It was becoming a nuisance to be preceded by this friendly urchin who kept staring at Maigret with inquisitive eyes, as if trying to solve the mystery of this strange being who had descended into his universe.

So much for that! He could go down now. He stopped to light his pipe, and he still sniffed at the air about him: he imagined a slender, blond young man climbing this same staircase with a violin case under his arm, another, his hair thinning already, who played a clarinet by the window while looking down into the street.

'Hello.'

He scowled instantly. The expression on his face must have been rather unusual, for the man who was climbing the stairs to meet him, and who was none other than O'Brien, could not keep from bursting into a resounding laugh.

It was to hide his feelings a bit that Maigret appeared embarrassed and muttered awkwardly:

'I thought you weren't having anything to do with this business.'

'And who says I'm having anything to do with it?'

'Are you going to tell me you've come to see some relatives?'

'For one thing, that wouldn't be entirely impossible, for all of us have all kinds of family.'

He was in a good mood. Had he realized what Maigret had come looking for in the house? He had sensed, in any case, that his French colleague was feeling a certain quality of emotion that morning that did not leave him unmoved, and his eyes expressed a greater friendliness than usual.

'I don't want to play cat and mouse with you. I came to find you. Let's get out of here, shall we?'

Maigret had walked down one flight before he turned and walked back up to give a dime to the little boy, who looked at it without thinking to say thank you.

'Are you beginning to understand New York? I wager you've

learned more this morning than you would have learned in a month at the St Regis or the Waldorf.'

They had paused instinctively on the doorstep and both were looking at the shop opposite, and at the tailor, the son of old Angelino, who worked at his pressing table, for the poor have no time to loiter over their grief.

A car bearing the emblem of the police was parked a few yards away.

'I went by your hotel. When they told me you'd gone out early, I thought I'd find you here. What I didn't know was that I'd have to climb four flights of stairs.'

A little flicker of irony, an allusion to a certain sensibility – perhaps a certain sentimentality – that he had just discovered in this heavy-set French inspector.

'If you had *concierges*, as we do, I wouldn't have had to climb all those stairs.'

'Don't you think you might have done it just the same?'

They got in the car.

'Where are we going?'

'Wherever you like. It really doesn't matter any more. I will simply drop you off in a slightly more central section, which will make you a little less gloomy.'

He lighted his pipe. A chauffeur was driving.

'I have bad news for you, my dear Inspector.'

Why, in that case, did he say it in a voice full of mild satisfaction?

'Jean Maura has been found.'

Frowning, Maigret turned and stared at him hard.

'You don't mean that your men –'

'Come! Don't be jealous!'

'It isn't jealousy on my part, but –'

'But?'

'It wouldn't fit with the rest,' he finished under his breath, as if to himself. 'No. It wouldn't tally.'

'Well, well!'

'What's so surprising?'

'Nothing. Tell me what you're thinking.'

'I'm not thinking. But if Jean Maura has reappeared, if he's alive . . .'

O'Brien nodded affirmatively.

'. . . I bet he was simply found settled at the St Regis with his father and MacGill.'

'Bravo, Maigret! That's exactly what happened. In spite of the individual freedom I told you about, maybe exaggerating a little bit to tease you, we do have a few small ways of investigating, especially in a hotel like the St Regis. Now, this morning, one breakfast more than usual was ordered for Little John's apartment. Jean Maura was there, settled in the big bedroom right next to his father's bedroom-office.'

'He hasn't been questioned?'

'You forget we have no reason to question him. No federal or other law requires passengers who disembark to rush forthwith into their fathers' arms, and the father never signed a complaint or notified the police of his son's disappearance.'

'One question.'

'Provided it's a discreet one.'

'Why does Little John, who maintains a luxurious suite of four or five rooms at the St Regis, personally occupy a bedroom that looks like a maid's room in France, and why does he work at a plain deal table, when his secretary sits in state behind an impressive mahogany desk?'

'Does it really surprise you?'

'A little.'

'Here, you see, it doesn't surprise anyone, any more than the son of a millionaire insisting on living in the Bronx, which we are just leaving, and going to his office every day by subway when he could have as many expensive cars as he'd like.

'The detail you mention about Little John is public knowledge. It's part of his legend, and it's smart publicity; the papers and magazines are only too happy to write about them.

'The man grown rich and powerful who has recreated, in the St Regis, the bedroom of his humble beginnings and who lives there simply, scorning the luxury of the other rooms.

'As to whether Little John is sincere, or if he's careful of his publicity, that's another question.'

Why did Maigret find himself replying without hesitation:

'He is sincere.'

'Ah!'

Whereupon they were silent for a good minute.

'Perhaps you would like to know the pedigree of MacGill, whom you don't seem to be too fond of? These are things I was told by chance, remember, it's not police information.'

This perpetual double-talk, even if it was only joking, exasperated Maigret.

'I'm listening.'

'He was born in New York, twenty-eight years ago, probably in the Bronx, parents unknown. For a few months, I don't know for just how long, he was brought up by a children's aid society just outside New York.

'He was taken from the orphanage by a man who stated he was willing to be responsible for him and who furnished the moral and financial guarantees required in such cases.'

'Little John . . .'

'Who was not called Little John yet and who had just set up a small business in secondhand phonographs. The child was put in the care of a certain Mrs MacGill, a Scotchwoman, the widow of a funeral-parlour employee. This woman and the child left the country to live in Canada, at St Jerome. When he grew up, MacGill studied in Montreal, which explains why he speaks French as well as English. Then, around the age of twenty, he disappeared, to reappear six months ago as private secretary to Little John. That's all I know and I don't guarantee that this gossip is correct.

'And now, what are you going to do?'

He was smiling his softest, most irritating smile.

'Are you going to call on your client? For, after all, it was young Maura who asked for your help and who –'

'I don't know.'

Maigret was furious. Because, actually, it was no longer Jean Maura and his fears that interested him, but his father, Little John, and the house on 169th Street, and a certain cabaret programme, and finally an old Italian by the name of Angelino Giacomi, who had been run down like a dog as he was crossing the street.

He would go to the St Regis, obviously, because he could not do otherwise. He would undoubtedly be told again that he was not needed; he would be offered a cheque and a boat ticket to France.

The wisest thing to do was to go back the way he had come, even if it meant being on his guard for the rest of his days against all the young men and all the d'Hoquélus of creation.

'Shall I drop you there?'

'Where?'

'At the St Regis.'

'If you like.'

'Shall I see you again this evening? I think I will be free for dinner. If you are too, give me a ring and I'll call for you at your hotel or anywhere else. Today is my lucky day; I have one of the office cars at my disposal. I wonder if we will be drinking to your departure?'

And his eyes said no. He had understood Maigret so well! But he needed to escape, by way of a joke, from the least emotion.

'Good luck!'

It was a disagreeable prospect, an irksome task. Maigret could have predicted almost exactly what was going to happen. Nothing unforeseen, nothing important, and yet he did not feel he had the right to avoid it.

He said to the desk clerk, as he had done on arriving:

'Will you please tell Monsieur Jean Maura that I am here to see him?'

The desk clerk was already briefed, for he simply picked up the telephone.

'Mr MacGill? There is someone here asking for Mr Jean Maura. I think so, yes. Wait a moment until I make sure. Could I have your name, please?'

And when the Inspector had given it:

'That's right. Very well. I will send him up.'

So, MacGill had immediately guessed it was he.

A bellboy took him up once again. He recognized the floor, the corridor, the apartment.

'Come in!'

And a smiling MacGill, with no trace of resentment in his bearing, a MacGill who seemed freed of a great weight, came towards him and held out his hand without appearing to remember that Maigret had refused it the day before.

Since Maigret ignored it again, he exclaimed equably:

'Still annoyed, my dear Maigret?'

Well! Before he used to say 'Inspector', and this little touch of familiarity was perhaps not without significance.

'You see we were right, the Chief and I, and you were wrong. By the way, let me congratulate you on your police friends. It didn't take you long to hear about the prodigal's return.'

He went to open the communicating door. Jean Maura was in the next room, with his father. The young man saw the Inspector first, and blushed.

'Your friend Maigret,' announced MacGill, 'would like to talk to you. You don't mind, Chief?'

Little John, also, came into the office, but he contented himself with a vague nod in the Inspector's direction. As for the young man, he came over and shook hands, embarrassed and constrained. He stammered, looking away:

'I beg your pardon.'

MacGill preserved his gay, easy manner while Little John, on the contrary, seemed troubled, weary. He must not have slept the night before. His glance, for the first time, was evasive, and to look self-assured, he felt the need to light one of the plump cigars made specially for him and stamped with his initials.

His hand trembled a little as he struck the match. He probably was in a hurry, also, to get this unavoidable farce over with.

'What are you apologizing for?' inquired Maigret, who knew perfectly well this question was expected of him.

'For having left you so shabbily. You see, among the reporters who came aboard I saw a fellow I met last year. He had a flask of whisky with him and made me drink some because he was set on celebrating my home-coming.'

Maigret did not inquire where on the boat this scene had taken place, for he knew it was purely imaginary, that it had been suggested to the young man by either Little John or MacGill.

By MacGill, probably, who was looking a little too detached, too indifferent during his pupil's recitation, like a teacher who refrains from prompting his favourite student.

'He had some girls with him in the taxi.'

How plausible, this journalist who went to work, at ten o'clock in the morning, with a cabful of young women in tow! They weren't taking the trouble to make up a good story. They were tossing him an explanation like any old bone to chew on, not caring whether he believed the tale or not. Why bother? Wasn't he out of the picture now?

Curiously enough, Jean Maura was much less tired than his father. He had the look of a young man who's had a good night's sleep and he seemed more embarrassed than upset.

'I should have let you know. I did look for you on deck.'

'No!'

Why had Maigret said that?

'You're right, I didn't look for you. I'd been on my good behaviour too long during that trip. I didn't dare drink in front of you, except that last evening. You remember? I even apologized for that.'

Little John, as the day before, had gone to plant himself before the window and had drawn back the curtain with one hand, in a gesture that must be habitual with him.

MacGill, for his part, pretended to busy himself like a man who is only moderately interested in the conversation and he indulged in the luxury of making a routine phone call.

'A cocktail, Inspector?'

'No, thank you.'

'As you like.'

Jean Maura was concluding:

'I don't know what happened then. It's the first time I have ever been completely drunk. We went to a lot of places, drank with a lot of people I wouldn't know if I saw them again.'

'At the Donkey Bar?' inquired Maigret, glancing ironically at MacGill.

'I don't know . . . It's possible . . . There was a party at the house of somebody my friend knows –'

'In the country?'

This time the young man looked quickly at his father's secretary, but, since MacGill wasn't facing him, he was forced to answer on his own and he said:

'Yes . . . In the country . . . We drove out by car.'

'And you came back only yesterday evening?'

'Yes.'

'You were brought back?'

'Yes ... No, I mean, I was brought back as far as town.'

'But not as far as the hotel?'

Again a glance at MacGill.

'No ... not as far as the hotel ... I didn't want them to, I was ashamed.'

'I suppose you don't need me any more?'

This time it was his father he looked at as if asking for help, and it was odd to see Little John, the typical man of action, shun the conversation as if it did not concern him. Yet it concerned his son, to whom he wrote letters so tender they might have been taken for love letters.

'I've had a long talk with my father ...'

'And with Mr MacGill?'

He did not answer yes or no. He almost denied it, changed his mind, continued:

'I am embarrassed to have made you come so far because of my childish fears. I know how concerned you have been. I wonder if you will ever forgive me for having left you in the dark as to what had happened to me.'

As he spoke, he too seemed surprised by the attitude of his father whom he was begging with his eyes to come to his rescue.

And MacGill, once again, took the situation in hand:

'Don't you think, Chief, that this would be the time to settle unfinished business with the Inspector?'

At that, Little John did turn, flicked the ash from his cigar with his little finger, walked over to the mahogany desk.

'I think,' he said, 'there's not much to settle. I apologize, Inspector, for not having received you with all the cordiality that might have been wished for. I thank you for having concerned yourself with such solicitude about my son. I ask you simply to accept the cheque which my secretary will hand over to you and which is only slight compensation for the trouble my son and I have caused you.'

He hesitated a second, wondering, no doubt, if he would shake hands with the Inspector. He finally bowed rather stiffly and walked towards the connecting door, nodding to Jean to follow him.

'Good-bye, sir,' the young man said, hastily shaking Maigret's hand.

He added, with what seemed complete sincerity:

'I'm not afraid any more, you know.'

He smiled. A pale smile, like the smile of a convalescent. Where-upon he disappeared behind his father into the next room.

The cheque was all ready in the chequebook lying on the desk. Without sitting down MacGill tore it out and handed it to Maigret, perhaps expecting to see him refuse it.

But Maigret calmly glanced at the amount: two thousand dollars. Then he folded the piece of paper with deliberate care and slipped it in his wallet, saying:

'Thank you.'

That was all. The irritating business was over and done with. He went out. He did not even say good-bye to MacGill, who had followed him to the door and finally closed it behind him.

Despite his horror of cocktails and of exclusively luxurious places, Maigret stopped in the bar and downed two manhattans.

Then he struck off in the direction of his hotel and, as he walked, he shook his head now and then and moved his lips like a man absorbed in a long discussion with himself.

Hadn't the clown promised him to be at the Berwick at the same time as the day before?

He was there, on the bench, but his expression was so sad, so heart-rending, that it was obvious he'd been drinking.

'I know you're going to call me a backslider,' he began, rising to his feet. 'And it's true, you know, I am a coward. I knew what would happen, but I couldn't resist.'

'Have you had any lunch?'

'Not yet, but I'm not hungry. No, strange as it may seem, I'm not hungry. I'm too ashamed of myself. I'd have done better not to let you see me in this condition. And yet I've only had two little drinks – gin – and see, I picked gin because it's the weakest hard liquor there is. Otherwise, I'd have taken scotch. I was so tired, and I said to myself: "Ronald, if you have one gin, just one ..."

'Only I had three ... Did I say three? I don't know now ... I'm disgusting, and it was your money I spent. You'd better fire me. Oh no, don't fire me yet, I've got something for you ... Wait. Something important, it'll come back to me. If only there were some air in here ... Could we get a little air?'

He sniffed, wiping his nose.

'I'll eat a bite, after all, not before I've told you. Wait a second ... yes ... I saw my friend again, yesterday evening ... Germain. You remember Germain? ... Poor old Germain! Imagine a man who's led an active life, who's travelled with circuses all over the world, and who's nailed to a wheelchair.

'He'd be better off dead, wouldn't he? ... What am I saying? ... Don't go thinking I wish he would die. But if it had to happen to me, I'd rather be dead. That's what I meant.

'Well! I was right to say Germain would do anything for me ... There's a man who would turn himself inside out for other people.

'He doesn't look like much ... He grumbles ... You'd take him for a self-centred old man. And yet he spent hours leafing through his notebooks to find some trace of *J and J*. Look, I've got another paper.'

He paled, turned green, searched frantically in his pockets, and seemed on the verge of bursting into tears.

'I deserve to be ...'

No. He deserved nothing at all, since he finally found the document under his handkerchief.

'It's not very clean, but you'll understand why.'

This time it was the programme of a road company that had toured the United States thirty years ago. In big letters the name of a dance-hall queen whose photograph was on the cover, then other names, a pair of tightrope walkers, Robson the comic, Lucille the Medium, and finally, at the very bottom of the listing, the musical comedians, *J and J*.

'Read the names carefully ... Robson died in a railroad accident, ten or fifteen years ago, I don't remember ... Germain told me about it. You remember I told you yesterday Germain has an old friend who comes to see him every Wednesday? Don't you think that's touching now? ... And, you know, there was never anything between them, not one single thing!'

He was going to melt into tears again.

'I never saw her. They say she was very fragile and pale in those days, so fragile that she was called The Angel. Well! Now she's so fat that – We are going to eat, aren't we? ... I don't know whether it's the gin, but I've got pains in my stomach. It's disgusting to ask

you for more money. What was I saying? ... The Angel, Lucille ...
Germain's old friend ... Today's Wednesday ... She's sure to be at
his house around five o'clock. She'll bring a little cake, like every
week ... I swear I won't touch a piece if we go, because this old
woman who used to be called The Angel and who brings a cake to
Germain every week –'

'Did you tell your friend we would come?'

'I told him perhaps – I could come and pick you up at four-thirty.
It's pretty far, especially by subway, because the line isn't direct –'

'Come on!'

Maigret had suddenly made up his mind not to let his decidedly
too lugubrious clown out of sight and, after feeding him, he took
him back to the hotel and bedded him down on the green plush sofa.

Then, like the day before, he wrote a long letter to Madame
Maigret.

6

Maigret followed his clown up the creaking stairs and because Dexter, God knows why, felt some need to walk on tiptoe, the Inspector caught himself doing the same.

The melancholy man, however, had slept off his gin and, if his eyes were dull and his tongue a bit thick, he had abandoned his wail for a slightly firmer tone.

It was he who had given the taxi driver an address in Greenwich Village and Maigret had discovered, in the heart of New York, a few minutes away from the skyscrapers, a little city set within a city. It was almost a provincial town, with houses no taller than those in Bordeaux or Dijon, with little shops, quiet streets along which one could stroll leisurely, and inhabitants who appeared to pay no heed to the monster metropolis surrounding them.

'Here we are,' he had announced.

Just then Maigret had noted something like fear in his voice and he had looked his companion in the shabby trench coat squarely in the face.

'You're sure you said I was coming?'

'I said you might come.'

'And who did you say I was?'

He was expecting as much. The clown became upset.

'I was going to talk to you about that . . . I didn't know how to handle it, because Germain has grown pretty cantankerous. When I came to see him the first time, he made me take one or two quick ones. I don't know now just what I did tell him, that you were a very rich man, and were looking for a son you'd never seen. You mustn't be mad at me . . . I did the best I could . . . to the point where he was touched and why, I'm sure, he hurried to see what he could find.'

It was silly. The Inspector could imagine what the clown, with a few drinks under his belt, had invented.

And now Dexter, the nearer they came to the house of the former Mr Loyal, seemed hesitant. Wasn't he capable of having lied the whole way down the line, even to Maigret? No, for there was the photograph and the programme.

Light under the door. A slight murmur of voices. Dexter, stammering:

'Knock ... there's no bell.'

Maigret knocked. Silence. Someone coughed. The sound of a cup being set down on a saucer.

'Come in.'

And then one got the impression, simply by stepping across a worn straw door mat, of taking an immense voyage in time and space! Of no longer being in New York, two steps from the skyscrapers that, at that hour, flung their fires across the Manhattan sky. Was this still the age of electricity?

The lighting in the room could have come from an oil lamp: this impression was caused by the thick, pleated red silk that shaded the standard lamp.

There was a single circle of light in the middle of the room, and within this circle of light sat a man in a wheelchair, an old man who must once have been very stout and was still corpulent, but who was now so flaccid that he looked as if he had been abruptly deflated. Long wisps of white hair floated around his shiny bald skull, as he bent his head to stare at the intruders over the rims of his glasses.

'Forgive me for disturbing you,' Maigret said, the clown hiding behind him.

There was another person in the room, as fat as Germain, purple-faced, with incredibly blonde hair, and she was smiling with a small, smeared red mouth.

Surely this was some corner of a waxwork museum? No, for the figures did move, the tea was steaming in the two cups set on a table beside a sliced cake.

'Ronald Dexter told me that you might have the information I want.'

The walls were covered with posters and photographs. A long whip, the handle still encircled with multi-coloured ribbons, occupied a prominent position.

'Will you offer chairs to the gentlemen, Lucille?'

The voice had remained what it no doubt was in the days when the man, at the entrance to the ring, used to summon the clowns and the stars, and it thundered strangely in this too small and crowded room, which overflowed so that poor Lucille had difficulty clearing two black chairs with red velvet seats.

'This young man who knew me long ago ...'

Was this opening remark not a poem? First Dexter, in the eyes of the old circus man, became a young man. Then the phrase 'who knew me long ago' and not 'whom I used to know ...'

'... has informed me of your painful situation. If your son had belonged to the circus world, even if only for a few weeks, I can assure you that you would have had only to come to me and say:

'"Germain, it was in such and such a year ... He played in such and such a number ... He was thus and so ..."'

'And Germain would not have had to leaf through his records.'

His gesture indicated the stacks of paper one saw everywhere, on the furniture and on the floor, even on the bed, for Lucille had had to put some there to clear two chairs.

'Germain has all that here.'

He pointed to his head and tapped it with his finger.

'But, the moment it's a question of the cabarets, I tell you this:

'It is to my old friend, Lucille, that you must appeal. She is here ... She is listening to you ... If you will, please, speak to her.'

Maigret had let his pipe go out and yet he needed it to regain a toe-hold on reality. He was holding it in his hand, sheepishly, no doubt, for the fat lady said to him with a fresh smile that resembled, because of her clumsy make-up, the smile of a doll:

'You may smoke. Robson used to smoke a pipe too. I smoked one myself, in the years after his death ... Perhaps you won't understand that, but it was still a bit of him.'

'You did a very interesting number,' murmured the Inspector out of politeness.

'The best of its kind, I don't deny it. Everybody will tell you so. Robson was unique – his bearing, especially, and you can't imagine how much bearing counts in an act like that. He used to wear a frock coat, with tight-fitting breeches and black silk stockings. He had magnificent calves ... Wait a moment.'

She searched, not in a handbag, but in a silk reticule with a silver clasp, and drew out a photograph, a publicity print in which her husband figured in the costume she had just described, a black velvet mask over his eyes, moustaches waxed, legs flexed, brandishing a magician's wand at the invisble spectators.

'And here I am, at the same time.'

An ageless woman, slender, sad, with hands crossed under her chin in the most artificial of poses, stared vacantly into nothingness.

'I may say we travelled all over the world ... In some countries, Robson would wear a red silk cape over his evening clothes and, with a red spotlight, he really did look diabolic doing the magic coffin number ... I hope that you believe in mind-reading?'

It was stifling. One longed for a breath of air, but thick, faded plush curtains hung before the windows, as heavy as a theatre drop. Who knows? Maigret guessed that these curtains had perhaps been cut down from some old stage curtain.

'Germain has told me that you are looking for your son or your brother.'

'My brother,' he hastened to confirm, thinking suddenly that neither Joseph nor Joachim could possibly be his son.

'That's what I thought ... I hadn't quite understood ... That's why I expected to see an old man. Which of the two was your brother? The violin or the clarinet?'

'I don't know, madame.'

'What do you mean, you don't know?'

'My brother disappeared when he was a baby. It's only recently, by chance, that we found a trace of him.'

This was absurd. It was odious. And yet, it was impossible to tell the simple truth to these two who dosed themselves with make-believe. It was almost an act of Christian charity towards them and, topping it all, that fool Dexter, who knew it was all a hoax, seemed to be taken in and was even beginning to sniffle.

'Stand in the light, so I can see your features ...'

'I don't believe there was any resemblance between my brother and me.'

'How do you know, if he was kidnapped so young?'

Kidnapped! No less! Now, the comedy had to be played out to the end.

'In my opinion, it would probably be Joachim ... No, wait ... There's something of Joseph in the forehead. Yet, I don't know, maybe I'm confusing their names ... Imagine, I never could tell them apart ... One of them had long blond hair, like a girl's, hair almost the colour of mine ...'

'Joachim, I think,' said Maigret.

'Let me remember ... How would you know? The other one was a little broader in the shoulders and wore glasses ... It's funny! We lived together for almost a year and there are some things I don't remember at all, others that I see now as if it were yesterday ... We had all signed up for a tour through the South, Mississippi, Louisiana, Texas ... It was very hard, for the people down there were still practically savages. Some of them came to the show on horseback ... One night they killed a Negro during our number, I don't remember why.

'What I wonder is, which of them was Jessie with?

'And was it Jessie or Bessie? Probably Bessie ... No, Jessie! I'm sure it was Jessie, because once I said that it made three J's: Joseph, Joachim and Jessie ...'

If only Maigret had been able to ask questions, quietly, to get exact answers! But he had to let her talk on, follow the involved meanderings of an old woman's mind that must never have been very logical.

'Poor little Jessie. She was touching ... I had taken her under my wing, for she was in a delicate condition.'

What kind of delicate condition? That would come out in time, no doubt.

'She was slender and frail ... I was slender and frail too, in those days, fragile as a flower. I was called The Angel, did you know?'

'I know.'

'Robson gave me the name. He didn't say, "My Angel," which is banal, just "The Angel" ... I don't know if you catch the nuance ... Bessie – No, Jessie was very young. I wonder if she was eighteen. And one felt that she had been unhappy. I never knew where they'd found her. I say "they" because I don't know if it was Joseph or Joachim. Since the three of them were never apart, one inevitably wondered which of them it had been.'

'What part did she play in your show?'

327

'None. She was not an artist. She was an orphan, certainly, for I never saw her write to anyone. They must have plucked her from her dying mother's arms.'

'And she followed the company?'

'She followed us everywhere. It was very strenuous. The manager was a beast. Did you know him, Germain?'

'His brother is still in New York ... Someone was talking about him last week. He's selling programmes at the Garden.'

'He used to treat us like dogs ... Robson was the only one to stand up to him. I think, if he'd been allowed to get away with it, he'd have fed us dog biscuits to save on the food. We lived in flea-ridden hovels. He finally left us stranded fifty miles from New Orleans, running off with the house receipts, and once again it was Robson –'

Happily she suddenly decided to nibble on a piece of cake. It provided a brief respite, but soon she went on, wiping her lips with a lace handkerchief.

'*J and J*, excuse me for putting it like that since one of the two is your brother – I wager it is Joseph – *J and J* were not artists like us, with top billing, but they were listed at the very end of the programme ... There's no disgrace in that ... Don't hold it against me if I've hurt your feelings.'

'Not at all. Not at all!'

'They made very little money, really nothing to speak of, but their travelling expenses were paid, and their food, if one can call that food. Only, there was Jessie ... They had to pay for Jessie's train fare, and for her meals. Not always her meals. Wait, I remember ... I believe I am in contact with Robson.'

And her enormous bosom heaved under her dress, her fat little fingers fluttered.

'Pardon me, sir. I suppose that you do believe in the after-life? If not, you wouldn't put so much passion into searching for your brother, who may, after all, be dead. I feel that Robson has just entered into communication with me ... I know it, I am sure of it. Let me commune with him and he will tell me himself everything you need to know.'

The clown was so moved that he let out a kind of groan. But was it not at the sight of the cake, of which no one had thought to offer him a piece?

Maigret stared fixedly at the floor, wondering how much longer he could stand this.

'Yes, Robson ... I am listening ... Germain, won't you dim the light?'

Both of them must have been used to these spiritualistic séances, for Germain, without leaving his wheelchair, turned off one of the two bulbs under the red silk shade.

'I see them, yes ... Beside a broad river ... And there are cotton plantations all around ... Help me again, Robson, my darling ... Help me as you used to do ... A big table ... We are all there and you are the guest of honour ... *J and J* ... Wait ... She is between the two of us. A fat black woman is waiting at the table ...'

The clown groaned again, but she went on in the monotone that she must have assumed formerly in her medium act:

'Jessie is very pale ... We have been travelling by train ... We've travelled a long time ... The train stopped in the middle of nowhere ... Everybody is worn out ... The manager has gone off to put up the posters ... And *J and J* each cut a piece of their meat to give to Jessie.'

It would have been simpler for her, obviously, to recount these things without any mystico-theatrical claptrap. Maigret longed to say to her:

'Facts, please ... And talk like the rest of us.'

But if a Lucille had begun to talk like the rest of them, if a Germain had begun to look squarely at his mementoes, would either of them have had the strength to go on living?

'... And everywhere I see them, it's the same ... They are both near her and they share their meals ... Because they haven't enough money to buy a real meal.'

'You said that the tour lasted a year?'

She pretended to struggle, painfully raised her eyelids, stammered:

'Did I say something? ... I beg your pardon ... I was with Robson.'

'I was asking how long the tour lasted.'

'Over a year. We had left for three or four months. But it's always like that ... A lot of things go wrong on the road. Then there's the question of money ... There's never enough money to come back. So, on it goes, from town to town, and even to little villages.'

'You don't know which of the two was in love with Jessie?'

'I don't know. Was it Joachim, maybe? He's your brother, isn't he? I am convinced that you look like Joachim ... He was my favourite and he played the violin wonderfully, not during his act, because in his number, he only did improvisations. But when we happened to be in the same hotel for a day or so ...'

He could visualize her, in some frame hotel in Texas or Louisiana, darning her husband's black silk stockings, and this Jessie, who at meals humbly nibbled a little of the two men's portions.

'You've never known what happened to them?'

'As I told you, the company broke up in New Orleans because the manager left us high and dry. Robson and I got another engagement right away, because our act was well known. I don't know how the others earned enough money to pay their fares.'

'You came back to New York immediately?'

'I think so. I don't remember exactly, but I know that I saw one of the two *J*'s again in a booking agent's office on Broadway – it must have been soon afterwards. What makes me think so is that I'd put on one of the dresses I wore on the tour ... Which of the two men was it? ... It struck me, seeing him all alone, you never saw one without the other.'

Abruptly, taking them all by surprise, Maigret stood up. He felt he could not last five minutes more in that stifling atmosphere.

'Forgive me for this intrusion,' he said, turning to old Germain.

'If it had been a question of the circus instead of the cabaret ...' the old man repeated, like a damaged record.

And she:

'I'll give you my address ... I still give private consultations ... I have a nice little group of clients, who trust me ... And, to you I can tell this, which is the truth: it's Robson who keeps on helping me ... I don't always admit this, because some people are afraid of spirits.'

She handed him a card that he stuffed in his pocket. The clown gave one farewell glance at the cake and seized his hat.

'Thank you again.'

Phew! Never had he gone downstairs faster and, once out on the street, he gulped in the air. He felt as though he were setting foot again on man's earth. The lamp posts were suddenly like old friends encountered after a long absence.

There were lighted shops, passers-by. A flesh-and-blood boy was hopping on the edge of the pavement.

True, the other one was still there, the clown, who could still murmur in his mournful voice:

'I did my best . . .'

Another five dollars, obviously!

They were dining together again in a French restaurant. On returning to the Berwick, Maigret had found a telephone message from O'Brien asking him to call back as soon as he came in.

'My evening is my own, as I hoped,' O'Brien had said. 'If you're also free, we can have dinner and a talk together.'

They had been sitting opposite each other for more than a quarter of an hour and he had still said nothing; he contented himself, as he ordered his meal, with smiling faintly at Maigret in his at once ironic and satisfied way.

'You didn't notice,' he murmured finally, attacking a magnificent Châteaubriand, 'that you were being followed again?'

The Inspector frowned, not because of any immediate alarm, but because he was annoyed not to have been aware of it.

'I noticed it immediately when I came to pick you up at the Berwick. This time it isn't Bill, but the person who ran down old Angelino. I bet you anything you like that he's outside now.

'We'll easily see when we leave.

'I don't know when he started on the job. Did you leave the hotel this afternoon?'

This time Maigret looked up with anguished eyes, sat thinking a moment, and finally brought his fist down on the table, uttering a 'damn' that made his redheaded companion smile again.

'Were you on some very compromising errands?'

'Your man is swarthy, obviously, since he's a Sicilian. He wears a light grey hat, doesn't he?'

'Exactly.'

'In that case, he was in the hotel lobby when I came down from my room with my clown, around five. We bumped into each other as we were both hurrying to the door.'

'So, he's been following you since five o'clock.'

'And in that case . . .'

Was it to be the same thing, again, as with poor Angelino?

'Can't you do anything, you people on the police force,' he asked testily, 'to protect people?'

'That depends perhaps on the danger which threatens them.'

'Would you have protected the old tailor?'

'If I knew what I know now, yes.'

'Well, there are two other people who need protection, and I think you would do well to take the necessary steps before you finish your steak.'

He gave O'Brien Germain's address. Then he took out of his pocket the card of the superlucid medium and handed it to him.

'There must be a telephone here.'

'Excuse me, please.'

Well! Well! The imperturbably curly-haired O'Brien was not mocking now, was not urging the famous individual freedom!

He was a long time telephoning and Maigret took advantage of it to glance out into the street. On the pavement opposite he recognized the light grey hat he had glimpsed in his hotel lobby, and when he sat down again, he drank two large glasses of wine.

O'Brien returned presently and he was polite enough – or perhaps malicious enough – not to ask a single question and to go on quietly with his meal where he'd left off.

'In short,' grumbled Maigret, eating without relish, 'if I hadn't been there, old Angelino would not be dead, no doubt.'

He was waiting, hoping, for denials, but O'Brien simply said:

'Probably not.'

'In that case, if other accidents were to happen . . .'

'They would be your fault, is that it? Is that what you're thinking? Well, it's what I've thought, myself, from the very first. Do you remember the dinner we had together the evening you arrived?'

'Does that mean those people must be left alone?'

'It's too late now.'

'What do you mean?'

'It's too late, because we are also involved now, because, in any event, even if you drop out, if you sail for Le Havre or Cherbourg tomorrow, they will still feel hunted.'

'Little John?'

'I have no idea.'

'MacGill?'

'I don't know. I must add at once that I'm not the one who is conducting this case. Tomorrow or the day after, when the right moment comes, when my colleague expresses a wish to, for this is no business of mine and he's in charge of his own investigation, I'll introduce you to him. He's a good man.'

'Like you?'

'Just the opposite. That's why I say he's a good man. I've just telephoned him. He'd like me to give him a few details about these people he's to protect.'

'It's a lunatics' tale!' growled Maigret.

'What?'

'I say, it's a lunatics' tale! Because it involves, if not two authentic lunatics, at least two poor fools who risk paying with their lives for indiscretions they've committed to help me. And, to top it off, without meaning to, because of that fool of a crying clown, I played on their sympathies to soften them up.'

O'Brien was startled to see Maigret so nervous, biting off his words and eating his food in a kind of rage.

'You'll probably tell me that what I found out doesn't amount to much and that the game was not worth the candle. But perhaps we don't share the same ideas about police investigations.'

His companion's bland smile exasperated him.

'My visit this morning to the house on 169th Street amused you, too, didn't it, and you'd probably have exploded with laughter if you'd seen me, marching on the heels of a little boy, sniffing in all the corners and knocking at all the doors.

'That doesn't prevent me, who arrived in America only a few days ago, from maintaining that I now know more than you do about Little John and the other *J*.

'Question of temperament, doubtless. You have to have facts, isn't that so, precise facts, while I –'

He stopped short, seeing his companion about to burst into laughter, despite the effort made to hold it back, and he chose to laugh too.

'You must excuse me . . . I lived through the most idiotic moments of my life a little while ago. Listen to this . . .'

He related his visit to old Germain, described Lucille in her trances or her fake trances, and wound up:

'Do you understand why I'm afraid for them? ... Angelino knew something and they didn't hesitate to put him out of the way. Did Angelino know more than these two? It's likely. But I stayed one whole hour at the former Mr Loyal's. Lucille was there.'

'I see ... And yet, I don't think the danger's as great.'

'Because you think as I do, I bet, that it's on 169th Street that those people smell danger?'

An affirmative nod.

'What we need to know is whether Jessie also lived in the apartment house opposite the tailor's. Is it possible to unearth, in police records, traces of any tragedy or accident that might have occurred in the house some thirty years ago?'

'It's more complicated than in your country, especially if the tragedy was not what I might call an official tragedy, if there was no investigation. In France, I remember, a record would be found at police headquarters of all the tenants who lived in the house, and of their deaths, if any.'

'Because you also believe –'

'I don't believe anything. I repeat that I'm not in charge of this investigation ... I'm on a very different assignment, which will take me weeks more, if not months. Presently, when we've had our brandy, I'll phone my colleague. I know that he went to the immigration office this afternoon. There, at least, they keep a record of every person who has entered the United States. Wait ... I wrote that down somewhere on a piece of paper.'

Always the same nonchalant movements, as if to minimize the importance of what he was doing. Perhaps, after all, it was more a kind of modesty towards Maigret than bureaucratic caution?

'Here's the date of Maura's entry into the United States. *Joachim-Jean Maire Maura, born in Bayonne, age twenty-two, violinist* ... The name of the ship, which has been out of service for a long time: the *Aquitaine*. As for the second *J*, he can't be anyone but *Joseph-Ernest-Dominique Daumale, age twenty-four, born in Bayonne* too. He's not listed as a clarinettist, but as composer ... I suppose you catch the difference?

'They gave me one other item of information which is perhaps of no importance, but which I think I should pass on to you ... Two years and a half after his arrival, Joachim Maura, who was already

334

going by the name of John Maura, and who gave as his address in New York the building you know on 169th Street, left America for Europe, where he stayed a little less than ten months.

'We find a record of his return, after this lapse of time, on board an English boat, the *Mooltan*.

'I don't think my colleague will trouble to cable France on this point. But, knowing you ...'

Maigret had thought of it the moment his friend had mentioned Bayonne. Already he was mentally composing the cable to the police of that city:

Request urgently all details re Joachim-Jean-Marie Maura and Joseph-Ernest-Dominique Daumale, who left France the ...

It was the American's idea to order two Armagnacs in snifters. He was also the first to light his pipe.

'What are you thinking about?' he asked as Maigret sat, impassive and thoughtful, his glass held close under his nostrils.

'About Jessie.'

'And you're wondering what?'

It was almost a game they were playing, the man with an everlasting smile that he kept vague, and the other with a scowl of assumed peevishness.

'I'm wondering whose mother she is?'

For a second the redhead's smile vanished as he murmured, swallowing a sip of his liqueur:

'That will depend on the death certificate, won't it?'

They had understood each other. Neither wished to define his thoughts further.

Maigret, however, could not help growling, feigning a bad temper that had already passed:

'If it's ever found! ... What with this precious individual liberty of yours preventing you from keeping any record of who lives or dies!'

'Another round, waiter!' O'Brien contented himself with ordering as he pointed to their empty glasses.

And he added:

'Your poor Sicilian must be dying of thirst out there on the pavement.'

7

It was late, probably close to ten o'clock. Maigret's watch had stopped and the Berwick, unlike the St Regis, did not go so far in its solicitude for its guests as to install electric wall clocks. What was the point of knowing the time, anyhow? Maigret, that morning, was in no hurry. To tell the truth, he had nothing to do. For the first time since he had disembarked in New York, he was greeted on awakening by truly springlike sunshine: a little bit of sun found its way into his bedroom and bathroom.

Moreover, because of this sunshine, he had hung his mirror on the window sash, and there he was shaving, exactly as in Paris, where he always had a ray of sun on his cheek when he shaved in the morning. Isn't it wrong to think that big cities are so very different, even New York, which a whole body of literature makes out to be a kind of monstrous man mixer?

Here he was, in New York, he, Maigret, and there was a window sash at just the right height for shaving, a slanting sunbeam that made him blink, and opposite, in some office or workshop, two young women in white overalls were laughing at him.

But he was to shave himself, that morning, in instalments, for twice the ringing of the telephone interrupted him. The first time the voice sounded far away, a voice that recalled recent memories but that he did not recognize.

'Hello . . . Inspector Maigret?'

'Yes.'

'Is this Inspector Maigret?'

'Yes, indeed.'

'Is this Inspector Maigret on the phone?'

'Yes, blast it!'

Then the voice, so mournful that it verged on the tragic:

336

'Ronald Dexter speaking.'

'Yes. Well?'

'I am terribly sorry to disturb you, but it's absolutely necessary that I see you.'

'You have something new?'

'Please, just let me see you as soon as possible.'

'Are you far from here?'

'Not very far.'

'It's urgent?'

'Very urgent.'

'In that case, come to the hotel right away.'

'Thank you.'

Maigret had begun by smiling. Then, on second thoughts, he had detected something in the clown's tone of voice that disturbed him.

He had scarcely begun to lather his cheeks again when the telephone called him back into the bedroom. He dried his face hastily.

'Hello.'

'Inspector Maigret?'

A clear and distinct voice this time, almost too distinct, with a strong American accent in very careful French.

'Speaking.'

'This is Lieutenant Lewis!'

'Yes?'

'My associate O'Brien has told me it would be wise for me to get in touch with you as soon as possible. Can I meet you this morning?'

'Excuse me, Lieutenant, for asking you this, but my watch has stopped. What time is it?'

'Ten-thirty.'

'I would have been glad to come to your office. Unfortunately, just a moment ago I made an appointment. It's possible, and even likely, that it may be about something that interests you. Do you mind coming to see me in my room at the Berwick?'

'I'll be there in twenty minutes.'

'Is there something new?'

Maigret was sure that the other man was still on the telephone when he asked the question, but the lieutenant pretended not to have heard and hung up.

Two down! All he had to do now was finish shaving and dress.

He had just phoned Room Service to order his breakfast, when someone knocked at the door.

It was Dexter. A Dexter whom Maigret, for all his understanding of the phenomenon, looked at in amazement.

Never in his life had he seen a man so pale and giving so much the impression of a sleepwalker loose in New York in full daylight.

The clown was not drunk. Moreover, he did not wear the tearful expression of his drunken moments. On the contrary, he seemed entirely self-possessed, but in a special way.

To be exact, he looked, standing there in the doorway, like actors in slapstick comedies who have just been hit on the head with an axe and who stand upright for a good minute, glassy-eyed, before they collapse.

'Inspector . . .' he began, articulating with some difficulty.

'Come in and shut the door.'

'Inspector . . .'

Then Maigret saw that the man was not drunk, but had a frightening hangover. Only by a miracle did he keep on his feet. The slightest movement must have made his head spin and whirl. His face wrinkled with pain, and his hands mechanically sought the support of the table.

'Sit down!'

He shook his head. No doubt, had he sat down, he would have sunk into a comatose sleep.

'Inspector, I am a louse.'

His shaking hand, as he spoke, had fumbled in his coat pocket, and he placed on the table some folded notes, American bank-notes, which the Inspector stared at in astonishment.

'There is five hundred dollars.'

'I don't understand.'

'Five big hundred-dollar bills. They're new. They are not counterfeit, don't worry. It's the first time in my life that I have had five hundred dollars in my possession all at once. Do you understand that? *Five hundred dollars all at once in my pocket.*'

The waiter came in with a tray of coffee, eggs, bacon, jam. Dexter, gluttonous Dexter, who had always been hungry, as he had always longed to have five hundred dollars at once, felt his stomach turn at the smell of the bacon and eggs. He averted his head, as if about to vomit.

'Don't you want to drink something?'

'Water.'

And he drank two, three, four glasses without pausing for breath.

'Excuse me. I'll go to bed in a little while. First I had to come and see you.'

Drops of sweat beaded his pale forehead and he held fast to the table, which did not prevent his tall, thin body from swaying helplessly backwards and forwards.

'You must tell O'Brien, who has always taken me for an honest man and who recommended me to you, that Dexter is a louse.'

He pushed the money towards Maigret.

'Take them. Do what you like with them. They don't belong to me. Last night ... last night ...'

He looked as if he were gathering his strength to accomplish the most difficult part of his task.

'... last night I betrayed you for five hundred dollars.'

Telephone.

'Hello! ... What? ... You're downstairs? ... Come up, Lieutenant. I'm not alone, but that doesn't matter.'

And the clown questioned him with a bitter smile:

'Police?'

'Don't worry. You can talk in front of Lieutenant Lewis. He's a friend of O'Brien.'

'They can do what they like with me. It doesn't matter. Only, I'd like it to be quick.'

He stood there swaying.

'Come in, Lieutenant. I'm glad to meet you. You know Dexter? It doesn't matter, O'Brien knows him. I think he has some very interesting things to tell me. Won't you take this armchair while he talks and I have my breakfast?'

The room was almost gay, thanks to the sun that slanted across it and filled it with a swarm of fine golden dust.

Maigret, however, was wondering if he had done the right thing in inviting the lieutenant to be present at the conversation. O'Brien had not been lying when he said the evening before that this was a man as different from himself as could be.

'Delighted to make your acquaintance, Inspector.'

But he said it without a smile. It was obvious that he was there on duty, and he sat down in the chair, crossed his legs, lighted a cigarette, and, though Dexter still had not opened his mouth, he pulled a notebook and pencil from his pocket.

He was of medium height, of rather less than average weight, with the face of an intellectual, of a professor, for instance, with a long nose and thick glasses.

'You can take down my statement, if necessary,' Dexter said in English, speaking as if he saw himself already condemned to death.

The lieutenant did not stir, but observed him coldly, pencil poised.

'It was about eleven o'clock,' Dexter continued in French. 'I'm not sure. Maybe almost midnight. Near City Hall. But I was not drunk. I swear I was not drunk, and you can believe me.

'Two men came over and leaned against the bar beside me and immediately I knew that it was no coincidence, but that they were looking for me.'

'Would you recognize them?' the lieutenant asked.

Dexter looked at him, then he looked at Maigret, appearing to ask to whom he should be speaking.

'They were looking for me. Those are things you can feel. I had a feeling they belonged to the gang.'

'What gang?'

'I am very tired,' he enunciated carefully. 'If I am to be interrupted all the time . . .'

And Maigret could not keep from smiling as he ate his eggs.

'They offered me a drink, and I knew it was just to make me talk. You see that I am not trying to lie or to make excuses. I knew also that, if I drank, I was lost, and still I accepted and had four or five scotches, I don't exactly know now.

'They called me Ronald, although I hadn't told them my name.

'They took me to another bar. Then to another, but this time by car. And, in that bar, we all went upstairs to a billiard room where there was nobody else.

'I wondered if they wanted to kill me.

'"Sit down, Ronald," the bigger one of the two said to me after he'd locked the door. "You're a poor bastard, aren't you? All your life you've been a poor bastard. And, if you've never been able to amount to anything, it's because you never had the capital to start with."

'You know, Inspector, what I'm like when I've been drinking. I told you so myself. People should never let me drink.

'I saw myself when I was little. I saw myself at every stage of my life, always broke, always running after a couple of dollars, and I began to cry.'

What notes could Lieutenant Lewis be taking? For from time to time he jotted down a word or two in his notebook, and he was as grave as if he were interrogating the most dangerous of criminals.

'Then, the bigger fellow pulled some bills from his pocket, beautiful new bills, hundred-dollar bills. There was a bottle of whisky, and some soda on the table. I don't know who brought them, because I don't remember seeing the waiter come in.

'"Drink, you fool." That's what he said to me.

'And I drank. Then he folded the bills, after counting them under my nose, and he stuffed them in the outside pocket of my jacket.

'"You see, we treat you right. We could have got you some other way, by scaring you, because you're a coward. But we prefer to buy off cowards like you, see?

'"And now, down to business. You're going to tell us all you know. Everything, understand?"'

The clown looked at the Inspector out of his pale eyes, and said very distinctly:

'I told everything.'

'Told what?'

'The whole truth.'

'What truth?'

'That you knew everything.'

The Inspector still did not understand and, with a frown, he lighted his pipe and thought for a moment. He was actually wondering if he should laugh or take seriously his clown, afflicted with the worst hangover Maigret had ever seen in his life.

'That I knew what?'

'First of all, the truth about *J and J*.'

'But what truth, damn it all?'

The poor fellow stared at him in astonishment, as if he wondered why Maigret was suddenly playing cat and mouse with him.

'That Joseph, the clarinet one, was the husband or the lover of Jessie. You know that.'

'Is that so?'

'And that they had a child.'

'I beg your pardon?'

'Jos MacGill. Look at that first name, Jos. And the dates match. I saw you figuring them out yourself. Maura, that's Little John, was in love with her too, and he was jealous. He killed Joseph. Maybe he killed Jessie, later. Unless she died of a broken heart.'

The Inspector was staring now, astonished at his clown. And what amazed him most was to see Lieutenant Lewis feverishly taking notes.

'Later, when Little John had made some money, he had a bad conscience and he took care of the child, but without ever going to see him. Instead, he sent him off to Canada with a Mrs MacGill. And the boy, who had taken the name of the old Scotchwoman, did not know the name of the man who paid for his keep.'

'Go on, old man,' sighed Maigret resignedly, speaking to Dexter for the first time in a more familiar tone.

'You know this better than I do. But I told everything. I had to earn the five hundred, see? Because I still had, even so, a little bit of honesty left.

'Then Little John got married too. In any case, he had a child who was brought up in Europe.

'Mrs MacGill died. Either that, or Jos ran away. I don't know. Maybe you know, but you haven't told me. But last night I told them you were sure.

'They kept on pouring me big glasses of whisky.

'I was so ashamed of myself, believe it or not, that I wanted to carry it through to the end.

'There was an Italian tailor up on 169th Street who knew the whole story, who might have witnessed the crime.

'And one day Jos MacGill met him. I don't know how, by accident, I guess. And that's how he learned the truth about Little John.'

Now Maigret had settled down to smoking his pipe benignly, like a man listening to a child relate some fanciful tale.

'Go on.'

'MacGill had fallen in with some undesirable characters, like the ones last night. And they got together and decided to blackmail Little John.

'And Little John got scared.

'When they found out that his son was arriving from Europe, they wanted to tighten the screws a little more and they kidnapped Jean Maura when the ship docked.

'I couldn't tell them how Jean Maura got back to the St Regis. Maybe Little John coughed up a pile of money. Maybe, being no fool, he discovered where they were hiding the boy.

'I swore you knew everything.'

'And that they were going to be arrested?' inquired Maigret, rising.

'I don't remember. I think so. And that you also knew they had done it –'

'They, who?'

'The ones who gave me the five hundred.'

'That they had done what?'

'Killed old Angelino with the car. Because MacGill had found out that you were going to find out everything. There. Now, you can arrest me.'

Maigret had to look away to hide a smile, while Lieutenant Lewis remained as serious as a judge.

'What did they say to all this?'

'They made me get into the car. I thought they were taking me for a ride and would kill me in some back street. They could have had their five hundred dollars back that way. They simply dropped me opposite City Hall and they said ...'

'What did they say?'

'"Go get some sleep, you fool!" What are you going to do?'

'Tell you the same thing?'

'What?'

'I'm telling you to get some sleep. That's all.'

'I suppose I'm not to come back?'

'On the contrary.'

'You still need me?'

'We might.'

'Because, in that case . . .'

With a sidelong glance at the five hundred dollars he sighed:

'I haven't kept a cent. I couldn't even take the subway to go home. Today, I'm not asking you for five dollars like the other times, but just for one. Now that I am a louse . . .'

'What do you think of it, Lieutenant?'

Instead of bursting into laughter as Maigret longed to do, O'Brien's colleague contemplated his notes gravely and said:

'It was not MacGill who had Jean Maura kidnapped.'

'By jove!'

'You know that?'

'I'm convinced of it.'

'We know it to be a fact.'

And he had an air of dotting the i's in this distinction between an American certainty and a mere French feeling.

'Young Maura was taken off by an individual who delivered to him a letter from his father.'

'I know.'

'But we know, also, where he took the young man. To a cottage in Connecticut which belongs to Maura but where he hasn't set foot for several years.'

'That's entirely plausible.'

'It's certain. We have proof.'

'And his father had him brought back to the St Regis.'

'How do you know?'

'I surmise as much.'

'We do not surmise. The same individual went two days later to fetch young Maura.'

'Which means,' murmured Maigret, puffing on his pipe, 'that for two days there were reasons why this young man should be out of circulation.'

The lieutenant stared at him with comic astonishment.

'One could note a coincidence,' pursued the Inspector. 'That the young man reappeared only after old Angelino's death.'

'From which you reason . . . ?'

'Nothing. Your colleague O'Brien will tell you that I never reason.

He no doubt will add, with a dash of malice, that I never think. Do you think?'

Maigret wondered if he had gone too far, but Lewis, after a moment's reflection, replied:

'Sometimes. When I have sufficient elements in hand.'

'At that stage, there's no point in thinking.'

'What is your opinion of the story Ronald Dexter told us? It is Dexter, isn't it?'

'I have no opinion; I enjoyed it no end.'

'It is true that the dates coincide.'

'I'm sure they do. They also coincide with Maura's trip to Europe.'

'What do you mean?'

'That Jos MacGill was born one month before Little John came back from Bayonne. Or, to put it the other way round, eight and one-half months after he'd left.'

'So?'

'So, MacGill can as easily be the son of one as of the other. We have a choice, as you see. That's always handy.'

Maigret could not help himself. The scene with the hung-over clown had put him in a fine fettle and the peevish attitude of Lieutenant Lewis was well calculated to keep him in this frame of mind.

'I've ordered a check into all the death certificates of that period which might relate to Joseph Daumale and to Jessie.'

And Maigret, sharply:

'Provided they're dead.'

'Where would they be?'

'Where are the other three hundred tenants who lived in the house on 169th Street at the same time?'

'If Joseph Daumale were alive . . .'

'Well?'

'He would probably have looked after his son.'

'Provided it is his son.'

'He'd have turned up in the wake of Little John.'

'Why? Merely because two young men, just starting out, do a cabaret number together, are they bound together for life?'

'What about Jessie?'

'Mind you, I don't claim she is not dead, or that Daumale is not dead. But one of them could just as well have dropped dead in Paris or Carpentras last year and the other be living today in an old ladies' home. The opposite is just as possible.'

'I suppose, Inspector, that you are joking?'

'Hardly.'

'Do follow my line of reasoning.'

'You have been reasoning?'

'All night long. We have, to begin with, exactly twenty-eight years ago, three individuals.'

'The three J's . . .'

'What?'

'The three J's . . . That's what we call them.'

'Who is we?'

'The medium and the old circus man.'

'By the way, I've had a watch put on them, as you asked. So far, nothing has happened.'

'And probably nothing will happen, now that the clown has betrayed me, as he puts it. We were talking about the three J's – Joachim, Joseph and Jessie. Twenty-eight years ago, as you say, there were these three individuals, and a fourth whose name was Angelino Giacomi.'

'Right.'

He began to take notes again. It was a mania.

'And today –'

'Today,' the American hastened to intervene, 'we are again confronted with three individuals.'

'But they're no longer the same. Joachim, first of all, who, with time, has become Little John. MacGill and another young man who seems to be undeniably Maura's son. The fourth individual, Angelino, existed up to two days ago, but, no doubt to simplify the problem, he was suppressed.'

'To simplify the problem?'

'I'm sorry . . . Three people twenty-eight years ago and three people today. To put it differently, the two who are missing from the old cast of characters have been replaced.'

'And Maura seems to live in fear of his so-called secretary.'

'You think so?'

'O'Brien told me that was your impression also.'

'I believe I did say to him that MacGill showed great self-assurance and often spoke for his employer.'

'It's the same thing.'

'Not entirely.'

'I thought coming to see you this morning, that you would tell me with complete frankness what you think of this business. O'Brien passed on to me –'

'He told you more of my impressions?'

'No, just his own. He informed me that he's convinced you have an idea and that it may very well be the right one. So I hoped that, in comparing your ideas and mine –'

'We would reach the solution? Well! You heard my hired clown.'

'Do you believe what he said?'

'Not at all.'

'You think he's wrong?'

'He made up a nice story, almost a love story. Right now Little John, MacGill, and maybe some others must be in seventh heaven.'

'I've got proof of that.'

'Can you tell me about it?'

'This morning MacGill reserved a first-class cabin on a ship which is leaving at four for France. In the name of Jean Maura.'

'That's quite natural, don't you think? This young man, who is in the middle of his studies, suddenly leaves Paris and the university to run to New York, where his papa decides he had no business being. So he's sent back where he came from.'

'That's one way of looking at it.'

'You see, my dear Lieutenant, I understand your disappointment perfectly. You've been told, and it was a mistake, that I am an intelligent man who, in the course of his career, has solved a certain number of criminal cases. My friend O'Brien, who goes in for irony a bit, must have exaggerated somewhat. But, first of all, I am not intelligent.'

It was funny to see the officer as cross as if he were being made fun of, whereas Maigret had never been more sincere.

'Secondly, I never try to make up my mind about a case until it is finished. Are you married?'

'Of course.'

347

Lewis was taken aback by this absurd question.

'For years, no doubt. And I'm sure you are convinced that your wife doesn't always understand you.'

'It does happen, sometimes –'

'And your wife, for her part, has the same feeling about you. Yet you live together, you spend evenings together, you sleep in the same bed, you have children. Two weeks ago I'd never heard of Jean Maura or of Little John. Four days ago I didn't even know that Jos MacGill existed and it was only yesterday, in the house of a helpless old man, that an elderly medium talked to me about a certain Jessie.

'And you would like me to have a definite idea about each of them?

'I'm at sea, Lieutenant. No doubt we are both at sea. Only you, you fight against the tide, you try to go in one fixed direction, while I let myself go with the current, catching hold here and there at a passing branch.

'I'm waiting for some cables from France. O'Brien must have spoken to you about them. I'm also waiting, like you, for the results of your people's research into the death certificates, marriage licences etc . . .

'In the meantime, I don't know anything.

'By the way, when is the boat leaving for France?'

'You want to take it?'

'Not in the slightest, although it would be the wisest thing to do. The weather is nice. This is my first sunny day in New York. It will be a nice walk to go and see Jean Maura off and I wouldn't mind shaking hands with this boy with whom I had the pleasure of making a delightful crossing.'

He rose, put on his hat, his overcoat, while the officer, disappointed, regretfully closed his notebook and slipped it into his pocket.

'What about a drink before lunch?' proposed the Inspector.

'Don't be offended if I refuse, but I never touch alcohol.'

A tiny sparkle in Maigret's eye. He almost said, but he caught himself in time:

'I'd have sworn as much!'

They left the hotel together.

'So! My Sicilian's no longer on the job. They must think that now that Dexter has spilled the beans, there's no need to watch my comings and goings.'

'I have my car, Inspector. May I drop you somewhere?'

'No, thanks . . .'

He wanted to walk. He reached Broadway without incident, then a street where he hoped he would find the Donkey Bar. At first he was lost, but he finally recognized the façade, and he went into the bar, which at this time of day was practically deserted.

At one end of the bar, however, was the reporter with the yellow teeth, to whom MacGill and the detective-boxer had spoken that day. He seemed to be writing an article as he sipped a double whisky.

He looked up, recognized Maigret, made an ugly face, and then nodded a greeting.

'Beer,' ordered the Inspector because the air already smelled of spring and it made him thirsty.

He savoured it like a peaceable man who has before him long hours of leisure.

8

At the Quai des Orfèvres, only a year ago, they used to say about Maigret in such moments:

'This is it, boys. The Chief's gone into his trance.'

The irrepressible Sergeant Torrence, who actually worshipped the Inspector, would say more bluntly:

'The boss is in another world.'

'In a trance' or 'in another world' was in any case a state that Maigret's associates saw approaching with relief. And they had come to recognize it by little storm warnings, could foresee before the Inspector the moment the crisis would break.

What would a Lewis have made of the behaviour of his French colleague during the next few hours? He would not have understood, that's certain, and doubtless would have looked on him with a kind of pity. Would O'Brien himself, so subtly ironic under his heavy-handed manner, have been able to follow the Inspector that far?

It would happen in a rather odd way, which Maigret had never been curious enough to analyse. He had finally come to know it by dint of hearing his associates of the Police Judiciaire discuss it in endless detail.

For days, sometimes weeks, he would plod through a case, do what had to be done, no more, give instructions, keep tabs on this one and that one, with an air of being moderately interested in the investigation, sometimes of not being interested in it at all.

Because, during that period, the problem only appeared to him in a theoretical form. This or that man has been killed under such and such circumstances. So and so are the suspects.

These people, basically, did not interest him. *Did not interest him yet*.

Then suddenly, when one least expected it, when he might have seemed discouraged by the complexity of his job, something clicked.

Who was it who maintained that, at the very same time, he seemed to become more ponderous? Wasn't it a former chief of the PJ who had watched him work for years? It was only a joke, but it hit the mark. Maigret, all of a sudden, would appear to take on more depth, more weight. He had a different way of clenching his pipe between his teeth, of smoking it in short, widely spaced puffs, of looking about him with an almost secretive air, actually because he was completely absorbed by his interior activity.

It meant, in short, that for him the characters in the drama had ceased to be abstractions, pawns, or puppets and had become human beings.

And Maigret put himself in their shoes. He doggedly strove to put himself in their shoes.

Whatever a fellow human being had thought, had lived, had suffered, was he not capable of thinking it, reliving it, suffering it as well?

Such and such an individual, at a given moment in his life, under given circumstances, had reacted in a certain way, and it was a question, briefly, of kindling identical reactions from the depths of his own being, by dint of putting himself in the other's place.

Only, this was not done consciously. Maigret was not always aware of it. For example, he thought he remained Maigret, and nothing but Maigret, as he lunched alone at a counter.

But, had he looked at his face in the mirror, he would have caught there certain expressions of Little John. Among others the expression of the former violinist, when, coming from the far end of his St Regis apartment, from the bare room he had set up as a kind of refuge, he had looked at the Inspector for the first time through the half-open door.

Was it fear? Or rather a kind of acceptance of the inevitable?

The same Little John walking towards a window, at difficult moments, pushing back the curtain with a nervous hand and looking out, while MacGill automatically took charge.

It was not enough to decide:

'Little John is this or that . . .'

It was necessary to feel it. It was necessary to become Little John.

And that is why, as he walked through the streets, then hailed a taxi to take him to the docks, the outside world did not exist.

There was the Little John of long ago, the one who had arrived from France on the *Aquitaine* with his violin under his arm, accompanied by Joseph the clarinettist.

... The Little John who, during his wretched tour of the South, would share his dinner with a thin, sickly girl, with Jessie, whom they fed by setting aside part of two servings.

He scarcely heeded two men from the police whom he recognized on the quay. He smiled vaguely. Obviously Lieutenant Lewis had sent them just in case, and Lewis was doing his job properly, so no one could hold it against him.

Just fifteen minutes before sailing time a long limousine stopped outside the customs house and MacGill jumped out, then Jean Maura, wearing a light tweed suit that he must have bought in New York, and lastly Little John who seemed to have adopted, once and for all, navy blue or black for his clothes.

Maigret made no effort to keep out of sight. The three men had to pass near him. Their reactions were different. MacGill, who was walking first and carrying Jean's light cabin bag, frowned, then, perhaps out of defiance, made a slight, somewhat scornful face.

Jean Maura hesitated, looked at his father, walked over to the Inspector, and shook hands.

'You're not leaving ... Once more, please forgive me ... You should have taken the boat back with me ... There's nothing, you know ... I've behaved like a fool.'

'Of course.'

'Thank you, Inspector.'

As for Little John, he walked on and waited a little way off, then he bowed to Maigret, simply, discreetly.

The Inspector had never seen him except in his apartment. He was a bit surprised to find him, outside, even smaller than he had thought. And also he found him older, more worn by life. Was that recent? It was as if a veil hung about this man, despite the prodigious energy that could be sensed in him.

All this added up to nothing. These were not even thoughts. The last passengers were going aboard. Relatives and friends were lined up along the quay, faces upturned. A few English people, in keeping

352

with their own custom, were throwing streamers towards the rails and the departing travellers gravely held one end between their fingers.

The Inspector caught sight of Jean Maura on the first-class gangway. He saw him from below and for a moment he thought he saw, not the son, but the father. He thought he was present, not at today's sailing, but at that one long ago, when Joachim Maura had left to go back to France, where he was to remain almost ten months.

Joachim Maura had not travelled first-class, but third. Had he come alone to the dock? Had there not been, for him also, two people standing on the quay?

Those two people, Maigret automatically looked around to find them; in his mind's eye he could see the clarinettist and Jessie, who must have waited as he had, faces upturned, to see the moving wall of the ship slide from the quay.

Then . . . Then they left together . . . Did Joseph take Jessie's arm? . . . Or did Jessie instinctively lean on Joseph's arm? . . . Was she crying? Did he say to her, 'He'll soon be back'?

In any case, there were only the two of them, then, in New York, while Joachim, standing on the deck, watched America shrink and finally sink into the evening mist.

This time, also, two people who remained behind, Little John and MacGill, left side by side, walking in step towards the car that awaited them. MacGill opened the door and stood aside.

It's no good to move too quickly, like Lieutenant Lewis. No good to run after the truths one wants to grasp. The only thing is to become permeated by the truth pure and simple.

And that is why Maigret wandered off, hands in pockets, towards a part of town he did not know. No matter. In thought he was following Jessie and Joseph into the subway. Did the subway exist in those days? Yes, probably. They would have gone directly back to the house on 169th Street. And there, did they leave each other on the landing? Would Joseph not have comforted his companion?

Why did a very recent memory strike him then? At the time the incident occurred he had paid no attention.

At noon he had slowly sipped his beer at the Donkey Bar. He had ordered a second, because it was good. Just as he was leaving, the reporter with the bad teeth, Parson, had looked up and tossed at him:

'A very good day to you, Monsieur Maigret!'

But he had said it in French, with a strong accent, and he had pronounced the name 'Mégrette'. He had an unpleasant voice, too shrill and cutting, with crude or rather vicious intonations.

This was a bitter man, a malcontent, for sure. Maigret had looked at him, a little surprised. He had muttered a vague greeting and gone out without giving it another thought.

He suddenly remembered that when he had gone to the Donkey Bar the first time with MacGill and his gum-chewing detective his own name had not been mentioned. Nor had Parson said that he knew French.

It probably was unimportant. Maigret did not linger over the point. And yet this detail became embodied in the mass of his unconscious preoccupations.

When he arrived at Times Square, he looked automatically at the Times Square Building, which blocked the horizon. It reminded him that Little John had his offices in this skyscraper.

He went in. He was not looking for anything in particular. But of the Little John of today he knew only the intimate setting at the St Regis. Why not see the other?

He looked in the directory for the Automatic Record Company and an express lift took him to the forty-second floor.

It was uninteresting. There was nothing to see. All those automatic record players, those dream dispensers found in most of the bars and restaurants, actually ended up in here. Here, in any case, was where the hundreds of thousands of nickels coughed up by the machines were transformed into bank accounts, into stocks, and into entries in the big ledgers.

A sign on a glass door:

GENERAL MANAGER: JOHN MAURA.

More glass doors, numbered, bearing the names of a whole general staff, and lastly an immense room with metal desks and fluorescent lighting, where at least a hundred men and women were working.

He was asked what he wanted and he replied tranquilly, wheeling about after tapping his pipe against his heel:

'Nothing.'

To take it in, that was all. Wouldn't Lieutenant Lewis understand that?

And walking once again along the street, he stopped before a bar, hesitated, shrugged. Why not? It did him no harm in moments like these, and he didn't weep like Ronald Dexter. All alone at a corner of the bar, he downed two drinks, paid, and went out as he had come in.

Joseph and Jessie were alone, from now on, alone for ten months in the house at 169th Street, opposite the tailor's shop.

What came over him to make him say suddenly, aloud, startling a passer-by:

'No . . .'

He was thinking of old Angelino, of the wretched death of old Angelino, and he was saying no because he felt sure, without knowing exactly why, that it had not happened as Lewis imagined.

There was something that did not fit. Again he saw Little John and MacGill walking towards the black limousine that awaited them and he repeated to himself:

'No . . .'

It had to be simpler. Events can afford the luxury of being complicated or of appearing so. Men are always simpler than one thinks.

Even a Little John . . . Even a MacGill . . .

Only in order to understand that simplicity, one had to probe the depths and not be satisfied with exploring the surface.

'Taxi . . .'

He forgot he was in New York, and began to speak French to the astonished cabdriver. He apologized, and repeated in English the address of the medium.

He had to ask her one question, just one. She also lived in Greenwich Village, and the Inspector was quite surprised to find an attractive house, a four-storey, middle-class house, with a clean, carpeted staircase and straw mats before each door.

MADAME LUCILLE

EXTRA-LUCID MEDIUM

BY APPOINTMENT ONLY

He rang and the bell on the other side of the door gave a

smothered sound, as in all elderly people's homes. Then there were padded footsteps, a pause, a very faint sound of a bolt being carefully pulled back.

The door scarcely opened and, through the crack, an eye studied him. Maigret, smiling in spite of himself, said:

'Maigret.'

'Oh! I beg your pardon. I didn't recognize you. Since I had no appointment at this hour, I wondered who could be coming ... Come in ... Excuse me for opening the door myself, but the maid is out.'

There was surely no maid, but that was unimportant.

It was almost dark and no lamp had been lighted. An armchair, opposite an iron parlour stove, reflected the glow of a coal fire.

The air was warm and soft, a little stale. Madame Lucille went from switch to switch and lamps lighted up, invariably shaded in blue or pink.

'Sit down ... Have you news of your brother?'

Maigret had almost forgotten the story that the clown had told to arouse the sympathy of Germain and his elderly friend. He looked around him, with surprise, for, instead of the bric-à-brac he had expected, he found a tiny Louis Seize sitting-room that reminded him of so many others like it, in Passy or Auteuil.

Only one thing, the heavy, clumsy make-up of the old woman, gave the room an equivocal note. Her face, under a crust of cream and powder, was as wan as a moon, with the crimson lips and long bluish eyebrows of a doll.

'I've thought a lot about you and my old friends *J and J*.'

'I would like to ask you a question about them.'

'You know .. : I am almost sure ... You remember you asked me which of the two was in love ... I believe, now I think back, that they both were.'

Maigret brushed that aside.

'What I would like to know, madame, is – But wait a moment ... I should like you to understand my thinking on this ... It is rare that two young people of the same age, with more or less the same background, have the same vitality, the same strength of character. There is always one who has the edge over the other ... Let's put it this way, there's always a leader ... Just a minute ...

'In such a case, the second man may react in different ways, depending on his character.

'Some accept domination by their friend, even seek that domination sometimes . . . Others, on the other hand, rebel every step of the way.

'You see that my question is rather delicate. Don't answer in a hurry . . . You lived with them for almost a year . . . Which of the two left the stronger impression on you?'

'The violinist,' she replied without hesitation.

'So Joachim . . . The blond one with the long hair, the very thin face?'

'Yes . . . And yet, he wasn't always pleasant.'

'What do you mean?'

'I couldn't say exactly . . . It's an impression . . . Look! . . . *J and J* were the very last on the programme, weren't they? Robson and I were the stars . . . in cases like that, there is a kind of hierarchy. About luggage, for example . . . Well! The violinist would never have offered to carry my bag.'

'While the other one?'

'He did many times. He was more polite, had better manners.'

'Joseph?'

'Yes, the one with the clarinet. And yet . . . Heavens! How hard it is to explain! Joachim had an uneven temper, that's it. One day he would be charming, delightfully friendly, and the next day he wouldn't so much as speak to you. I think, he was very proud, that he suffered from his position. Joseph, on the other hand, took it with a smile. And there again I'm saying something wrong, because he didn't smile often.'

'Was he a sad man?'

'Not that, either! He did things correctly, properly, he did his best, no more. If he had been asked to help the stagehands or to fill in for the prompter, he would have done it, while the other one would have gotten on his high horse. That's what I mean. It didn't prevent me from preferring Joachim, even when he was curt.'

'Thank you.'

'Won't you have a cup of tea? Don't you want me to try to help you?'

She had said this last with a strange shyness and Maigret did not immediately understand.

'I could try to see.'

Only then did he remember he was calling on an extra-lucid medium and he nearly, out of kindness, so as not to disappoint her, agreed to a consultation.

Really no! He could not bear to watch her silly performance, listen again to her whining voice and the questions she put to her dead Robson.

'I will come another time, madame ... Forgive me if, today, I do not have the time.'

'I understand.'

'But no ...'

There he was spoiling things. He was genuinely sorry to leave her with a bad impression, but there was no avoiding it.

'I hope you find your brother.'

Downstairs, in front of the house, stood a man he had not noticed on arriving and who stared at him hard. One of Lewis's men, no doubt. Was this still necessary?

He took a cab back to Broadway. Already it had become his home base and he was beginning to know his way around. Why did he unhesitatingly go into the Donkey Bar?

He had, in the first place, to make a telephone call. But, above all, he wanted, for no precise reason, to see again the reporter with the grating voice, and he knew that by this time the fellow would be drunk.

'Good afternoon, Monsieur Mégrette.'

Parson was not alone. He was surrounded by three or four characters whom he had apparently been amusing for some time with his sallies.

'Will you have a scotch with us?' he continued in French. 'True, in France, you don't like whisky. A cognac for the retired Inspector of the Police Judiciaire?'

He was trying to be funny. He knew, or thought, he was the object of attention of the whole bar, where few people, actually, were paying any attention to him.

'A beautiful country, France, is it not?'

Maigret hesitated, put off his call until later, and leaned on the bar next to Parson.

'You know France?'

'I lived there two years.'

'In Paris?'

'Gay Paree, yes ... And in Lille, Marseille, Nice ... The Côte d'Azur, right?'

He said it spitefully, as if his slightest word had a meaning for him alone.

If Dexter was a sad drunk, Parson was the disagreeable aggressive drunk.

He knew he was skinny and ugly; he knew he was dirty; he knew he was despised or disliked, and he bore a grudge against the whole of humanity, which, for that moment, took on the form and face of this placid Maigret, who was looking at him with calm, untroubled eyes, the way one looks at a fly buffeted by the gale.

'I bet when you get back to your beautiful France you will say every nasty thing possible about America and Americans ... The French are all like that ... And you'll tell how New York is full of gangsters ... Ha! Ha! ... Only you'll forget to say that most of them come from Europe.'

And, breaking into a mean laugh, he pointed his index finger at Maigret's chest.

'You'll also forget to add that there are as many gangsters in Paris as there are here. Only, yours are bourgeois gangsters ... They have wives and children ... and, sometimes, they even get decorated ... Ha! Ha! ... Another round, Bob!' he went on in English. 'A brandy for Monsieur Mégrette, who doesn't care for whisky.'

Then, turning back to Maigret:

'But there ... will you be going back to Europe?'

He looked slyly around at his companions, very proud of himself for having flung this question straight in the Inspector's face.

'Eh? Are you sure you're going back? Suppose our gangsters don't want you to? Eh? Do you imagine that the excellent Mr O'Brien or the honourable Mr Lewis can do anything about that?'

'You weren't at the boat when Jean Maura left?' inquired the Inspector casually.

'There were enough people there without me, weren't there? To your health, Monsieur Mégrette ... To the health of the police of Paris.'

These last words seemed so funny to him that he literally shook with laughter.

'In any case, if you do take the boat back, I promise to ask you for an interview ... "*The renowned Inspector Maigret today stated to our brilliant correspondent Parson that he is very pleased with his contacts with the Federal Bureau of Investigation and ...*"'

Two of the men who made up the group went off without a word and, strangely enough, Parson, who saw them leave, did not say a word to them, nor did he appear surprised.

At that moment Maigret regretted having no one on call to tail them.

'Another drink, Monsieur Mégrette ... You see, it's better to take it while the taking's good ... Just look at this bar ... Thousands and thousands of people have leaned on it, the way we are this minute ... There've been some who refused a last whisky, saying:

'Tomorrow ...

'And, the next day they weren't around any more to drink it.

'Result: one good scotch lost ... Ha! Ha! When I was in France, I always had a tag with my hotel address pinned to my coat ... That way, people knew where to take me ... You don't have a tag, do you?

'It's very practical, even for the morgue, because it speeds up the formalities ... Where are you going? ... You're turning down the last drink?'

Maigret had had enough. He left after looking the shrill-voiced journalist straight in the eye.

'Good day,' he said.

'Or good-bye,' the other retorted.

Instead of telephoning from the booth in the Donkey Bar, he chose to walk back to his hotel. A telegram lay in his box, but he did not open it before reaching his room. And, even then, out of a certain fastidiousness, he laid the envelope on the table and dialled a number.

'Hello ... Lieutenant Lewis? ... This is Maigret ... Have you traced a marriage licence? ... Yes ... What date? ... One second ... In the name of John Maura and Jessie Dewey? ... Yes ... What? ... Born in New York ... Right ... The date? ... I don't understand what you're saying ...'

In the first place, English was much harder to understand over the telephone than in ordinary conversation. Furthermore, Lieutenant Lewis was explaining something rather complicated.

'Good ... You say that the licence was taken out at City Hall ... Excuse me ... What is it, City Hall? ... Oh, I see ... Good ... Four days before Little John's departure for Europe ... And then? ... What? It does not prove they were married?'

That's what he found hard to understand. Fortunately Lewis switched to his too precise French.

'Yes ... A marriage licence can be secured and not used ... In that case, how can one know if they were married? ... Eh? ... Only Little John could tell us? ... Or the witnesses, or the person who would be in possession of the licence today? ... Obviously, all this is easier in any country ... Yes ... I don't think it's important ... I say: I do not think it is important ... Whether they were married or not ... What? ... I assure you, I have nothing new ... I've been taking a walk, that's all ... He said good-bye, politely ... Adding that he was sorry I was not making the return trip with him ...

'I suppose now that you have Jessie's family name, you will be able to ... Yes ... Your men are already working on it? ... I can't hear you clearly ... Not found any trace of her death? ... That doesn't mean anything, does it? ... People don't always die in their beds ...

'No, my dear Lieutenant, of course I am not contradicting myself. I said this morning that people who cannot be located are not necessarily dead and gone. I never claimed that Jessie was alive ...

'One second ... Will you hold on? I've just had a cable from France in reply to my request for information ... I haven't opened it yet. Indeed not! I wanted first to have you on the line.'

He laid the receiver down, tore open the yellow envelope containing the very long cable, which said in substance:

Joachim-Jean-Marie Maura: born Bayonne on ... Son of town's most important ironmonger. Lost mother early. Attended lycée. Studied music. Bordeaux Conservatory. First prize violin at nineteen. Left for Paris shortly after.

Did not return Bayonne until four years later, on death of father of whom he was sole heir, whose business affairs were somewhat confused. Must have cleared two or three hundred thousand francs.

... Cousins still living Bayonne and outskirts claim he had made fortune in America, but never answered their letters ...

'Are you still there, Lieutenant? Forgive me for taking so much of your time ... As far as Maura goes, nothing important to note ... May I go on? ...'

Joseph-Ernest-Dominique Daumale: born Bayonne on ... Son of postal clerk and schoolteacher. Mother widowed when he was fifteen. Studied lycée, then Bordeaux Conservatory. Left for Paris, where must have met Maura. Quite long stay in America. Presently conducts spa orchestras. Spent last season in La Bourboule, where he has built villa and must currently be. Married to Anne-Marie Penette, of Sables-d'Olonne, by whom he has three children ...

'Hello ... Are you there, Lieutenant? ... Well, I've found one of your dead men ... Yes, I know, they aren't yours. It's Joseph. Yes, the clarinettist. Well! Joseph Daumale is in France, married, a father, owner of a villa, and director of an orchestra ... Are you continuing your investigation? ... What? ... Indeed not, I assure you, I'm not joking ... I know, yes ... Obviously there is still old Angelino ... You really want ...'

Lewis had begun spouting English at the other end of the line with such animation that Maigret no longer even tried to understand. He muttered indifferently:

'Yes ... yes ... As you like ... Good-bye, Lieutenant ... What am I going to do? That all depends on what time it is in France ... What did you say? ... Midnight? That's a little late. Telephoning from here at one in the morning, it would be seven over there. About the time people should be getting up, if they own a villa at La Bourboule. A time, in any case, when they're pretty sure to be found at home.

'Meanwhile, I'll go quietly to a film. They must be showing a funny one somewhere on Broadway. I confess I only like funny films.

'Good-bye, Lieutenant. My regards to O'Brien.'

And he went to wash his hands and face, and brush his teeth. He put one foot after another up on the armchair to wipe the dust off his shoes with a soiled handkerchief, which at home would have earned him a scene with Madame Maigret.

After which he went downstairs, light of heart, pipe between his teeth, and selected with care a good little restaurant.

It was like a private party all for him. He ordered his favourite dishes, an old bourgogne and a fine, mellow Armagnac, hesitated between a cigar and his pipe, finally chose his pipe, and found himself once more among the moving lights of Broadway.

No one knew who he was, fortunately, otherwise his prestige would certainly have fallen in American eyes. Slouching, hands shoved in his pockets, he looked like a mild, bumpkin-like stroller who pauses to window-shop, allows himself the pleasure of gazing occasionally after a pretty woman, and hesitates in front of the posters of the various cinemas.

Somewhere a Laurel and Hardy was showing, and Maigret, having found what he wanted, went up to the window to pay for his ticket, and followed the usherette into the darkness of the theatre.

Fifteen minutes later he was laughing with such gusto and abandon that his neighbours were pointing him out to one another.

One minor drawback, however. The usherette came and politely asked him to put out his pipe, which he regretfully stuffed in his pocket.

9

As he left the cinema, around eleven-thirty, he was calm, a little deliberate, without nervousness or tension, and it reminded him of other investigations during which, at a certain moment, he had had the same feeling of quiet strength with just a little uneasiness deep in his throat – stage fright, in other words. For a few seconds he forgot he was on Broadway and not on the Boulevard des Italiens and wondered which street to take to get to the Qaui des Orfèvres.

First he drank a glass of beer at a bar, not because he was thirsty, but from a kind of superstition, because he had always had a beer just before he was to begin a difficult interrogation, indeed during the interrogation itself.

He remembered the half pints Joseph, the waiter from the Brasserie Dauphine, used to bring up to his office on the Quai, for him and often also for the poor, pale devil facing him, who was awaiting his questions with the near certainty that he would walk out of the office with handcuffs on his wrists.

Why, that evening, did he think of the longest, the hardest of those interrogations, the one that had become almost a classic in the annals of the Police Judiciaire, the questioning of Mestorino, which had lasted no less than twenty-six hours?

By the end of it the office had been filled with pipe smoke, the air was unbreathable; there were ashes, empty glasses, crusts of sandwiches everywhere, and the two men had taken off their jackets and ties; both faces were so haggard that a stranger would have been hard put to say which of the two belonged to the murderer.

He went into a telephone booth a little before midnight, dialled the number of the St Regis, and asked for Little John's apartment.

He recognized MacGill's voice at the other end of the line.

'Hello ... This is Maigret ... I'd like to speak to Mr Maura.'

Was there something in his voice that indicated clearly this was no longer the time to try to be clever? The secretary replied, simply, directly, with obvious truthfulness, that Little John was at some affair at the Waldorf and would probably not be back before two in the morning.

'Will you phone him, or better still, go and join him?' replied Maigret.

'I'm not alone here. I have a girlfriend in the apartment and –'

'Send her away, then, and do as I tell you. It is absolutely necessary, do you hear, it is essential, if you prefer, that Little John and you be in my room at the Berwick at ten minutes to one, at the latest. I repeat, at the latest ... No, it is not possible for us to meet somewhere else. If Little John should hesitate, tell him that I want him to be present at a conversation with someone he used to know long ago. No, I am sorry. I can't say anything more now. *Ten minutes to one.*'

He had placed a call to La Bourboule for one and he had some time to spare. At the same unhurried pace, his pipe between his teeth, he walked over to the Donkey Bar, where there were a lot of people, but where, to his great disappointment, he did not see Parson.

He drank another glass of beer nevertheless, and it was then he noticed another, smaller room at the back of the place. He went over. A pair of lovers in one corner. In the other, on the black leather wall bench, the reporter slouched, legs spread wide, eyes vacant, a glass spilled on the table before him.

He recognized the Inspector, however, but made no effort to move.

'Can you still hear me, Parson?' the Inspector growled, planting himself in front of the other man with perhaps as much pity as scorn.

The man mumbled, scarcely moving his lips:

'How d'you do?'

'This afternoon, you talked about having a sensational interview with me, didn't you? Well! If you have the strength to follow me, I think you'll get the biggest story of your career.'

'Where do you want to take me?'

He had trouble speaking, and he was past trying to match Maigret's French. Even in English the syllables could not quite take shape on his fuddled tongue; yet in the depths of his drunkenness he quite evidently retained a certain if not complete lucidity. His eyes showed distrust, perhaps fear. But his pride was stronger than his fear.

'Third degree?' he inquired insultingly, referring to the vigorous interrogations conducted by American police.

'I will not even question you. It isn't necessary any more.'

Parson tried to get up and, before making it, fell back twice on the bench.

'Just a minute ...' Maigret intervened. 'Are there any of your friends in the bar at the moment? I'm asking for your sake. If there are, it would be better for you, perhaps, if I went out first and waited for you in a taxi about a hundred yards up the street, on the left.'

The reporter tried to grasp the full meaning, but failed; uppermost in his mind was the will not to appear to lose his nerve. He glanced out into the room, leaning against the door for support.

'Go ahead ... I'll follow you.'

And Maigret did not try to find out which of the customers at the bar belonged to the gang. It did not concern him. That was Lieutenant Lewis's business.

Outside he hailed a cab, ordered it to park by the kerb at the agreed place, sat back in the darkness. Five minutes later a Parson who staggered only slightly but had to keep staring fixedly ahead in order to stay on his feet opened the car door.

He joked allusively again:

'Taking me for a ride?'

'To the Berwick,' Maigret ordered the driver, ignoring Parson's remark.

It was just a step away. The Inspector helped his companion to the lift and in the tired eyes of the journalist lingered that same mixture of panic and pride.

'Is Lieutenant Lewis upstairs?'

'No, nobody from the police.'

He turned on all the lights in the room. Then, having seated Parson in one corner, he called Room Service, ordered a bottle of whisky, glasses, soda, and, lastly, four bottles of beer.

About to hang up, he had a second thought:

'Send up a couple of ham sandwiches, too.'

366

Not because he was hungry, but because it was his habit at the Quai des Orfèvres and had become a kind of ritual.

Parson was slumped down again, as he had been at the Donkey Bar, and from time to time he shut his eyes and dozed off, waking with a start at the slightest noise.

Twelve-thirty. Quarter to one. The bottle, glasses, and the plate of sandwiches stood in a row on the mantelpeice.

'May I have a drink?'

'Certainly. Don't move. I'll get it for you.'

How drunk he was didn't matter, at this point. Maigret poured him a whisky and soda, which the other man accepted with a bewilderment he could not conceal.

'You're a queer fish. Damned if I know what you want to do with me.'

'Nothing at all.'

The telephone rang. Little John and MacGill were downstairs.

'Ask them to come up.'

And he went to wait for them by the door. He watched them walk the length of the corridor, Little John in tails and white tie, more spare, more nervous than ever, his secretary in a dinner jacket, smiling vaguely.

'Come in, please. Forgive me for having disturbed you but I think it was essential.'

MacGill was the first to see the journalist collapsed in his chair, and his look of surprise did not escape the Inspector.

'Pay no attention to Parson,' he said. 'I wanted him to be present for certain reasons that you'll understand presently. Sit down, gentlemen. I advise you to take off your overcoats, because this will take a while, no doubt.'

'May I ask you, Inspector –'

'No, Mr Maura. Not yet.'

And he gave an impression of such quiet strength that the two men did not protest. Maigret had sat down in front of the table where he had set the telephone and his watch.

'I must ask you to be patient for a few more minutes. You can smoke, naturally. Forgive me for not having any cigars to offer you.'

He was not trying to be funny and, as the moment approached, his throat grew tighter and he puffed more quickly at his pipe.

The room, in spite of all the lamps, was quite dim, like all third-class hotel rooms. Through the wall they could hear a couple getting ready for bed.

Finally the telephone rang.

'Hello ... Yes ... Maigret ... Hello, I'm calling La Bourboule ... What? ... I'll hold on.'

And, turning to Maura, the receiver at his ear:

'I'm sorry your American phones don't have an extra receiver, like ours, for I should like you to hear the entire conversation. I promise to repeat, word for word, the important parts. Hello! Yes ... What? ... No answer? ... Keep trying, mademoiselle. Maybe everyone is still asleep?'

He was moved, for no reason, to hear the operator in La Bourboule who was greatly shaken at getting a call from New York.

It was seven o'clock in the morning, over there. Was the sun shining? Maigret remembered the post office, opposite the steam baths, on the banks of the mountain stream.

'Hello! Who is speaking? ... Hello, madame! Excuse me for waking you ... You were up? ... Would you be kind enough to call your husband to the phone? ... I'm sorry, but I'm calling you from New York and it would be hard for me to call back in half an hour ... Wake him ... Yes.'

He avoided looking at the three men he had brought together in his room to witness this strange interrogation.

'Hello! Monsieur Joseph Daumale?'

Little John could not stop crossing and uncrossing his legs, but he gave no other sign of emotion.

'This is Maigret speaking ... Yes, the Maigret of the Police Judiciaire, as you say. I hasten to add that I am retired from Quai des Orfèvres and that I am calling you in a private capacity. What? ... Just a moment. Tell me, first of all, where the phone is located in your house. In your study? On the first floor? ... One more question. Can you be heard from downstairs or from the bedrooms? ... That's right. Close the door. And if you haven't already done so, put on a dressing gown.'

He would have bet that the conductor's study was done in Renaissance style, with old, heavy, well-polished furniture, and that the walls were decorated with photographs of the various orchestras that Jos Daumale had directed in the little casinos of France.

'Hello! Wait a second until I have one more word with the young lady who is plugged in on this line and listening to us ... Will you be kind enough to get off the line and to take care that we are not cut off? ... Hello! ... Very good ... Are you there, Mr Daumale?'

Did he wear a beard now, a moustache? A moustache, almost certainly. Greying, very likely. And thick glasses. Had he had time to put on his glasses when he jumped out of bed?

'I am going to ask you a question which may seem to you both impertinent and indiscreet, and I ask you to think before you answer. I know that you are a temperate man, mindful of your responsibilities as a family man ... What? ... You are an honest man?'

He turned to Little John and repeated without irony:

'He says he is an honest man.'

And he resumed:

'I don't doubt it, Mr Daumale. Since this concerns a very serious matter, I am sure that you are going to answer me very frankly. When was the last time you were really drunk? ... Yes, you heard me ... I said drunk. Really drunk, you understand? Drunk enough to lose your self-control.'

Silence. And Maigret pictured to himself the Joseph of the past, the one he had visualized as he listened to the medium unburden her memories. He must have grown quite stout. Doubtless he had been decorated? Wasn't his wife on the landing, listening?

'You better go and make sure no one is listening at the door ... What did you say? ... Yes, I'll wait.'

He heard footsteps, the sound of a door opening and closing.

'Well! Last July? What? It hasn't happened to you more than three times in your life? Congratulations.'

A noise in the room, near the fireplace. Parson, who had got up, was pouring himself a whisky with an uncertain hand, knocking the neck of the bottle against the glass.

'Give me the details, then, will you please? In July, therefore at La Bourboule. At the Casino, yes, I imagined so ... By chance, obviously ... Wait. I'll help you ... You were, were you not, in the company of an American? A man by the name of Parson ... You don't remember his name? It doesn't really matter. A tall fellow, sloppily dressed, tow-headed, with yellow teeth ... Yes ... For that matter, he's right beside me now ... What?

'Keep calm, please. I can assure you that no unpleasantness will result from it for you.

'He was at the bar ... No. Forgive me for repeating your answers, but I have here several people interested in your story ... Of course this has nothing to do with the American police. Don't worry about the peace of your household or about your position.'

Maigret's voice had turned scornful and it was almost a glance of complicity he threw at John Maura, who sat listening, his forehead in his hand. MacGill played nervously with his gold cigarette case.

'You don't know how it happened? One never knows how those things happen. A man has a drink, then a second, yes. It was years since you'd drunk whisky? Obviously. And you enjoyed talking about New York ... Hello! ... Tell me, is the sun shining over there?'

It was absurd, but since the very beginning of the conversation he had been wanting to ask this question. As though from a need to see the character in his usual setting, in his usual atmosphere.

'Yes. I understand. Spring comes earlier in France than here. You talked a lot about New York and your early days, didn't you? *J and J* ... It doesn't matter how I found out about it.

'And you asked him if he knew a certain Little John ... You were very drunk ... Yes, perfectly, I know it was he who was forcing you to drink. Drunkards don't like to drink alone.

'You told him that Little John ... Oh, but you did, Mr Daumale ... I must ask you ... What? You don't see how I could force you to answer? Let's suppose, for example, that you were to have a visit tomorrow or the next day from an Inspector of the Brigade Mobile armed with a summons duly and properly made out?

'You have done a great deal of harm, without wishing to, possibly. But you have done harm just the same.'

Furious, he let his voice rise, and he motioned to MacGill to pour him a glass of beer.

'Don't tell me you don't remember. Parson, unfortunately, remembered everything you told him. Jessie ... What? ... The house on 169th Street ... By the way, I have some bad news for you. Angelino is dead. He was murdered and you are, all things considered, the one responsible for his death.

'Stop snivelling, will you?

'That's right, sit down if your knees are shaking. I have time. The telephone connection is reserved and they won't cut us off. As to who will pay for the call, we'll see about that later. Don't worry, it won't be you ...

'What? That's it: tell me everything you want to, I'm listening. But remember that I already know a great deal and there's no point in lying.

'You're a poor specimen, Mr Daumale.

'An honest man, I know, you said that before ...'

Three silent men in a dimly lighted hotel room. Parson had sunk down in his chair again and he stayed there, his eyes half closed, mouth half open, while Little John still rested his forehead in his delicate white hand and MacGill poured himself a glass of whisky. The white splashes of the two shirt fronts, of the cuffs, the black of the dinner jacket and tails, and this single voice that resounded through the room, now heavy and scornful, now vibrating with anger.

'Talk ... You loved her, naturally. And hopelessly, too ... Yes, yes! ... I tell you I do understand, and, if you want that, I even believe you ... Your best friend ... Given your life for him.'

How disdainful were the lips through which these words were uttered!

'All weak men say that and it doesn't keep them from rebelling. I know. You didn't rebel. You only took advantage of the opportunity, isn't that it? ... No, she did not ... Please don't besmirch her into the bargain. She was a child and you were a man.

'Yes ... Maura's father was dying. I know that. And he left ... You both went back to 169th Street. She was very unhappy, I expect so ... That he would not come back? ... Who told her that? ... Never! You're the one who put that idea into her head. It's enough to see a photograph of you at the time. Exactly, I do have one. You don't any more? Well, I'll send you a print.

'Poverty-stricken? Hadn't left any money? How could he have left you any money, when he had no more than you did?

'Of course. You couldn't do the act alone. But you could have played the clarinet in cafés, cinemas, in the street, if necessary.

'You did? Congratulations.

'A pity you did something else, too. Made love, I mean.

'Only, you knew perfectly well there was another love, two other loves, Jessie's and your friend's.

'So what? Be brief, Mr Daumale. You're talking rot.

'Almost ten months, I know ... It wasn't his fault if his father, whom they'd practically given up for dead, wouldn't die. Nor if he had difficulties, later, in straightening out his affairs.

'And, during that time, you had taken his place.

'And, when the child was born, you were so afraid, because John had written he would be returning soon, that you put it in an orphanage.

'What do you swear? ... What? ... You want to go and look behind the door? ... Please do. And drink some water while you're at it, because you seem to need it.'

It was the first time in his life that he had conducted an interrogation like this, from a distance of three thousand miles, knowing nothing about the man he talked to.

Drops of sweat beaded his forehead. He had already emptied two bottles of beer.

'Hello! It isn't you, I know. Stop telling me that it isn't your fault, will you? You had taken his place and he came back. And, instead of telling him the truth, of keeping the woman you claim to have loved, you gave her back to him, like a filthy little coward.

'Oh yes, Joseph. You are a filthy little coward. A shabby, spineless coward.

'And you didn't dare tell him a child had been born. What are you saying?

'That he wouldn't have believed the child was his? Wait a second until I repeat your words.

'"*John would not have believed that the child was his ...*"

'Then you, Joseph, did know it was not yours ... What? ... Otherwise, you would never have put it in an orphanage? And you've got the nerve to say that? ... I forbid you to hang up, do you hear? If you do, I'll have you locked up before the day's over. Good! ...

'Maybe you have become an honest man or something that looks like one on the outside, but at the time you were a first-class rat.

'And the three of you continued to live next door to each other.

'John resumed the place you had occupied in his absence.

'Talk louder. I don't want to miss a word . . . John had changed? What do you mean? He was worried, nervous, suspicious? You must admit he had cause. And Jessie wanted to tell him everything? Naturally! It would have been better for her, wouldn't it?

'No, of course, you couldn't foresee. You prevented her from telling him.

'And John kept wondering what there was around him that was so strange . . . What? She used to cry at the drop of a hat. I like the way you put it. You have a real gift for words. *She used to cry at the drop of a hat.*

'How did he find out?'

Little John stirred as if he wanted to speak, but the Inspector waved him back into silence.

'Let him tell it! . . . No, I wasn't speaking to you . . . I'll tell you in a moment . . . He found a bill from the midwife? . . . Indeed, one can't think of everything . . . He didn't believe it was his?

'Put yourself in his place . . . Especially in a state orphanage.

'Where were you during this scene? . . . Come now, you heard everything. On the other side of the connecting door, yes. Because there was a connecting door between the two rooms! And for . . . for how long, in fact? . . . Three weeks . . . For three weeks after he came back, you slept in that room, next to the room where John and Jessie, Jessie who had belonged to you for months . . .

'Finish quickly, will you . . . I'm sure you're not a very pretty sight just now, Mr Daumale . . . I'm no longer sorry to be questioning you by phone, for I'd have a hard time not bashing your face in.

'Be quiet! Answer my questions and that's all. You were behind the door.

'Yes . . . Yes . . . Yes . . . Go on . . .'

He was staring at the cloth on the table in front of him and, now, he refrained from repeating the words he heard. His jaws were clenched so tightly that at one point the stem of his pipe snapped between his teeth.

'And then? Hurry up, damn it! . . . What? . . . And you did not intervene sooner? ... Capable of anything, yes! ... Put yourself in his place. Or rather don't, you couldn't ... On the stairs ... Angelino delivering a suit ... Saw everything ... Yes.

'No! You're lying again ... You did not try to get into the room! You tried to sneak away. Only, as the door was open ... That's it ... He saw you ...

'I can imagine it was too late!

'This time I believe you without hesitation. I'm sure you didn't tell that to Parson. Because you could have been accused of complicity, couldn't you? And remember, you still can be ... No, no statute of limitations, you're wrong ... I see the wicker trunk very well. And all the rest ... Thanks. I don't need to know more. As I told you at the beginning, Parson is here. He's drunk, yes, as usual.

'Little John is here too. You don't want to talk to him? I can't force you to, obviously.

'Nor to MacGill, whom you so kindly dispatched to the state orphanage? ... Exactly, he's here in my room, too.

'That's all. The smell of Mrs Daumale's coffee must be drifting up to you ... You'll be able to hang up, draw a deep sigh of relief, and go downstairs to a family breakfast.

'I can guess how you're going to explain this telephone call. An American impresario who has heard about your talents as a conductor and who ...

'Good-bye, Joseph Daumale. I hope I never meet you!'

Maigret hung up and sat motionless for a long while, as if drained of all his strength.

No one stirred around him. He rose heavily to his feet, picked up the bowl of his broken pipe, and laid it on the table. It happened to be the pipe he had bought the second day after his arrival in New York. He went to get another from his overcoat pocket, filled it, lighted it and poured himself a drink, not beer, which would have seemed too weak now, but a big tumbler of straight whisky.

'And that's that,' he sighed at last.

Little John still had not stirred, and it was Maigret who poured him a drink and set it down beside him.

Only when Maura had drunk it, had pulled himself together a bit,

374

did the Inspector speak in his normal voice, which sounded strange at first.

'We'd better finish first with this one,' he said, pointing to Parson, who was mopping his forehead in the depths of his armchair.

Another weakling, another coward, but of the worst kind, the aggressive kind. At that, didn't Maigret prefer it to the cautious, measly cowardice of a Daumale?

Parson's story was easy to reconstruct. He knew, from the Donkey Bar or elsewhere, some gangsters in a position to exploit the information that chance had put in his hands during his stay in Europe.

'How much did you get?' Maigret asked him listlessly.

'What's it to you? You'd be only too glad to know I'd been had.'

'A few hundred dollars?'

'Barely.'

Then the Inspector took a cheque from his pocket, the cheque for two thousand dollars that MacGill had given him in Little John's name. He picked up a pen from the table, endorsed it over to Parson.

'That will be enough for you to clear out while there's time. I had to have you on hand, in case Daumale refused to talk, or in case I had been wrong. You shouldn't have talked to me about your trip to France, you see. I would have found out just the same, in the end, perhaps much later, for I knew that you knew MacGill and that, on the other hand, you went around with the people who killed Angelino. Note that I am not even asking you their names.'

'Jos knows them as well as I do.'

'That's right. That is not my affair. What I am trying to spare you, I don't know why, perhaps through pity, is seeing you come up before a jury.'

'I'd blow my brains out first.'

'Why?'

'Because of a certain person.'

It smacked of the soap operas, maybe, and yet Maigret would have been willing to bet that Parson was referring to his mother.

'I don't think it is wise for you to leave the hotel today. Your friends surely imagine that you spilled the beans and, in your circles, people don't like that much. I'm going to phone for a room near mine.'

'I'm not afraid.'

'I'd rather nothing happened to you tonight.'

Parson, with a shrug, took a drink straight from the bottle.

'Don't put yourself out for me.'

He took the cheque, staggered towards the door.

'So long, Jos,' he flung out, turning round.

And, in a last attempt at irony:

'Bye, bye, Mr Mégrette.'

Premonition? The Inspector came close to calling him back, and forcing him to sleep at the hotel, locking him in a room, if necessary. He did not. He was unable, however, to stop himself from walking over to the window, where he lifted the curtain in a gesture unusual for him, and which belonged to Little John.

A few minutes later some muffled explosions were heard, a burst of machine-gun fire, surely.

And Maigret, turning back to the two men, sighed:

'I don't think there's any point in going down. He must have had his account squared.'

10

They sat on for another hour in the room, which, like the office on the Quai des Orfèvres, filled, little by little, with the smoke of pipes and cigarettes.

'I apologize,' Little John had begun by saying, 'for the way my son and I have tried to put you off.'

He, too, was tired, but a great release, an infinite, almost physical relief could be sensed in him.

For the first time Maigret saw him other than tense, withdrawn, checking with painful energy his impulse to lash out.

'I've been holding out against them for six months now, giving ground only by inches. There are four, two of them Sicilians.'

'That part of the affair is not my business,' Maigret declared.

'I know. Yesterday, when you came to the hotel, I nearly spoke to you and Jos stopped me.'

His face hardened, his eyes grew more inhuman than ever – but now Maigret knew what anguish gave them that terrible coldness.

'Can you imagine,' he said in a low voice, 'what it is to have a son whose mother you have killed and to love her still?'

MacGill had discreetly gone to sit in the corner armchair, the one Parson has occupied, as far away from the two men as possible.

'I won't speak to you of what happened then. I'm not seeking excuses for myself. I don't want any. Do you understand? I am not Joseph Daumale. It's he I should have killed. But you must know.'

'I do know.'

'That I loved, that I love still as I think no man has ever loved. Confronted with total collapse, I – No, it's no use.'

And Maigret repeated gravely:

'It's no use.'

'I believe I have paid more dearly than the justice of mankind would have made me pay. A little while ago you stopped Daumale from going on to the end. I think, Inspector, that you believe me?'

And Maigret nodded twice in an affirmative gesture.

'I wanted to go with her. Then I decided to give myself up. He prevented me, for fear of being involved in a scandal.'

'I understood that.'

'He was the one who went to get the wicker trunk from his room. He suggested we throw it in the river. I couldn't. There is one thing you cannot have guessed. Angelino had come. He had seen. He knew. He might denounce me. Joseph wanted us to go away immediately. Well! For two days . . .'

'Yes. You kept her.'

'And Angelino didn't talk. And Joseph was nearly out of his mind with fear. And I was in such a state that I endured his being there, and gave him the last money I had to do what had to be done.

'He bought a secondhand truck. We pretended to be moving and we loaded everything we owned . . .

'We went out into the countryside, about fifty miles away, and there in a wood near the river, I –'

'Father, don't,' begged MacGill's voice.

'That's all. I say that I paid, paid in every way. Even with doubt. And that was the most frightful. For months I continued to doubt, saying to myself that the child was perhaps not mine, that Jessie perhaps had lied to me.

'I put him in the care of a decent woman I knew and I did not want to see him . . . Even later, I believed I had no right to see him . . . One hasn't the right to see the son of –

'Could I tell you all this when Jean brought you to New York?

'He is my son, too.

'But he is not the son of Jessie.

'I confess, Inspector, and Jos knows it, that after a few years I hoped I might become again a man like any other, and no longer a kind of automaton.

'I married . . . without love . . . the way one takes a medicine . . . I had a child . . . and I was never able to live with the mother. She's still alive. It was she who asked for a divorce. She's living somewhere in South America, where she has made a new life for herself.

'You know that Jos disappeared, when he was about twenty. He was running around in Montreal, with a gang which was rather like the one Parson was mixed up with.

'Old Mrs MacGill died. I lost track of Jos and I never suspected he was living a half block away from me, on Broadway, among the people you know.

'My other son, Jean, as he admitted to me, showed you the letters I used to write him and you must have been surprised.

'It was, you see, because I thought only of the other one, of Jessie's son.

'I forced myself to love Jean ... I did it with a kind of rage ... I wanted at all costs to give him an affection that in my heart I devoted to another.

'And one day, about six months ago, I saw that boy turn up.'

What infinite tenderness in that word 'boy', in that gesture towards Jos MacGill!

'He had just learned, through Parson and the others, the truth. I remember his first words when we met face to face:

'"Sir, you are my father ..."'

And MacGill, at that, pleadingly:

'Dad, don't!'

'All right, Jos. I'm only saying what must be said. Since then, we've lived together, we've worked together to save what can be saved, and that explains the transfer of funds that Monsieur d'Hoquélus spoke to you about ... because I felt the catastrophe to be inevitable sooner or later. Our enemies, who had been Jos's friends, were quite heavy-handed and, when you arrived, one of them, Bill, staged an act to put you off.

'You thought Bill was working for us, when it was he who was ordering us about. They couldn't persuade you to leave ...

'They killed Angelino on account of you, because they felt you were on the right track and they didn't want to be deprived of their best business.

'I'm worth three million dollars, Mr Maigret ... In six months, I've paid off almost half a million, but it's the whole of it they want.

'Go and explain that to the police.'

Why did Maigret think just then of his sad clown? It was Dexter, much more than Maura, who suddenly stood as a symbol, he and, paradoxically, Parson, who had just been shot down in the street at the moment when he had finally earned, almost honestly, two thousand dollars.

Ronald Dexter, in the Inspector's eyes, embodied the bad luck and all the misery that can overwhelm humanity. Dexter, who also had made a small fortune, five hundred dollars, by betrayal, and who had come to lay the money on this table where the beer bottles and the whisky glasses stood side by side now with the sandwiches no one had touched.

'You might perhaps go abroad,' Maigret suggested without conviction.

'No, Inspector ... A Joseph would, but not I ... I have fought alone for almost thirty years ... against my worst enemy: myself and my own suffering ... A hundred times I've wished the thing would break wide open, you understand? ... I have truly, sincerely wished to make an accounting.'

'What would that accomplish?'

And Little John spoke a phrase that truly expressed his innermost thought, now that he had permitted his nerves to relax:

'It would allow me to rest ...'

'Hello ... Lieutenant Lewis?'

Maigret, alone in his room, at five in the morning, had called the officer at his home.

'You have something new?' the other man asked. 'A crime was committed last night, not far from you, in the middle of the street, and I wonder –'

'Parson?'

'You know about it?'

'It's so unimportant, you see!'

'What?'

'It is not important! He would have died anyhow in two or three years of sclerosis of the liver and he'd have suffered more.'

'I don't understand ...'

'It doesn't matter. I'm calling you, Lieutenant, because I believe there's an English ship sailing for Europe tomorrow morning and I plan to take it.'

'You know that we haven't found any death certificate in the young woman's name?'

'You won't find any.'

'What?'

'Nothing. In short, there has been only one murder committed. No, I'm sorry, the one last night makes two! Angelino and Parson ... In France, we call them crimes of milieu.'

'What milieu?'

'Of people who care nothing for human life.'

'I don't follow.'

'It doesn't matter! I wanted to say good-bye to you, Lieutenant, because I am going back to my home in Meung-sur-Loire, where I will always be very happy to welcome you if you come to visit our old country.'

'You're giving up?'

'Yes.'

'Discouraged?'

'No.'

'I don't mean to annoy you.'

'Certainly not.'

'But we'll get them.'

'I'm convinced of that.'

Moreover, it was true, for three days later, at sea, Maigret heard over the radio that four dangerous criminals, two of them Sicilians, had been apprehended by the police for the murders of Angelino and Parson, and that their lawyer was denying the evidence.

At the sailing time there had been a few people on the quay who pretended not to know each other but who kept looking in the direction of Maigret.

Little John, in a blue suit and a dark overcoat.

MacGill, nervously smoking cork-tipped cigarettes.

A gloomy person attempting to slip through and whom the stewards treated with sovereign disdain: Ronald Dexter.

There was also a curly-haired redhead, who stayed on board until the last moment and to whom the police showed the greatest courtesy.

It was O'Brien, too, who inquired over a last drink in the ship's bar:

'In other words, you give up?'

His face was at its most innocent and Maigret tried hard to match that innocence in replying:

'As you say, I give up.'

'At the moment when –'

'At the moment when people could be forced to talk who have nothing interesting to say, but when, in the valley of the Loire, it is high time to thin the melon plants in the hotbeds . . . And I've become a gardener, you see.'

'Satisfied?'

'No.'

'Disappointed?'

'Not that, either.'

'Checkmate?'

'I don't know about that.'

At that moment it still depended on the Sicilians. Once arrested, they would or would not talk.

They judged it more prudent and perhaps more profitable not to talk.

And ten days later Madame Maigret inquired:

'Actually, what did you go to America for?'

'Nothing.'

'You didn't even bring back a pipe as I wrote and told you to . . .'

It was his turn to play Joseph and he replied like a coward:

'Over there, you see, they're much too expensive . . . and not well made . . .'

'You could at least have brought me a little something, a souvenir, I don't know . . .'

As a result of which, he permitted himself to cable Little John:

PLEASE SEND PHONOGRAPH.

It was all he kept, together with a few pennies and a couple of nickels, from his trip to New York.

Saint-Marguerite-du-Lac-Masson, PQ

MORE ABOUT PENGUINS, PELICANS
AND PUFFINS

For further information about books available from Penguins please write to Dept EP, Penguin Books Ltd, Harmondsworth, Middlesex UB7 0DA.

In the U.S.A.: For a complete list of books available from Penguins in the United States write to Dept DG, Penguin Books, 299 Murray Hill Parkway, East Rutherford, New Jersey 07073.

In Canada: For a complete list of books available from Penguins in Canada write to Penguin Books Canada Ltd, 2801 John Street, Markham, Ontario L3R 1B4.

In Australia: For a complete list of books available from Penguins in Australia write to the Marketing Department, Penguin Books Australia Ltd, P.O. Box 257, Ringwood, Victoria 3134.

In New Zealand: For a complete list of books available from Penguins in New Zealand write to the Marketing Department, Penguin Books (N.Z.) Ltd, Private Bag, Takapuna, Auckland 9.

In India: For a complete list of books available from Penguins in India write to Penguin Overseas Ltd, 706 Eros Apartments, 56 Nehru Place, New Delhi 110019.